"That's t

"What do we do now?" Justine asked.

The Tonkawa said, "Won't be any Indian tracks left after this buffalo herd goes by. Even Kicker couldn't find any."

"Kicker?"

"The Tonks' name for Elijah Thompson," Duggan said. "Butt Kicker. That old man doesn't like anybody very much, especially Indians. Even friendly ones. Pete's right. Not even Thompson can track Indians through a buffalo herd."

"Speaking of which, what happened to Thompson? I never saw him at the fort," Justine said.

Duggan shrugged. "Rode in, parleyed with Mackenzie, resupplied, and rode out again the next day." He pointed toward the west. "Most likely, he's back out there again. Somewhere."

"Alone?"

"That's the way he hunts Indians."

RED RIVER WAR

RAY ROSSON

BERKLEY BOOKS, NEW YORK

If you purchased this book without a cover, you should be aware that this book is stolen property. It was reported as "unsold and destroyed" to the publisher and neither the author nor the publisher has received any payment for this "stripped book."

This is a work of fiction. Names, characters, places, and incidents are either the product of the author's imagination or are used fictitiously, and any resemblance to actual persons, living or dead, business establishments, events, or locales is entirely coincidental.

RED RIVER WAR

A Berkley Book / published by arrangement with the author

PRINTING HISTORY
Berkley paperback edition / August 2000

All rights reserved.
Copyright © 2000 by Gene Shelton.
Cover illustration by Bruce Emmett.
This book may not be reproduced in whole or in part, by mimeograph or any other means, without permission.
For information address:
The Berkley Publishing Group, a division of Penguin Putnam, Inc.,
375 Hudson Street, New York, New York 10014.

The Penguin Putnam Inc. World Wide Web site address is
http://www.penguinputnam.com

ISBN: 0-425-17543-X

BERKLEY®
Berkley Books are published by The Berkley Publishing Group,
a division of Penguin Putnam Inc.,
375 Hudson Street, New York, New York 10014.
BERKLEY and the "B" design
are trademarks belonging to Penguin Putnam Inc.

PRINTED IN THE UNITED STATES OF AMERICA

10 9 8 7 6 5 4 3 2 1

This one's for Poodle and Lucille.
They know why.

AUTHOR'S NOTE

This is a work of fiction based on historical events in the Red River War during the period 1871–1875. While many of the characters in this story actually existed, no conclusions should be drawn as to their real-life personalities, motivations, and actions on the basis of this work.

Any factual errors are strictly the responsibility of the author.

—R.R.

1

SMOKE FROM THE wagons spread along the valley floor, flattened on the wings of the wind.

The young Kiowa Tabi unuu—the Badger—sat astride his roan war pony an arrow's flight from the ambush site, his ears deaf to the jubilant whoops and cries of his companions on the raid. The exaltation of the kill pounded through his veins. He held a fresh scalp overhead. A droplet of blood from the trophy snaked down his forearm. Badger's spirits soared.

He was now a warrior.

Despite the mild spring air and the cooling wind, a thin rivulet of sweat trickled from beneath his yellow headband. The afternoon sun pressed warm against the black war paint covering the left side of his face from hairline to throat. Streaks and dots of yellow and vermillion marked the other brow and cheek. The wind stirred his single long braid of dark brown hair, greased almost to black and bound near the end by a single red cloth strip. The braid lay across his left shoulder, against the smooth muscle of his chest.

A gust of wind ruffled the gray-streaked brown hair clutched in Badger's hand. He stared at the trophy held toward the sky, a sight that would remain forever burned deep into his memory. His heart threatened to burst with pride. He felt a deep warmth within, a oneness with the spirit of his father. He could not speak his dead father's name aloud. To do so was forbidden. Yet he felt the warrior's presence, a spirit as tangible as the wind.

Badger knew that Hawk Chaser also was filled with pride. Pride for his only son, a man now, even though the youth had not yet seen his twentieth summer.

It was enough.

Badger lowered the trophy.

His father had seen, and smiled. Hawk Chaser's spirit now would be at peace, knowing his warrior's blood had this day passed to a new generation. Hawk Chaser's bones lay hidden near the place where he had fallen while defending his family in the long-ago battle with the soldier chief called Yellow Hair, in the fight at Black Kettle's camp on the Wichita.

The memory of the battle tightened Badger's heart along with the scar tissue on his right side, the puckered dent where the horse soldier's rifle ball had struck. He had been little more than a child then, barely grown past the Rabbit Society status of young boys of his mixed Kiowa-Comanche band. Yet he had fought at his father's side. He had helped hold the horse soldiers at bay until many women and children, his mother and sister among them, escaped. Hawk Chaser was among the last to fall in battle.

It was expected.

Hawk Chaser was Koisenko, a member of the elite warrior society whose ranks were reserved for only the bravest and most feared Kiowa fighting men.

Badger had vowed that bloody, painful morning on the Washita that one day he would take his father's place among the Koisenko.

Approaching hoofbeats brought his thoughts back to the present. Yellowfish pulled his sorrel-and-white paint pony to a stop alongside Badger. The slender Comanche was younger by two snows than was Badger. Over the years he also had become the brother Badger had never had.

Yellowfish sat silently for a moment, staring toward the burning wagons and the mutilated bodies. "Our medicine is strong today, Badger." His soft voice, surprisingly deep for a young man of slight build, reflected a quiet satisfaction. Not the pulsing exuberance of triumph that raced through Badger's heart, but a contented calmness. And perhaps, Badger thought, a hint of disappointment.

Badger nodded. "Yes. Our medicine was powerful throughout this raid. Even before we found the hide hunters. There are now four less white men on our hunting grounds." As he spoke, he tied the dead hunter's scalp to the horn of the scarred Mexican saddle his father had ridden.

"More will come," Yellowfish said.

"Let them. We will kill them, too."

Yellowfish's brow furrowed. "Perhaps the peace chiefs back on the reservation are right. That we cannot stop the white man. That they are like the river that flows forever. That the old ways are lost to our people. That we must remain on the land the white man sets aside for us and scratch in the dirt like the Kickapoo and Caddo." He spat the names of the two tribes as if they were curse words.

Badger snorted in disgust. "The peace chiefs have become old women, afraid of their own shadows. Let them disgrace our fathers' memories by taking up the white man's big arrowhead that wounds the earth." He turned to glare at Yellowfish, irritated with the young man for speaking words that doused his exuberance like water on a fire.

The flush of aggravation quickly passed. It was impossible for him to stay angry with Yellowfish. The young Comanche's only fault was that he listened too much and believed the words of those who had betrayed The People. The embers of excitement flared anew in Badger's heart.

He said with confidence, "While those old women dig in the dirt, we, too, will use the white man's tools—the rifles they give us for hunting, the weapons and bullets we take from their dead. We will drive the white hunters and horse soldiers from our land. We will turn them back from the hunting grounds and camps that have been ours since before my father's grandfather's father's time."

The frown faded from Yellowfish's brow. "It must be

so. Wiser, stronger men than the peace chiefs have said it will be so."

Badger shifted his gaze back to the killing field. The buffalo slayers had paid with their lives for their laziness and stupidity. They had followed the easy trail, past the low ridge above the arroyo. Had they chosen to cross the rolling, rocky land above the valley, such a quick and decisive ambush would not have been possible. They had ridden their wagons straight into the guns and arrows of the war party. The white man might be many, Badger mused, but he made up for his numbers with a shortage of common sense.

Throaty whoops and shrill victory cries of the other young men in the party still rang over the valley. Badger had spoken the truth. It had been a good raid, even before the spirits delivered these buffalo killers into their hands. The bodies of four other white men already marked their backtrail. Today, the count had reached eight. Twice the sacred number, four. And now the raiders had more than four times four horses and mules, and four times two guns more than when they had ridden south across the Red River.

Not a man among the war party had suffered so much as a scratch. They had crossed the river as eager young men. They would return in triumph. As proven warriors.

"Why do you not join in the celebration, Badger?" Yellowfish asked. "You took your first scalp today."

"I choose to spend this time with the spirit of my father." Badger glanced at his companion, an ache for his friend in his heart. Yellowfish had had no opportunity to claim a scalp of his own during this raid. As the youngest member of the party, his duty was to hold the horses—no small responsibility, yet one that kept him from the fight. He had done his job well and without complaint. One day soon, Yellowfish would have the chance to prove his courage in battle.

"Your father would have been proud."

"He is. I feel his hand on my shoulder and his smile upon my face."

Yellowfish nodded. "It must be so. I will speak for you when it is time to tell of your deeds before the council fire. You will advance to warrior rank after this day—" His words abruptly stopped.

Badger's gaze followed Yellowfish's stare toward a low butte a rifle shot away at the southern edge of the valley.

A lone rider sat astride a big horse atop the butte, staring toward the scene in the valley below. Badger's breath caught in his throat. The horseman was Satank, he who wore the elkskin sash of the Koisenko, the man revered as the greatest living warrior of the Kiowa nation. It was uncommon for a senior war chief to observe the conduct of a band of young men during a raiding party. Custom held that the party simply rode from camp, to return either in triumph or in disgrace.

"Where did he come from?" Yellowfish's quiet voice reflected the awe that showed in his deep brown eyes.

"Satank appears and vanishes as he chooses." Even as Badger spoke, the war chief reined about and disappeared from atop the butte.

"Should we tell Jonopitz of Satank watching us?" Yellowfish asked.

"No. That is for Satank to say to Bat, should he choose."

Badger shifted his gaze to the men gathered around the smoking remains of the wagons. Jonopitz, the Bat, motioned for Badger and Yellowfish to ride in.

The stocky, dark-skinned Kiowa Apache wiped the blood from his knife on the leg of a dead hunter and sheathed the blade as the two rode up. Bat's face pinched into its usual frown. He always looked like a man with an ache in his belly, Badger mused. He couldn't remember having heard Bat laugh aloud. The Apache blood in him, Badger thought.

"It is enough," Bat said. "We will go home now. There may be other white hunters nearby with their long rifles.

They might be drawn to the shooting and the smoke."

"Let them come," one of more eager men said with a snort of disdain. "We will kill them as we killed these."

Bat glowered at the anxious one. "No. The spirits have been kind to us so far. It is best we not ask for more good hunting this day."

Badger glanced at the Cheyenne called Wah-ho-lah, who sat solemnly atop his paint war pony, and caught the slight nod of agreement. There were those who said the young Cheyenne was cautious to a fault, bordering on timidity. Badger knew differently. Wah-ho-lah simply wasn't as hot-blooded as many of the others. He had the ability to think beyond the moment, to sense when it was time to strike and when to fade away to fight another time. One day, Badger thought, Wah-ho-lah would be a great war leader.

Badger nodded himself. The ambush had been so quick and decisive that the hide hunters managed but one shot, and that one hurried and wild. Yet he, Bat, and Wah-ho-lah knew the short rifles, bows, and lances of the war party were no match for the long-range guns of the buffalo slayers. Stealth, a quick strike, and flight were the raiders' friends; an extended duel with big rifles in the hands of men who knew how to use them was an unnecessary risk. To scorn one's enemies was acceptable. To underestimate those enemies was to invite death—or worse, disgrace.

For a moment, Badger thought the eager one would protest. To do so would be a breach of the code. The leader of the party was not to be challenged without cause as long as his decisions were sound. Bat's heart and instincts had been true these twelve suns. Had Bat failed and a warrior been injured or killed, his leadership would have been challenged. Not in words. Those who chose to no longer follow him would simply ride away.

Badger relaxed when the eager one dropped his gaze and grunted a reluctant agreement.

"When we cross into the land where the white soldiers are forbidden to ride, we will divide the fruits of our raid,"

Bat said. His gaze settled on Badger. "You fought well, Tabi unuu. You will be rewarded. Scout ahead. Lead us across the river and on to our home."

Badger's heartbeat quickened still more as he nodded and reined his horse toward the line of trees that marked the path of the river the white man called the Salt Fork of the Brazos, a short ride away. To lead the party home was an honor, an act of praise for a man's courage and tenacity, as was the equally important post of riding in the rear guard. And Badger would no longer be a poor man. He would have still more ponies. Perhaps not more than two or three from this raid, to join the five he had stolen from the despised Kickapoos. Not yet enough horses to approach the family of the girl he had chosen. But it was a start.

If Bat held to tradition, he would profit little from the raid himself. Custom held that the leader of a successful war party distribute most of the bounty to those who rode with him. Such an act of unselfishness would add to Bat's prestige—a message to all of his complete confidence that he could always get more ponies, more guns. If Bat defied that tradition and kept the most or best for himself, he would be marked as a man of greed, unworthy to lead. And few, or none, would ride with him.

Badger's deep greenish-brown eyes narrowed as his gaze swept the countryside. He saw nothing but the lazy soaring of an eagle on the hunt, its wings brushing the sky above the far bank of the river, and the quick white flash as an antelope's raised tail flared a warning to its tribe grazing downstream.

He turned to glance back at the battle site one last time. The smoke from the wagons had dwindled to a faint, gray-white smudge against the dark cedars and red sandstone slopes of the hills that flanked the valley. The wind at his back carried the muted sounds of laughter and high spirits of his companions to his ears. Despite his keen hearing, he could not make out the words. He didn't have to. He knew they would be recounting the battles fought and the enemies slain during the last few suns.

There would be much dancing and feasting in the isolated valley at the west end of the Kiowa reservation when the party returned in glory. The thought deepened Badger's sense of pride and contentment. His sister and her husband would be proud, as would the spirit of his mother, lost four snows ago to the bad chest disease. Their brother and son was now a warrior.

Badger reined in for a moment at the edge of a willow thicket on the south bank of the river. He unsheathed his knife, leaned from the saddle, and sliced off a willow limb the size of his small finger. As he rode, he stripped the delicate leaves from the branch, then cut thin slits in the still-oozing scalp. He threaded the limb through the skin until the supple branch formed into a hoop that held the scalp open to the wind and sun. He would ride into camp with the scalp hoop raised overhead, tied to the muzzle of his short rifle, a proclamation to all that the youth who had ridden away as a boy returned as a man.

He forced himself to put aside thoughts of homecoming as his war horse snorted, shook its head, and stepped gingerly into the muddy red trickle that marked the main channel of the river. He gave the horse its head. The red roan gelding had been raised in river country. Scorpion could read the treacherous ground for quicksand bogs and deep holes better than could any man.

Badger reined in at the top of the narrow pass between rocky hills that overlooked the river ford. After a moment, satisfied that no surprises waited on the rolling plains ahead, he turned to watch as the other members of the party made the crossing. The captured horses and mules stepped into the muddy stream, snorted nervously at the strange sights and smells around them, then followed Yellowfish's pony across. There were no problems.

The wind pressed harder against Badger's face, gaining strength as the day warmed. The wind and sun had darkened his skin, but beneath the war paint it remained a shade lighter than that of his companions.

Many of the Comanches, Kiowas, and Kiowa Apaches with whom he rode and camped were almost as dark as the buffalo soldiers, the black warriors with curly hair who wore the white man's uniform. The lighter tone of Badger's skin was more obvious when he bathed or swam. Beneath his breechclout, moccasins, and leggings, Badger's skin was white as the antelope's tail, the legacy of the birth parents he no longer remembered.

It was of no concern to him.

To the white man, he was a captive turned Indian renegade, one of their own kind gone savage. To the Kiowas, he was Kiowa. His heart was Kiowa. Nothing else mattered.

He could recall almost nothing of the raid that had made him and his sister Kiowas. His own memory brought forth only a blurred swirl of horsemen and smoke and a long, jolting ride, the strong arm of Hawk Chaser holding him on the horse's withers. He remembered nothing of his white father except that he was big. But when one is only three summers, all grownups are big. His sister, who had seen six summers at the time, remembered more. When she chose to do so. She had told him what she recalled of the adventure, of her terror, as the raiding party left the blazing white man's lodge behind.

Her fears proved unfounded.

The Kiowas and Comanches welcomed the children, not as white captives, but as children. No more, no less. When Hawk Chaser took them into his lodge, the warrior's wives had seen that they were fed and clothed well and bathed often. Hawk Chaser became their father and Sings-All-Time, the older of Hawk Chaser's three wives, their favored mother. But the entire village had raised them. Among the Kiowas and their close allies, the Comanches, a child belonged to all members of the tribe, not to just one set of parents.

As the years passed, the times of plenty and the times

of hunger, Badger and his sister played with the other children without suffering any teasing or torment from youngsters born to the tribe. The elders hid them when the white man came searching for captives to ransom or take back by force. The elders, the storytellers, and their new parents taught them the true way.

By his tenth summer, Badger was Kiowa.

He knew no other world.

He rode to the highest point of the rolling hills, pulled Scorpion to a stop, and studied the surrounding land with care. He saw no threat. Soon he would switch his saddle to his bay long-riding horse to preserve his war pony's strength, endurance, and battle medicine.

He kneed Scorpion to the northeast. Two days' travel and the band would reach the sprawling village just inside the line that was not there, yet marked the western boundary of the reservation. They would be home.

The party would camp overnight an hour's ride from the village. They would send a messenger ahead to spread the word of their great success. That would give the people of the village time to prepare a proper welcome to the returning band.

A serene warmth settled in Badger's chest in anticipation of the festive homecoming. That the celebration and victory dance would be held on land grudgingly granted them by the white man did not dampen his spirit. One day soon, the Kiowas, Comanches, and other bands would return to their true home on the vast plains, the reservation little more than a bitter memory.

Badger knew it would be so.

The great war chief Satank had seen it in a vision. So had Maman-ti, the most powerful medicine man among the Kiowas. Thus, it must be so.

2

THE COACH FROM Fort Worth to Jacksboro lurched into a deep rut, then in a heartbeat jolted over a big rock.

Try as he might, the young man on the rear left seat couldn't keep his shoulder from constantly shoving against the beefy merchant who rode in the center of the thinly padded bench.

The jounces and lunges triggered a brief burst of mild profanity from the driver, the raspy curse words faint over the wind, the creak of running gear and harness. The curses were mild in deference to the one woman riding in the cramped coach.

Ned Justine muttered another apology to the big man with the florid face and the heavy wool suit now soaked dark with sweat at the armpits. Justine pulled away from the contact as quickly as he could. It wasn't possible to lean far on the crowded coach. Four people could travel in reasonable comfort in the rig. On this trip it held six.

On the bench facing Justine, a slight smile lifted the lips of the pleasant, somewhat round face of the middle-aged woman in the center seat. Her husband, slight of build and sharp of features, tightened his arm protectively around her shoulders. Justine knew they were a team, had been for many years. Even their clothing was similar, down to the considerable dust trapped in the folds of heavy black cloth. Her dress, swollen by many petticoats, covered her from neck to ankle. Despite the layers of cloth and the thick, sultry air in the coach, she didn't appear to be sweating.

The man seated directly across from Justine was the opposite image of the Quaker couple. His heavy shoulders stretched the cloth of a plain blue homespun shirt worn thin at the elbows. He filled more than his allotted third of the bench seat. A battered, trail-stained hat tilted low over a lined face the color of saddle leather. The flat crown of the hat almost touched the roof of the coach. The frontiersman had spoken only a handful of words in his deep, rumbling baritone since the stage pulled out of Fort Worth.

The sixth occupant of the coach, barely visible to Justine across the girth of the salesman seated between them, was as talkative as the big man was reticent; his jutting chin had barely stopped moving the whole trip. That came as no particular surprise to Justine. He hadn't known many politicians, but the ones he did know all had active tongues.

At least, Ned thought in relief, the heavy sway and jolt of the coach over the rough section of road put a momentary end to the argument—a quiet argument, the words carefully phrased in deference to the lady, no doubt, but still an argument—that had simmered through most of the long ride. Justine's gaze caught the look in the big frontiersman's pale blue eyes and saw his own relief at the sudden, blessed silence reflected there.

"She'll smooth out in a bit, folks," the driver yelled over the clatter of hooves and jangle of bits. "This here's the worst stretch. Be in Jacksboro near on time."

Justine hoped the rough stretch would be over soon. He had never been to sea, but if the deck of a ship pitched and rolled as violently as the coach, he was glad he hadn't chosen the navy.

The canvas flaps, rolled and tied partway up the coach windows, let an occasional breath of fresh air into the sticky interior, along with wisps of dust raised by the coach wheels. Through the open space beneath the rolled canvas, Justine watched the countryside flow past. Rolling hills mostly covered in rocks and junipers, the occasional stand of stubby post oak trees, and flat layers of prickly pear marched past, one hill seemingly identical to the next.

The rugged landscape left Justine relieved that if he had to serve at all, at least he was cavalry and not infantry. The idea of walking through this godforsaken country packing a fifty-pound rucksack and toting a rifle and ammunition, all the while clad in a stifling blue woolen uniform in the tormenting Texas sun, left a ghost ache in the muscles of his thighs and back.

Something else ached a bit, too, though Justine hid it well.

This wild, rocky country was nothing like the tall pines and sugar maples and other majestic trees back home. Trees that seemed to reach out and touch the sky, or caress the abrupt slopes of steep granite mountains. About the only thing northern Texas and Maine shared were rocks. Even the rocks were different.

"I tell you again, sir," the square-chinned politician said in his raspy voice, "your policy toward the Indians may be admirable in theory back in Washington, but not out here on the frontier. It won't work."

The slight man in the black suit merely smiled as if indulging a wayward child. "Reasonable men may differ, sir. But I see no reason why the Indians cannot be taught to work the land, to embrace the one true God, become one with the white man. All they need is teachers—teachers to lead them along the proper path. Then this unnecessary and terrible bloodshed between the red race and the white will stop. We are all God's children."

The politician snorted in derision. "The Quaker policy was drafted by men who don't know the red savages." He turned his gaze to the big man across from Justine. "You, sir. You have the look of a man who knows the frontier and the Indian. What is your opinion on the matter?"

The leathery face wrinkled in a frown. "Easier to teach a possum to play the harp than teach a Comanche to farm," he said. "Ain't part of their culture, not since they got the horse. Even before then."

"And you, young man?" The Quaker man cast a quiet, almost benevolent gaze on Justine. "What do you, as a soldier, think of Washington's plan to pacify the Indian?"

Justine shook his head. "I don't know, sir."

"But surely you must have a personal opinion," the Quaker wife said.

"No, ma'am. I don't know the first thing about Indians, and the policy makers in Washington don't make it a practice to consult raw young cavalry troopers on such matters."

The woman's dark eyes studied Justine. "You don't seem to be the typical soldier, sir. I sense a gentleness in you. Still, you must have some feelings on the matter."

Justine again shook his head. "I merely go where my orders send me and do what my superiors tell me to do."

The beefy salesman snorted in disgust. "Just like the army. Send green kids to do men's work. Young boys who know nothing about fighting Indians."

"Nobody in the U.S. Army knows anything about fighting Indians," the frontiersman said, "except maybe one man who might be able to figure it out. You headed for the Fourth, son?"

"Yes, sir."

"Then you'll learn. Fourth's a good outfit. Bad Hand Mackenzie's the only officer in the white man's army who just might learn to cut the cheese against Indians. It's a different kind of war out here."

The Quaker man cleared his throat. "Gentlemen, please. Let's have no more talk of fighting. It will merely upset my wife. Besides, I do not believe it will be necessary to engage in outright warfare."

"It'll take it," the politician said with a snort of disgust. "Only way to solve the Indian problem is wipe them out. To the last man, squaw, and louse-bitten papoose. Then there'll be peace on the frontier."

The woman's eyes widened in an expression of revulsion. "Eliminate an entire race of human beings?"

"Not human beings, ma'am. Indians."

"Jacksboro in five minutes, folks!" the coach driver called.

Relief flooded through Justine. The discussion left him uncomfortable. And, for some reason he didn't understand, feeling a touch of shame and guilt. Worst of all was the talk of fighting. It rekindled the nagging fear that was never far from Justine's conscious mind: whether, if an actual battle started, he could face the prospect of shooting another man or being shot at himself—or if he would turn tail and run.

He didn't know the answer to that question.

It was one he'd never wanted to face.

As the passengers began to gather personal items carried aboard the coach, the frontiersman spoke softly to Justine. "Listen to Mackenzie and his noncoms, son. Watch and listen for the unexpected. Then maybe some redskin won't have your hair on his lodgepole."

The coach lurched to a halt, swaying and creaking on the running gear.

Justine stepped down stiffly, his joints and muscles protesting the long ride in cramped quarters. For someone who hasn't yet seen his twentieth birthday, he thought, I'm moving like an old man.

He caught a flicker of movement at the edge of his vision and jumped aside just in time to keep from being slammed to the street by the shoulder of a big bay horse moving at a fast trot. The man in the saddle never acknowledged the near miss.

The streets of Jacksboro teemed with people who scurried about like ants whose mound had been disturbed. Men clad in everything from rough teamster garb to neatly pressed suits, and women whose dresses ranged from coarse farmwife homespun to expensive gowns, jostled for space with blue-clad soldiers. In addition to horsemen, buckboards, buggies, and wagons of every size and design jockeyed for passage, oaths tingeing the air when wheel hubs ground against each other or a slow-moving team of oxen blocked part of the packed roadways.

Every man seemed to be armed. Sidearms of all varieties, as well as rifles and shotguns ranging from ancient percussion longarms to metallic cartridge repeaters, were in open view. And an unseen but palpable tension cut through the thick dust raised by many wheels and hooves.

It was Justine's first taste of life on the frontier.

He wasn't at all sure he liked it. Or knew where he fit in. For an instant he had the strange sensation of standing outside himself and watching a young man of average height and slender build glance about in confusion.

"New recruit?"

Justine started slightly at the voice from beside him, then nodded to the short, sunbrowned, bowlegged man in a uniform faded by sun, wind, and repeated launderings, a single chevron on the visible arm. A darker image in the cloth marked the spot where a second stripe had been. The man had been reduced in rank for some infraction not long ago. A ragged scar puckered the trooper's left eyebrow and set the cloudy eye to looking off at an odd angle.

"You'd be bound for Richardson, then. Grab your stuff. My buckboard's right over there. Long walk elsewise, and I personal never took much to walkin' when I could ride. 'Specially since a man walkin' alone's fair game for any bad hombre around, and we got plenty of that breed in Jacksboro." He offered a hand. "Name's Sam Cooper. B Company, Sixth Cav."

Justine took the hand, surprised at the strength in the grip. "Ned Justine. Newly assigned to the Fourth Cavalry Regiment. Pleased to make your acquaintance."

"We'll get buddied up later, Justine," Cooper said. "Right now, get your truck together. It's a week to payday, so I got no reason to hang around town." He gestured toward a buckboard nearby. A roan mule stood in the traces, ears flopped, half-asleep. "Hope you wasn't expectin' a brass band to escort you into the Fourth, son."

"Just a ride out to the post will be fine, thank you."

Justine retrieved his few belongings and settled into the

passenger's side of the buckboard. The seat was a single hard wooden plank, unpainted but worn smooth enough to eliminate the threat of getting a splinter in his backside.

The two men sat in silence as Cooper threaded the rig through the mass of humanity and turned onto the road toward Fort Richardson a mile southwest of town. Finally, Justine turned to the aging private.

"You said you were with the Sixth?"

Cooper worked a chew of tobacco and spat over the side of the buckboard. "Sixth is pullin' out, a few companies at a time. Turnin' the place over to Mackenzie's Fourth. You boys are sure enough welcome to it." He cocked his one good eye at Justine. "Got your weapons with you?"

"Just my personal sidearm. My father's old Colt Army revolver. I was told I would be issued firearms and other equipment when I reported to Fort Richardson."

"Better grab that old Henry of mine from behind the seat there. You ride shotgun in case there's any trouble."

After a moment's groping, Justine's fingers touched the brass receiver. The rimfire rifle showed considerable wear.

"Careful with her, son. She's got a round in the chamber and a hair trigger on her," Cooper said casually. "Just cock her, point, and pull."

"You always carry a round in the chamber, Mr. Cooper?"

"Empty carbine ain't nothin' but a club."

"Do you think there might be trouble, even though it's such a short distance to the fort?"

"Out here a man stays ready. For anything. You handle a rifle?"

"Handle it, yes. Hit something with it, I don't know. I wasn't the best shot in my training company."

Cooper chuckled. "I be damned. All these years in this man's army, I finally meet an honest recruit. Most youngsters won't admit they can't knock a gnat's eye out at a hundred yards with a carbine. How you rate with a handgun?"

Justine allowed himself a wry smile. "As much as I hate to admit it, I'm better with a rifle. In short, not very good."

"Then you're as good as most I've rode with out here," Cooper said. "Been my experience there's maybe four, five really good shooters in each company. Rest of 'em just make noise, burn powder, and hope an Injun runs in front of the slug."

"Have you been in many Indian fights?"

"Not many. Little skirmish here and there. With Injuns, you mostly hunt. Mighty seldom you find 'em. Or even then get close enough to shoot. Well, there's home, just ahead."

Except for the broad, square parade ground in the center, the cannon parked in rows, and the uniformed soldiers drilling, picking up litter, or lounging about, Fort Richardson looked more like a frontier settlement than an actual fort, Justine thought.

Only a few of the buildings even hinted at permanence. What he assumed to be the powder magazine, hospital, commissary, and guardhouse were made of native stone. A few small buildings made of rough-cut logs appeared to be officers' quarters. Most of the buildings were of picket construction, thin timber poles with bases sunk into the soil and chinked with mud and grass. Not much protection from the elements, Justine thought. Enlisted men tended equipment or lounged beneath the shade of a canvas awning that served as a veranda at the front of one of the long, shotgun-style structures.

On a flat beyond the southwestern edge of the fort itself, numerous tents stood in sharply defined rows. Cooper reined the mule past the quadrangle toward the tent settlement.

"Most of Mackenzie's outfit's livin' under canvas," Cooper said. "What with the Fourth moving in before all the Sixth has moved out, there ain't much room in the fort itself. And there's more units of the Fourth on the way. From experience, son, I'd say you're gonna be more comfortable in the tents, anyway. Just watch out for scorpions, snakes, and spiders."

Justine was a bit surprised that no sentries were picketed at the fort itself. But the tent compound was well patrolled. A dusty, sweating private with shoulders almost as wide as the buggy and carrying an old rifled musket converted from percussion to cartridge waved them to a stop, then nodded to Cooper.

"New recruit, Sam?"

Cooper nodded. "Ned Justine, meet Olaf Svenson. Best Swede in the Fourth, even if he can't play poker for spit."

"I still have two dollars of your money, old man," Svenson said with a smile that crinkled blue eyes under a mane of yellow hair. He held out a hand. "Let's have a look at your orders, Justine. See where to get you started."

Justine handed over his papers. Svensen studied them for a minute, then nodded. "Corporal Charlton's over at the smithy's. He'll take it from here." The Swede returned Justine's papers, then gripped his hand in a squeeze that would have made a bear wince. "Welcome to the Fourth, Justine. Expected you two days ago. More than one of you, in fact."

"Mixup in orders at Fort Worth," Justine said, a note of apology in his tone. "I was delayed in getting them straightened out, then again waiting for transportation. I don't know about any others."

"That's the U.S. Army for you, trooper. There's always a mixup. If you need something, see Charlton. He's a good man. Just don't cross him." Svenson put his rifle at right shoulder arms and waved the buggy past.

"Svenson's right, Justine," Cooper said as he clucked the mule into motion. "Charlton's as good a soldier I ever met. I'd add a word of advice, for what it's worth. Was I you, I'd keep out of Mackenzie's way—and out of his sight—every chance you get."

"I've heard rumors he's . . . well . . . difficult sometimes," Justine said.

"That ain't the half of it. Some say Mackenzie's a bit

tetched in the head." Cooper had unconsciously lowered his voice to a near-whisper. "He's moody, that's for sure. But from what I hear, there ain't a better commander in the field when it comes to fightin' Injuns. Just do your job, stay sober on duty, listen to Charlton, and you'll be all right."

Cooper eased the buggy to a stop near a tent where the crackle and rumble of a field forge underlay the clang of a blacksmith's hammer. The old soldier nodded toward a figure holding the headstall of a wide-eyed, rangy sorrel horse. "That there's Charlton. I'll be droppin' you off here, Justine. Got to get back to my own outfit." He extended a hand. "Good luck to you, son. As the old sayin' goes, keep your hair on."

"Thanks for the ride," Justine said as he gathered his bundle of personal belongings and stepped down, "and for the advice. I'll take it to heart. Hope we meet again soon."

Cooper chuckled again, and scraped scarred knuckles across the stubble on his chin. "All due respect, son, I hope it ain't for a spell. You're welcome to my share of Bad Hand Mackenzie's Comanches and Kiowas."

As Cooper reined the buggy about, Justine waited for a moment before striding to the man holding the sorrel's bridle.

"Corporal Charlton? Ned Justine, reporting for duty."

Charlton glanced at Justine, but quickly turned his attention back to the sorrel. He was a man of medium height, but powerfully built, and he carried his muscular frame in a confident manner that hinted at a quickness not often seen in strong men.

"Be with you in a minute," Charlton said. "We've been half an hour trying to get this jugheaded idiot of a horse shod, and I'm not about to let go now. I can't spare any more skin."

Justine waited patiently until the regimental farrier finally released the snorting sorrel's left rear foot and pronounced him shod, in rather colorful terms.

Charlton handed the reins over to a trooper on stable duty, then turned to Justine. "All right, Justine, let's get you settled in to life in the Fourth Cavalry. Hope you've got a tolerance for abuse of body, mind, and soul, because this is no place for the weak of heart and weary of butt. And it's about to get worse."

"How's that?"

"Normally, Mackenzie doesn't put much stock in formal inspections, spit-and-polish type," Charlton said. "But we got some nervous lieutenants. High-ranking brass coming in. Doesn't believe we've got a real Indian problem and wants to find out for himself. We're about to get a visit from General William Tecumseh Sherman."

"The general-in-chief of the army?"

"Himself," Charlton said. "Provided the Indians don't get him first."

3

FROM THE COVER of a juniper stand at the crest of a low, rocky ridge, Badger squatted beside the two other men and stared toward the soldiers moving across the prairie below.

Badger wondered if the others could hear the quickening thump of his heart against a chest still swollen with pride. To be personally chosen by the great Satank to ride the warpath would have been enough. To then be selected to ride at the storied war chief's own side had been almost more honor than a young man could bear without bursting.

In the valley below the observation point, a small band of blue-coated men rode on either side of a single wagon, its canvas sides open to the fresh spring breeze. Two other men rode inside, beneath the shadow cast by the covered roof.

The soldiers who rode with the wagon carried rifles unslung, draped in the crooks of elbows or with the buttstocks propped against thighs, muzzles pointed toward the sky. The soldiers were few, only a handful to face the four times four times four of the war party waiting at the base of the ridge behind the leaders.

The bluecoats were not true horse soldiers. Badger could tell from the way they rode. These were the walk-a-heaps, the ones the white men called infantry, but now mounted, as they often were. They would be formidable foes, but less so than a true horse soldier skilled in the handling of a war mount.

Badger's muscles tingled in anticipation. The fight would be brief. So many warriors would quickly overwhelm the few soldiers. He intended to be among the first to strike.

Maman-ti dashed Badger's hopes. The medicine man shook his head and glanced at Satank. "Not these," he said, his words soft but firm. "We let them pass. A greater prize will come soon. Many wagons, carrying guns, food, blankets."

Maman-ti lifted his broad, yellow-painted face to the skies. His nostrils flared, testing the breeze—or perhaps conferring with his many and powerful spirits. Badger did not know which. Only the medicine man knew. After a moment he turned to Satank.

"Soon after we have taken the wagons that follow this small band, much rain will come to wash away our tracks. This also I have seen in my vision."

Badger swallowed his disappointment and checked his impatience. And his tongue. A young warrior did not argue with such a powerful medicine chief, any more than he would argue with Satank. Showing disrespect to one's elders was unthinkable; showing disrespect to men of such status could mean trouble. And showing disrespect to a medicine man could bring much worse than mere trouble down upon a young man's lodge.

Satank glanced at Maman-ti and grunted in agreement. "We will wait," he said.

* * *

William Tecumseh Sherman peered out the open side of the ambulance, then flashed a wry smile at his traveling companion.

"Well, General Marcy," Sherman said, "in all these miles, I have yet to see a single one of your storied red marauders. I've suspected all along that the many reports of atrocities along the frontier were mostly rumors."

Inspector General Randolph B. Marcy did not return

Sherman's smile. He had ridden these hills, broken new trails, led survey parties through northern Texas and the vast lands to the west, long before most white men ever set foot on the sundown side of the Trinity River.

"Not seeing them doesn't mean they aren't there, General Sherman," Marcy said solemnly. "I've personally seen the slaughter and destruction from Indian raids all across the frontier, and especially near Jacksboro. There are graves of murdered settlers in almost any direction one cares to look."

Marcy paused for a moment and gazed across the seemingly empty stretch of land known as Salt Creek Prairie. "There are not nearly as many white people in the Brazos watershed as were here when I visited eighteen years ago. General, if these Indian marauders are not punished, and punished severely, this entire country will be depopulated of civilized people."

Sherman waved a hand. "I'll not dispute your personal observations, Randolph. Lord knows, you're more familiar with this particular region of Texas than any other man alive—at least among those in uniform. I merely wish to point out that, at this time and to my own eyes, it appears all the reports that have crossed my desk regarding Indian depredations are somewhat exaggerated."

"With all due respect, General," Marcy said, "the reports were not the least bit exaggerated to the many who have died here. If we don't see Indians, it's most likely the result of Colonel Mackenzie's sending company-sized patrols out to scour the countryside from the first day his advance units arrived at Fort Richardson."

Sherman nodded. "Mackenzie does have a reputation for getting things done. I seem to recall General Grant once expressed his personal admiration for Mackenzie. At any rate, it was most considerate of the colonel to offer us an entire cavalry company for the remaining leg of the inspection tour."

Marcy's brow furrowed. "Yes, it was. I must admit, I rather wish you had taken him up on his offer. We aren't that far from the reservation lands. It wouldn't greatly surprise me, sir, if we are being watched by a war party even as we speak."

Justine blinked through eyes stung with sweat and dust kicked up by the hooves of the troop's horses as he threw his weight and muscle against the near side rein.

The big, rawboned bay—sixteen hands and well over a thousand pounds—fought the rein for half a dozen strides before finally starting the turn. Justine had ridden cold-jawed horses before, but not one quite this bad.

Justine's arm and shoulder muscles burned from the effort of controlling the stubborn bay, and his ears stung from the constant tongue lashing of the troop sergeant. Three hours on the open prairie in constant maneuvers had taken its toll of both men and mounts. What should have been a simple wheel right, the guidon bearer as pivot rider, once again had degenerated into a ragged line of unequally spaced, cursing horsemen. Veteran cavalrymen on trained mounts executed the basic exercise flawlessly. It was a different matter entirely with new recruits and untrained, untested horses, most of the mounts barely broken to saddle.

Justine didn't complain about the bay assigned to him. The gelding might be cold-jawed, but at least he didn't buck. For the first few minutes after boots and saddles sounded for the recruits, it seemed to be raining cavalrymen. Justine alone had retrieved the mounts of three men bucked off by ranker horses than his.

Any mounts at all were welcome at Fort Richardson.

It was a problem shared by all frontier outpost cavalry units: never enough horses or equipment, even ammunition in short supply. The glamor of cavalry duty in the United States Army was significantly overrated, Justine wryly admitted for perhaps the hundredth time since his enlistment.

Still, it beat walking.

The disgusted first sergeant, a weathered veteran of campaigns from Pennsylvania to the Rio Grande, finally called an end to the exercise.

The troop straggled into something resembling an inspection line. Only the creak of saddle leather, jangle of bits and curb chains, and puffs from the nostrils of winded horses broke the silence as the sergeant rode slowly down the line. He fixed a baleful glare on each of the recruits in turn, then wheeled his sleek, well-trained sorrel to the front center of the command.

After a moment, the sergeant leaned in the saddle, spat a glob of tobacco juice, and shook his head.

"Jesus," he said, sarcasm heavy in his words, "Colonel Mackenzie asks for cavalry replacements. He gets store clerks who don't know which end of a horse the bit goes in." His gaze drifted from one end of the line to the other. "Might be half a dozen of you boys make it as cavalry. What I see here mostly is a bunch of cooks, wagon drivers, latrine diggers, and infantry. And that's an insult to our fine infantry troops."

He shrugged. "We'll sort out the assignments later. Tend your mounts and wash up. Dress uniforms this afternoon. The general's due in shortly. You boys may not be soldiers, but, by God, at least you can look like 'em. Maybe we can fool Sherman into thinking we've got men here. Dismissed."

Justine sighed in relief. At least he might have a few hours away from the iron-jawed bay. He started a steady pull on the left rein.

"You, there. Trooper Justine!" the sergeant called.

Justine's heart sank. The image of himself on the business end of a shovel flashed through his mind. He eased the pressure on the rein and straightened in the saddle, trying to sit at attention.

"Yes, Sergeant?"

"You handled that idiot of a horse reasonably well. Better than most could have. Where you from?"

"Maine, Sergeant."

"Vermont, myself. At least I think so. Been so long since I've seen home I'm not sure any longer. Good to have a neighbor of sorts in the Fourth."

Justine started to reply, but the sergeant cut him short with a brusque wave of the hand. "Corporal Charlton seems to have taken a liking to you, Justine. Asked for you to be assigned to him. After general inspection, report to him. He'll teach you what you need to know to keep alive and find Indians."

"Right away, Sergeant," Justine said, relieved at having been spared the indignity, blisters, and aching back of digging trenches, but at the same time feeling a tingle of dread—or some feeling between his shoulders he couldn't quite pin down. The sergeant's parting remark about "find Indians" lingered in his unease.

Charlton's primary job in the field was as chief of scouts.

Justine sawed at the rein again and finally got the bay headed back toward the tent settlement of the Fourth.

The spit-and-polish inspection anticipated by junior officers when General Sherman arrived at Fort Richardson amounted to little more than a cursory glance and a few casual salutes.

Justine stood in the ranks, feeling the armpits of his wool dress uniform dampen with sweat, as the group of officers passed with barely an acknowledgment of the troopers' presence. The polishing of boots and buttons and the meticulous cleaning of the issue Spencer .56–50-caliber carbine, which he had yet to fire and now held at right shoulder arms, seemed to Justine a waste of time. But it was the army way. At least the occasion provided him with his first look at his new commanding officer.

Colonel Ranald Slidell Mackenzie, breveted major general for heroism during the war between North and South, strode past only a few yards from Justine. Mackenzie, Justine thought, didn't look the part of a frontier field commander. He stood a bit more than medium height, slightly built, an intense expression on his round face, lips set firm below a bushy brown mustache. He walked with a stiff gait that reflected a series of war wounds, the most obvious of which was the two fingers missing from his right hand. That wound was the reason the Indians and many troopers referred to the commander as "Bad Hand."

Of the two visiting generals, Sherman seemed pleasant enough, but Marcy wore a preoccupied, even worried, expression. Sherman smiled frequently as he strode past the assembled troops.

The trio picked up an honor guard at the northeastern edge of the Fourth's tent headquarters, climbed into ambulances, and made their way toward Fort Richardson proper.

Charlton dismissed his company and fell into step between Justine and Al Duggan, the stocky, grizzled veteran who always looked as if he needed a shave and a fresh uniform.

Charlton said, "Word is the general still doesn't believe we've got a problem here. Maybe he'll change his mind after a session or two with the folks who live in this area."

"How big a problem do we have?" Justine asked.

"Big enough," Charlton said. "A dozen settlers killed over the past four months. More than a hundred in this county alone since the fall of '59, not quite two years back. It'll get worse if Mackenzie can't convince Sherman we're sitting on a powder keg and the Indians are holding the match."

After a moment, the older man glanced toward the western horizon. "Gonna rain tonight. Not just a little shower, neither. Real catfish-floater on the way." Duggan said to Justine, "Bad as heat and dust is, mud's worse when it comes to soldierin'. But I reckon you'll find that out soon enough. By the by, don't get crossways with the colonel. Bad Hand Mackenzie ain't a man you want mad at you."

"So I've heard." Justine said. The steady stream of warnings wasn't necessary. Justine hadn't been in uniform that long, but he'd already discovered the enlisted man's primary rule of survival: Keep as much distance as possible between yourself and the nearest officer. Less often seen, less often in trouble.

Later that evening, Justine lay on his canvas cot, unable to sleep despite the weariness that weighted down his bones. The trooper with whom he shared the tent had started rattling the canvas with snores a few seconds after his back hit the blankets.

Justine again found himself wondering if he'd made a mistake. But then again, when he enlisted, it had been the first time in his memory that his father had actually touched him, shaken his hand, even admitted he was proud of him. He'd said it in sort of a grudging way. At least he'd said it.

Justine would rather have been in the classrooms at William and Mary, studying engineering and architecture, than out here in the middle of nowhere facing a life he couldn't yet comprehend.

That didn't change the fact that there had been at least one Justine in every armed conflict since the French and Indian War, and probably before then. His father, his father's father, back through the entire history of the Justine family.

Ned was the last male in his particular line.

Enlisting had been a desperate bid to finally gain a measure of respect from his father. That and the fact he hadn't had the courage to defy his father and break family tradition.

The more he thought on it, the more he wondered. Was joining the army an act of courage or an act of cowardice on his part? He suspected the latter. Which brought up the other question, never far from his thought, bubbling back into his brain. When or if the time came, would he stand and fight in the tradition of his ancestors? Or panic in the face of the enemy and be cashiered from the service? Would the last of the Justines prove to be a coward? Was he his stern, strong father's son, or his sensitive and gentle mother's?

The answers still eluded him as he finally slipped into the comforting darkness of sleep.

Badger, riding his honor post as the rearmost of the rear guard, twisted in the saddle to stare through the heavy rain toward the crossing point of the Red River.

Maman-ti's medicine was strong.

As Maman-ti had predicted, a long string of wagons had appeared on the prairie barely half a sun after the lone wagon had passed. Seven white men lay dead or dying within minutes of the attack. The gurgled screams of the one chained to the wagon tongue, facedown over the fire with his tongue cut out, lingered comfortably in Badger's mind.

Then the rains came, as Maman-ti had seen in his vision. Already, the river's rolling red waters spread and deepened. Soon it would be in full flood. Even if the horse soldiers managed to follow the raiders' trail through the heavy mud, the river would stop them in their tracks.

It was yet another sign.

The Great Spirit had sent the rain to aid his children.

If Maman-ti had been wrong in one respect, it was but a small matter. The wagons had not yielded great quantities of guns, bullets, and goods. They carried only corn, forage for the horse soldiers' mounts and mules. Yet the raid was a success. Six fresh scalps dangled from Kiowa saddles and bridles. One of those six rode at Badger's right knee, along with the scrotal pouch of the biggest wagon driver. The skin sack would make a powerful medicine bag.

Best of all, the spirits had given Badger the white man

while the mule driver still lived, pinned to the ground by Badger's lance. The sharp memory of the man's agonized screams as Badger slowly sliced off his genitals, then his scalp, brought a warm glow to Badger's breast.

The big man had been the second to fall. Satank had taken the first, Badger the second. None could dispute Badger's claim to the trophies. He had taken them under the approving gaze of Satank.

Ahead, four times ten captured mules plodded through the mud, flanked on either side by warriors.

Yes, it had been a good raid. Especially for Badger. He could feel the power of his medicine surge through his veins. Not since the days of Satank's youth had a young warrior so quickly earned such respect among his Kiowa and Comanche brothers as had Badger.

Best of all, the raid had been almost under the noses of the horse soldiers from the place called Fort Richardson. If the handful of white men who did escape made it back to the fort, so much the better. The soldiers and other whites then would know the strength and courage of the Kiowa and Comanche nations. The alliance of the people who once, long ago, had been enemies would drive the white man back beyond the Big River. The reservation lands would be but a memory.

And the young woman Tiesuat tatzinupi—Small Star—would be his.

It was a good time to be young.

Badger shook himself from his musings and peered through the rain toward the hills beyond the river. He saw no sign of life and was reassured. Even if the horse soldiers' medicine led them to the trail, even if they found the magic to cross the flooded river, it would be of no consequence. The raiders were now safe on reservation lands. The white man would not follow. Badger did not fully understand why it was so, why some unseen line across the land would stop the horse soldiers but not the raiding parties. It was enough that it did.

He reined his long-riding horse toward the sheltering

hills ahead, the roan war pony trailing close behind on loose lead. The heavy rain pounded against the paint on his face, turned it into small rivulets of red and black and yellow. That also was of no concern. The raid was over.

Soon, he would tie ponies before Small Star's lodge.

4

"ROLL OUT, TROOPER. We've got Indians to find."

Corporal Charlton's call jarred Justine awake. Seconds later the Boots and Saddles bugle call sounded, muted by the drumroll of raindrops against the canvas tent.

"What's going on, Corporal?" Justine asked as he reached for his uniform. A tingle of apprehension raced up his spine.

"Indians hit a wagon train yesterday afternoon on Salt Grass Prairie. Two men lived through it. They reached the post about midnight. Mackenzie's ordered two full companies formed up. Get cracking, Justine. We move out in thirty minutes."

It didn't take the full half hour.

Justine had barely pulled the cinch tight, checked his weapons, and mounted the cold-jawed bay before Charlton and six other scouts, blacker blobs against a black night, moved out at the trot.

Within a half mile, Justine realized with a start bordering on panic that he was totally lost in the pitch black of the night and pounding rain in unfamiliar terrain. If he fell behind the others, he would never be able to find the fort again.

It was all the incentive a man needed to keep up and pay attention. Charlton and the others knew where they were going.

The small party slogged through mud that grew deeper by the moment. Horses' hooves slipped and skidded on the surface that now seemed as slick as Maine ice. The mounts snorted and tossed their heads, uneasy with the insecure footing. At least, Justine thought, the simple act of moving kept the bay's attention on something other than fighting the bit.

By the time the sky had begun to brighten a bit, the landscape still a muted dark gray in the steady downpour, Justine was soaked through to the skin. The oiled canvas field coat seemed to collect more rain than it turned. Water poured from the brim of his hat, trickled beneath his collar, and traced an icy finger down his back.

The faint light eased some of Justine's fears about being left behind and lost, but the cold knot in his belly didn't go away. Something about riding toward an unseen enemy with only seven men had a way of putting a twist in a man's gut. He gradually maneuvered the bay alongside Charlton's buckskin. The corporal cut a quick glance at Justine.

"Ever do any tracking, Ned?"

"Just deer, bear, and the like back home. Not men."

"All the same. An animal's an animal, four legs or two. Kiowas and Comanches are a lot tougher to track, though. Not as predictable in their habits, and a sight trickier when it comes to hiding a trail." Charlton paused and waved a couple of hand signals. Two of the men reined their mounts aside, spreading out from the rest. Within seconds the two disappeared behind the wall of water. "Looks like you'll just have to learn on the job, Justine. Too bad we couldn't spend a little more time training before tossing you to the wolves on your first time out."

"I wish you had phrased that a bit differently, Corporal," Justine said through jaws clenched to keep his teeth from chattering. "About the wolves, I mean. How many Indians do you think are out there?"

"One of the teamsters who lived through it said he thought a hundred, maybe more," Charlton said casually.

"What . . . what if we find them? Before the others catch up?"

"They'll kill us. If they're feeling generous about it.

Wouldn't worry too much. Indians being Indians, they're long gone by now. Best we can hope for is to cut their sign before it completely washes out, then track them to wherever they're going. Probably back to the reservation, where they'll feel safe. It won't do them any good this time."

"What do you mean, this time?"

"For once, we got orders that make sense. Until now, troops have been barred from going onto reservation land. This time—if we can follow the trail—we don't stop at the Red River. We go onto the reserve and get them. Direct order from Sherman. All of a sudden the general's convinced we've really got Indian problems out here."

Justine rode in silence for a time, glancing at the grim expressions of the men riding with them. Four were seasoned cavalrymen. The two who now ranged far ahead and to either side were Charlton's best Tonkawa Indian scouts. He asked Charlton about those two.

"An Indian can find another Indian a lot quicker than a white man can," Charlton said. "There's a generations-long feud between the Comanches and Tonkawas. Tonks hate Kiowas with a passion, and don't like Comanches even that much. Tonks catch a Comanche, they eat part of him. Big medicine. Gives them the Comanche's power."

Justine shuddered, but not from the cold and wet. He had never ridden with cannibals before.

"Whiskey Pete, the older one, has been tracking the Southern Plains tribes for years," Charlton said. "George, the young one out on left flank, is nearly as good a tracker as Pete. They're good men. Just don't eat supper with them after they've made a kill." The corporal sighed. "Still, I sure would like to have old Lige with us."

"Lige?"

"Elijah Thompson. Civilian. Scouts for the army from time to time. Hates Kiowas and Comanches even worse than the Tonks do. Despises anybody with a red skin, in fact, and hasn't got much use for white folks, either.

Grouchy old cuss, but the best tracker I've ever seen, white or red. That old man can follow one snowflake through a blizzard. The colonel doesn't like Thompson much personally, but Mackenzie's smart enough to use every edge he can get."

Charlton peered into the rain-shrouded distance. Justine wondered why the corporal bothered. He couldn't see twenty feet past his own horse's ears. "Won't be long now, if that teamster had his directions right." He turned to Justine. "Ned, I've got to warn you. What we'll find up ahead isn't going to be pretty."

Justine sagged against a scorched wagon wheel, the driving rain forgotten as his belly tried to come up through his teeth.

There wasn't much left of the six naked bodies that lay scattered among the wagons. Dozens of bullet holes and lance and arrow wounds gashed the scalped and mutilated things that once had been living, breathing men. The wounds, washed clean of blood by the rain, looked like angry, dark-edged specks and slashes surrounded by skin the color of chalk. Bits of skull exposed by scalping knives and axe blows glowed white in the weak light.

It was the remains of the seventh man that finally had broken Justine's resolve and sent the contents of his stomach burning up through his throat and nose to spew into the mud until the heaves brought up nothing but aching ribs and gasps for air between bouts of retching.

Chains from the mule hitches held the charred body of the teamster fast to the tongue of the lead wagon. The rain had doused the blaze set beneath his head, but not before the skin seared black and cracked open. The man's face was burned beyond recognition, but the jaw remained open in a final, agonized scream.

The man's tongue had been cut out.

Justine felt a light touch on his shoulder.

"You all right now, trooper?" Charlton asked.

Justine managed a weak nod and willed his cramped stomach muscles to straighten. He wiped a rain-drenched hand across the foul matter on his lips. "Sorry, Corporal. I—"

"Don't be ashamed, Justine. It happens to all of us the first time. And usually again when the body's that of a woman, and again if it's a child. What they do to suckling infants is worst of all."

"My God, what sort of person . . . could do that . . . to another human being?" Justine tried to turn his face from the charred horror chained to the wagon tongue. His gaze stayed there as if nailed in place by a power stronger than his own will.

Charlton said, "It's the Indian way. When it comes to captives or dead enemies, they *aren't* human. At least by white man's standards. It's part of their culture. Before the whites came, they did the same to other Indians. Don't try to understand it, Ned. Just accept it. And remember it, if you ever find yourself surrounded." Charlton gave Justine a final reassuring pat on the shoulder. "Take a few minutes to get yourself together. Whiskey Pete'll be back soon with Mackenzie and the boys."

Justine managed to regain control of his churning gut by the time the advance unit of the Fourth appeared. To Ned's surprise, Mackenzie himself rode at the head of the detachment astride his prized iron gray gelding.

"I didn't think commanders of his rank actually led their troops in the field," Justine said to Charlton, as much to keep his mind off the mutilated bodies as to invite comment on his commanding officer.

"Mackenzie's a different bird," Charlton said.

Mackenzie reined in. For a time he didn't speak. He surveyed the carnage with a steady gaze, a jaw muscle twitching, eyes narrowed and glinting in anger. Then he turned to Charlton. "Corporal, get your scouts back on the trail while we can still find it. I'll get a burial detail together and do what we can for these poor souls, then follow you. Relay riders to keep us informed of your progress. Your appraisal, Corporal?"

Charlton shook his head. "Not promising, Colonel. They've got a twenty-four-hour head start on us, and the way this rain's coming down the trail won't last long."

"Just do your best. And then a bit better." Mackenzie stared off toward the north for a moment. He flipped the stumps of his damaged fingers together, the light snaps audible through the steady hammer of raindrops. "I want the Indians who did this, Corporal Charlton."

"Yes, sir." Charlton swung into the saddle and nodded to Justine and the other scouts. "Let's get to work, men. We've wasted enough time here."

Justine rode at Charlton's right. His belly still cramped. Whether it was the sight of the dead teamster burned into his brain or sheer, selfish terror that he could wind up facedown over a fire with his own tongue cut out, he didn't know. Part of his brain hoped they could find the butchers. Another part prayed they wouldn't.

Within a couple of miles, a distance that could be covered in thirty minutes on dry ground but now consumed the better part of two hours, the faint trail of torn prairie grass and overturned rocks that marked the raiders' retreat faded into a watery quagmire churned by the incessant rain.

The two Tonkawas reined their mounts away from the main trail, one headed to the left, the other to the right, without a word or signal from Charlton. The corporal, water cascading from the brim of his hat, turned to Justine.

"We're losing them," Charlton said bitterly. "Damn this rain. The colonel's already mad enough to eat a wagon rim. Notice how he was snapping those finger stumps of his?"

"Yes, I did," Justine said.

"When Mackenzie starts doing that, trooper, he's mad through to the bone. A word of advice. If possible, stay clear of him when he's doing that." Charlton wiped a saturated sleeve across his face.

The corporal's curses turned sharper as the miles passed, the winded horses laboring through the sucking mud. Justine felt the bay's sides heave against his thighs, heard the rapid puffs through the horse's nostrils as the animal struggled for air. The gelding's muscles already quivered from fatigue. Justine had never imagined that struggling through deep mud could sap a horse's strength and endurance as quickly as fighting through drifts of Maine snow.

After another half hour, Charlton called a halt. "Dismount and lead," he said. "No need to kill good horses in a lost cause."

Justine stepped from the saddle. His boots sank past the ankle. Mud grabbed his feet and wouldn't let go. Within minutes, his thighs and calves burned from the effort of battling the clinging goop. He idly wondered if he would ever be able to salvage his boots. Red mud attacked and climbed his legs until he felt encased to the knee. Each foot seemed to weigh a hundred pounds. He couldn't pull enough air into his lungs.

Charlton called a halt shortly after what Justine assumed was midafternoon; it was hard to judge time, with the sun obscured by the dense cloud cover.

Whiskey Pete appeared through gloom, leading his horse, man and animal as coated with mud as any of the others. The Tonkawa leveled a steady gaze at Charlton and shook his head silently.

Charlton's shoulders slumped. He muttered a curse. "That's it. We've lost them." He turned to one of the veteran troopers. "Franklin, get back to Mackenzie. Tell him it's no good. It looks like they were headed for the reservation, but we can't tell for sure. Inform the colonel we'll wait for him at the banks of the Wichita."

The trooper struggled into the saddle and reined his mount back the way they had come.

"What do we do now, Corporal?" Justine asked.

"Nothing much we can do." Charlton snorted in disgust. "You just had your first real lesson in scouting, Justine. We find two hundred trails, we'll lose a hundred ninety-nine of them. If we're that lucky. For now, we go on to the river and see if there's any way to ford, which I seriously doubt, and wait for Mackenzie. What we do after that depends on the colonel."

Badger squatted beside his lodge on the western edge of the Kiowa-Comanche reservation, as far as his band could settle from the agency at Fort Sill and still be on ground safe from the horse soldiers.

The sun, now midway down the western sky, warmed his bare chest as he stroked the edge of his knife against the sharpening stone to restore the keen edge blunted against skin and bone during the raid on the wagon train. The scalp and scrotal sack hung from crossed sticks, scraped clean of fat and bits of flesh, the trophies now drying in the blaze of spring sun.

Pride still stirred within Badger's breast.

The homecoming, with its trophies and spoils of war, had been more subdued than it would have been off reservation lands. The scalp dance had lasted but one evening, but the brief celebration would remain in his memory forever. The praise of Satank and the other war leaders still rang in his ears.

And in the first light of the following dawn, Small Star had come to him at their private meeting place. He could still feel her softness, see in his mind's eye the way she stretched, contented, sunlight through the trees dappling her bare dark skin and black hair.

She had chosen him.

All that remained now was to acquire two more ponies and she would be his. Six fine horses and the medicine pouch he would make from the white man's scrotum should be enough of a bride price for Holds-His-Horses's youngest daughter—

"Badger." The soft voice cut through his musings. "I was hoping to find you here. There is news. It is not good."

Badger turned to Yellowfish. "What is it, my friend?"

"The big war chief of all the horse soldiers, the one called Sherman, is now at Fort Sill. He is very angry about the raid on the wagons. Even as we speak, soldiers from the fort and Agent Bald Head Tatum search the whole of the reservation for those responsible for the raid. It is said they will be taken in chains and tried under the white man's law. And the news gets worse."

Badger's own brow furrowed. "In what way, Yellowfish?"

"Satank was very angry that others tried to claim credit for the raid. He rode to the fort and personally boasted to Bald Head that he and he alone was the leader."

Badger's lips thinned in a grimace. If Satank had a weakness, it was an overabundance of pride. Even if it meant being taken away in chains, Satank intended that no other would be given the glory of such a raid.

"What of the others? Eagle Heart, Big Tree, Satanta? Maman-ti?"

"Eagle Heart slipped away before the soldiers could get him." Yellowfish's eyes narrowed. "Maman-ti has vanished. I suggest that you and I do the same, Badger. There are those among our own people who would sell us to the white soldiers for a haunch of mouldy beef. Your name is more well known than mine, but it is common knowledge we both were among those who rode against the wagons. I do not wish to rot in the white man's iron cage."

Badger fell silent for a moment, his heart sinking. "But what of Star? What if Scar Nose ties ponies before her lodge?"

Yellowfish's hand settled reassuringly on his friend's shoulder. "I have spoken with her. She will wait. She wishes only for you to be safe, and to return when the white man's fire of anger has died away."

Again, Badger did not make an immediate reply. The gamble was great. To stay likely meant banishment forever to the white man's cage. To leave might cost him Small Star—to the despised Scar Nose, the one whose warrior's heart had softened in the last of his thirty summers. The one who beat his wives for no reason, who sometimes cut their flesh and disfigured them so other men would not try to steal them. The thought of Star in Scar Nose's blankets was almost more than Badger could bear.

It was as if Yellowfish could read his friend's mind.

"Scar Nose will not get her, Badger. No matter how many ponies he ties before her lodge, how many blankets and guns he offers, she will not be his."

"But if Holds-His-Horses accepts Scar Nose's price? What then?"

"If you are in chains, Badger, you cannot return to claim her. She has promised to wait for you, and you only. Is her word not enough?"

"I wish to consider this," Badger said.

Yellowfish's hand tightened on his shoulder. "Consider quickly, my friend. Bad Hand is on his way to Fort Sill."

Badger glanced at the lowering sun. His shoulders slumped. From the stories he had heard and had no reason to doubt, Bad Hand Mackenzie was a determined war chief among the horse soldiers. The tribes far to the south had felt Bad Hand's wrath soon after the white men stopped shooting each other. If either he or Yellowfish fell into Mackenzie's grasp, nothing good would happen.

"I wish to see Star, to discuss this with her."

"There is no time," Yellowfish said. "Spies among us may be watching her lodge, waiting for you to appear so they can alert the soldiers. Also, we must assume the horse soldiers know of this place. If not, someone soon will tell them."

"Where would we go?" Badger finally asked, his words soft, his tone weary.

"To Quanah's band in the land of the Quahadis. I have relatives and friends among Quanah's people. We will leave this cursed patch of rocks and dirt." Yellowfish paused for a moment, staring toward the southwest. "We cannot drive the white man from our land if we are in his chains."

Badger sighed. "Then we must go to the land of the wide grass. Not even Bad Hand will find us there. Before the time of falling leaves I will return to the reservation. To Small Star. And bring her with me, to live as Quahadi Comanche."

5

JUSTINE SAT ASTRIDE his big bay outside a cluster of lodges and listened as Charlton interrogated the Penateka Comanche band leader.

"Watching" might have been a better term than "listening," Justine mused. The corporal and the Indian stood in the wash of warm early June sunshine, speaking a mixture of Spanish, English, and Comanche. The polyglot of tongues defied Justine's attempts to follow the conversation.

He didn't need any linguistic talent to understand how the conversation unfolded. The Penateka shook his head vigorously at almost every question put to him by Charlton. The Indian obviously claimed to have no knowledge of any of his band, or the names of any others, who had participated in the Salt Creek Prairie massacre.

Justine tended to believe the Penateka. There was no evidence to the contrary visible in the village. No mules stolen in the raid, no personal possessions of the slain teamsters. Or much of anything except poverty.

Despite the Salt Creek images still fresh in his mind, Justine felt a twinge of sympathy for the reservation Indians. The shortage of decent food and basic necessities was evident in the gaunt faces of the adults. But it was the vacant, listless dark eyes of the children that knifed into Justine's heart.

One of the traits he had inherited from his mother was a soft streak where children were concerned. No boy or girl, regardless of skin color, should have a youthful spirit broken by want at such an early age. Justine thought for a moment of sharing his meager field rations with the children, but just as quickly abandoned the idea. He did not have enough for all.

Charlton abruptly mounted, glanced at the five troopers on this detail, and shook his head. "Might as well head back to the fort. We're not likely to find any Indian who knows a solitary thing about the raid. At least we've got the leaders."

Justine suppressed a sigh of relief at the prospect of returning to the relative comfort of Fort Sill. As he rode, he tried to shake the sense of sympathy with the Indians and their struggle to survive on insufficient supplies. He knew it wasn't Lawrie Tatum's fault. The agent the Indians called Bald Head constantly battled the government for more food, more blankets, more medicines, more everything, for his charges.

Nobody listened.

The government, Justine thought, either didn't care, or the Indian Bureau was heavily laced with graft and corruption. Or both. Either way, the reservation Indians were the losers. On the other hand, many of these reservation tribesmen slipped guns and ammunition supplied to them by the government for hunting purposes to their wilder friends and relatives, who then turned the weapons against the white man.

Justine's head buzzed in confusion. He wasn't sure he would ever be able to sort it all out.

He shook the nagging questions aside. It wasn't his job to understand. His job was to be a soldier. Or at least try to be. For now, he actually looked like one again. He hadn't thought it would be possible, but he finally felt clean.

The past few days in Fort Sill had given him a chance to chip away the mud accumulated during almost three weeks on the trail, counting the time the Fourth spent waiting for the flooded Wichita and Red rivers to drop enough that the column could safely cross.

It helped that Fort Sill had numerous laundresses. Within a day he had had his field uniform back, washed and pressed. It was worth the five cents not to have to tackle such a chore on his own. Some of the laundresses obviously made more money between the sheets than washing them. Justine wasn't interested in that. He had better things to do with what little money he could save from his army pay. College was expensive to a young man of limited means.

The stay at Fort Sill provided a welcome break for both men and mounts. Compared to the struggle through mud hock-deep to horses and the nervous crossing of flooded rivers, scouting for raiders and renegades on reservation lands had been almost a ride on the parade ground. The Fourth had accomplished little in the search, but, as Charlton had told Justine up front, they hadn't expected to.

The Tenth Cavalry troopers stationed at Fort Sill had more to show for their efforts. Satank, Satanta, and Big Tree, the major leaders of the Salt Creek Prairie massacre, were now in chains. Most of the warriors suspected of being involved in the raid had simply vanished.

"Don't get too comfortable, Justine," Charlton said. "We'll be heading back to Fort Richardson before the rest of the troops. The colonel's detailed us to take the prisoners back to Texas for trial. We move out in the morning."

Justine and Al Duggan rode a few yards behind the two wagons carrying the prisoners and their guards. Satank rode in the first wagon, Satanta and Big Tree in the second. All three Indians were shackled. Two armed troopers rode in Satank's wagon, Charlton in the one carrying Satanta and Big Tree.

Though they were less than a mile from Fort Sill, Charlton carried his Spencer carbine across his lap, his thumb on the hammer. Justine wondered why the corporal seemed so edgy. The Indians weren't going anywhere. He sneezed from the rooster tails of dust kicked up by the wagon wheels despite the soaking rains that had fallen only a few days ago.

Justine heard the soft moan and glanced at Duggan. The stocky veteran wiped a hand across his forehead, then squeezed the bridge of his nose between thumb and forefinger. "Feels like my head's about to pop wide open," Duggan said.

"If you'd go a bit easier on the payday whiskey, Al, maybe your head wouldn't hurt."

Duggan groaned again. "Ain't the quantity, it's the quality. Worst panther spit I ever tangled with. That whiskey runner ought to be chained to a wagon tongue and burnt like that teamster was."

Justine stifled a grin. "All I can say is, you'd best watch your step, Al. If the colonel catches you drinking when you're supposed to be on duty, he'll skin you alive himself—" He sat bolt upright in the saddle. "What's that?"

"What's what?"

"That singing. More like a chant, from the front wagon."

Duggan shrugged. "Who the hell knows? Injuns are always singin' some song or other."

A shrill yelp of pain sounded. A split second later, the two guards flung themselves from the front wagon. Through the sudden blur of action, Justine saw Satank half rise, grab one of the troopers' dropped carbines, and try to work the action.

Justine froze. It was if his brain had locked up; his heart raced, but his muscles refused to move. He could only sit in the saddle and stare as Charlton stood in the trailing wagon. Smoke belched from Charlton's carbine. Satank's body spun halfway around under the impact of the slug. The Kiowa twisted back toward Charlton, still yanking at the lever of the carbine. The corporal's Spencer cracked four more times, the muzzle blasts seeming to merge into a single harsh roll.

Satank tumbled from the wagon.

Justine finally managed to move. He pulled his carbine and spurred the bay forward, past one of the men who had dived from the wagon. Charlton still stood in the bed of the second wagon, rifle muzzle leveled at the bleeding body in the road.

"Watch out!" Charlton shouted without looking up from the sights. "He might not be dead yet!"

"What happened?" Justine's voice quavered.

"He had a hideout knife. Slipped his shackles somehow. Stabbed the driver and grabbed a rifle."

Justine cautiously dismounted and studied the body crumpled in the dust. "He's dead, Corporal."

Charlton lowered his carbine. "Better check on our men. We've got two down."

By the time Justine and Duggan had examined the two troopers' wounds, a bugler from Fort Sill had skidded his lathered mount to a stop. "The colonel heard shots and sent me," the bugler said. "What happened here?"

"We got a dead Kiowa," Duggan said, crouched beside the injured driver. "Satank made a break for it. He had a little pocket knife. Stabbed this man in the leg. Ain't bad. Should heal fine unless it gets infected."

The downed man at Justine's side moaned, his face twisted in pain and shock, eyes closed. "This one took a bullet in the hip," Justine said shakily, still stunned at the suddenness with which everything had happened. "He needs a surgeon."

"I'll get Mackenzie." The bugler whirled his mount and spurred into a run toward the fort.

Mackenzie obviously had started from the fort shortly after dispatching the bugler; the colonel reined his iron gray to a halt beside the wagons moments later. "What happened here, Corporal Charlton?" Mackenzie's eyes narrowed to little more than slits as he glanced around.

Charlton briefed the colonel. "I think one of my slugs went through Satank and hit the driver. Nobody else was shooting," he concluded. Justine saw Charlton square his shoulders and brace himself for an expected tongue-lashing.

The explosion never came.

Mackenzie turned to the half dozen cavalrymen who had ridden out with him. "Sergeant, put the wounded men in the empty wagon. See that they get proper medical attention back at the fort."

"Sir," one of the shaken guards said haltingly, "it's strange. Satank was chanting something before—before it happened."

"His death song, trooper," Mackenzie said. "He decided to end it here instead of facing the hangman's noose."

Charlton muttered, "Dammit, I should have known. Could have kept this from happening."

"What's done is done, Corporal," Mackenzie said, the sharp edge gone from his words. "Don't flog yourself over it." He glanced around the gathering of troopers. "You men remember that sound. If you hear it again, kill the Indian who's singing it on the spot. Before he kills one of you."

"What should we do with the body?"

"Leave it lay, Corporal," Mackenzie said. He turned a cold glare at the two remaining Indian captives. "Somebody slipped Satank that knife. Search these two again. Make sure they don't have any concealed weapons. I'll assign two more outriders to your escort, Charlton. Continue to Fort Richardson. Put the prisoners in the guardhouse and post as many guards as you feel necessary for absolute security."

"Yes, sir." Charlton thumbed fresh loads into the butt port of his Spencer.

"In the meantime, stake them out, spread-eagled, each night. Offer them absolutely no opportunity to escape. They must be made examples of what happens to Indians who butcher white men."

Mackenzie didn't wait for an acknowledgment of his orders. He wheeled the iron gray and started back toward Fort Sill.

Justine's fingers trembled as he sheathed his carbine and watched the colonel ride away. The uninjured guard who had leapt clear of Satank's wagon stood quietly, his head lowered, while other troopers loaded the injured men into the wagon. Justine felt a quick surge of compassion for the trooper. The man might have panicked in the face of an armed enemy, but Justine knew he had committed an equally severe sin himself. Surprise and fear had nailed him to the saddle, unable to react until too late. Shame and embarrassment flooded his cheeks.

His first exposure to a fight and the coward inside him surfaced.

None of the others seemed to have noticed his lack of response. That didn't matter. Ned had noticed. A heavy weight settled in his gut.

The last of the Justine line was unfit to wear the uniform, a disgrace to generations. . . .

The second night after Satank sang his death song, Justine stood first watch over the prisoners. He had never been quite so miserable in his life, and not just from the lingering sense of shame and disgrace.

The legacy of the hard rains of a few days past now rose in vast clouds and all but obscured the pale crescent of moon overhead. There had been mosquitoes in Maine, but nothing like this. Every exposed spot of his skin stung and itched. Welts burned even beneath the heavy cloth of his uniform. Only the snorting, stamping, and tail swishing of tormented horses penetrated the droning buzz of the swarm. A few yards away, soldiers slept fitfully under the insect assault, blankets pulled over their faces despite the muggy, oppressive heat.

Justine removed his hat, fanned the mosquitoes from his face and neck, and glanced at Satanta. The Kiowa, arms and legs spread by ropes tied to heavy stakes driven into the ground, twitched and winced in obvious agony.

Satanta's flesh was black with mosquitoes. The Indian's muscles quivered and strained against the restraints in a futile attempt to shake away the plague of insects.

On impulse, Justine knelt beside Satanta, alternately fanning himself and the Indian with his hat. The action brought some relief to the Indian. In the half light of the moon Justine couldn't be sure, but he thought he saw a brief flicker of gratitude in the black eyes that so far had reflected only hate of the white soldiers.

The sound of a footstep brought Justine to his feet. Charlton stepped to his side, waving his own hand in front of his face. Justine braced himself for a dressing down for his show of sympathy toward the men who had tortured and killed whites.

Instead of directing a tongue-lashing at Justine, the corporal stood silently for a moment, stared down at Satanta, then shook his head.

"Not even an Indian deserves to be eaten alive by mosquitoes when he can't move," Charlton said. "Justine, you've got the right idea." The corporal squatted beside Satanta. "Well, old man," he said to the Indian, "we may be in a war and war may be hell, and you may be nothing but a bloodthirsty, murdering savage, but I'm not. I'll be damned if those mosquitoes are going to torture you while you're helpless."

The corporal rose. "Time for guard change, Justine. Give me a few minutes. I'll roust out a couple of the others, have them fetch branches with plenty of leaves, and fan the mosquitoes away from the prisoners. Maybe they're going to hang for murder, but I won't have them suffer like this in the meantime."

Justine fully understood the true meaning of the word "misery" now.

He had never been so sick in his life.

The extended search for Indian sign through the upper

Brazos watershed already had earned its wry nickname, Mackenzie's Picnic, among the troops.

Justine sagged in the saddle, the cramps that knotted his intestines all but leaving him permanently bent at the waist, abdominal muscles so weak from vomiting, diarrhea, and exhaustion that he could barely stay astride.

Even the tough, cold-jawed bay between his knees seemed to be near his limit. The gelding had long since stopped fighting the bit. The horse stumbled often. Each unexpected jolt of the horse's missteps set off a new gurgling stab in Justine's lower belly. It seemed he had spent more time out of the saddle than in it, his pants around his ankles.

The humiliation of those first few attacks of loose bowels hadn't lasted long. Almost every man in the ragged Fourth Cavalry column was as pale and drawn as Justine. Even the surgeon, the normally spriteful Julius Patzky, could barely stay in the saddle. Of them all, Patzky seemed to have come down with the worst case of what had become known throughout the ranks as the bad water trots.

They had found no Indian sign. And no palatable water for days. The water holes indicated on Marcy's map, a document now nearly twenty years old, had dried up or otherwise turned foul.

Several troopers too ill to ride had to travel on litters suspended between two horses. A quarter of those who could mount seemed to spend half their time out of the saddle, squatted or bent over with dry heaves.

The Tonkawa scouts, roving far ahead of the main column with Charlton and Justine, weren't immune. Another myth about Indians shot down, Justine thought. They couldn't go for days without good water any more than a white man could.

Water holes fouled by the offal of huge buffalo herds and sluggish streams laced with gypsum salts didn't differentiate between officers and enlisted men.

Mackenzie himself often quickly dismounted to avoid

churning bowels or vomit up gypsum-laced coffee. Still, the colonel kept to his routine of riding at the front of the main column.

The animals suffered along with the men. More than a dozen horses and mules, crippled, exhausted, sick, or too weak to keep up, had been left behind in the past week.

Justine had never thought he would look back fondly on the long ride through driving rain from Salt Creek Prairie to Fort Sill. Today he gladly would have sold a big chunk of his soul for at least a quick, drenching shower of cool rainwater.

There wasn't a cloud in sight.

Just a high, brassy sun in a washed-out sky, further broiling a land scorched to shades of tan and brown.

Justine tried to stand in the stirrups to peer over a rocky ridge ahead; a scout was supposed to be a scout, even if he didn't feel exactly parade-ground sharp at the moment. He soon gave up the effort. If they rode into a nest of painted warriors, at least the Indians would put him out of his misery.

From the top of the ridge, he glanced over his shoulder. The Fourth Cavalry column a mile behind the scouts moved like an army of ants against the desolate landscape. As miserable as Justine was, he had to admit he was thankful to be a scout. At least out here in front, the air was reasonably clear and a man could breathe. The dust raised by the two hundred or so mounted men laid a choking fog over the troopers in the main column.

Al Duggan, riding alongside Justine—and often reaching out to prop Ned back into the saddle—was one of the few who had escaped the worst.

Duggan, a twinkle in his smoke-colored eyes, said, "Well, Ned, how do you like the glamour, romance, and adventure of the cavalry now that you've got yourself a real taste of life on the campaign trail? Think the ladies would be all a-flutter over the dashing young uniformed man on the bay horse now?"

Justine fought to control the sudden cramp in his already ravaged colon. "Have to say it's not exactly what I'd been led to expect, Al," he said. It seemed he could barely hear his own words. His voice croaked painfully through cracked lips.

"Yep," Duggan said, "reality has a way of sticking its thumb up a cavalryman's butt, time to time. And not a single redskin spotted the whole month. Or even Indian sign less than six weeks old. Worst may be yet to come, though."

"Worst?" Justine muttered. "How can it get worse?"

"I hear that as soon as we get back, Mackenzie's gonna turn us around and do it all over again. But this time, clear out onto the Staked Plains, where there ain't nothin'. And I mean nothin'. No trees, no shade, no water. Not even *bad* water. Just miles of empty piled on more miles just like 'em."

Justine moaned. "I've heard no man can survive out there."

"Mackenzie says if an Indian can survive it, a good horse soldier can. Much as I hate to admit it, I reckon he's right about goin' out there. You want to catch redskins, you got to go where they are. Take the fight to 'em on their own ground, where they think they're safe."

Justine abruptly reined in the bay. He half dismounted, half fell from the saddle, and dropped his trousers.

Duggan reined in his own mount and waited. His gaze continued to sweep the rugged hills broken by twisted arroyos, dry streams, and canyons. "Just as well we didn't find any Indians this time out," he said. "Shape this outfit's in now, we couldn't whip five Kickapoo kids too young to be in breechclouts. Hang in there, Ned. At least it'll get better—for a while anyhow—when we get back home."

Badger and Yellowfish reined at the rim of a deep canyon, its almost vertical walls streaked by tan, gray, red, and near-white strips of soil and stone. The scent of junipers lay thick in the hot breeze.

Yellowfish grinned, suddenly pleased with himself, and lifted a finger. "Our new home, my friend."

Relief flooded Badger's chest. The long search had finally ended. After two moons of cold trails, talks with travelers, and finding little but abandoned camps, all the while dodging the occasional party of Utes or other longtime enemies of the Kiowa-Comanche alliance, they had found this fresh trail. It led them to the main band of the Quahadi.

It was Badger's second time to see the canyon, with its ribbon of pure, sweet water glittering as it flowed between stands of trees. The first time he had been but a youth of barely nine summers.

Then, as now, it filled him with a sense of awe, of his own smallness.

The slash in the earth seemed out of place in the vast, flat expanse of grass that stretched as far as the eagle could see. He knew that among the Comancheros, this great canyon was called Palo Duro. To the Comanches, it was the Place of the Chinaberry Trees, a safe haven provided by the spirits to protect The People from enemies and from the cold winds that swept down from the plains during the time of snows. It gave them fresh water, wood for fires, forage for ponies, and abundant game in the many twisting side canyons below and on the flat grasslands above.

For a time, neither of the two men spoke, their gazes sweeping the distant string of lodges along the banks of the stream.

"Quanah's band," Yellowfish said. "I was not sure we would find them here at this time of year. The spirits have guided us well, my friend. It seems many others have left the reservation to join Quanah since we rode out, Badger. While we rode the long trail, others came directly here. Perhaps Quanah sent riders to tell them where to meet. Let us go and greet my kinsmen among them."

Halfway down the steep, twisting trail to the canyon floor, a passage barely wide enough for one horse to descend at a time, Badger's breath caught in his throat.

One of the lodges far below seemed to glow in the rays of the sun, the symbols painted on the skin sides unmistakable.

It was the lodge of Holds-His-Horses.

And where that lodge was, Small Star would be.

6

JUSTINE'S HEART SKIPPED a beat as he opened the door of the stage from Fort Worth.

The bright flash of white teeth and the warmth of the young woman's smile, reflected in eyes of such a deep blue as to seem almost indigo, swept the dust and tumult of the Jacksboro street from Justine's conscious mind. Along with everything else except the cascade of blond hair that fell about her shoulders and the satin ribbon around the trim neck. She was the most beautiful young woman he had ever seen.

For a moment he simply stood, stunned, his manners forgotten, before the sudden warmth in his cheeks told him he had been staring like a stricken schoolboy.

He quickly removed his hat. "Mrs. Hopkins?"

"Yes, I'm Elaine Hopkins." Her voice was soft, musical, and carried the inflections of New England.

"Trooper Ned Justine, ma'am, at your service. I am to escort you to your quarters at Fort Richardson." He inclined his head in a slight bow. "Lieutenant Hopkins extends his apologies at being unable to greet you in person because of pressing duties on the post."

If her husband's absence distressed her, it didn't show. She merely nodded, her smile dimpling smooth cheeks. "Thank you, Mr. Justine. I truly appreciate the courtesy."

He extended a hand to help her from the stage. The touch of her fingers sent a tingle through him. She stepped from the stage and stood at his side for a moment. Her hand lingered in his. She was fine boned, little more than five feet tall, and appeared to be in her late teens. Justine thought she seemed awfully young to be married to a first lieutenant who was pushing forty, and pushing even harder for a promotion. Her bright smile and gentle warmth stood in stark contrast to her husband's sour coldness. It was no secret the lieutenant was universally disliked and mistrusted—even hated—in the enlisted ranks.

"How was your trip, ma'am?" Justine asked as she released his hand. The warmth of her touch seemed to linger on his skin.

She brushed back a stray strand of golden hair. "A bit dusty at times, and occasionally the ride was somewhat rough. It was quite an adventure, however. My first trip on a real frontier stage line. On the whole, I must say it was thoroughly enjoyable. So many new experiences."

Justine replaced his hat and tugged it down against the stiffening west wind. A gust swirled the skirts of her blue gown, lifted her petticoats to reveal the trim ankle of a small foot clad in lace-up shoes.

"Perhaps you will find the officers' quarters acceptable, Mrs. Hopkins," Justine said, "but I would be remiss not to warn you that housing and facilities are somewhat crude out here."

"I'm sure I will find it satisfactory, Mr. Justine," she said. "I wasn't exactly expecting a fine hotel like those back home."

Justine reached for the bags the driver handed down. "If I may be so bold, ma'am, may I ask where 'home' is?"

"Boston, originally. From your accent and phrasing, I would place you as a Northeasterner as well."

"Maine, Mrs. Hopkins. You will find that there are a number of New Englanders in the Fourth Regiment. Several of the women are from the East."

"Are there many women at the post?"

"More than one would expect, ma'am. Wives of officers and higher ranking noncommissioned officers, first sergeants and the like." He didn't mention the laundresses and camp followers. He loaded her bags into the spring buggy, the newest available at the post, with well-padded leather seats. She traveled light. Instead of the half dozen Gladstone bags and heavy steamer trunk he expected, she had only three small cases.

Justine introduced her to the two mounted outriders, Duggan and a new recruit named Smith. Both men removed their hats and bowed slightly. Justine couldn't help but notice that Smith's gaze raked her body as if peeling away the blue gown to see what was underneath. The look irritated Justine. It took a moment for him to realize the source of his irritation.

It was jealousy.

He tried to push the absurd thought aside. How could he possibly be jealous of the attention a beautiful young woman naturally attracted, especially one he had just met? A married one at that?

He again offered a hand, helped her into the buggy, and climbed onto the driver's seat. Before releasing the brake, he checked the action of his Spencer to reassure himself that a cartridge was chambered, and placed the carbine within easy reach.

Her eyes widened as she watched him handle the rifle. "Is it true that everyone on the frontier is armed?"

Justine clucked the mare into motion. "Yes, ma'am, just about," he said. "It is hazardous country. In addition to the white outlaw element, we've had several Indian raids, some practically within a stone's throw of Fort Richardson." He heard her quick gasp and added, "Please don't be alarmed, ma'am. There have been few incidents of late. Most of the Indian raids happened before I arrived."

He reined the mare around a big Conestoga freighter onto the dusty road toward Fort Richardson. "I hope weapons don't make you nervous."

Her smile returned. "Not really. It just seems that I've seen more guns today than in all my years back East."

"There are more dangers in the West." Justine hesitated a moment, wondered if he were about to step over the line drawn between officers' wives and enlisted men, then added, "If you will pardon my boldness, Mrs. Hopkins, those dangers increase for such an attractive young woman as yourself."

She placed a hand on his forearm. Justine felt the warmth of her touch even through the heat of the afternoon and the sleeve of his heavy wool dress uniform. "Thank you for the compliment, Mr. Justine. Would you please call me Elaine?"

Justine shook his head. "It would be best if I didn't, ma'am. It isn't appropriate for enlisted men to address the wives of officers by first name." He glanced at her, felt the full impact of that devastating smile and the giddy swirl it triggered in his head.

"I apologize, Mr. Justine. I'm afraid I have much to learn of military ways. Lieutenant Hopkins and I were married only a few months ago. Three days after the ceremony, he was assigned to frontier duty with the Fourth. Perhaps you and I will see each other from time to time."

The thought both intrigued and concerned Justine. Where common soldiers were concerned, undue familiarity with an officer's wife could mean a quick trip before a court-martial board and the guardhouse. If the husband didn't kill the enlisted man first.

Duggan and Smith moved out of earshot as the outskirts of Jacksboro fell behind. Duggan took the left flank, twenty yards away. Smith had the right flank. Justine was relieved. For some reason he couldn't explain, he didn't want the two men listening in on his quiet conversations with her.

"Is there a Catholic chapel and priest on the post, Mr. Justine?" she asked. "I've had such few opportunities to attend Mass or confession during the trip west."

"Yes, ma'am. Of a sort. The Fourth Regiment has chaplains conversant in most major faiths." He idly wondered what sins such a young woman might feel the need to confess. He didn't dare ask.

"Are you a religious man?"

"Raised as a Baptist, ma'am." Justine chanced a grin and a glance. "I got over it, though." The small joke brought her musical laugh bubbling to the surface.

They rode in silence for a time. For once, there was little traffic on the road from Jacksboro to the fort. The chestnut buggy mare knew the road well. Justine didn't have to drive, just hold the lines. He made a conscious effort to avoid staring at the woman beside him, but couldn't resist an occasional furtive glance. Each time, he saw Elaine Hopkins studying something, her dark blue eyes wide in wonder.

"This is such a beautiful country," she finally said.

The remark took Justine by surprise. He hadn't been able to see much of anything but heat, dust, mud, rocks, bugs, snakes, cold, and misery in this land. But when he thought on it, he recognized a sort of stark, subtle beauty to the series of rocky hills that seemed to roll on forever like ocean breakers, with their wind-twisted and stubby post oaks, the frequent patches of sprawling prickly pear or bush cactus, the clumps of sun-seared, tall buffalo grass sprinkled here and there against the backdrop of rocks and predominately red soil.

"Yes, I suppose it is, in its own way," Justine said. "It's certainly . . . different, I suppose the word would be—from the forests and mountains back home."

"Do you miss it, Mr. Justine? Home, I mean?"

He sighed softly and mouthed a partial lie. "I've been too busy to think about it much, Mrs. Hopkins." It was true he had been kept occupied. He couldn't tell her that he rode at least part of each day with a hollow ache in his chest. Pride wouldn't permit a man to openly admit to homesickness. She seemed satisfied with his answer.

The ride to the fort seemed entirely too short to Justine. He dutifully delivered Elaine Hopkins into the hands of the corporal of the post guard and the clutches of a flock of military wives, all peppering her with questions about news and fashions from back East and a dozen other topics of interest to women isolated on the frontier.

He parked the buggy beside the stables and led the mare into the picket corral. Duggan strode alongside, humming an old Civil War marching song, leading his mount. Neither animal had been overworked during the short trip, but that didn't matter. In the cavalry, and in Mackenzie's command in particular, a trooper cared for the animals in his charge.

Justine was relieved that Smith didn't accompany them. He knew it was no concern of his, but he didn't much care for the way Smith looked at Elaine.

He realized with a start he had thought of her by first name.

"Damn shame," Duggan muttered in disgust as he unsaddled.

"What's that?"

"The girl. Damn shame to waste such a fine-looking young woman on a horse's ass like Hopkins. It ain't fair, Ned."

Justine sighed. "Nobody said life was fair." He wondered why his throat had suddenly tightened up.

"Maybe you'll get lucky and the Indians will kill him."

"Why would that be lucky for me?"

"I seen the way she looked at you, Ned. That gal's took an interest in you. Don't know why, you bein' as ugly as a wet possum, but it's plain as war paint on a Kiowa."

"Oh, come on, Al. You're imagining things." Justine's cheeks flushed despite the protest.

"Maybe. Maybe not. Either way, I don't reckon I have to remind you to be mighty careful around an officer's wife. 'Specially that officer's."

"No, you don't."

Duggan sighed, racked his saddle, dipped his fingers into the tallow used to keep leather soft, pliable, and somewhat waterproof, and started rubbing the stirrup leathers. "May not matter anyhow, at least for a spell. Lige Thompson's back. That old man don't show unless he's cut Indian sign somewhere. Big parley goin' on with the colonel right now. And Mackenzie's called in every unit of the Fourth from the Rio Grande north."

Justine frowned at Duggan. "Think this Thompson fellow has found an Indian encampment?"

"Likely. Or he'd still be out lookin'. I got a feelin' we'd best not get too used to soft cots, good water, and regular grub, Ned. Whether we find any Injuns or not, we're gonna be seein' a sizeable chunk of Comanche country this time out."

The night seemed never to end for Badger.

He squatted against a stone outcrop halfway up the steep side of the wall of stone and brush overlooking the Place of the Chinaberry Trees, unable to sleep, his heart heavy in his chest.

He peered through the starlit darkness toward the ponies tied before the lodge below. Star's lodge.

They were not his ponies.

They belonged to Scar Nose.

Embers of hate smoldered beneath the icy dread that gripped Badger's chest. Hate for the short, bandy-legged, ugly Comanche called Scar Nose.

He was an easy man to hate, one held beneath the contempt of the true warriors of the Comanches. None of Scar Nose's claims of many enemies slain in battle and coups counted had been witnessed. Those who had secretly examined the scalps that dangled from Scar Nose's seldom-used lance said the trophies appeared to be not from warriors, but of women and captive Mexicans. Yet no one disputed the claims. Scar Nose had taken the sacred oath on each of his claims, and the spirits had not struck him down. Therefore, the claims must be true.

Badger did not question the power of the sacred vow. But in his heart, he knew Scar Nose to be a liar and coward.

Unfortunately, Scar Nose also was a wealthy man. He

owned many ponies, blankets, knives, and two wives—both of whom he often beat nearly to death. Badger could not believe Star's father would sell his favorite daughter to such a man. But the offer of eight fine ponies, a stack of blankets, and several cooking pots might prove to be more than Holds-His-Horses could resist. If the price were accepted, Star would be forced to become Scar Nose's woman. If she refused despite her father's acceptance of the bride price, Holds-His-Horses had the right under Comanche custom to force her into marriage. Or even kill her.

Badger could do nothing but wait.

A lifetime seemed to pass before the first light broke the eastern sky.

Badger's heart chilled as the lodge flap opened and Star emerged. He held his breath as she stood still for a moment before reaching for the knots in the rawhide ropes securing the ponies. If she drove the offered horses into her father's herd, Badger had lost her—

His heart pounded against his ribs as she untied the last of the ponies. The moment of reckoning was at hand.

Star drove the horses back toward Scar Nose's herd.

Badger almost whooped aloud, his heart near bursting with joy. The offering had been refused.

He was on his feet in an instant, half running, half skidding, down the steep slope of the canyon wall. He fought back the urge to run straight to her; such a thing was not done.

By the time the new sun had climbed a hand span above the far wall of the canyon, Badger was in place, waiting for her.

His breath almost left him again as she strode toward him along the path through the cottonwoods to the river, a water bag crooked in an arm. She pretended not to expect him. But the small clearing in the trees a few strides from the path had been their secret meeting place since Badger had ridden in almost a moon ago.

Star stopped as Badger stepped from behind the broad trunk of an ancient cottonwood.

Badger's heart seemed to flutter, as it always did in her presence. Star's beauty, her trim, lithe body beneath the loose doeskin dress she wore, never failed to awe him. For a girl of only fifteen winters, she carried herself with an erect confidence and dignity beyond her years. Her wide brown eyes softened as she gazed into his face.

"You refused Scar Nose," he said. "My heart sang when you returned his ponies."

"You saw?"

As if she thought he could do anything else, Badger mused inwardly. "I waited all night on the far canyon wall. For the first time in my life, Star, I felt fear."

She smiled, a gentle lifting of the corners of her mouth. "You had nothing to fear, Badger. It is you I have chosen."

"Your father . . ." His voice trailed away.

"He was stubborn. Even now I do not know if his arguments were to tease me, or if his words were serious. The discussion lasted most of the night. Finally, my mothers and I convinced him that you would be the better husband and provider. That you would bring an even richer offering."

Her smile widened slightly. "I think it most likely he was teasing me, and my mothers, who all threatened to banish him from their sleeping robes if he accepted the offering. Still, it could not have been easy for him to refuse such a rich price."

Badger swallowed. His mouth had gone dry. "I do not yet have so many ponies."

"You will have. I will wait. And when you bring them, I will turn them into my father's herd." She brushed her fingers against his arm and glanced around. Voices and laughter sounded, louder and closer now, as other women came for water. She slipped her hand inside his arm and led him to the private place.

There, they would not be disturbed.

Badger ignored the hot, hard stare from the dark-skinned, stocky man seated across the council fire. A quick glance into the narrowed black eyes was enough to reaffirm what Badger already knew.

The potbellied man with thin, bowed legs, the left nostril missing from a mutilated nose, would kill him at first chance. Badger knew Scar Nose lacked the courage to voice an outright challenge. But he vowed not to turn his back on Scar Nose, even in battle against a common enemy.

Judging from the expression on Quanah's face, that battle might come soon.

Quanah was only a few summers older than Badger, but his standing as a warrior and leader already had reached the status of legend. His stature alone was impressive—tall for a Comanche, lean and smoothly muscled like the mountain cat, the expression in the eyes confident.

That Badger and Quanah shared a somewhat similar background—Quanah the son of a chieftain father and a captive white woman—was of no consequence. Nonetheless, Badger was pleased and flattered that Quanah had personally invited him to this council. Other warriors had been summoned by messenger; Quanah had ridden out to the horse herd, where Badger stood watch, to request his attendance. It was not an honor to be taken lightly. Only a few others had been so invited.

Badger's acceptance into the Quahadi band, and on occasion into Quanah's own lodge, had been quick and complete. And to Badger, welcomed. The Quahadis were the last truly free people of the southern plains. They had never signed a paper with the white man. Their customs were not that much different from those of the Kiowas. Badger felt at home half a sun after he and Yellowfish had ridden into the Place of the Chinaberry Trees.

There were few preliminary ceremonies for this meeting. The ceremonial fire was small. It was to be a less formal council, involving only a few tribal elders, two medicine men, the veteran subchiefs Para-a-coom and Mow-way, and the best warriors of the Quahadi. All waited, silent and expectant, as Quanah rose, the pipe ceremony completed.

"Our scouts have confirmed the whispers we all have heard," Quanah said. He did not raise his voice. There was no need. His words were strong and clear. "The time of turning leaves nears. Even now, the soldier chief Bad Hand gathers his men at the place called Fort Richardson. The soldiers are many. They have many wagons, many horses. Bad Hand has summoned more of the Tonkawas to guide them."

Quanah paused for a moment, let the murmur of rage at the mention of the hated Tonkawas fade. "After the leaves turn, these soldiers will leave their village. They will try to come into our lands, our camps, to kill our women and children and drive us from our sacred canyons and wide grass hunting grounds. They will try to force us onto the small patch of earth they call a reservation. This we will not allow to happen. We will meet them. And we will stop them."

A murmur of agreement rose from the throats of the gathered warriors. Badger cut a quick glance at Yellowfish, seated beside him. Excitement glittered in Yellowfish's eyes as he silently nodded to Badger. The same expression showed on the faces of many others. Several bands—Comanches, Kiowas, Cheyennes, even an occasional Arapaho—were represented here. Trouble and times of hunger on the reservation in the wake of the Salt Creek raid had swollen the ranks of Quanah's Quahadis.

"In three suns," Quanah continued after the mutterings faded, "the war pipe will be passed. Those who choose to smoke will ride with me against the horse soldiers."

7

"NED, CHARLTON WANTS us."

Justine looked up from the letter he was composing to his folks. Al Duggan stood in the doorway of the picket quarters, wearing a field jacket. The draft from the open door carried the evening chill inside. The candle beside the paper flickered.

Justine wiped the remaining ink from the quill pen and set it aside on the wooden chest that served multiple duties as his uniform storage closet, table for cleaning weapons and repairing equipment, and it was a functional if uncomfortably low writing desk. He puffed out the guttering candle and followed Duggan outside.

By the time he had taken a dozen strides, Justine wished he had worn his jacket. The north wind that was about to usher September into history held more of a bite than his uniform blouse could turn.

Curiosity soon pushed awareness of the chill from Justine's mind. A summons to a meeting more than an hour after sunset and not long before lights out was unusual, even for Fort Richardson.

"Any idea what he wants, Al?" Justine asked.

"Reckon we'll find out soon enough. I got a hunch we're about to start that long ride out into the big lonesome."

Justine sawed at the reins, brought the tough-mouthed bay to a stop at the crest of a high ridge, and stared in disbelief.

The rolling grassland ahead should have been green from recent rains. It was black.

"What the devil?"

Duggan, riding alongside, tapped his ancient briar pipe against his knee to empty the bowl of ash. "You never see buffalo before, Ned?"

"A few, in small bunches. Nothing like this. There must be a million of them." He heard the awe in his own words.

The black mass stretched as far as the eye could see between the Salt Fork of the Brazos and the South Wichita rivers. The coarse, grunting coughs of the bulls sounded like the steady pound of surf against Maine shoreline rocks.

"Double damned nuisance, those brutes," Duggan said. "Foul the water, wreck the grass. And a walking commissary for the Indians. Supply the redskins meat, lodge skins, robes, clothes, needle and thread—anything a Plains Indian could need to keep himself and his family alive. What this country needs is more hide hunters."

Justine shook his head. "I've never seen anything like it." He tore his gaze from the undulating black mass and glanced at Duggan. "Hide hunters?"

"Yep. Kill off the buffalo, starve out the redskins."

"It doesn't seem possible. I mean, there's so many of them. There couldn't be enough hide hunters to get rid of them all."

"Man can always hope. Hides are worth money. Money brings shooters." Duggan sighed. "Mackenzie's not going to be happy about this. Nothing slows down an army column like a big herd of shaggies."

"Can't we just ride around them? Or wait for them to pass?"

Duggan lifted an eyebrow at Justine. "Ned, you got a lot to learn about buffalo. It'd take a week, maybe more, for them to drift on, and longer'n that to go around. Mackenzie's got no choice but to work his way through. Besides, where there's buffalo, there's usually Indians not far away."

"That's not the most reassuring thing you could have said, Al." Justine instinctively glanced around. There was no sign of Corporal Charlton or the scout troop's commanding officer, Lieutenant Peter Boehm. Or any of the Tonkawa scouts except the three who rode with Justine and Duggan.

Mackenzie's force of six hundred soldiers trailed two days behind the scouts and a full day behind the company that rode as advance guard for the main troop body. If they happened across a sizeable band of Comanches . . . He didn't let himself finish the thought.

Duggan turned to the Tonkawa who rode at his left. "Pete, I reckon we ought to let the colonel know what he's headed into."

Whiskey Pete shook his head, his gaze still on the seething mass that stretched to the horizon. "Bad Hand will know soon. One of Boehm's boys rode past us an hour ago."

Justine started inwardly at the news. He hadn't seen another rider since the scouting party had split up and fanned out in the search for fresh Indian sign.

"What do we do now?" Justine asked.

The Tonkawa said, "Won't be any Indian tracks left after this buffalo herd goes by. Even Kicker couldn't find any."

"Kicker?"

"The Tonks' name for Elijah Thompson," Duggan said. "Butt Kicker. That old man doesn't like anybody very much, especially Indians. Even friendly ones. Pete's right. Not even Thompson can track Indians through a buffalo herd."

"Speaking of which, what happened to Thompson? I never saw him at the fort," Justine said.

Duggan shrugged. "Rode in, parleyed with Mackenzie, resupplied, and rode out again the next day." He pointed toward the west. "Most likely, he's back out there again. Somewhere."

"Alone?"

"That's the way he hunts Indians."

After relieving his aching bladder, Justine settled back into his blankets at the Fourth Cavalry's camp in Blanco Canyon, almost within cannon shot of the steep, rugged escarpment known as the Caprock that separated the southern Staked Plains from the western Brazos watershed.

The heaviness of his arms and legs and the ache in his knees reminded Justine he had been in the saddle eighteen to twenty hours a day with the scout company until his bay pulled a shoulder muscle fighting quicksand during the crossing of the Salt Fork of the Brazos.

At least, he thought, the cold-jawed idiot of a horse had done him one favor. He would be issued a remount the next day. For now, he could luxuriate in warm blankets, decent food, and real sleep. Except that now he couldn't doze off, despite his weariness.

He idly wondered if he had forgotten *how* to sleep during the last few days—days of weary boredom broken by an occasional jolt of excitement and fear. But now he had something to write home about if he ever had the chance to finish the letter.

He had seen his first wild Comanches. Four of them.

The chase lasted little more than two miles before Charlton called it off. The cavalry horses were too worn down to keep up with the fresh Indian ponies. And, Charlton pointed out, Comanches often set traps—troopers chasing a small band could turn a bend in a draw and find themselves facing a hundred mounted warriors. Charlton was no coward, but he wasn't dumb, either. The troopers and their Tonkawa guides had never closed to within rifle shot of the wild Indians. Justine had to admit he wasn't disappointed with the outcome of the pursuit.

Under Charlton's and Duggan's tutelage, Justine was quickly picking up the rudiments of reading sign.

They had found plenty of opportunities for him to do so. Several times they had come across campsites and cart tracks of Comancheros, the Mexicans and others who traded with the Plains Indians. His group and other scouts also had found a few Indian trails, but never more than a handful of pony tracks at a time.

Justine knew he was still a fawn in a forest of mountain lions when it came to Indian fighting; he was still green as grass at the trade that had been thrust upon him. But he had learned enough to recognize one unsettling possibility.

It seemed to Justine that the Indians were scouting the scouts. . . .

In the ravine between the soldier camp and the river, Badger patiently awaited the signal.

It would be a great feat, a story to be told and retold for many summers in Comanche lodges. To steal the white soldier's horses from beneath their very noses while outnumbered by five to one would bring much honor to Quanah's raiders.

Perhaps Quanah would see fit to present Badger with two ponies. Perhaps even more. They would be a welcome addition to his growing wealth. Soon, he would tie ten fine ponies and other less valuable offerings before Star's lodge. Her father could not resist such a high price.

The memory of Star in his arms in their private meeting place among the trees warmed him through the bite of the cold wind that whistled down from the faraway mountain country—

The whisper came down the line of waiting warriors. It was time.

* * *

A sudden explosion of whoops and yells and the thunder of hooves shattered the quiet night.

Justine sat up in his blankets, unable to move or think, his mind and muscles frozen by surprise and sheer terror. Above the high-pitched, blood-chilling whoops and the startled yelps of sentries, he heard the squeals of panicked horses fighting picket ropes. The muzzle flash of a rifle shot, followed by a ragged volley, illuminated the scene for a split second. Mounted figures raced along the cavalry picket lines, waving blankets, shouting, clanging cowbells.

"The horses! Comanches!" someone yelled.

The cry jolted Justine from his stunned disbelief. He groped for his rifle, wasted a few seconds before shaky fingers closed on the cold metal, then scrambled to his feet and sprinted toward the picketed horses a few yards away. One terrified animal raced past Justine. He heard a faint whistle, felt a sharp blow to his left shoulder, a quick stab of pain, and the thought he'd been shot flashed through his brain; he'd expected it to hurt more. . . .

After a moment he realized what had hit him wasn't a slug, but a whirling iron picket pin torn from the earth by the frantic horse.

He crouched, swinging his rifle first in one direction, then another, unable to find a sure target and unwilling to risk shooting one of his comrades in the swirling mass of confusion. In the muzzle flash of a nearby carbine, an apparition appeared, a horseman with but half a face, charging toward the picket line. Justine again froze, unable to will his muscles to bring the Spencer into play. Something hummed past his head as fire popped from the shoulder of the rider with half a face; the concussion of the muzzle blast hammered Justine's ears.

"Stand by your lines! Save your horses!" The shout barely penetrated Justine's ringing ears over the commotion of gunfire, pounding hooves, and squeals of horses. He shifted his rifle to his left hand and lunged for the halter of a horse fighting its picket rope. The animal's flailing head cracked against his cheek. Justine's vision blurred from the jolt. He managed to keep his grip on the halter and struggled to control the lunging, rearing animal.

The raid ended with the same abruptness in which it had begun. A stunned silence gripped the camp as the sound of whoops and hoofbeats faded into the distance. Justine's heart almost burst itself against his ribs as the reality hit him that he had been shot at and barely missed. His ears rang. The pain in his shoulder and cheekbone grew more intense.

The silence lasted only seconds before officers began to shout orders. Justine clung to the halter until the spooked horse finally quit fighting him and began to calm down.

"Secure the remaining mounts!" an officer called from nearby. Justine realized with a start that the voice was Mackenzie's. "Johnson, take your men to the top of the ridge! Be ready to lay down covering fire if they come back! Carter!"

"Yes, sir?"

"Assemble as many men and mounts as possible. Stand by to pursue at first light."

Justine still clung tight to the halter of the horse he had been able to reach. He started at the touch on his arm.

"Are you all right, son?" Mackenzie asked.

"I . . . I think so, sir."

"Good. Saddle your mount and stand by with Lieutenant Carter." As quickly as he had appeared, Mackenzie was gone, barking commands as he strode into the darkness.

It seemed to Justine that order was a long time returning to the Blanco Canyon camp.

By the light of rebuilt fires, the surgeon tended troopers

who had been run down by stampeding horses or had the skin peeled from their hands as picket ropes ripped through flesh. One man's face was raw and bloody, part of an ear torn away; he had become tangled in a picket rope and been dragged almost a hundred yards. Another bled profusely from a deep gash along his temple, put there by a whirling iron picket pin.

Nobody had been shot, or hit by arrow or lance.

His horse saddled and equipment checked, Justine stood by the animal, shivering from time to time as his sweat-soaked uniform chilled in the sharp breeze. He knew the shivering wasn't from the cold. Or that he had almost caught a ball in the head. It was the empty hollowness of disgrace, of failure.

His first real fight with the enemy, and he had frozen, paralyzed by an intense fear he had never before experienced. He hadn't even fired his weapon. His father would have had him court-martialed and possibly shot for cowardice under fire had he been in command.

Justine wasn't exactly measuring up to family standards.

He tried to shake the feeling. It wouldn't go away. If anything, the promise of dawn fueled the emptiness and dread. If he failed again, men could die. *He* could die.

The bitter twist of fate left a brassy taste in Justine's mouth.

For each fighting man, the army needed dozens, tens of dozens, in support. Engineers, teamsters, blacksmiths, cooks, armorers, supply personnel, medical units, musicians, orderlies, and clerks who transcribed orders and saw to communications. Thousands of chances to spend his tour of duty back East, or in the southern occupation forces.

Now he stood to horse in a small group of nervous troopers amid the rocks and cactus of a shallow valley in the middle of a hostile wilderness, awaiting an officer's call to boots and saddles. He was one of the fighting men. The one thing he had never wanted to be. It didn't seem fair. Justine hadn't beaten the odds. The odds had beaten him.

He slowly became aware of the brightening sky above the flames of the refueled fires. At the far side of the camp, Captain E. M. Heyl moved the first mounted detail in pursuit of the Indians. The handful of troopers had disappeared from sight when Lieutenant Robert Carter, his long Burnside-style whiskers rippling in the breeze and his close-set eyes flashing in anger, strode up to the five waiting troopers.

"Mount up," Carter said, his tone abrupt. After the creak of saddle leather died, he said, "Our primary job is to recover the stolen horses. If we get a chance to take down a few Comanches, all the better, but the horses are more important. A cavalry regiment without mounts is worthless in the field. Stay alert for anything. Move out. By the twos."

Justine reined his salvaged mount, a nervous, long-legged black with a deep chest that held the promise of speed and endurance, alongside a young trooper named Gregg. He knew the man only by last name and a supper shared by chance back at the camp on Duck Creek.

Gregg's horse was breathing heavily by the time they had covered half a mile. Justine knew the sorrel horse better than he knew the man in the saddle. The animal was one of the advance guard troop's mounts, returned just last night after days in the field. It was obvious to Justine that the mount was worn down, near the limit of its endurance.

"Dammit," Gregg said bitterly. "Heyl wasn't supposed to move out without us. We won't have a chance in hell if we run across a bunch of Indians before we catch up with the others."

Justine didn't have to reply. It was just as well. His mouth was too dried up to talk.

Only five men followed Lieutenant Carter toward the unknown.

Badger reined in his roan war pony a few yards beneath the highest point of the rim of the canyon wall.

He tied the horse to a juniper and climbed the rest of the way on foot. At the crest, the morning sun warmed the black paint covering half his face.

It had been a great raid. The horse soldiers hadn't known what hit them until too late. Not a single warrior had been injured. The large raiding party already had split up into smaller bands, driving stolen army horses toward the camp miles upstream on the river of sweet water.

Now it was time to spring the trap.

He glanced over his shoulder. The decoy force was ready below. Quanah and the others waited astride their best war ponies. A herd of soldier horses, chosen as those less likely to be of much value, stood with heads down, too worn out to go farther. Even from this height he could see the rapid puffs of steam from the nostrils of the winded army horses. Quanah and his men casually checked rifles and other weapons.

Badger stared toward the southeast and grunted in satisfaction. A band of soldiers hurried up the banks of the river, chasing the raiders. He glanced upstream and saw many warriors lined up on the far banks of the river. Badger scrambled back from the crest, flashed hand signs to Quanah, then half ran, half skidded the few strides downslope to his own war pony.

Badger fought back the strong urge to yelp in triumph. The horse soldiers were riding straight toward the trap.

Justine ignored the sharp, slicing pain in his left shoulder and pounding ache in his bruised head as he checked his already winded black.

Carter had set a fast pace after Heyl; now he waved his

detachment to a stop for a quick parley with four of Heyl's troopers who herded a band of recaptured horses back toward camp.

It was a short break.

Rifle fire cracked in the near distance.

Carter whirled his mount. "Heyl's closed with the Comanches! Let's ride!"

Justine's aches and pains faded as he leaned over the neck of his sorrel, only a few strides behind Carter's rangy bay. The lieutenant's horse stumbled and went down hard on its right side. Justine heard Carter's sharp yelp of surprise and pain. He yanked on the reins and leaned from the saddle to grab the bay's bridle as the snorting mount scrambled to its feet, Carter still in the saddle.

"You all right, sir?" Justine asked.

Carter, his face pale, jaw set and grim, winced but nodded. "I'm okay. Let's go. We're wasting time."

Moments later the troopers topped a low ridge. Justine's pounding heart skipped a beat, then leapt into his throat as the scene ahead unfolded. At the same instant, Carter barked a sharp curse.

A broad, almost featureless valley a mile long and nearly as wide, flanked by canyons, arroyos, and stands of junipers, stretched ahead. In a shallow depression in the middle of the plain, a handful of troopers milled about in total confusion. Less than a mile away to the north, at least a hundred mounted Comanches whooped and yelled in triumph as they raced toward the troopers.

"Dammit, Heyl, you rode into a trap! Get those men back here!" Carter shouted in vain. There was no way Heyl could have heard him over the distance, the yelling, the hoofbeats, and the sporadic crack of gunfire. Carter pointed to his left. "To the flank! We've got to cover their retreat!"

The Comanches closed to within five hundred yards, then four hundred, of the milling troopers on the plain below as Carter's small band spurred forward. Justine's eyes began to water from the wind and dust. He blinked away the blurring tears.

"Dismount! Fight on foot!" Carter called as he yanked his bay to a stiff-legged, bounding halt. The lieutenant glanced to his right. "Dammit, Heyl! Get control of your men! Get them out of there!" To his own troops he yelled, "Pick your targets! We've got to at least distract them!"

Justine thumbed the hammer of his rifle to full cock, aimed, and fired at a warrior on a paint horse. Even as he pulled the trigger, he knew the shot had fallen short. The range was too great for the Spencer. Other rifles cracked alongside Justine as he racked the action to chamber another round. The ragged volley had no more effect than his own shot. Justine cocked the weapon, fired again, hit nothing.

"We can't make a stand here!" Carter called. "Remount! Get back to the cover of the ravine behind us!"

As Justine swung into the saddle, he caught a quick glimpse of Heyl's detachment, finally brought under some measure of control, as troopers broke away from the milling confusion and spurred back toward the ravine.

Justine glanced over his shoulder as his horse broke into a run. A dozen Indians broke from the main body and charged toward them. The ravine seemed an impossible distance away. A rifle ball buzzed past Justine's shoulder, passed between him and the officer.

"Ride, men!" Carter shouted. "If they catch us out here, we don't stand a chance!"

Justine settled in to urge on his black, glanced over his shoulder again, and all but cried out in dismay.

Gregg's horse, stumbling badly, weaving as it tried to run, had fallen far behind the others.

"Help me! My horse is done!"

Gregg's cry for help seemed faint to Justine's ears. He started to rein in. Carter leaned over in the saddle and swatted Justine's horse on the rump. "We can't help him now, trooper! Not and stay alive ourselves! Keep riding!"

The cold knot of fear tightened its grip on Justine's

belly. After what seemed hours but in reality was only minutes, the winded cavalry mounts reached the ravine.

"Dismount! Covering fire for Gregg!" Carter yelled.

Justine jumped from the saddle and scrambled to the lip of the arroyo. The Indians were still three hundred yards from the ridge, closing rapidly on Gregg.

"Come on, Gregg! Ride!"

The shout of encouragement had barely sounded when an Indian mounted on a roan horse, half his face painted black, bore down on Gregg and pulled up alongside. Justine started at the sight, sure it was the same Indian with half a face who had fired at him during the raid.

The Indian's right arm rose, fell. Gregg's head snapped forward under the blow of the war axe. The trooper fell from the saddle as the Indian whooped and waved the axe overhead, urging his roan horse into a dead run toward the arroyo.

Justine fired at the warrior and again missed. Four other rifle shots also fell short or went wild overhead before the Indian charge wavered, then broke at a rattle of gunfire from farther down the ravine. Heyl's men had reached cover and finally were beginning to fight back.

Through the swirl of dust and powder smoke, Justine saw an Indian pony stumble and go down. The rider kicked free, rolled once, and came to his feet. A rifle ball kicked dirt at the dismounted Indian's feet seconds before two other Comanches swept toward him, leaned from the backs of their horses, hooked forearms beneath his armpits, and picked the man up on the dead run. One of the riders swung the dismounted Indian up behind him. The three were out of rifle range within a few heartbeats.

The main body of Indians wheeled toward the ravine. Justine wiped the dust and sweat from his eyes with a sleeve, heart pounding, fumbling to reload the Spencer, as he awaited the charge. One of the Indians, feathers trailing from his headband, pointed off to Justine's right. The warriors reined their mounts to the north, kicking ponies into a run.

Another trap? Justine wondered. He glanced to his right. A skirmish line of cavalrymen bore down on the ravine from the rear. Reinforcements.

Air burst in relief from Justine's parched lips. The Indians had broken off the fight and were in full retreat up the valley floor.

Justine turned to Carter. "Pursuit, Lieutenant?" he asked.

The officer shook his head. "Our horses are done in. Chase them now and we'd just ride into an ambush like Heyl did. Take two men and retrieve poor Gregg's body. And, Justine . . ."

"Yes, sir?"

"Thanks. For helping out when my horse fell."

Justine noticed for the first time that Carter carried all his weight on his left leg. "Are you sure you're all right, Lieutenant?"

"May have broken a leg. Don't worry about it. Take one man with you. Get Gregg out of there before some buck comes back to take his scalp. We'll cover you, but watch yourself. One dead trooper is one too many."

8

JUSTINE LEANED AGAINST the black horse's lathered shoulder and struggled to regain control of his fingers.

The tremors had begun on the way back from the fight in the valley. They wouldn't go away. Justine's stomach fluttered as much as his fingers. Despite the fact that he hadn't eaten since last night and the sun was halfway up the eastern sky, he felt no hunger. He knew that if he did eat something, it would come back up faster than it went down.

It was worse now.

At least until a few minutes ago, he had kept busy tending the black mount he had salvaged from the picket line. The leggy, tough animal had carried him into and safely through his first battle. Now there was nothing to distract Justine from the vision of Private Gregg's crushed head, hair matted with blood and brains.

Justine ran a shaky hand through the black's mane, wondering whose horse it was. His own crippled bay had been among the handful of horses and mules abandoned by the Indians in the wake of the raid and fight in the valley. The bay was useless now as a cavalry mount. The long run had broken its wind and spirit. Justine didn't mourn the loss of the bay. It hadn't been much of a horse to begin with.

Colonel Mackenzie's personal mount, the gaited iron gray, was among the missing animals. Somewhere, Justine thought, a painted Indian might even now be mounting the colonel's prized horse—

"Justine? You all right?"

Justine turned to John Charlton. The corporal's frown mirrored the concern in his eyes. "I'm all right," Justine said, a bit surprised that his voice didn't quaver. "Just still scared, I guess."

"Your shoulder's bleeding. Sure you didn't get hit? Sometimes a man doesn't realize it until the fight's over. Let's take a look." Charlton helped Justine slip his uniform blouse from the shoulder. The movement rekindled the sting of pain. For a moment, Justine couldn't figure out what the dark stain on the cloth was—then realized it was blood. His own.

Charlton peered at the injury. "You've got a gash as long as my thumb and the makings of a big, nasty bruise there, Justine."

"A picket pin hit me during the raid. I never felt the blood. It couldn't be too bad."

"Better get the surgeon to take a look anyway," Charlton said. "Infection from a small cut can be just as bad as from a big one. By the way, I heard Carter say you did well out there. Carried yourself like a veteran instead of a recruit."

Justine held out his hand to show the quavering fingers. "Does that look like the hand of a combat soldier?"

Charlton half smiled. "As a matter of fact, it does. Typical reaction to almost losing your hair. Now, haul yourself over to the surgeon's tent and get checked out. If he says it's okay for you to take the field again, report back to me. Mackenzie's mounting as many men as he can with the horses we have left. We're going to see if we can get some of our stolen mounts back."

Justine winced as Dr. Julius Patsky swabbed the cut with something that stung like the blazes.

"You got lucky, trooper," the surgeon said. "I'll just whip a stitch or two in this and it'll heal fine. If it doesn't get infected. Couple of the men caught picket pins or hooves in the head. Believe you know Svenson. He got it worst."

"Olaf? How is he?" Justine couldn't bring himself to watch Patsky thread a wicked-looking curved needle.

"The hard-headed Swede'll make it. Rattled his brain some, though. Still doesn't know where he's at."

"Lieutenant Carter?"

"Splinted his leg. I tried to convince him he should ride in a wagon, but he wouldn't hear of it. Insisted he could still fork a horse. Hold still."

Justine's breath whistled through his teeth as the surgeon's needle pierced his flesh. "Will I be fit to ride?"

"Unless you want to spend the rest of this campaign on foot, sure." The surgeon took another stitch, knotted the thread, and tugged Justine's blouse back over his shoulder. "You're fixed up, son. Get on back to your company. And congratulations."

"On what?"

"Your first battle wound. Something to tell your grandkids about. When you've got 'em." The surgeon winked at Justine. "If you know you've got 'em."

Two hours later Justine was back in the saddle aboard the black, field pack filled with a hundred rounds of ammunition and five days of rations, and his shoulder stinging like a dozen angry bees had nailed him in the same spot.

"All right, move out," Charlton said to his squad. "Whiskey Pete and the boys found us some Indians to chase."

Justine stood beside the body of one of the two Indians, his shoulders slumped, the weight of the Spencer like a wagon tongue in his aching arms, the scent of gunpowder, blood, and death sharp in his nostrils. The bitter north wind cut through the thin cloth of his summer uniform.

He turned away as two of the Tonkawa scouts approached the bodies, the weak October sunlight glinting from knives in their hands.

On the slope below, a handful of men clustered around Mackenzie. The feathered shaft of an arrow protruded from the colonel's thigh. Mackenzie had insisted on leading the squad assault up the side of rocky, brush-covered canyon wall where the Indians had made their final stand. He caught the arrow for his troubles.

Another group clustered around a fallen soldier. The trooper had been at Justine's side when the Indian's rifle ball tore through his intestines. He might or might not live.

The two Indians had been unlucky enough to be caught in the path of the cavalry's retreat.

Two dead Comanches to show for more than a week in the saddle. A week of fresh trails that became fresher by the day. A week that had brought them to within a cannon shot of a big Indian encampment. A week of ignoring the painted horsemen who stalked the column, just out of rifle range, and tried in vain to taunt the soldiers away from the broad trail and into another ambush. And a couple of particularly miserable nights of bitter cold and rain mixed with snow and sleet, sharpened on the fangs of the norther.

Then, practically within hailing distance of the main Indian camp, Mackenzie called off the campaign.

A number of the younger troopers openly groused about the colonel's decision. Justine wasn't one of them. He knew as well as Mackenzie that the horses and men were too worn out to chance a full-fledged attack on an encampment of Indians at least equal to the troops in number, mounted on rested horses and willing to die in battle against Bad Hand's warriors.

It *might* have been a major victory for the Fourth, had Mackenzie attacked. But, as Charlton snapped to one of the griping troopers, it could just as easily have been a major disaster. The Fourth had no remounts. Men and horses alike were cold, miserable, hungry, stumbling from exhaustion, on half rations as supplies dwindled. Mackenzie and his entire command could have died back there. It would have been a close call either way.

Justine didn't know, and didn't want to know, if one or more of his slugs were in the bullet-riddled bodies on that rocky canyon wall. In death, the two weren't enemies who had killed Justine's own kind. They were just men. He idly wondered if they had families. Wives and mothers to mourn them. Children who would grow up without fathers.

It was a disturbing thought, tempered only by the lingering memory of Private Gregg's bashed-in skull and the charred remains of the teamster burned over the wagon tongue at Salt Creek.

Justine tried to shake free of the detached feeling that had again settled over him, the sensation that he stood apart from the scene and watched through another set of eyes. He had done his duty. It should have been enough to ease the emptiness in his belly, the bright fear carried from rock to tree up the steep slope through the slugs and arrows.

He sucked in a deep gulp of the dusty haze, tried to snort the scent of black powder and blood from his nostrils, shouldered his Spencer, and made his way back down the steep bluff. He still couldn't fully believe he had voluntarily followed Mackenzie and Lieutenant Boehm up that slope into the face of an armed and desperate enemy. He didn't even remember making the decision. He just went.

Justine's fingers trembled, but not as badly as they had after the fight in the plain above Blanco Canyon. He knew it wasn't because he had become a more seasoned soldier. He was simply too cold and exhausted to work up a good shiver.

The yelps of the Tonkawa scouts as they finished their work on the bodies followed Justine on his descent. He didn't look back.

It was time to go home.

➤ ➤ ➤

Atop a distant hill, Badger watched as the column of horse soldiers re-formed into ragged ranks in the canyon and began to move away.

A heaviness pushed the exuberance of the successful raid from his heart. There had been no way to warn the two warriors they were riding straight into the horse soldiers' guns. All he and his small rear guard band could do now was wait until the soldiers were well clear of the canyon, then retrieve the bodies.

"This soldier chief Bad Hand learns quickly," Yellowfish said at Badger's side. "This time he did not chase our decoys away from the main trail. He knew where our village was, but he did not attack."

Badger snorted in disgust. "I wish he had. We could have stopped Bad Hand, wiped out his entire band."

"Perhaps," Yellowfish said, brow wrinkled in thought. "But at least the women and children are safe. We captured many horse soldier ponies. Bad Hand will not return."

"He will return," Badger said. "I can feel this white soldier chief; he is like a wolf on the trail of a wounded deer. But for now, he is beaten, and the horse soldiers do not fight during the time of snows. Soon we return to the Place of the Chinaberry Trees. There will be no hunger in our lodges when the cold winds come."

Yellowfish's frown vanished, replaced by a knowing grin. "And you, my friend, shall have something besides a fire to warm your lodge."

The comment lifted the cloud from Badger's heart.

"You have spoken with Holds-His-Horses?"

"I have. He agrees that ten ponies, two blankets, and the medicine pouch made from the white man's testicle sac is a fair price. Even for such a beloved daughter as Small Star."

Badger, heart racing, placed a hand on Yellowfish's shoulder. "It is agreed, then?"

"It is agreed. With the success of this raid, you have plenty of fine ponies. And yet another coup, striking the horse soldier from his mount with your war club. Do you wish me to lead your ponies to her lodge?"

Badger shook his head. "That is a thing I must do myself." He stared into his friend's eyes, saw the twinkle there, knew it must be mirrored in his own. "You should begin looking for a woman of your own, Yellowfish. You are no longer a holder of horses. You are now a respected hunter, horse thief, and warrior. You fought well in this meeting with Bad Hand."

"As a matter of fact, there is one who shares my soul. The youngest daughter of Para-a-coom." The twinkle faded from Yellowfish's black eyes. "The price will be great, and I am a poor man. I have few ponies."

"You aim your arrows high, my friend," Badger said. "The daughter of a war chief. Do not worry about your lack of ponies. If you do not have the price when the time comes, I will have. They are yours, as many as you need."

Yellowfish bared his teeth in a wide smile. "You are a true friend to make such a generous offer. It is the mark of a great warrior to share his wealth so. But by then, you will perhaps have another friend. A son."

"If the spirits will it, perhaps."

"They will. I have seen this in a dream. Not a vision, but twice in a dream. And twice in a dream should be at least part of a real vision." The smile again faded from Yellowfish's face. "We must go now and retrieve our dead."

The grim job of strapping the mutilated bodies onto the backs of spare horses seemed to bring less hurt to Badger's heart. The news that Star would soon be his eased the heaviness.

As they rode back along the broad trail left by the move of the village toward the distant canyon, Badger realized with a start that there was a problem he had not yet addressed.

He had only a sister. No brother. No one to take Star into his lodge, no husband to care for her, should he die. He realized the answer rode at his side. From this day forth, Yellowfish would be his brother. . . .

Justine stood beside the door of the town meeting hall in Jacksboro and listened to the laughter and music from just beyond the portal.

The Christmas ball hosted by town officials and businessmen in honor of the officers of the post was well under way. Justine turned up the collar of his greatcoat against the cold wind that whipped around the corner of the building.

For a few wistful moments he had fancied himself an officer, and thus eligible to dine and dance in the presence of the petite young blond woman inside. The fancy soon passed. Even if he had the ambition and the political inclination to have bars on the collar of his uniform instead of just serving his time to fill an obligation to family tradition, she would still be out of his reach.

Even officers didn't consort with the wives of fellow officers.

Just being near her—although the distance could have been measured in miles instead of a few feet or yards, and the cold ache of knowing he could never be closer—was sufficient for now.

He found a measure of comfort in the gentle smile and the warm expression in those deep blue eyes when she had stepped from her quarters and seen him waiting by the surrey, and the upward lilt of her voice when she greeted him by name.

The familiarity of her greeting also brought a flutter of discomfort when Lieutenant Hopkins pinned a hard, cold stare on Justine. Did he suspect something? Justine thought not. He had been careful to give Hopkins no reason to believe he was attracted to Elaine. Hopkins *always* glared at enlisted men as if they were some kind of bug to be squashed underfoot.

All in all, Justine counted himself fortunate to be detailed to escort duty. He stood guard to keep the rougher elements of Jacksboro from interrupting the grand ball. The detail had permitted him to ride at the side of Elaine's coach from Fort Richardson. Despite the chill, the windows of the surrey were open to the evening air. He caught an occasional glimpse of her golden hair, her slight form in the elegant, dark green gown, heard her musical laugh at some remark from time to time.

That alone would have been worth bearing the cold—but Justine forced himself to stop thinking along those lines. He inwardly chided himself that he was acting like some schoolboy smitten by a third-grade teacher.

The detail had other compensations. The hosts hadn't forgotten the enlisted men who served as guards or stood stable duty while the officers partied. They had been well fed, served at their posts—heaping platters of roast beef, wild turkey, quail, baked yams, boiled potatoes, and even green beans canned from some matron's garden, along with freshly baked bread and coffee brewed in a civilized manner. After months of camp coffee on the trail or in the enlisted men's mess at the fort, the civilian coffee seemed a bit weak to Justine's taste buds. But it was the first truly sumptuous meal he had had since his last Christmas at home in Maine.

The only holiday fare not shared with enlisted men outside was liquor. Colonel Mackenzie didn't mind his men having an occasional drink, but not while on duty. Holiday rations of whiskey, rum, brandy, and even wine would be available at the post later for those who wished it. The lack of spirits didn't bother Justine. He had never developed much of a taste for liquor.

He stiffened as a big, broad-shouldered, unshaven man

who reeked of cheap gin and unwashed skin lurched to a stop in the lamplight.

"Party goin' on?"

"Yes, sir," Justine said. "The officers' Christmas ball."

The big man's crooked grin revealed a gap where a front tooth had been. "Well, now. Sure sounds like a mighty good time a-happenin' in there. Reckon I'll join in." He took a step forward.

Justine moved to his right, put himself between the big man and the door. "Admittance is by invitation only, sir. Do you have an invitation?"

The man's pale blue eyes turned hard in the lamplight. "No, I ain't, boy."

"Then, I'm sorry, sir, but I can't admit you."

For several heartbeats the big man stared at Justine. A muscle in his jaw twitched. Justine held his gaze, unblinking, knowing the big man could stomp him into a small, bloody puddle if he took a notion to do it.

"You gonna stop me, soldier pup?" The man's hands clenched into fists that looked to be the size of smoked hams.

"If I have to," Justine said.

"Reckon you can do that?"

"It's a possibility, sir."

"All by your little self?"

Justine said, "If I can't, I'll yell for help."

The silence dragged on through almost two bars of a waltz playing inside. Then the big man shook his head and laughed aloud. "Gotta hand it to you. You got balls like a Mexican stud hoss."

"And if it's all the same to you, sir, I'd like to keep them awhile longer," Justine said calmly.

"Aw, hell, son. I like a man with grit. You'll do to ride the river with." The big man glanced past Justine's shoulder. "Sure looks like they're havin' a good time in there. But I reckon I'll mosey over to Big-Eared Mary's. Find me a *real* party. Merry Christmas."

"Merry Christmas to you, sir."

Justine realized his palms were sweaty as the big man strode away, a bit unsteady on oversized feet.

"Well done, trooper."

Justine started at the voice from behind him. He hadn't heard the door open. He turned, found himself face-to-face with Ranald Mackenzie, and snapped a salute. The colonel returned the salute with a casual wave.

"That man was twice your size, Trooper . . . Justine, is it?"

"Yes, sir."

"Remind me never to play poker with you. I couldn't tell whether you were bluffing or not, but I do believe you could have stopped that man." Mackenzie reached into the pocket of his crisp blue dress uniform, produced a slim cigar, and offered it to Justine.

Ned shook his head. "Thank you, sir, but I don't use them."

"Felt the need for a smoke, myself. It's hot and crowded in there. Too much perfume and too many petticoats, too."

Justine had heard that the colonel, for all his quick temper and cool confidence afield, was painfully shy and uncomfortable around women. He now felt sure the rumors were true.

"Yes, sir. If I may ask, Colonel, how is your leg?"

"Mending nicely." The faintest hint of a smile touched the colonel's lips. "The surgeon gave that leg a slight tug a few days after he dug the arrow out. Patsky told me, with a straight face, he was going to have to amputate." Mackenzie gripped a match between the stubs of his fingers, swiped it against the veranda railing, and fired his smoke. "I wasn't in a particularly good mood at the time, given the failure of the campaign. I would have parted his hair with my crutch if he hadn't run. Looking back, I guess it was a bit amusing. Anyway, I hardly notice it anymore."

So the story of the surgeon's little joke had been true, Justine mused. And the colonel *had* been in a foul mood at the time. Even his senior officers avoided him whenever possible on the long trip back.

Justine found himself wishing the colonel would move on. He had never been especially comfortable in the company of officers, especially those of high rank. Standing there at attention, he wondered if that were part of the Justine legacy as well; as best he knew, only two of his ancestors had ever gained more than sergeant's stripes.

"Stand at ease, trooper," Mackenzie said after a couple of minutes passed in silence. "There's no need for formality. It's Christmas Eve."

Justine's muscles relaxed a bit, but his mind raced. He couldn't think of anything to say in the way of small talk with the man breveted major general for heroism in an earlier war, and who now commanded an entire regiment of cavalry.

The door opened and the regimental sergeant major—the highest ranking noncom in the outfit, invited to the ball along with the Officers' Corps—stepped to Mackenzie's side. The two spoke in soft voices for a moment before the sergeant major turned and strode back into the building.

"Justine, how long have you been on duty here?" Mackenzie's words held a tinge of anger; frown wrinkles formed between his thick brows.

"A bit over three hours, sir," Justine said.

"That's long enough. I'd ask a favor of you."

"Yes, sir."

"Escort Mrs. Hopkins and Mrs. Temples back to their quarters at the post. The sergeant major will have the surrey brought around and arrange for someone to take over here."

Justine's spirits lifted at the prospect of seeing Elaine again so soon, but at the same time he wondered why anyone would want to leave the party so early in the evening. "Yes, sir," he said. "It will be my pleasure, sir."

Mackenzie tossed his half-smoked cigar into the street,

started to turn away, then paused. "Merry Christmas, Trooper Justine."

"Merry Christmas to you, sir."

Elaine Hopkins and Mrs. Temples—the latter the matronly wife of a career officer in the Quartermaster Corps who currently was confined to the post hospital with a recurrence of a stomach problem—stepped onto the veranda moments before the surrey arrived.

Justine's chest tightened as he formally greeted both women and noticed the lantern light glint on unspilled tears in Elaine's lower lids. Mrs. Temples had a hand on Elaine's arm.

"Don't be too upset, dear," she said softly to Elaine. "It was just the whiskey talking. I'm sure he didn't mean it."

"I think he did." Elaine obviously struggled to maintain her composure. "It isn't the first time my husband has criticized me in public. . . ." Her voice trailed away as the surrey pulled up, Justine's horse tied to the iron hitch ring in the rear.

Justine stowed his carbine beneath the driver's seat and helped both women into the surrey. Elaine tried to force a smile as he took her hand, but the hurt was plainly visible in her eyes. The lightness of Justine's mood faded, scorched by an ember of anger at Lieutenant Hopkins. How could any man reduce a woman to near tears in public? Especially one as obviously sensitive as Elaine? Lord, she deserved a man who worshipped the ground she walked on, he thought with some bitterness as he clucked the surrey horse into motion.

He tried not to think of it on the way back to the fort. It helped some that he couldn't make out the words of the muted conversation in the closed carriage behind him.

As they neared the officers' quarters, Mrs. Temples leaned from the surrey and called to Justine. "Leave us both at my quarters, if you please, young man."

"Yes, ma'am." Justine tugged lightly on the leathers, bringing the surrey horse to a stop before the Temples' door in the string of small log homes reserved for officers and their families. He helped the two women from the coach, painfully aware of the wetness on Elaine's cheeks, glinting in the lantern light. He wished there was something he could say. There wasn't.

"Mr. Justine, you must be quite cold," Mrs. Temples said as he released her hand. "Would you like to come in for coffee? Or perhaps a cup of warm cider?"

Justine glanced at Elaine and shook his head. "Thank you, ma'am, but I must respectfully decline. It appears you two ladies need to talk without a man underfoot."

The older woman smiled, the lift of her lips smoothing the wrinkles in her brow. "A most sensitive observation, Mr. Justine. Thank you for understanding. Merry Christmas, young man."

Justine lifted his fingers to his hat brim. "Merry Christmas to you also, ladies."

As he climbed onto the seat for the short drive to the stables, he overheard the older woman's words as she opened the door to her quarters:

"Now, there is a young man who will some day make a young woman very happy—"

The compliment only pushed Justine's mood into darker territory. Why is it, he wondered, that the right people so seldom wind up together?

The question left only a bitter taste on his tongue.

It was an absurdly presumptuous assumption on his part.

And there wasn't a damn thing he could do about it, anyway.

9

BADGER LAY ON the soft bedding of juniper boughs and blankets topped by a buffalo robe and listened to the soft sigh of wind through the bare limbs of the cottonwood trees beside the lodge, conscious of the warmth of Star's thigh resting lightly across his leg.

A contented smile lifted the corners of his mouth.

His heart also smiled. It had done so throughout the three moons since Star emerged from her father's lodge that cool evening as the last leaves fell, untied his bride price offering of ponies, and led them to her father's herd. She then gathered her few personal belongings and moved into his lodge. No further ceremony was needed. They were husband and wife.

It had been the best time of snows in Badger's memory. Not a child whimpered from hunger in the sprawling camp along the clear, sweet stream in the Place of the Chinaberry Trees.

Except during the worst weather, young boys played at the arrow-and-wheel sport or other games. Sometimes they amused themselves by playing practical jokes on their elders. Once, two boys had slipped into Quanah's lodge during the night and tied his leggings into so many knots that it took the great war chief almost half a day to untie them. Another time, the youths had backed a nervous colt into the lodge where the elders were meeting and made the yearling buck. The entire camp had quite a laugh from that stunt. It was yet another sign of the time of plenty.

The fall hunt had been a success unlike any other Badger had known. Even the elders of the band could not recall a more bountiful buffalo harvest.

Each lodge, even those of the poorest of the poor, had more than enough dried meat from the buffalo, deer, elk, and antelope, and many containers of dried berries, nuts, honey, wild plants, and mesquite beans gathered and prepared for storage by the women. What they could not find themselves, they obtained in trade. Dried squash and pumpkins woven into mats lined the inside of lodges, along with bags of dried beans, sugar, salt, and coffee.

The *jebistzitzi*—old women often known for their biting tongues—honked their laughs as they mercilessly teased the younger men about their inadequacies as warriors and shortcomings as husbands and lovers. When women passed the age of bearing children, they were entitled to jest at will with the men of the village. They especially delighted in teasing the young ones.

It seemed to Badger that even the old man of the cold breath smiled on The People. He had held back the worst of the bitter winds. The snows that had fallen did not reach higher than a man's knees, and melted within a few suns.

It was a good time to be young.

Star, her head tucked against the side of his neck, snored softly. When the sun came, Badger again would tease her about that. She would deny it, even to the point of mock threats. It had become a game they played in the moments of privacy when no friends or relatives came to visit.

The lodge was warm and snug, the tanned buffalo hides easily turning the wind's breath. A robe to lie on and one for cover, and a small fire, were all that were needed on even the coldest of nights.

Badger and Yellowfish now commonly called each other brother. Badger found much comfort in that. Should something happen to him, Star would become Yellowfish's wife. He would see that she and her family were cared for, would not be in want.

Even the ponies fared well this winter. Many of them now were showing ribs, but enough dry grass remained that it had not been necessary to strip the bark from the cottonwood trees to keep the animals from starving.

Soon the greening of the grass would come. A short time later, the ponies again would be sleek and fat, fit and ready for the hunt and the raid.

The only times Badger felt incomplete were when Star's bleeding moon came and she was banished to the special lodge for five to seven suns. Until her time passed and she could bathe in the purifying icy waters of the stream, Badger occupied himself on the hunt. Deer, elk, and antelope were plentiful and easy to stalk less than half a sun's ride from camp. When there was no desire for fresh meat, he tended his weapons and cared for his pony herd.

There were moments when he regretted not being able to visit his sister and her girl child back on the reservation. Even if he risked the trip, he could do little more than speak briefly with his sister. He didn't even know her that well, for among The People, familiarity between sister and brother was taboo. He had not spoken directly with her since they were but children. The practice of brother-sister avoidance kept the tribal bloodlines pure. At first, Badger greatly missed his talks with his sister. The loneliness passed with the changing seasons. He never questioned the custom. Things were as they were.

While Quanah's band had prospered the previous summer and autumn, Mow-way and his people had become even more wealthy. While Quanah's warriors stole many of Bad Hand's horses and beaten back his soldiers, Mow-way's men raided behind the bluecoats. They had taken more than a dozen scalps, many horses and mules, and large numbers of the white man's cattle for trade with the Comancheros. The lodges of both bands now were well equipped with rifles and ammunition, cooking pots, blankets, trinkets for the men and women to adorn their clothing and bodies, metal arrow and lance heads, even the white man's small fire sticks called matches.

A few of the warriors followed Quanah's lead and carried revolvers, though Badger and many others scorned the small guns in favor of rifles, bows, and lances. The one-hand guns were good only for close-quarter fighting. Most warriors preferred the club or short lance for such combat. Those weapons were easier to use when face-to-face with an enemy.

The distant yips and mournful yells of Coyote, the Trickster, sounded above the brush of wind in the quiet village. There was no need to place sentries to watch over camp. Like the red warriors, the white soldiers did not take the field during the time of snows. Even if the horse soldiers did, they would never find this village. The Place of the Chinaberry Trees had been given to The People by the greatest of all spirits.

Badger became aware that Star's soft snoring had stopped. The light touch of her delicate hand warmed a spot on his belly.

"Are you unable to sleep, husband?" she asked, her words soft as the night outside. Her eyes sparkled in the faint light from the glowing coals of the fire.

"Merely awake and enjoying life, Star. It is a good time."

Her hand slipped lower on his belly. "Yes, it is a good time. Perhaps a good time to make a son, if my great warrior husband is not too tired from his wake-dreams."

Badger smiled, pulled her even closer, and whispered, "If ever I should be *that* tired, may Father Sky roar and send his forked arrows into my breast."

The sharp blast of light, followed almost instantly by the explosive crack of thunder, jarred Justine from the twilight of near sleep. A strange sizzling sound lingered as he sat upright on his cot, heart hammering against his ribs.

An odd, sharp scent tickled his nostrils; the squeals of frightened horses reached his ears for an instant before the next flash and instantaneous crack of thunder penetrated the pounding rain and rattled the walls of the Fort Concho enlisted men's barracks. That one, he thought, had been close. Possibly inside the compound.

He lay still, listening to the thunderstorm crack and rumble outside, knowing it would soon pass. And that he wouldn't get back to sleep. Already, other troopers had begun to stir, lighting oil lamps and placing pans or buckets beneath the steady drips from the roof. It was less than two hours to reveille, anyway. Justine rose, dressed, and rolled his bedding.

He had welcomed the reassignment to Concho when Mackenzie dispersed many of his units to ease the overcrowding at Fort Richardson for the winter.

Here, the enlisted men's barracks held the bitter wind at bay. While the buildings still leaked in such heavy storms, they provided more effective shelter than those at Fort Richardson. And here, he wasn't haunted so often by the sight of a small figure with golden hair and a bright smile, often waving to him as she strode across the compound for Mass in the small chapel. Elaine Hopkins and her husband remained at Fort Richardson. Out of sight didn't mean out of mind, but not seeing her on an almost daily basis did ease the ache a bit.

He felt a brief gust of rain-washed wind as the door opened and closed.

"Lookin' for a trooper named Justine."

The statement, little more than a snarl, brought Justine back to the present. A lean, almost rail-thin man stood inside the doorway, rainwater dripping from his battered hat and oiled canvas duster. Wild gray hair splayed from beneath his hatband to brush against stooped shoulders and frame a lined face weathered to the color of saddle leather. A handlebar mustache bristled below a skewed nose flattened at the bridge. The man wore high-heeled riding boots spattered with mud and cradled a Henry rifle in the crook of his left elbow.

It was the eyes that startled Justine more than the man's overall appearance. They were light blue, so pale as to be almost colorless in the lantern light, the look in them cold and hard.

"I'm Ned Justine."

"I hear tell you're a middlin' fair soldier and got the makin's of a halfway decent scout, given time. Get your field stuff together. We're gonna see how good you are. We move out in two hours."

"What—"

"Ain't got time for jawin' right now. Draw rations for two weeks, a hundred rounds for the Spencer. Plenty of powder, cap and ball for that Dragoon handgun. You got good horses?"

"Yes, sir."

"Be at the stable. Two hours."

The man turned and left as quickly as he had appeared.

A veteran private seated two bunks down from Justine whistled softly. "Man, I never heard ol' Lige say that many words at one time in a mess of years."

"Lige?"

"Elijah Thompson. Justine, you're going to be riding with a sure-enough legend for a spell. And I ain't especially envyin' you. Better get hoppin'. When Lige Thompson says two hours, he don't mean two hours and a minute."

"Is he always that curt? Like he's mad at the world?"

The private chuckled. "You just seen Lige Thompson in one of his rare good moods. Don't do nothin' to rile him out of it."

"Why me?"

"Ask him. But you best be polite about it."

An hour and fifty minutes later, Justine stood at the halter of his saddled black in the reluctant dawn. Lightning flickered from distant clouds as the storm sped toward the northeast. Justine rechecked his field kit and bedroll strapped onto the chestnut that would alternate under saddle and pack, and studied the group assembled with him.

They were an assorted bunch, only three of whom Justine knew by name—Whiskey Pete, Sam, and Little Joe, Tonkawa scouts who had ridden with him and Charlton. Two other Indians, whom Justine assumed by their clothing and broad, dark-skinned fetures to be Lipan Apaches, sat scowling astride wiry mustang-type ponies. Four troopers who had the look of men who knew their way around a horse and rifle and one new recruit rounded out the group.

The soldiers straightened and squared their shoulders as Thompson rode up. The Indians remained slouched and glowered at the aging frontiersman. The glares from five pairs of dark brown or obsidian eyes reflected the scorn in Thompson's pale blue eyes when his gaze brushed over the Indians.

"For Christ's sake, relax, soldier boys," Thompson said. "I ain't no damn officer. Bad Hand wants Comancheros. I know where some are at. Anybody can't keep up gets left behind." He turned that brittle stare on the Indian scouts. "First one of you damn heathens gets lazy or don't pull his weight, I'll put a pistol ball in your red gut. Time's wastin'."

"Mr. Thompson?" the new trooper asked hesitantly.

"What the hell do you want?"

"Where's the rest of the patrol?"

"There ain't a rest. We're it. Less one." He stabbed a bony finger at the questioner. "You stay and knit with the other women. I can't abide a man yammers all the time."

Justine decided he wouldn't ask Thompson why he'd been chosen. Not just yet. . . .

Justine felt like he carried an elk across his shoulders. His eyelids seemed sprinkled inside with gravel, the tender inner skin of his knees raw from endless hours of rubbing against stirrup leathers.

Six days out, and Fort Concho was but a distant memory.

Five nights of jerky, hardtack, and dry camps. In those five nights, a total of not quite twelve hours of sleep, riding at a fast walk or trot over seemingly endless, rolling land dotted with thornbush, catclaw, cactus, spiny Spanish dagger clumps, and scattered patches of bunch grass. Through rugged ravines and rocky, broken badlands. Justine had no idea how many miles the group had covered, but even his tough black and stout chestnut were showing signs of miles passed by.

He sat beside the small camp fire at the edge of a thornbush and leaned back against his bedroll, too tired to fully savor his first cup of rank coffee in more hours than he could count. He battled constantly to keep his sagging lids open.

He became aware of the presence beside him, a sense more than any sound. He glanced at the lean frontiersman. Elijah Thompson didn't show any signs of wear and tear from the long, hard ride. Justine was beginning to think the old man wasn't human. Thompson's eyes seemed to soften a bit as he lit his battered pipe and peered at Justine.

"Been watchin' you, son," Thompson said after a couple of drags on the pipe. "Lookin' behind you, studyin' how a hill or ridge looks from the far side. Ain't heard you whinin' or gripin' about bein' tired. I reckon you maybe got what it takes."

"Thank you, sir," Justine said. It was the first time the old man had made any effort to speak with him—or any of the others, for that matter—in private. Especially in a civil tone.

"Knock off the 'sir' crap, Justine. Like I said, I ain't no officer. Lord willin' and a cyclone don't hit me, I'll never be one, neither. That was to happen, I reckon I'd bite the end of this ol' Remington Army and drop the hammer. Only army officer I ever seen who's got sense enough to pour pee out of a boot's Bad Hand Mackenzie. He's makin' mistakes, but he's learnin'."

Justine nodded and sipped the bitter coffee. After a moment's silence, he said, "Sir—I mean, Mr. Thompson—I know it irritates you when people talk. But I've been wanting to ask a couple of questions, if you don't mind."

Thompson dragged at the pipe for time, then grunted. "Reckon I can tolerate a few, long's they come from somebody tryin' to learn and willin' to bust his ass on the trail. Fire away. I'll answer 'em if I want, ignore 'em if it ain't none of your business."

"Mind you, I'm not implying a criticism of anything you've done, so please don't take offense. It's just that I'm green as grass at this business."

"Good start," Thompson said. For a split second, Justine thought amusement twinkled in the old man's eyes. The expression seemed totally out of place. "Man's gotta admit his faults before he starts to fix 'em."

"I've noticed that you always have soldiers stand night watch, not the Indian scouts. And that when we split up hunting sign, there's always at least one white man to each group. I know you have a reason. I'm just curious as to why."

The hard look came back to Thompson's eyes and the set of his jaw. "Simple enough. Never leave one of them damned savages in charge of the horses. They'll steal the ponies and guns. Maybe lift your scalp in the process. Gotta watch the heathen butchers all the time."

"But these Indians are our allies, our friends—"

"Ain't no such thing as a redskin ally, Ned," Thompson interrupted, his tone sharp. "Tuck that in the front part of your head to remember. It's their nature to steal from and cut up white folks. That's the same reason I keep a trooper alongside 'em when we scatter to hunt sign."

"May I ask why you distrust Indians so much? Even those you ride with?"

Thompson didn't immediately answer. For a time, Justine feared he'd stepped over some invisible line. Then the old man sighed. "Reckon you might as well hear it from me as somebody else, since we're likely to be ridin' together more, off and on. I put up with 'em 'cause they're damn good trackers. No other reason." A muscle in his weathered jaw twitched. "I don't like 'em because I had me a family once. Wife, two daughters, a son. We had a place on the East Fork of the Trinity."

Thompson fell silent for a time, staring into the distance of memory. Justine didn't press the issue. He figured he'd pushed far enough as it was.

Finally, the old man knocked the wattle from the bowl of his pipe and refilled the scarred meerschaum. "Comanches come one day when me and some other men was out chasin' Kiowa hoss thieves. Killed my wife and older daughter. Took Sarah, my youngest girl, and my little boy, John, off with 'em. That was sixteen, seventeen year ago this summer."

Justine's heart tightened in his chest. "I'm sorry."

Thompson glanced at Justine as if surprised. "Weren't your fault. Anyhow, I been huntin' Injuns and my two kids ever since."

"What will you do when you find them? Your son and daughter?"

Thompson abruptly stood. "Get some sleep, Justine. You look plumb tuckered. I'll take first watch, Callahan second, Jurgenson third. We move out come first light." The old man strode away into the growing darkness.

Justine finished his coffee, wiped the residue from the tin campaign cup, and spread his blankets. He was asleep seconds after his head touched the saddle he used for a pillow.

It seemed he had barely dozed off when he awakened, groggy but somewhat rested, as the first faint gray streak of the coming dawn lightened the eastern horizon. He'd soon noticed why the Indians called Thompson "Kicker." A boot toe none too gently applied to ribs or hip, accompanied by a snarl—"Get up, you lazy red bastard"—was his standard way of rousting out the Indian scouts.

The sun was two hours above the horizon when Justine reined his chestnut to a stop in a swale between two brushy hills. As had seemed to have become custom, Whiskey Pete was his scouting companion. Pete sat astride his blue roan, staring at the ground.

"Comancheros. Fresh tracks," the Tonkawa said. Whiskey Pete spoke better English than most white men when he wasn't playing Indian for the benefit of those he didn't like or trust, or just wanted to aggravate. He also spoke fluent Spanish, passable Comanche, and several other Indian tongues. Pete didn't drink, which Justine found strange in light of the name tagged to him. He had asked Pete about it one day. "No like white man poison water," Pete had said in his pidgin dialect act, but with a grin. "Pete try it once. Wake up next sun with bad head, sick belly, beside Kickapoo squaw ugly as scorpion spit. No drink stuff since."

Justine dismounted and studied the sign. The dry grass had been crushed by the wheels of several carts and the hooves of oxen, horses, and mules. There was no dew on the tracks, yet small droplets lingered on the grass and rocks flanking the trail.

"What you think, white man?" Pete asked.

"Two hours. No more."

The Tonkawa's thin lips lifted in a half smile. "You're learning pretty good." He nodded to a pile of droppings to one side of the cart tracks. "Horse or mule?"

"Horse," Justine said. "Mule stops to relieve himself and won't take another step until the job's done. Horse just lifts his tail and keeps on walking." He picked up a twig and stabbed one of the droppings. It was fresh. Beside the droppings a damp spot remained, a few inches from a pair of tracks left by flat leather sandals. "The mule rider relieved his bladder here, I'd say. We're close."

"Yep. You're learning quick. Ol' Whiskey Pete'll make a tracker out of you yet." The Tonkawa pulled a twist of tobacco from a pouch and bit off a plug. "Better fetch Kicker. Mebbe so put ol' bastard in better mood. Cranky 'stead of just mean. Don't bet your best pony on it, though." He reined his horse to the crest of a hill overlooking the trail, waved his hat overhead, and rode back down a minute later.

"Kicker'll be along soon. We wait."

While they waited, Justine turned to Pete.

"Why the colonel's sudden interest in Comancheros?"

The Tonkawa shrugged. "In the spring, the time the Comanches call the greening of the grass, they trade with the Comancheros. Replenish supplies that aren't available from their friends and relatives on the reservation. Then they start raiding the white man's farms and ranches."

"What do they have to trade this early in the year?"

Pete worked the chew for a moment, then spat. "Buffalo robes. Gold and silver taken from settlers and soldiers in fall raids. But mostly captives. Men, women, and children. Sometimes whole families, but usually they split up the families so the ones left won't be tempted so much escape. Later, after the summer and fall raids, the Indians trade stolen cattle to the Comancheros. Stopping them's not what were out here to do. Bad Hand wants a Comanchero. A live one."

Justine's brow furrowed. "He sent us out here after a prisoner?"

"Comancheros know where the Plains Indian camps are, where they're most likely to be hanging out. They also know the way across the country the Comanches call the big flat grass. The Staked Plains. Bad Hand plans a big campaign against Comanches. He figures that where Indians live, horse soldiers can also live. Water's the big problem. Comancheros know where the water is."

Pete paused for a moment, staring in the direction the cart tracks led. "Pretty soon now, Bad Hand'll know where that water is."

10

JUSTINE WIPED THE sweat from his palms, checked the action of the Spencer one last time, then loosened the flap covering the Colt's Dragoon revolver holstered in proscribed cavalry crossdraw style at his left hip.

The four other troopers also double-checked weapons. The Indian scouts, faces already streaked with slashes and dots of war paint, waited beside their ponies, normally stoic faces showing a restrained eagerness for the battle soon to unfold. Even Whiskey Pete's broad face sported a couple of swipes of vermillion descending from hairline to brow above each eye. The two Lipan Apaches squatted side by side, whetting the edge of knives on their leather leggings.

Atop the low ridge fifty yards ahead, Elijah Thompson lay on his belly beside a Spanish dagger clump, his battered hat beside him as he stared into the shallow valley below. The old man's silver-gray hair riffled in the soft spring wind.

Thompson had picked the spot. It was obvious the man knew the ambush trade.

The long, circular ride around the Comanchero band left the mounts winded, but in two hours of waiting the animals regained their air. Even the horses seemed eager, snorting and pawing the ground.

Justine tried to ignore the queasy feeling in his belly. It came to him before each engagement when he had time to know a fight was coming instead of being thrown into one by sudden ambush. This time they had the element of surprise on their side. It could help even the odds some.

He knew what they were up against. At Thompson's side atop a low butte, Justine had watched the approach of the Comanchero band through the old scout's worn brass spyglass. The train included four mule-drawn wagons and three two-wheel *carretas* pulled by sluggish oxen. Counting the drivers, eight armed men guarded the train proper. Two of them rode saddled mules. Behind the wagons, four other riders trailed a herd of rangy Longhorn cattle, many of which had yet to shed long winter coats. All but three men in the band wore the broad-brimmed sombreros favored by Mexicans.

Justine knew it wasn't going to be easy. The main challenge wasn't just to take down the Comancheros, but to do so without accidentally killing any of the half-dozen captive women and children crowded into the open bed of the second wagon—and to take one specific Comanchero alive. More if possible. The traders were armed with rifles, shotguns, and handguns, wagon drivers and horsemen alike.

Justine's heartbeat quickened at the hand signals from Thompson.

"Looks like the dance is about to open," the wiry trooper at his side said. "Let's mount up and get into position."

A quarter hour later, Justine lay between Whiskey Pete and the surly Lipan called Dead Horse on the northwest flank of the narrow pass. One soldier and two other Indian scouts held the south flank. Thompson, the third trooper, and the remaining Indians held the front where the road, its ruts worn deep by the passage of many wagons and carts, angled between the low hills. The other two troopers, the best riflemen in the squad, waited with Sam and Little Joe at the far end of the pass, ready to close off any retreat. The scouts' horses were tied below the crest of the ridge, out of sight from the road but near at hand.

The leading Comanchero passed barely a stone's throw beneath Justine's post on the ridge, closely followed by other riders flanking the wagons and carts. Justine recognized one of the outriders from Thompson's description—the man Lige especially wanted alive.

Justine cocked the Spencer's hammer and drew a bead on a big man riding beside the second wagon. The man in his sights wore a buffalo headdress, the horns seemingly out of place above thick, sloping shoulders. The horse he rode seemed like a small pony beneath his bulk—

The whack of lead against flesh sounded a split second before the crack of Thompson's rifle reached Justine's ears. The lead rider tumbled over the rump of his horse.

Justine squeezed the trigger. The big man in his sights jerked in the saddle, obviously hit, but didn't go down.

Another horseman went down and a wagon driver slumped in the seat at the first rattling volley from rifles and carbines on the ridges overlooking the Comanchero caravan. A pair of riders trailing the beeves at the rear of the column spun their mounts and spurred back up the trail, toward the waiting guns of the rear guard.

Justine chambered a second cartridge, felt the sting of a pebble against his cheek as a slug from below kicked dirt beside his head. He fired at one horseman who had brought a handgun into play. The shot missed as the man's horse spun away.

The mules pulling the wagonload of captives bolted as the driver went down amid a rattle of gunfire. Justine gritted his teeth, lined the Spencer's sights, and dropped the offside mule. The animal's harness mate went down in a tangle.

The initial fight lasted only a few seconds before the Comancheros rallied from the initial shock and surprise; those still mounted turned and spurred hard up a narrow side spur of the ridge a hundred yards to Justine's left, wagons and goods abandoned. Justine fired again, a snap shot that hit nothing but dirt, then scrambled back down the ridge to his horse.

Moments later he was in the saddle, his chestnut a few

strides behind Dead Horse's mustang, closing on the fleeing Comanchero Thompson had described. The rider's mount rapidly lost ground to the faster horses of the pursuers. Justine sheathed the rifle and pulled his Dragoon. The revolver would be easier to handle in a close-quarter scrap.

The fleeing rider's mount stumbled and went down. The Comanchero rolled, then came to his knees, shaking his head, stunned. He made no attempt to pull the revolver at his waist. Justine's chestnut pulled alongside the Lipan's mustang only a few strides from the kneeling Comanchero. Justine saw the glint of sunlight on steel as Dead Horse raised his war axe.

"No!" Justine yelled. He reined his chestnut sharply to the right. The powerful gelding's shoulder slammed against the Lipan's smaller mount. The Indian's horse staggered, regained its footing, and the two men sped past the downed trader. The shoulder of Justine's horse missed him by inches.

Justine pulled the chestnut to a stop, spun the mount and dismounted, his Dragoon aimed at the dusty Comanchero's chest.

"What for you stop me kill Mexican?" The Lipan, still mounted, glared at Justine. Fury danced in his black eyes.

"Thompson said we were to bring this one back alive. You heard him."

"Mebbe so I take your scalp. Then Mexican's."

Justine's gaze flicked from the downed man to the Lipan. "Try it and I'll kill you," he said, surprised at the calm tone of his own words. "I've got this one. Go help the others. Maybe *they'll* let you kill somebody. I won't."

The Lipan stared at Justine for a few heartbeats, then barked a curse and reined his horse toward the sporadic gunfire in the distance.

Justine dismounted, keeping a close watch on the Comanchero, who was still on his knees. "You speak English?" Justine asked.

"*Sí, señor. Un poco.* A bit."

"Unbuckle that gun belt and toss it over here. Don't make any sudden moves." Justine waited until the Comanchero complied, then asked, "Are you hurt?" He scooped up the worn gun belt and holstered revolver.

"I think no. Only bruised. *Gracias, señor.* The Apache, he would have bashed in my head. Mexicans they don't like."

"They don't like a lot of people. You are Polonio Ortiz?"

"*Sí, señor.*" The Comanchero swept the big hat from his head.

"I'm Ned Justine. You are a prisoner of the United States Army, Mr. Ortiz, and will be treated as such. Do as you're told and you won't be hurt. Now, sit down. We'll wait until Mr. Thompson and the others get here."

"Thompson? Kicker Thompson?" Ortiz's brown face paled beneath the dust, terror lighting his dark brown eyes. "No wonder you find us. Perhaps you have not done me such a favor after all."

"Supplying guns to Indians is a serious offense, Mr. Ortiz. But if you fully cooperate, maybe Mr. Thompson won't nail you to one of your own wagons and skin you alive." Justine surprised himself at the confidence of his tone and the ease with which the words rolled from his tongue despite the tremors in his belly. "Now, be quiet and wait."

Ortiz nodded. "*Sí, Señor* Justine. You have the big *pistola.*"

"And I tend to get the nervous shakes after a fight. Don't do anything to startle me and maybe this thing won't go off."

Just over an hour later, Justine stood at Thompson's side between two captured wagons. None of the rescued captives had been injured, nor had any of the scouts. The surviving Comancheros, securely bound, all but Ortiz bleeding and moaning in pain, sat before a semicircle of rifle and handgun muzzles. Whiskey Pete and two others guarded the recovered Longhorns fifty yards away.

"Not a bad day's work," Thompson said. "Two Comancheros dead, three hit hard enough they might or might not make it. No need trackin' down the ones got away. Reckon this bunch has done their last tradin' with redskins."

The old scout turned to Callahan. "Make up a full team for the captive wagon. Pile these Comancheros in a couple of the carts. Go through the stuff they traded for, take what we can use. Burn the rest."

"How about the horses, mules, and cattle?"

"Trail 'em back. Company C's just a day or so behind us. Turn the whole gaggle over to 'em when you meet up." Thompson turned to Justine.

"Son, you done good here. I seen you make sure that damn heathen Lipan didn't kill Ortiz. You hadn't stopped the redskin, we might not of had Bad Hand his prize Mexican." He turned away to tighten his saddle cinch. "You and the boys get ready to move out, Justine. See you later." He swung into the saddle and looped the lead rope of his packhorse through a cinch ring.

"Aren't you going back with us?"

"Ain't through huntin' yet. Be seein' you again when I find us some Injun sign."

"I don't know where I'll be stationed."

"Don't matter. I need you, I'll find you." The old scout reined his mount toward the north without another word. Within minutes, moving at a fast trot, he had disappeared from sight.

"Tough old coot," said the trooper standing beside Justine. "He'd do to ride with if he didn't hate everybody so much. We might as well get a move on. It's a long ride from here back to Concho."

Badger kept a firm grip on the red-haired boy seated before him on the roan war pony's withers and smiled at his good fortune.

The child, who appeared to be nearing his fourth summer, shivered in fear and confusion. But the boy no longer cried or struggled against his captor. He was strong of spirit for his age. Already he had proven his bravery. He had darted from his hiding place in the woodpile to kick Bat in the rump moments after Bat spread the legs of the screaming red-haired girl. The raiders had a good laugh over that. Badger snatched the boy away before Bat brained him.

The boy would be a fine son, a great warrior, the pride of Badger and Star, whose lodge had not yet yielded a child. This was a fitting prize to end a great raid.

Badger kept his pony facing away from the whoops and cries of the others as the band sacked the isolated house not a day's ride from the horse soldier's camp called Fort Griffin. There was no need for the child to see what had happened—and was happening—to his family.

The white man had fought well, but in vain, to protect his people. The man and a suckling infant now lay dead. Several of the raiders toyed with the young red-haired girl and the older white woman before putting them to the knife. Badger felt no need to put himself between the legs of a white woman. He had his prize in the saddle before him.

Others of the band plundered the buildings and gathered the white man's cattle.

Badger glanced over his shoulder toward the house, which now began to smolder as torches ignited the green, uncured logs. Between the woodpile and house, Bat finished with the girl and turned her over to another warrior.

Yellowfish reined his paint war pony alongside Badger, reached out and ruffled the fiery red hair on the boy's head. "A fine child, a brave boy. He will grow tall and strong." Yellowfish chuckled. "Maybe we call him Bat Butt Kicker. It will be a good story to tell around the fire."

Badger grinned, his breast already swollen with the pride of fatherhood. "He will bring much pleasure to our lodge. Star will be proud."

"And perhaps soon he shall have a young friend of his own in that lodge." Yellowfish fell silent for a moment, fiddling with his breechclout to adjust it after taking his turn with the older white woman. "It has been a good time of the greening grass. We chose well to ride with Mow-way. Many horses, guns, mules, and white man's buffalo. And now, a son for Badger and his brother, Yellowfish."

Badger grunted an agreement, barely listening. At the moment his thoughts were with Star in the lodge several days' ride to the northwest. He was pleased that this raid was at its end. Soon he would be with her again, to see the delight in her face when she first gazed upon their new son.

"You look far into the distance, brother," Yellowfish said. "Your eyes are at peace, yet I sense your heart is troubled."

Badger sighed, his elation over the success of the raid and the capture of the boy momentarily diminished. "There are signs I do not like, Yellowfish."

"The killers of buffalo?"

"In part, yes. The Cheyennes say the big guns of the hunters already prey on the great herds north of the Arkansas River. Those who have come to join the Quahadi say the buffalo become harder and harder to find."

Yellowfish snorted in derision. "The long guns cannot kill so many as to cause problems."

Badger cut a questioning glance at Yellowfish. "Is this the same speaker who but two snows past told me that he feared for the buffalo? And hence for The People?"

"And is my brother the same who spoke at that time that the visions of Maman-ti and others must be true? That the whites would be driven from our lands? The same man whose mind is now clouded like the rain sky?"

Badger hesitated, listening to the crackle as flames gained a foothold on the white man's house, the fading cries of the victorious raiders. Finally, he sighed. "It is an emptiness feeding in my breast, like the bear feeds in the rotting log."

"Your visit to your sister in the last moon of the time of snows still haunts you."

"Yes. There is much hunger on the reservation. Children's bellies swell from lack of meat. The white man's promises to fill empty bellies are as empty as the bellies of those children. My sister and her child suffer. The sight both weakened and angered my heart."

Yellowfish nodded. "It is so. And thus more important to the future of The People to drive the white man away. This is why I have changed my mind. I have since dreamed—perhaps it was even a vision—that Quanah and my brother Badger, at the head of a great many warriors, descended upon the white hunters' camps and killed them all. Then the buffalo returned from a hole in the earth, in greater numbers than ever before. And all the Great Spirit's children from then on no longer feared The Starving Time."

"Perhaps this will be so, brother. But what of the horse soldiers? Even now, their war chief Bad Hand rides across the wide grass country, the land the white man calls the Staked Plains."

Yellowfish snorted again. "White men cannot survive in the big grass country. Only the red people know that land. Bad Hand and all his warriors will become lost and die of thirst. And have we not harvested many scalps, many horses, many prisoners, while Bad Hand is off chasing ghosts through the wide grass?"

"Again, perhaps." Badger paused to run his free hand gently over the brow of the captive boy and calm his squirming. "And perhaps we would be wise not to take this soldier chief Bad Hand and his warriors too lightly."

"Have we not defeated him in battle?"

"Yes, so far. But I feel in my heart that this *taibo* Bad Hand is no ordinary war chief. He has the cunning of the wolf and the courage of the big bear of the mountains, the grizzly."

Yellowfish cuffed Badger playfully on the shoulder. "You worry too much, brother. Like an old woman. Now, let us enjoy the spoils of our raid. It has been a good *puiseahcat*, this third month of the greening grass that the white man calls June. Let us take your new son to meet his mother. There will be plenty of time for more raids later, before the great hunt when the sun moves south."

Badger became aware that the rest of the raiders had begun preparations to move out; there was no more to be gained here. He kneed his horse into motion, Yellowfish riding alongside.

As the miles passed, the band split into smaller and yet smaller groups, a tactic which always threw the horse soldiers off the track. Some of the men trailed small herds of stolen livestock accumulated during the extended raid on many ranches and farms. Others simply reined their ponies in another direction. They would meet again in Mow-way's village, where the plunder would be distributed. Badger, as leader of this raid, would keep little for himself, except the only prize that counted—the small body before him. That, he would claim.

After a time, Badger called a brief stop and rigged a makeshift sunshade for the boy. White skin burned badly under such a strong sun. The wide-eyed child still trembled, but he did not cry. He was a strong boy.

"Brother," Yellowfish said as the ride resumed, "it is time for you to think of taking a second wife."

"Yes. Star would be pleased. Even such a hard worker as she will need more hands now, to tend camp and see to the growth of our son." He paused for a moment, frowning. "I have no idea which lodge to begin searching. Until now, Star has been the only wife I have needed."

Yellowfish laughed. "It will be no problem for such a warrior and hunter as yourself, a wealthy man, already with more than a hundred horses. You could have your pick of any young woman in the village."

Badger nodded. "This is something I must consider, and discuss with Star. It is a pity she has no unmarried sister. They make more agreeable second wives and get along much better than non-sisters. No arguments among wives brings peace and contentment to a man's lodge."

"It is true. Quarreling women can drive a man to sing his death chant," Yellowfish said. The young Comanche glanced at the sun, now lowering itself toward its bed in the west. "It will be good to be home."

Justine had never been able to picture Fort Richardson as home. But at the moment, it never had been more inviting or comfortable.

His duties ended for the day, he lounged in a rickety wooden chair outside his picket barracks, enjoying the cool September evening.

It was a welcome break from the long summer under the fierce sun in a wide, empty sky above the equally empty Staked Plains.

The campaign to penetrate and map the vast, unknown expanse, guided by information supplied by the captured Comanchero, had taken its toll on men and beasts alike.

Justine still shuddered inwardly at the remembered dread that flashed through his gut when the Fourth Cavalry detachment first topped out on the edge of that treeless, featureless, flat grass sea after ascending the Caprock. The sense of foreboding he felt there had been worse than any battle—as if some unheard voice said this was a land forbidden to man.

But Polonio Ortiz's information had been accurate. There was water to be had on the Staked Plains. Now they knew where that water was. Springs and flowing, freshwater creeks sprouted in the shallow draws and washes, and in the unexpected slashes of arroyos and deep canyons that a man could almost ride into before he knew they existed.

The Tonkawa scouts had all but balked at riding out onto the "big empty place." A few days later, the surliness and fear had passed, replaced by wide-eyed wonder at the metal shirts, long steel spear points, and rusted sword blades found in one shallow wash only a few miles north of the main Comanchero road.

Justine dug up a rusted spur as a souvenir and knew he held a piece of history in his hand. The site obviously had been the camp of a band of Conquistadors, the Spanish explorers who had crossed the plains in search of the cities of gold more than a century ago. Somehow, the slight weight of the rusted metal in his hand reassured Justine. The land seemed less hostile, knowing that men who were not Indian had passed that way.

Once, Charlton and Justine found signs of a large body of Indians moving toward the north. The band had been so large that the trail, though months old, seemed stamped indelibly into the ground at first. But the trail vanished after a few miles, obliterated by the passage of a huge buffalo herd. The herd must have been three miles wide, Justine thought, and no one could guess how long it had taken the shaggy beasts to pass this one point.

They found a few other Indian trails, also old—probably made before last winter's first snows, Whiskey Pete concluded after a brief examination of the sites. Half a dozen other places in canyons and valleys at the edge of, or just below, the sheer Caprock cliffs yielded signs of well-used Comanchero camps. In most of the sites the tracks of *carretas* and wagons, worn deep into passages over stretches of exposed flat rock or in the narrow bottoms of arroyos, told the scouts the camps had been used for generations of traders. But they found no live Indians, Comancheros, or fresh trails.

The names along the Comanchero Road remained indelibly stamped in Justine's mind. Muchaque, Quitaque, Blackwater Draw, Tierra Blanca Creek. And the place known as *El Cañon del Rescate*—Ransom Canyon, where captives were exchanged for Comanchero goods. He could have drawn the routes himself if Mackenzie hadn't had qualified surveyors and cartographers on his staff.

Long before the extended journey's end, Mackenzie began to fume and sputter that the expedition had found no live Indians, or even the New Mexicans who bought stolen cattle from the Comancheros. The buyers already had fled the New Mexico village of La Questa at the "request" of vigilance committees formed among ranchers and others who lived in or near the settlement.

Justine instinctively knew the long, hot campaign had not been a waste of time, at least in the long run. The Indians' vast stronghold had been penetrated by horse soldiers. If a white man could survive there, the wide grass country no longer provided a safe haven for the red man.

Like most privates, Justine was not schooled in overall military tactics. That was the province of generals. But he had followed the military maneuvers of the Civil War campaigns, and knew those tactics could not be applied to fighting Indians. This was a whole new style of warfare. The newfound knowledge of the terrain and water sources in Comancheria gave Mackenzie a powerful weapon in this unusual war.

The realization of what he had been thinking surprised Justine. He didn't know when he had become a soldier instead of a reluctant civilian trapped in uniform by family tradition.

At least he could lay aside one fear—until the next engagement. He hadn't panicked in the face of the enemy since that first brush with Indians in the Blanco Canyon raid. It was no guarantee he wouldn't panic the next time. If there was one, and, God willing, there wouldn't be. The sheer terror was still there. The shakes still came after the fight. And some nights, the vision of Gregg's crushed skull and oozing brain matter returned to haunt his sleep—

"Boots and saddles, trooper." The words jarred Justine from his thoughts. Elijah Thompson, leading a jaded blue roan, stood before Justine in the fading evening light. The old man's jaw was set, the expression in his eyes even colder than normal.

"What's up, Mr. Thompson?"

"Found us some real bygod Injuns, Justine. Mackenzie said you're mine for a spell."

"Why me?"

" 'Cause I asked Bad Hand for you. Need a man I can trust ridin' with me. Draw rations for a couple weeks, extra rounds for that Spencer, two of your best hosses. Fast ones, in case we get into a hoss race before Mackenzie's boys catch up to us. Get a move on. Time's a-wastin'."

Justine's spine tingled. He stamped into his freshly blacked boots. "Where are these Indians?"

"Cut sign on 'em four days back. Tracked 'em long enough to know they're headed up McClellan Creek. Mow-way's bunch. Mostly Comanch, few Kiowas and Cheyennes. Same bastards butchered the Lee family back in June and carried off one of their kids. Reckon they come back for more."

Justine nodded. A few minutes later he was ready for the trail. "Who's going with us?"

"Just you and me and a gaggle of these lazy damn redksin heathen Tonk thieves that call themselves scouts. Mackenzie'll bring a mess of troops a couple days behind us. For now, we're gonna track 'em down and find out where their main camp's at. When we find 'em, there's gonna be one helluva fight."

11

BADGER SQUATTED BESIDE a thick juniper atop the ridge overlooking the creek, rifle nestled in the crook of his elbow.

He stared for a long time into the rolling prairie beyond. Though the time of turning leaves approached, the sun's warmth bathed the land beneath a sweep of cloudless sky.

The absence of clouds concerned Badger. The second rain season should have begun. But only a bit had fallen during the last moon. The tracks of his small group would remain in the dry soil. He must be careful.

A light breeze ruffled the scalplock tied to the muzzle of his rifle as he studied the land. He saw only the flash of an antelope's tail, the soaring of a hawk high in the distance, and the scurry of a long-legged rabbit nearby. Once during his vigil he caught a quick glimpse of *tzena,* the trickster Coyote. The antelope and coyote were good signs. They were shy animals. They ran when danger approached. They gave him no sign of the white horse soldiers or the despised Tonkawas who served them as scouts.

Badger shifted his gaze to the small group of women and children in the shallow valley below.

Star's clear, liquid laugh from the creek where she gathered wild grapes caressed his ears. The captured boy stood at her side, neither defiant nor timid in his posture, but alert and observant. He seemed more a small man than a boy, clad in deerskin shirt, leggings, and moccasins Star had made. A battered elkhide hat with floppy brim protected his fair skin from the burn of sun and wind.

The boy would grow to be a strong warrior. All the signs were there, in the way he carried himself, the way he did not cry at some slight injury or discomfort. Badger looked forward to the moon after the leaves had fallen. Then it would be time to begin his son's training for his future role.

Even at such a young age and in his brief time with them, the boy had already excelled at the simpler games that taught the basic tactics of hunting and war. He held his own against older boys in the games.

Badger already had the boy's first mount selected, a gentle bay mare. By the time the grass again greened, the boy would be riding as well as any Comanche his age. Perhaps better. He had shown no fear of horses during his time in Badger's lodge. Already he spoke a number of words in the Comanche tongue and grasped the simpler signs of the hand language.

He had become a favorite among Mow-way's band, welcomed in any lodge as one of their own. That was not unusual. All children—red or white, born to the band or captives—were treasured by the Comanches and Kiowas, boys even more than girls. The future of The People rode on small male shoulders. It had always been so.

Though Badger did not remember his own first few months of captivity before he became Kiowa, and since his marriage to Star more Comanche than Kiowa, it was as if he now relived those times of long ago through the eyes and ears of the boy.

When they rejoined Mow-way's main band less than two sun's easy ride to the northwest, it would be time to seek out the most accomplished giver of names.

The boy said his white name was Billy. That would not do. Nor would Bat Butt Kicker. That was an entertaining story, but not a proper name. He must have a good Comanche name. Like Badger, he would be free to change that name at any time he chose. Badger had not seen fit to change his own name. It had been given to him by a wise medicine man before he had seen his sixth summer. It was a good name.

Badger would be generous with the naming price. The boy was worth a fine name, and he was the son of a wealthy man. Badger's herd now numbered well over a hundred fine ponies. The edges of his war shield boasted several scalps, the symbol of a great warrior, and an equal number of twists of the hair from horse's tails that told all he was an accomplished horse thief. Sign stories painted on the skin walls of his lodge portrayed his prowess as hunter and warrior. All were symbols of which to be proud. They were earned, not granted.

And now he was a father.

A man could ask for nothing more.

He caught Star's glance; even from this distance, half an arrow flight away, he sensed that her eyes twinkled in mischief. Or an unspoken promise of what sundown might bring, a notion that always warmed his loins.

Badger did not know why, but it seemed that Star somehow glowed from within now, even more than usual. It was a curious thing.

He remounted his long-riding horse. He paused, scanned the horizon one last time for danger, and saw none. His brief feeling of contentment cooled. He was not satisfied that the band of gatherers was safe from pursuit by the horse soldiers. It was a sense beyond those of sight and hearing, a squirm in the belly like the wriggles of a small snake. He knew he could not relax until the gatherers reached Mow-way's camp and the safety of numbers there, where many warriors waited.

His first duty this day was not to hunting or to warfare or glory or plunder.

It was to the women and children.

In his heart, he feared Mow-way might be underestimating Bad Hand. The white soldier chief had moved many of his warriors back to the place called Fort Richardson. That place was not so far away.

Badger's words of worry went unspoken in council, but

he had mentioned privately to Mow-way his concern that the main camp might best be moved farther up along the rivers, perhaps even as far as the red water called the Canadian, many miles from Bad Hand's main camp.

Mow-way listened with an honest ear, but just as politely dismissed the suggestion.

"We will be safe here," Mow-way had said, "and it is a good place from which to make more raids on the white men's lodges. The *taibo* who disturb the earth with their big mule-drawn iron arrowheads are fewer now. Soon they will leave the land that is rightfully our hunting ground. Our families will be happy here. There is plenty of wood, good water, much game."

Mow-way paused for a moment, then said, "In the time of the next moon, a council will be called to prepare for the move to the Place of the Chinaberry Trees and the snow time camp. If you wish, you may call the council sooner. It is your right."

"No," Badger said, "the council can wait. As you say, this is a good place." He turned to leave, then stopped. "Should we not post lookouts while we remain here?"

Mow-way shrugged. "There is no need. No enemy will find us."

Badger nodded and left. He had not pushed the argument. He had stated his beliefs. Mow-way had stated his. Who was to say which of the two different beliefs might be right?

Still, he wished Mow-way would put more men to watch over the women and children on gathering trips away from camp, such as this. Being a husband and father did not weaken a warrior's courage. It did bring a heightened sense of responsibility, the realization that something more important than that a man's own life might be lost.

He realized with a bit of a start that it was the first time he had ever seriously considered the possibility of his own death. That a warrior could die in battle or on the hunt was simply a fact. He did not fear death. But now he had a family, and more responsibility to the larger family of

The People as his reputation grew. The carefree days of his youth had passed with the changing seasons.

Badger pushed aside his musings and reined his horse down the slope toward the thick grape vines.

The packs on the two mules bulged with the harvest. The wild grapes had grown thick and fat this season. They would be a welcome addition to their meals both now and, when dried and mixed with other foods, during the time of snows.

As the gatherers finished their work and prepared to leave, Star reined her riding mare alongside Badger. The red-haired boy rode behind her, an arm around her waist. Star's eyes seemed to twinkle like her namesake as she placed a hand on Badger's leg and motioned for him to lean closer.

"I wish to share a secret with you, husband," she said, her voice soft but with the hint of a giggle that threatened to burst through her smile. "But not here. It is a secret that must be shared when the two of us are alone in our sleeping robes tonight. You must be the first to know, but what I have to tell you will not remain a secret for long."

Badger's brow furrowed for a moment, then smoothed as his hopes abruptly soared. The unnoticed obvious struck him like a thunderclap. For the past two moons, Star had not gone to the isolated lodge for women in their bleeding time.

His attempt at a stern glare failed miserably under his spreading smile. The glow in her deep brown eyes warmed him even more. "You should not tease me so, woman, or I shall have to beat you even more than usual. Speak of this secret."

She giggled aloud. "Later. When the sun goes to bed. Then I must share it with you before I burst open from its keeping."

Badger checked his anxious, hopeful curiosity, and nodded. Let Star enjoy her small game. Still, it was a long time until sundown.

He forced himself to concentrate on the job at hand, to

see the small band returned safely to the village. Not by the easiest trail, up the sandy bottom of the creek. There was a better way. Or at least a safer one. If any of Bad Hand's scouts were beyond the horizon, they must not find the trail to the main camp. He kept his rifle at the ready as he rode to the front of the column and led his people away from the creek.

He didn't relax his guard until the band was safely inside the protection of Mow-way's camp. Many lodges lined the valley along the creek, protected at the far end by a rocky ravine across the creek bottom, and on the sides by steep hills. The only smooth trail into the village was along the stream, where the water flowed eastward.

This was a happy camp, marked by laughter and contentment. The hunting and gathering had been good. Many fine raids, along with trade with other bands, provided all that Mow-way's people needed through the coming time of snows.

Badger still wondered why there were so few Comanchero traders this season. Only a handful had come instead of the usual wagon trains. That troubled him.

Still, it would not be the Starving Time when the old man of the north blew his icy breath upon them.

Badger's lodge stood near the flowing waters of the creek beside a tall pecan tree, a stone's throw from Mow-way's lodge at the center of the sprawling encampment.

Throughout the village, warriors tended their weapons, sat and smoked, gathered in small groups to gamble, or dozed in the shade of cottonwood, pecan, elm, and the clump of willows that grew beside a deep pool at a bend in the creek. Young boys followed by yapping dogs played at their games. Girls old enough for simple chores worked alongside the women, learning skills they would need when they came of age. The scent of wood smoke, broiling meat, and the fragrance of junipers wafted into the village by the gentle breeze from the hillside above. The smells left a gentle warmth in the nostrils.

The band's big horse herd grazed in the wide meadow

of a side canyon near the village, watched over by a few young men under the guidance of two older, more experienced warriors. The ponies were sleek and fat. The seasons had been good to The People and their ponies.

Despite the relaxed, playful mood of the camp and his eagerness to hear Star's secret, the snake still squirmed in Badger's belly. He did not know why the feeling refused to go away. Perhaps, he told himself sternly, he was acting as Yellowfish had said in jest—like an old woman, his mind fretting and fussing that all was not as it seemed. That something evil lurked just over the horizon. Yet, Mow-way had said there was no danger here, and Mow-way was a wise man with strong medicine. But he would not post watchers on the hills above the camp.

Badger gave in to the snake.

He led his long-riding horse to the grazing herd, caught up his roan war pony, staked the animal before his lodge, and fed it a double handful of grain to apologize for interrupting its grazing. He carefully cleaned and examined his rifle, then counted the brass shells upon which the weapon fed. He had only eight of the stubby cartridges left. It was of no great concern. He had other weapons in which he had more trust.

He retrieved his short war bow, made of strong wood called bois d'arc, or Osage orange, that could send an arrow many strides past the reach of most other bows. He checked the sinew bow string, found no frayed spots or signs of weakness, then returned it to the leather pouch that held it across his back by a sturdy thong. He gave equal care to his arrows. The shafts remained straight, the three feathers of each smooth, their iron tips sharp and securely fastened. Satisfied, he slipped the arrows back into their quiver.

The preparations seemed to help. They were not enough.

The snake still wriggled.

Badger went to see Yellowfish. He found the young

warrior seated before his lodge, staring at the backs of his hands, his expression glum.

"Something troubles you, brother?" Badger asked.

Yellowfish shrugged. "The sticks and bones game was not kind to me today, Badger. I gambled away the special robe from my lodge, the one I had been saving as part of my bride price offering to Para-a-Coom for his daughter, Runs-With-Antelope."

"That is no problem. You shall have an even finer robe from my lodge." The offer fell easily and without regret from Badger's lips. Among the Comanches, the possessions of one were the possessions of all. Only favorite horses and wives were considered personal property, their use allowed by permission only.

Yellowfish's frown faded. "Thank you, brother."

Badger casually waved a hand, that subject dismissed, and frowned. "I would ask a favor of you."

"It is yours."

"Should something happen here, see to Star and the boy. Picket your best ponies by your lodge, as I will picket Star's. If a fight begins, flee the danger. Do not rush to join the battle. Help Star and my son to safety."

Yellowfish's eyes widened, questioning. "My brother has a dream? A vision of danger?"

"Only a feeling," Badger said. "It is probably nothing. But my spirit will be less troubled if you promise to aid them. Just in case."

"It shall be as you ask, brother." Yellowfish paused for a moment, his gaze locked on Badger's face. "Do I see something else in Badger's eyes?"

A slight smile touched Badger's lips. "When the sun goes to bed, I shall know."

The glint of mischief, never far from the surface of Yellowfish's dark eyes, returned. "And you shall share this something with Yellowfish?"

"Of course. Are we not brothers?"

It seemed to Badger that sunset would never come.

Eventually, it did.

He and Star lay side by side on the soft bed of fresh juniper boughs draped with trade blankets. The faint light from the coals of the small fire cast a pale red glow through the near darkness. Their son snored softly on his bedding nearby, his unruly hair painted even redder by the soft light of the embers.

"Now it is time," Star whispered.

"The secret?"

She took his hand and placed it on her belly. "In seven moons you will have a small friend. Perhaps a brother to our already-son."

Badger stifled the urge to whoop aloud. "A child?"

"Yes. You have so honored me, husband." She nestled her head against his neck and shoulder, her breath light against his skin. "Your heart beats so fast."

"Because it is about to burst with happiness."

"As does mine." Her hand moved his fingers farther down her belly. "Sleep will be long coming tonight unless we do something to help us relax."

"But—will it not harm the baby?"

Her soft laugh held an even more musical tone than ever. "Ah, my brave husband. You know so much of life, but so little of women. It will not harm the child."

Justine leaned in the saddle to study the smooth, sandy soil below.

Nothing.

The trail had simply vanished.

For the last five miles, Lige Thompson's steady string of profanity had singed Justine's ears. The old scout had not taken kindly to losing the trail. He had, as usual, taken out his frustrations on the Tonkawa scouts. The Indians now fanned out over a mile-wide front, trying to pick up some sort of sign, but more importantly to get out of range of Kicker and his rage.

Thompson himself had ridden off, alone and still spewing invectives, leaving Justine to deal with Captain Wirt Davis and his company of troopers. Davis's detail, the advance unit of five cavalry companies, had caught up with the scouts just in time to hear the air turn blue around Thompson's battered hat.

Justine glanced at Davis and shook his head. "Sorry, sir. It appears we've lost them."

"Thompson said he was positive they were headed in this direction. That large a band had to leave a trail somewhere." The officer's brow furrowed. "Colonel Mackenzie wouldn't mount such a sizeable expedition if he didn't have faith in that old scout. As I do. Keep looking, Justine."

"Yes, sir." Justine sat motionless in the saddle for a moment, trying to think, then on impulse reined his sorrel toward the tangle of wild grape vines.

He dismounted, dropped to a knee, and studied the sandy soil beneath the vines. Fallen grapes, some squashed flat as if stepped upon, littered the ground beneath the natural arbor. He picked up one of the grapes and squeezed it between his fingers. It didn't seem ripe enough to have fallen from the vine on its own.

At the east edge of the arbor, a slight depression in the ground caught his eye. A mule's hoofprint. And beside it, the faint imprint of a small moccasin—a woman's foot. At the heel of the impression, an even smaller print lay over the first. A child's foot had left this.

"Captain, I may have found something here," Justine called.

Davis trotted his horse to where Justine waited, swung from the saddle, and peered at the prints. "Gathering party," he said after a moment. "Women and children. Picking grapes to take back to the main camp."

"Looks that way, sir." Justine removed his hat and wiped his brow, though the late September air held the first touch of the coming night chill as the sun lowered.

Davis stood and looked around. "Well, let's see what we've got before we lose the light."

Davis and Justine remained afoot, a couple of yards apart, scanning the ground. The tracks of the woman, child, and mule seemed to abruptly vanish, as if they had never been there.

Justine glanced up, caught the captain's faint head shake, and was about to remount when the oblong shadows of a few round objects on a stretch of hardpan near the edge of the arbor drew his attention. The small objects seemed out of place on the exposed flat rock. His heartbeat quickened as he neared the shadows.

The round objects were grapes.

"Captain," Justine called softly, "take a look at this."

Davis squatted beside Justine, then grunted in approval. "One of the packs carrying the grapes must be leaking. Justine, I do believe we've found our trail." He stood. "We'd better find Thompson."

Justine glanced over Davis's shoulder. "He's coming in now, sir."

Thompson reined in beside them, no longer swearing like a teamster. "Cut sign on top of that ridge. Injun sat there a long time. Unshod pony, couple piles of horse apples. Tracks headed back this way."

"It appears Justine's found what we've been looking for," Davis said. "The Indians left us a trail of grapes to follow, like a bird follows bread crumbs. Gather in your Tonkawas. I'll send a rider back to inform Colonel Mackenzie. We'll follow this sign as far as we can before sundown."

Thompson's gaze raked the ground, then shifted to Justine. "By God, Ned, you may turn into a tracker after all. These grapes are going to take us right to that butcherin' red bastard Mow-way and his bunch. Let's go find 'em."

Justine wiped a sleeve across his eyes, trying to clear away the gravelly feeling beneath his lids.

The weight of the miles and the strain of following the

faint trail lay heavy on his shoulders. The signs had been anything but easy to follow; the trail had led away from the wild grape arbor on the creek into dry, rolling country with sprawling mats of prickly pear, bush cactus, and stretches of exposed rock. Now, almost twenty hours later, the trail had returned to the softer, more readable sandy soil along the creek.

"This bunch's got one mighty trail-savvy redskin with 'em," Thompson groused as he reined his horse in at the edge of the creek. "But, by God, we got 'em now." The old man leaned from the saddle, spat, and lifted an eyebrow at Justine. "Look around and tell me what you see."

Justine took his time. When Thompson handed a man a test, he'd better make sure he found the right answers. Lige Thompson had a tongue that could take a man to the woodshed in a hurry and leave him feeling about as tall as a grasshopper, and equally as useless. Justine also knew that what he was learning might save his hair one day.

He blinked under the morning sun, which had lost much of its intensity and warmth in its late autumn movement southward. The light seemed to have more of a soft, golden cast to it now. It hadn't chased the chill from the long night in the saddle, the countless hours of leading horses and squinting at the ground under the faint light from a lowering moon. He studied the skyline, the sky itself, twisted in the saddle to stare in all directions, and finally leaned from the saddle to peer into the lazy trickle of water drifting down the creek.

Finally, he turned to the grizzled scout. "Buzzards up ahead, maybe a mile or so away. Lots of them."

"Which means?"

"An Indian camp. A big one."

"What else?"

"The creek water was clear half a mile back. Now it's muddy. A sizeable horse herd crossed upstream not long ago."

"How do you know it's hosses and not buffler?"

"We haven't seen fresh buffalo sign in weeks. And

there's wood smoke on the breeze. Buffalo don't make camp fires."

"Doin' good so far, Ned. Anything else?"

Justine sighed. "The tracks we've been following were left by two mules, and five horses, three of them mares. Six women, three children, and one man. A quarter of a mile back, they were joined by four other riders, likely men from the camp."

Thompson almost smiled through the hard set of his jaw and the chill in his almost colorless eyes. "Like I said, you're learnin'. Even got so's you can tell the sex of an animal, two legs or four, by the way it pees." He pulled his battered pipe from a vest pocket, tamped it with tobacco, and lit the smoke with a sulfur match. "Soon's you learn to smell Injun from five miles off, you'll be a passin' fair scout. I smell a heap of 'em up ahead."

The exhaustion faded from Justine's body, chased by a flutter in his belly. His fingers started to chill. "What now, Mr. Thompson?" he asked.

"We go fetch them sorry damn Tonk redskin cannibals, if they ain't got their worthless, thievin' selves lost. Tell 'em to bring up Wirt Davis and his boys. Mackenzie and the rest of the troops should have near caught up with Davis by now. You and me'll go check out the lay of this here camp."

"Just the two of us?"

"Two men can stay outta sight easier'n a bunch. And them Tonks might do somethin' stupid and tip off Mow-way we're out here. It's for us to tell Bad Hand what he's up against. Then we can go make good Injuns outta bad ones."

The sun was at its highest point in the sky, but the chill in Justine's spine and fingers deepened as he lay alongside Thompson at the rim of a bluff overlooking the Indian camp.

"Bad Hand's been wantin' Injuns," Thompson said softly. "By damn, we done found him a bunch of 'em. Mow-way's camp, all right. That bigger tepee near the middle's his. Got his lightnin' bolt sign on it. Brought along the squaws, whelps, dogs, and all. Real family gatherin' down there. No pickets out."

"Why wouldn't they post lookouts?"

"Ain't Comanche nature once they get bunched up like this. Long as they figure they're safe and snug down there, not a fret in the world, their breechclouts'll stay down. We'll be on ol' Mow-way like fleas on a fat hound before he knows anybody's around. You take the west side, I'll take the east. Move quiet like a field mouse. Study the layout. Real careful."

Better than three hours later, the two met again at the spot where they had parted. The old scout's jaw clamped hard onto the gnawed stem of his battered pipe as he listened to Justine's report. He nodded. "Let's go parley with Bad Hand, Ned."

"Do I have to go with you, Mr. Thompson? To the colonel, I mean?"

Thompson reined his horse toward the meeting ground agreed upon with Captain Davis. "Reckon so. Two sets of eyes sees more'n one set. And, dammit, you might as well start callin' me Lige. On account of we're fixin' to do us some serious Injun killin', side by side."

The cold spot in Justine's belly turned colder. "What do you mean, side by side?"

Thompson pinned an unblinking gaze on Justine for a few heartbeats. "Because, son, you and me are gonna be right out in front of that first charge. I don't want just anybody coverin' my flank in a fight. I want a man I can trust, not some damn redskin Tonk, or no green, wet-eared trooper. A white man who won't turn tail and run first time he sees a few feathers."

"Mr. Thompson—Lige—I'm not exactly a veteran, you know."

"Don't matter. You earned your spurs far as I'm concerned." Thompson looked away and snorted. "Damn if you ain't got me yammerin' like a mama duck, Ned. Ain't talked this much at one stretch in twenty-odd years, and

I be damned if I know why I'm doin' it now. So let's shut up a spell, give our ears a rest, and save our talkin' for Bad Hand."

The old scout's gaze drifted toward the distant village. After a time, he turned back to Justine. The wide grin on his lips jolted Ned; it was the first time he had ever seen Thompson smile.

Thompson said, "Yep, son, McClellan Creek's where we bloody some Comanche noses."

12

JUSTINE'S NERVES SIZZLED as if he were surrounded by half the Comanche nation in war paint instead of white men in blue uniforms.

He tried to remain as inconspicuous as possible, but a single private stood out like a skunk in the cluster of officers gathered around Colonel Mackenzie. The only civilian in the group was Lige Thompson, who squatted beside Mackenzie as the two studied the crude map sketched into the dry soil.

The colonel's eyes glittered in anticipation as he studied the map Thompson had drawn with a pocketknife blade. The old scout jabbed a finger at a bulge in the sketch. "Pony herd's in this side canyon here. Big remuda, lots of hosses and mules." Thompson's gravelly voice carried easily in the intense silence as men peered at the layout of the Indian encampment on McCellan Creek. "Mow-way didn't post no lookouts. Be easy to catch him nappin'. Somethin' under three hunnerd lodges. Ned, what'd you tally?"

Justine swallowed hard and hoped his voice didn't quaver. "Two hundred sixty-two by my count." The steady tone of his voice surprised him. It should have been as shaky as his belly.

Mackenzie nodded in satisfaction and glanced around the gathering. "Gentlemen, this may well be the battle we've been hoping for and which to date has escaped us—our chance to severely cripple the Indians' ability to fight. Escape routes?"

Thompson shifted his gaze to Justine. "Ned, that be your department."

Justine squatted and traced a double slash on the sketch with a chilled finger. At least, he thought with relief, his hands weren't shaking much. Yet.

"Here, Colonel," he said. "Across the ravine at the upstream, the west end of the village. The ravine isn't deep, but it offers considerable cover—fallen timbers and rocks—and provides a good field of fire into the valley proper for riflemen. The pass is narrow compared to the rest of the valley. The walls on either side would be difficult to climb on foot, let alone on horseback."

"And that's where you believe they'll run, Justine?"

"In my opinion, sir, it's the most logical way out for anyone trying to flee the camp. Or for the Indians to establish a strong rear guard. If we gain control of both the ravine pass and the broader eastern opening into the valley, the Indians will be trapped."

Mackenzie stared into Justine's eyes for a moment; Ned wondered if he had stepped across the line. It wasn't a trooper's place to even remotely suggest battle tactics to a man like Mackenzie. The colonel merely nodded, then dropped his gaze to the map. "One company can take and hold that pass. Lieutenant Hopkins, that's your assignment."

Hopkins's ruddy face seemed to pale a bit. Justine thought he caught a glimmer of apprehension, perhaps outright fear, in the lieutenant's eyes. "Yes, sir. My men should be able to handle it."

"Be sure they do, Mr. Hopkins," Mackenzie said. "Trooper Justine's analysis of the situation is correct. If the Indians dig in there, it could cost us heavily, and permit many of them to escape. While Company I secures the ravine pass, Company F and the Tonkawa scouts will lead the assault, Company L in the second wave. Company D will secure the Indian pony herd. Infantry and quartermaster units will remain here and establish multiple defensive perimeters. This site will be our base camp for the operation. Questions?"

There were none.

Mackenzie said, "Very well, gentlemen. We move out within the hour. Twelve miles at an alternating walk and trot to save the mounts. Five miles from the Indian encampment, a final equipment check and tighten saddle girths for the attack." He glanced at the sun. "We should be in position by four o'clock. That will give us two and a half hours before sunset to get the job done."

Hopkins cleared his throat. The man looked on edge, Justine thought. If he was, he wasn't alone. "Excuse me, Colonel, but wouldn't it be better to approach during the night and strike at dawn, when the village will still be asleep?" Hopkins asked.

Mackenzie shook his head emphatically. "Lieutenant, I've learned from painful experience that night marches only create confusion and leave troops scattered all over the countryside. And I don't want to spend that much time camped here. That would increase the risk of discovery and cost us the element of surprise. We will strike this afternoon."

He paused for a moment for emphasis. "I cannot stress strongly enough that we must hit them hard, fast and efficiently. I want this village destroyed with minimum losses to our own. See to your preparations, gentlemen."

Justine fell into step with Thompson as the war council broke up. The frontiersman's brow furrowed, his face dark, eyes narrowed. "Wish Bad Hand had left them damn Tonks out of it. I ain't trustin' no heathen redskins. 'Specially at my back."

"They haven't let us down yet, Lige," Justine said.

"They ain't been in no real full-blown scrap before, neither. Likely the bastards'll turn tail first time one of 'em gets bloodied a scratch."

Justine didn't argue. He knew it would be a waste of breath. As they reached the tethered horses, he asked, "Think your son and daughter might be in this band?"

Thompson shrugged. "Damned if I know."

"If they are, we'll get them back."

Thompson didn't reply. He rummaged in his saddlebag and brought out a Remington Army percussion revolver. "Know how to use this?"

"Yes. As well as I can use any sidearm. Which admittedly isn't very well."

Thompson handed the weapon to Justine. "Stick it in your belt just before we charge 'em. Quicker to change handguns than to reload. This's gonna be an eyeball-to-eyeball fight, Ned. Comanches'll run to save their own skins, but they'll fight like hell to save their squaws and whelps. Sidearm's easier to handle than a rifle on hossback. When we hit 'em, shoot anything wearin' feathers and buckskins."

"That include the Tonkawas?"

"They're Injuns, too."

"I was joking, Lige."

"I weren't." Thompson stripped his saddle from the mount he had ridden on the extended scout. "Catch up a fresh hoss, Ned. Use that big line-backed dun of mine. He's fast, got plenty of bottom, and he knows what to do. Just give him his head when the dance opens. Fight Injuns, not the horse. Get a move on now. We're burnin' daylight here, not powder up yonder."

Justine was mildly surprised at the near silence with which the column moved after the initial formation of ranks. Few of the men spoke, and then only in soft tones. Sergeants issued any necessary commands in subdued tones.

The Tonkawa scouts spoke even less than the white soldiers. The expressions on the dark faces mirrored that of Whiskey Pete's, who rode at Justine's right. A muscle in Pete's jaw throbbed. His free hand occasionally brushed the haft of the knife sheathed at his right hip. His eyes glittered in eagerness to wipe out an enemy in a frenzy of hatred bred of centuries of mutual destruction.

Even the mounts seemed to sense the impending battle.

The prevailing sounds of the moving column were those of horses snorting, bits jangling as they tossed their heads. Justine could feel the controlled power in the muscles of the line-backed dun beneath him. The horse's ears pointed straight ahead. Justine doubted the animal could smell Indians or their pony herd at this distance, despite the light breeze in their faces, but the gelding seemed to know what lay ahead. The dun was a veteran, well trained to battle under the firm hand of the old frontiersman.

Justine didn't share the enthusiasm of either the Indian scouts or the dun horse.

Despite the mild late September air, his fingers chilled more with each passing mile. The knot in his belly grew tighter and colder. He had learned to live with the fear. He also had learned he would never conquer it.

From time to time, the brown and tan tones of the rolling, rocky countryside faded beneath a brief flash of another scene in Justine's mind—the tall granite mountains of home, trees ablaze with autumn color, pumpkins and squash turning orange and gold in manicured fields.

He wondered if he would live to see those mountains, trees, and fields in autumn dress again.

"Rein in," came the call from behind. Justine recognized the voice. Mackenzie rode at the front of the Company F troops. "Rest the horses half an hour and see to your weapons, then tighten girths and prepare to move at the gallop."

At the top of a low hill overlooking the village, Wah-ho-lah reined in to scan the countryside in search of three horses that had strayed from the main herd.

Above the distant horizon, a smudge against the soft blue sky caught his attention. A dust cloud.

The Cheyenne stared toward the dust, brow furrowed, then turned his horse back toward the village below, the strayed ponies momentarily forgotten.

He found Mow-way seated in front of his lodge, smoking. Mow-way listened to Wah-ho-lah's report, then shrugged. "It is nothing. Buffalo on the move."

Wah-ho-lah frowned. "Should we not send scouts to look?"

The Comanche chief smiled as if indulging a wayward child, and shook his head. "We have more than enough meat and robes for the coming time of snows. There is no need to disturb our friend the buffalo."

The Cheyenne's frown deepened, but he knew that to argue with Mow-way was a waste of time and breath. The Comanche was a great war chief, with but one flaw—his stubborn refusal to admit even a possibility of danger here in this valley.

Wah-ho-lah tried to quiet the feeling of unease in his breast as he nodded to Mow-way, mounted, and went to resume his search for the missing ponies.

As he passed the lodge of Tabi unuu, his concern grew. Badger was applying war paint.

Badger's roan war pony stood saddled at his side. Behind the lodge, the mare ridden by Badger's wife waited, also saddled and with small packs slung over its withers. A few yards away, Yellowfish's long-riding horse stood hipshot, dozing. It, too, was under saddle. Another of Yellowfish's ponies nuzzled the long-riding horse's flanks. There were packs across the second horse's back.

Badger and his brother Yellowfish obviously sensed something was afoot. Something that was not good. . . .

Justine tightened the girth and glanced around.

The Tonkawas had taken advantage of the short break to apply war paint. Streaks of black, red, and ocher across foreheads, cheeks, and bared breasts emphasized the symbolic tattoos that adorned many chests, chins, and upper arms. Some wore necklaces made of dried human ears or fingers. Bits of colored cloth decorated horses' manes and tails. Shriveled scalps dangled from the hackamores of ponies.

The Tonkawas were ready for the attack.

The grim expressions on the Company F veterans' faces contrasted sharply with the pale, wide-eyed looks of the newer recruits.

Justine knew how the recruits felt. When it came to major battles, he was a recruit himself. The ice in his belly wouldn't let him forget they were not headed into some minor skirmish with a handful of raiders or the ambush of a band of unsuspecting Comancheros. What lay ahead was a full-fledged, pitched battle with scores of armed and competent warriors.

Almost a third of Mackenzie's command were men inexperienced in battle, green as grass. Even those troopers who had crossed and recrossed the Staked Plains during the long summer campaign had yet to go up against a live Indian who was doing his best to kill them.

Mackenzie held one last, brief conference with his officers, then sent the order down the line: "Mount up. At the trot, by the fours."

Wah-ho-lah couldn't shake the feeling of unease as he herded the strayed ponies back toward the village.The sun, now more than halfway toward its bed, shone warm on his breast but did not chase the chill from his heart.

The lead pony topped the lip of the shallow buffalo wallow. Its head snapped up; at the same instant, the unmistakable sound of many horses moving at a run reached Wah-ho-lah's ears. His heart seemed to stop, stunned to stillness as the three ponies abruptly bolted. The sound was louder now, a river of hoofbeats, the jangle of metal, war cries in tongues he did not understand.

Wah-ho-lah slammed heels into his pony's ribs. The stocky horse bolted up the last few feet of the wallow's edge and skidded to a stop. A cry burst from Wah-ho-lah's lips.

Less than an arrow's flight away downstream, a line of painted warriors thundered toward the village, followed by wave upon wave of blue-clad riders—horse soldiers.

Wah-ho-lah fought back the quick surge of panic that momentarily froze him in his tracks. He yanked at the rein. The village must be warned. He leaned low over his pony's neck, heels pounding the animal's ribs, and shouted as loud as he could; he carried no gun with which to fire the shot that would alert the warriors in the village.

He shouted again, a third time, and something heavy slammed into his back. Half a heartbeat later he heard the rifle blast from behind. He sagged over his pony's neck and clung in desperation to the horse's mane. He tried to cry out again. The shout would not come. The sun, so bright and warm moments ago, faded. His grip weakened. He slid from the pony's neck, struck the ground, and rolled.

The last thing Wah-ho-lah saw was the triumphant leer in the Tonkawa's eyes before the war club crashed into his skull.

Badger sprang to his feet as the first rattle of gunfire sounded from the east end of the village. He swept up his bow and quiver, slung them over his back, and yelled a warning to Star: "Go to Yellowfish! Take the boy! Stop for nothing else!"

He vaulted onto the back of his roan war horse and racked a cartridge into the chamber of his rifle. At that instant Yellowfish darted from his own lodge a few feet away.

"Soldiers!" Badger shouted to Yellowfish. "Stay with Star and the boy! See them to safety, then to Quanah's band!"

"You?"

"I fight the soldiers! Go, Yellowfish! Take only your weapons and what is already packed! Leave all else behind!" Badger ignored Star's frightened cry from the lodge opening. He kicked his horse into a run toward the dust and gunshots.

The sudden explosion of noise hammered Justine's ears, the shrill yelps of the Tonkawas clear and sharp above the muzzle blasts of carbines and handguns.

He instinctively ducked as a rifle ball sizzled over his head. He thumbed the hammer of his Dragoon and fired, saw the ball kick dirt at the knees of a kneeling Indian rifleman. The Indian tumbled backward as Lige Thompson's revolver blasted. Seconds later they swept past the first thin line of Comanche defenses, only half a dozen armed warriors, and closed rapidly on the first of the string of lodges.

An arrow whistled near his left ear. He slapped a quick shot toward a crouching Indian. The man dropped straight down as if hit between the eyes with a heavy club. Justine's eyes began to water from the hard ride into the wind and the sudden swirl of dust and powder smoke.

He fired once more, again missed. Then the first wave of real resistance rose up to meet the attackers. Tonkawas leaned from the saddle, wielding war clubs, firing carbines with one hand, the Company F troopers close behind, handguns barking.

The charge carried Justine beyond the first few lodges, his dun horse two strides behind Thompson's mount. Through the dust, smoke, and confusion, he saw Thompson point his revolver at a figure attempting to flee—a woman. Justine's sickened shout of "No!" vanished beneath the flat bark of Thompson's handgun. The woman staggered two strides and plunged forward, facedown, arms outspread.

Within seconds the fight was at close quarters as warriors poured from lodges. Justine momentarily lost contact with the other men in the maelstrom of dust and smoke. He fired point blank into the face of one warrior a split second before the Indian managed to raise his rifle. The range was so close that the tongue of flame from the Dragoon's muzzle actually touched the Indian's forehead. Justine winced as drops of blood and bits of flesh spattered his own skin.

Justine's horse stumbled over a downed Indian. Something tapped against Justine's hip as the horse caught its balance. The close-in fight swirled around Justine in blurred confusion, his ears battered by gunfire, the screams of injured men and frightened horses, the battle cries in Comanche, Tonkawa, and white tongues. Slashes of color flashed by in the heady haze of battle. Justine rode blind, unable to see more than a few feet; he slacked the reins and gave the dun its head.

The powerful horse's quick burst of speed carried Justine past the first few lodges into an unexpected wash of sunlight and clear air—and to within yards of an Indian mounted on a roan horse, nocking an arrow onto the string of a short bow. A quick jolt of recognition startled Justine; it was the same man with half a face he had glimpsed in Blanco Canyon.

The arrow point swung in Justine's direction. Justine fired a hurried, panicked shot, saw the Indian wince, and then his dun raced past the roan, the horses' shoulders almost brushing.

Justine felt a blow against his back. His right arm went numb. The heavy Dragoon slipped from fingers that suddenly refused to do his bidding. He couldn't feel the hand at the end of his arm, only an icy spot behind his right shoulder. He braced himself for the shock of the arrow or rifle ball that would end his life.

Neither came.

He glanced over his shoulder. There was no sign of the Indian with half his face painted black, only a wall of dust and smoke behind him.

Justine suddenly realized the racing dun had carried him beyond the last of the lodges, toward the cover of a stand of cottonwood trees at the south base of the valley wall. Rifle balls and arrows buzzed past as he leaned over the dun's neck. The icy spot in his back blossomed into a bright pain that lanced deeper with each stride of the horse's hooves. Then he was in the trees, pulling the winded dun to a stop.

He looked over his shoulder, saw the feathered shank of the arrow angling from his back, and fought back a wave of nausea. Beyond the feathered tip, he saw other riders break through the end of the village. Half a dozen blue-clad horsemen were less than three hundred yards behind him now.

Justine wavered in the saddle, then blinked away the dim haze that threatened to obscure his vision. Some feeling had returned to his right hand; at least he was able to flex his fingers. He shifted the reins to his right and fumbled to draw Thompson's spare Remington from his belt. He knew it was mostly an exercise in futility. If he placed a killing shot now, firing left-handed, it would be blind luck.

He gasped fresh air into his choked lungs, heard the whistle from the dun's nostrils as the horse fought to regain its wind. In the near distance the shapes of Indian men, women, and children ran toward the ravine at the west end of the valley. Toward the guns of Hopkins's I Company. But no gunshots poured into the running Indians; instead, muzzle flashes and powder smoke billowed from behind the lip of the gash in the earth, toward the soldiers exposed in the valley.

An Indian rear guard held the ravine and had opened a furious defense of the safe passage.

Where the hell was Hopkins?

Through the ringing in his ears, Justine heard a scattered volley from the direction of the Indian pony herd. Company D had closed with the herders. He doubted the few Indians guarding the ponies had been reinforced by many fighting men. Mackenzie's force had caught the village by surprise.

But without I Company in position, the troopers in the valley faced a murderous defense at the arroyo. A frontal charge could cost the Fourth a lot of men.

In the valley below, Thompson, hatless now, gray hair flowing in the wind, rode down and shot a young woman. A small bundle tumbled from her fingers as she went down. The scout shifted his revolver to his left hand, leaned from the saddle, plucked the baby from the ground, slammed the baby's head into a creekside tree trunk, then tossed the limp bundle of rags aside.

The pain in Justine's back paled beneath a burst of disbelief, horror, and rage.

He fought back the urge to raise his revolver and take a shot at the old bastard. Instead, he stared in stunned silence toward the gray-haired rider, then muttered a curse. There would be, he vowed, a day of reckoning for this—he forced the grisly vision from his mind. There was more pressing business at hand. Somebody had to do something about the Indians dug in at the arroyo.

He kneed the dun to the edge of the grove and reined in. He ignored the rifle balls and arrows that thudded into the tree beside him and frantically waved his good arm to the half dozen troopers now closing on his position. The lead rider shouted something over his shoulder to the others, then reined his bay toward Justine.

Justine led the troopers into the relative safety of the grove. The tree trunks and foliage helped muffle the sounds of battle still raging on the valley floor.

"Man, you're hit," a wide-eyed trooper said. "We better get you back to the surgeon."

"It can wait," Justine said with a grimace as a fresh stab of pain racked his shoulder and back. "Right now we've got another problem. The Indians have a rear guard dug in at the arroyo. We've got to get them out before we lose a lot of men."

Frown lines burrowed into the trooper's face, pale beneath smears of dust and powder smoke. "Where the hell's Hopkins?"

"All I know is he's not where he's supposed to be. Looks like we'll have to do I Company's job. With luck we can break the Indian defense before the main body of troops ride straight into their guns."

"How do we do that? Straight-ahead charge'd just get us all killed."

Justine lifted a shaky finger to point. "There's a game trail just behind these trees. I spotted it when I scouted the camp. It's steep and narrow, but we can make it up riding single file. The Indians below won't be able to see us. Once we get to the top, we'll have a clear field of fire into the Indian guard. How are you fixed for ammunition?"

"Forty rounds apiece, more or less."

"Let's get moving then. We don't have much time. Follow me." Justine reined the dun toward a narrow, deep slash in the canyon wall behind the tree line.

The switchback climb to the top seemed to take forever, but Justine knew it had been less than ten minutes since they'd left the trees. The effort of staying aboard a climbing horse sent the pain in his back climbing the scale toward agony. He gritted his teeth and waited out the dizziness that tried to overtake him.

From the top of the rim, the rifle fire and shouts from the ravine below seemed louder, as if only a few feet away from Justine's small band. He pointed to a jagged ridge of boulders and junipers and waved hand signals to the troopers.

Justine tucked the Remington back into his waistband and pulled the Spencer carbine. He knew it would be awkward to handle the weapon with only one hand. But even if he didn't hit anything, he could make some noise.

The firing from the ravine intensified as the seven men settled into position on the ridge. Justine rested the barrel of the Spencer across a stone, settled the stock against his left shoulder, aimed as best he could, and fired. Wood splinters flew two feet from the torso he'd picked as a target.

Two Indians went down under the first volley from the rim above. Others glanced around, confused, trying to pinpoint the source of the new attack. A third warrior dropped his rifle and sagged across a fallen tree trunk.

Justine had to slip the Spencer's stock between his thighs and work the stiff action with his left hand. It took time; when he had fired his first three shots, other troopers already were shoving reloading tubes into the stocks of their carbines.

Each time Justine fired, the recoil sent a fresh rip of pain along his back. The bright sear spread over his entire body, one blast of raw agony after another. The sound of the muzzle blasts from both his group and the Indians below seemed to gradually fade. A strange pinkish wash spread across his vision. A roaring sound filled his ears.

"They're giving it up, boys!" someone yelled. The words fell faint and blurred on Justine's ears. "They're running for it! Pour it on 'em! Company L's forming up for the charge!"

They were the last words Justine heard before the pink wash turned dark and blackness swept over him.

13

THE TONGUES OF flames that still flickered in the darkness of the valley cut into Badger's heart like a freshly honed knife.

The soldier chief Bad Hand's destruction of the village had been complete. He had spared not a single lodge, no blankets, no food from the torch. The darkness of the night, broken only by starlight and the pale sliver of moon, could not conceal Bad Hand's work here.

Even the escape of those who managed to flee had been costly to Mow-way's band. Bundles of clothing, food, robes, and other household goods lay scattered along many trails, abandoned in the desperate flight from the soldiers' guns. The running battle between red warriors and white had not stopped until darkness fell on the land.

Badger struggled to maintain his outward composure through the emotions that warred in his breast. This was no time to show weakness. There was work yet to be done. Until it was finished, he must control his swirling mix of rage, frustration, despair, determination—and above all, worry. The throbbing pain from the soldier's bullet in his thigh was but a fly's bite compared to the ache of his spirit.

The roan horse between his knees snorted and pawed a front hoof into the rocky soil of the rim above what had been, until a short, brutal time ago, home to a happy and contented people.

Badger became aware of a presence alongside and glanced at the stocky bulk of the Kiowa-Apache Bat.

"The horse soldiers left nothing, Badger," Bat said, his words bitter in the chill night air. "This season of snows will be a Starving Time."

Badger did not reply for a moment. His throat had gone tight. Then he nodded. "This Bad Hand is not like other white war chiefs. He is not satisfied to simply kill many of our best men here, to take many captives. He wars against women and children, destroys their homes and blankets, takes away the food from their bellies."

"He learns, Badger." Bat turned his head and spat. "He learns the war ways of the red man. Strike hard, kill, burn, destroy, then ride away to fight another time. And that makes him more dangerous than all the other white soldier chiefs combined. Mow-way underestimated Bad Hand. That mistake cost many lives, caused much suffering."

"A mistake that will not be repeated," Badger said, his tone grim. "We will speak of this later. We must go if we are to reach Bad Hand's camp before the night star is overhead." He gestured to the band of warriors who followed and nudged the tired roan into motion.

He tried to set aside his worry over Star, the unborn child, and their red-haired already-son. He had faith in Yellowfish. If anyone could see them to safety, it was his brother.

The faint glow from the ruins of the village fell behind. Badger probed the cloth wrapped around his upper thigh. His fingers touched fresh blood. It was of little concern. The bullet had passed through the muscle, missing bone. The wound might hamper him on the ground, but not on horseback.

The throb of torn flesh triggered Badger's memory. The wide-eyed, pale face of the young soldier who had shot him remained fresh in Badger's mind, a face he recalled from an earlier battle. He wondered if his arrow had dealt its death blow to the soldier.

Badger did not know the full extent of the losses in the valley, how many men had fallen, how many captives taken. He did not dwell on the unknown. That could be learned later, when there would be time to know. And mourn.

The most critical loss, aside from the many lives, was the pony herd. Bad Hand's warriors had taken more than five hundred horses and mules in the battle, including most of Badger's own herd. He did not bewail the loss of his personal fortune. The horses were more than measures of wealth now. They were the key to survival in the coming moons of cold. Without them his people could not hunt, could not travel to far places of safety and shelter, could not defend their lodges should Bad Hand press the attack beyond this valley.

And if they were to recover the mounts, it had to be done quickly, before the white soldiers drove them too near the army villages where they would be under the protection of many guns.

He twisted in the saddle, let his gaze drift over the line of warriors trailing behind, barely visible in the meager light. They were few. With Mow-way's band scattered in the hours since the battle, Badger had been unable to gather more than the thirty who now rode with him. They had little ammunition, few arrows. Half of them straddled horses of questionable quality.

It would be enough.

It had to be.

Badger had tried to climb into the mind of the soldier chief even as he gathered the small band of warriors. Bad Hand was learning, true. But so soon after such a resounding victory, he would be unlikely to expect a raid in the middle of the night. And then yet another the next night.

Badger and Quanah had bested Bad Hand before, taking many horses.

It could be done again. It *must* be done again. . . .

Justine struggled from the darkness and the nightmare into a strange world of rectangular tan squares. He lay still, shivering with cold but soaked in sweat, confused, fully aware only of the pain that pounded through his body with each beat of his heart and the heavy tightness around his chest. He had to fight for each breath.

After what seemed an eternity of bewilderment, he finally recognized the confusing rectangular squares. The pegged planks of a wooden floor. The odor in his nostrils seemed vaguely familiar, yet strange at the same time. He heard a soft moan and realized the sound had come from his own lips. He blinked against the tears in his lids, a response to the relentless pain.

He remembered where he had smelled that strange scent before. In the Bangor ward where his grandfather had breathed his last.

The muted notes of a bugle call sounded, nearby but seeming far away.

Justine realized then he was in a post hospital.

The pain was real enough. So were the recurring dreams. The swirl of smoke and dust and a spear of flame lancing into a broad, copper face. The feathered end of an arrow sticking from his back. A warrior with half his face painted black. Bits and pieces of scenes flashed through his mind, then vanished as quickly as they had appeared. The jolt of a wagon bed. Shouts. Gunfire. The sound of horses' hooves thundering in the darkness. The darkness made no sense. The battle in the valley had been in daylight, not the black of night—

"Well, Trooper Justine. Welcome back among us." The voice came from beside Justine's cot. He turned his head, the effort sapping what little strength he had. Post surgeon Julius Patsky stood beside him. "How are you feeling?"

"Thirs—thirsty." The word came in a raspy croak from Justine's parched lips. A hand appeared, held a tin cup to his mouth. He drank a couple of awkward swallows.

"We came mighty close to losing you, trooper. You almost bled out on us," the surgeon said.

"Back . . . hurts."

"No wonder. I had hell's own time digging out that

arrow point. I've got something here to ease the pain." The cup reappeared, this time with an odd smell. Justine managed to force down the bit of liquid. It left a sweetly bitter taste on his tongue.

Patsky said, "It's laudanum. Extract of opium with a wee touch of good Irish whiskey. Developed the formula myself and still had enough whiskey to mix up some for the troops. It'll take effect in a few minutes. Now, let's take a look at these two holes you got in you."

"Two?" Justine winced as the surgeon loosened the tight bindings around his chest.

"Yep, two. The bullet hole in your butt turned out to be a bigger worry than the arrowhead. Think the slug cracked a hipbone. No boots and saddle calls for you for quite some time, Justine." Patsky chuckled. "Good thing you didn't follow the Scripture and turn the other cheek, son, or you might have caught a slug in that one, too."

"Don't remember . . . getting shot."

"Not much fresh blood, just a small spot. That's good news." The surgeon swiped something wet and cold across Justine's shoulder. Within two heartbeats it stung like the devil's fire. "As far as not remembering the gunshot wound goes, that's not unusual. I've seen men get hit pretty hard in the heat of battle and not even know it until they either keeled over or the fight was done. Happened to Albert Sidney Johnston in the Shiloh scrap. Ball nicked in the back of his knee. Didn't even know he was hit bad until he keeled over. They poured a gallon of blood out of his boot."

"Didn't know you . . . were Confederate."

"Wasn't. My brother was. He's a surgeon, too. We swapped a few yarns after the war." Patsky swabbed Justine's right buttock. The stinging liquid raised a second blaze and brought fresh beads of cold sweat to his brow and upper lip. "No sign of infection here, either. You'll have trouble walking or even riding for a while, and it may pain you some during cold weather. Eventually, though, it'll just be a cute little dimple in your butt. I hear the ladies think dimpled butts are cute. You won't be sitting up for a few days."

"How long have I been here?" Justine asked.

"Little over a week. You were unconscious most of the time. It's the body's way of saving the brain a lot of pain. Or the other way around." Patsky replaced and tightened the bandages, again restricting Justine's breathing. Fingers probed the side of his neck, the back of a hand touched his forehead.

"Fever's going down. Pulse is strong. All good signs. You're one lucky young man, trooper. If that arrow had hit a tad lower or at a different angle, and if the point hadn't stuck in your shoulder blade—which stopped it from slicing through a lung—you'd have been a dead man for sure."

More bits of memory flashed in Justine brain. The flickers seemed unreal, as if they had happened to someone else. He still couldn't recall many details about the battle. "How many men did we lose?"

"Two dead. One on the field, another in camp the first night after the fight." Patsky's hand rested lightly on Justine's shoulder. His voice softened. "Sorry to be the one to break it to you, son. Your friend Svenson . . ." His voice trailed away.

A pain that wasn't physical cut into Justine's chest. "Olaf?"

"He didn't make it. Took four Indians to bring him down, I hear. He got three of them before he died. We buried him the next day." Patsky sighed. "Damn, but I liked that big Swede. Anyhow, we had you and one other trooper seriously wounded, several others with minor ouches. Two soldiers dead is two too many, but the way the military equation works it was a good trade. The Indians lost a lot of fighting men."

Justine's lids became heavy. The laudanum was beginning to take effect; the pain seemed to be easing. Patsky's hand rested for a moment on Justine's undamaged shoulder. "Get some sleep now, son. Lot of folks been asking about you. I'll tell them you can have a visitor or two in a couple days if you feel up to it." The soft voice faded as Justine's eyes closed and the darkness returned.

Justine didn't know how much time had passed. He was aware only that he had slipped in and out of consciousness. He faintly recalled awakening once, groggy and weak, and thinking it was all over, that he was dead, when the angel had come to him.

It had to have been an angel.

He remembered a halo around golden hair, the faint scent of flowers, the gentle touch of a delicate hand on his brow. Soft words he didn't understand from a gentle face—a face in shadow, framed by golden light. The bittersweet taste of laudanum. Then more darkness.

"Justine?"

The touch of a hand on his undamaged shoulder brought him awake. The first thing he noticed was that the pain seemed less; the second, that he was both hungry and thirsty. He struggled for a moment to focus his vision before he recognized the man seated on the low stool beside the cot.

"How're you feeling?" Corporal John Charlton asked.

"Not bad—considering," Justine said. His words still croaked a bit, but seemed stronger now.

"Can you sit up?" Charlton said. The chief of scouts slipped a hand beneath Justine's left armpit. The effort to rise from his belly sapped Justine's strength and triggered a fresh stab of pain in his back and shoulder, then a pulsing ache in his butt as he swung his legs over the side of the bunk.

Charlton grunted in satisfaction. "You're mending nicely, Doc Patsky says. Time for something more solid than beef broth and weak stew. I brought a plate from the mess tent." Charlton put a tray on the folding camp table beside the bunk and removed the cloth from the dish.

"Yearling steak, Ned. Better chow than the rest of us get. Thought you'd rather have it than what the doc prescribed. He wanted you to have liver. Said it built up the blood faster."

Justine grimaced, but not from pain. "I hate liver. Never could eat it." He became aware of moans and dry, hacking coughs from other cots. He glanced around. A quarter of the hospital cots were occupied. He hadn't noticed that before. "Battle casualties? Patsky said we only had a few people hurt."

"He told it straight. We got out light, considering the scope of the fight. Mostly thanks to you."

"Me? I didn't do anything."

"I know different. So does Mackenzie." Charlton paused, glanced around, then said, "The men in here aren't battle casualties. Just an outbreak of some sort of croup and a few busted bones from horses falling during drills. The usual run of ailments you'll find on any army post." Charlton nodded toward the plate. "Can you handle that, or do you need a hand?"

"I think I can manage." Justine drank a few swallows from a tin cup of water on the tray, then reached for a fork with his left hand. His right arm was wrapped against his body. "What happened after the fight in the valley?" he asked between bites. "I seem to remember something, but I'm not sure what." Eating with his left hand was more awkward than he'd expected, but someone had gone to the trouble of cutting the steak into bite-size pieces for him. It was tender and juicy. Justine couldn't remember meat tasting so good.

Charlton said, "The fight on McClellan Creek wasn't the end of it. The Indians didn't just run away to lick their wounds. At least a fair number of them didn't. They hit us twice on the way back, the first time about midnight after we pulled back from the village. They got a bunch of their ponies back then, plus a few of ours." Charlton flashed a wry grin. "Got most of the Tonkawas' mounts, too. Whiskey Pete wound up walking and leading a burro after that first raid. Embarrassed hell out of him. The Comanches hit the horse herd again the next night, eighteen miles farther downstream. They got back all but about fifty of the horses and mules D Company brought out of the valley."

"The colonel wasn't pleased about that, I'll bet," Justine said.

"He was fit to be tied. But he shouldered responsibility for the whole mess. Some of us tried to talk him into not holding the horses outside the camp itself, where the Indians could stampede them so easy. He says he won't make that mistake again. He's decided we'll shoot every Indian pony we take that we don't need ourselves."

Justine winced. "Seems pretty drastic. Killing horses, I mean."

"No cavalryman likes to shoot a horse," Charlton said, "but it's the only way to put the Indians afoot and keep them that way. Still and all, we hit Mow-way's bunch hard. Mackenzie counted twenty-some dead Indians. One of the captives we recovered, a Mexican woman, said the Indians dumped sixty-odd bodies in a deep pool in the creek before they fell back. Wanted to keep the dead ones out of the hands of the Tonks, so they wouldn't be mutilated." Charlton frowned at Justine's clumsy maneuvering of the fork. "Sure you don't need some help?"

Justine shook his head. "I'll manage, thanks. Guess we did some damage after all."

"Could have been better, if Hopkins had done his job. We could have bottled up just about all the Indians if he had." Charlton's tone held a touch of bitterness, even contempt. "Still, from a tactical standpoint, it was a success. We brought back over a hundred and twenty prisoners, mostly women and kids. Recovered some captives the Comanches had. Mow-way'll have to do some tough horse trading to get his people back. Plus, we've tied him to a bunch of bloody raids with what one of the captives we rescued told us. All in all, we pulled a mess of one Comanche war chief's teeth."

Justine had managed only about a quarter of the meal, but all at once he couldn't eat another bite. He leaned back from the plate with a muttered apology.

"You'll get back on your feed in a few days," Charlton said. "After all, it's been a while since you had anything but watery soup." He set the plate aside, leaving the water, and produced a bundle from beneath his chair. "Brought you a new tunic, Ned. Your old one was bloodied and torn too much to save." He unfolded the new blue cloth and held it up.

"Whose is it?" Justine asked, puzzled.

"Yours."

"Couldn't be mine. It's got two stripes on the sleeve."

Charlton grinned. "It's yours, Corporal Justine. Battlefield promotion, direct orders of Colonel Mackenzie. I sewed the chevrons on myself. Congratulations."

Justine stared at the dress tunic in disbelief. "But why? What if I don't want the stripes?"

"You wear them anyway, Ned." Charlton rose, and hung the tunic on a nearby wall peg. "Nobody turns down a promotion from Mackenzie. Besides, it's a dollar or two more for you come payday. And a few other privileges enjoyed by noncoms, even us lowly corporals."

Justine sighed. "If I give a dollar or two back, can I have a discharge instead?"

"Can't help you there," Charlton said with a chuckle. "I'll be seeing you around, Ned, but it may be a while. All but a couple companies of the Fourth are heading south in a couple of days. Apache trouble on the Rio Grande. You're staying here to heal up. Need anything?"

"Something has been worrying me." Justine became aware that the throb in his hip was building. "Al Duggan. Did he come through the fight all right?"

"Not only all right, but in fine fettle—except for the aftereffects of a payday battle with ol' John Barleycorn last night. He'll be around to see you when his head quits hurting, likely tomorrow. Along with someone else who's been fretting over you like a mama hen here lately. Now, settle back and grow some skin. I'll need a healthy scout when we get back from down south."

Badger's heart all but stopped as he reined his recovered long-riding horse to a stop at the top of the twisting switchback trail up the steep, rocky bluff and onto the edge of the big grass country.

A familiar figure waited, outlined against a red sky above the sun's bed.

Badger shivered inwardly, though the wind was not yet cold in this lingering warmth which seemed to hold back the time of falling leaves. Throughout the many miles of leading the handful of warriors who remained with him, and their share of horses recovered from the soldiers, he had tried and failed to force the worry from his mind.

The worry eased as he drew alongside the horseman and saw the smile on Yellowfish's face.

"Star and the already-son are fine," Yellowfish said as he placed a hand on Badger's shoulder. "They wait for your return in Quanah's camp only a few suns' ride from here. I will take you to them."

Badger swallowed against the knot in his throat. "Thank you, brother. I knew they were in good hands, yet my heart remained troubled. And it is good to see you safe, as well."

The two moved aside as the pony herd began to top out on the flat land the white man called the Staked Plains.

"There he is," Yellowfish yelped in excitement. "My paint war pony, *Tuaahtaqui.* You brought him back for me."

"We were fortunate enough to get your Cricket and most of the other ponies back, Yellowfish. At least now our people will not have to wear out their moccasins, and we will be able to find buffalo to fill their bellies."

"Already, Quanah rides to the hunt—" Yellowfish broke off the statement, his gazed fixed on the stained cloth tied around Badger's leg. "You are injured."

Badger waved a hand casually. "It is nothing. Already the healing begins. Come. Show the way to Quanah's camp. We will speak as we ride."

Yellowfish hesitated a moment, watched as the last of the mounts and warriors ended the long climb from below, then kneed his horse into motion. "Where are the others?"

"Scattered here and there, partly to confuse the horse soldier scouts should they follow, some to return to their own bands and to learn the fate of their families. Many still follow Mow-way. Those whose hearts are weak." Badger heard the bitterness in his own words. "Mow-way failed his people. He and those who do follow him will be forced onto the reservation or face starvation or freezing. The Kiowas who were among us return to their people, angry and eager to resume raiding."

"Badger, are you not Kiowa?"

"I have been Comanche for some time now, brother. My place is with Star, with the child who grows in her belly, and with our already-son who needs a good name. With Quanah's band."

The slight frown faded from Yellowfish's brow. "It is good. With Quanah there will be no Starving Time. There will be enough for all who were able to reach his camp. His raids into Mexico were good. Now, Asking-About-the-Buffalo points him on the hunt."

Badger nodded. The small horned lizard had great powers. All a hunt leader or medicine man need do was ask where the buffalo were, and the little animal would scurry in that direction. Asking-About-the-Buffalo was even more reliable than the raven when The People needed meat and robes. "How is the feeling in Quanah's camp?"

The frown again flashed across Yellowfish's face. "Among the survivors of Mow-way's band who came to Quanah, there is much wailing and cutting of flesh and hair for those who fell in battle in the valley, much worry for captives taken by the horse soldiers. But when the time of greening grass again comes, the grief will be past and all will be well."

Badger also frowned, but said nothing of the nagging concern in his belly. He turned in the saddle to stare toward the southeast. Things could not be well as long as Bad Hand and his horse soldiers stalked them.

As if reading his brother's mind, Yellowfish said, "The horse soldiers will never find our winter camp. The Place of the Chinaberry Trees will see us through this time of snows, and the next, and the next after that, as long as the winds blow over the big grass land. Quanah's band is strong, with many seasoned warriors and fine hunters."

"Let us not repeat Mow-way's mistake, brother," Badger said. "Do not take Bad Hand lightly. He is not like the other war chiefs of the white soldiers."

Yellowfish nodded. "It is so. He is the one now most feared and respected among The People. But for the color of his skin, he would in time become a great Comanche, I think. Yet, another, greater threat than one soldier chief faces not only our people, but all those whose skin is red."

Badger lifted a questioning eyebrow.

"Travelers from the north bring troubling news," Yellowfish said solemnly. "The white hunters slaughter great herds of buffalo in the land beyond the Arkansas. The children of the northern bands cry of hunger. Hunting parties from all villages, even those from the reservation, ride through piles of rotting flesh and bones, and find few living buffalo to fill their bellies. It is but a matter of time until the hunters violate the treaties made at Medicine Lodge, the papers forbidding them to cross into our lands. They will attack the great southern herd."

Badger's jaw set in a firm line. "They must be stopped."

"You speak true, Badger." Yellowfish's tone became animated, his words punctuated by sweeping gestures. "They will be stopped. Those who survive will retreat across the big river far to the east, never to return. I have seen this in a dream. A vision, perhaps. A vision shared by others. Quanah—and you, my brother—will lead the greatest war party ever known to a great victory over the white man, at the salty river that runs red through the big grass land. The river the whites call the Canadian."

"Others have seen this vision?"

"Yes." Yellowfish's lips parted in a wide smile. "But we will speak more of this later. Sun goes to bed now. We will camp at the springs just ahead. Soon, you will be with Star and your already-son once more."

14

THE ANGEL WAS back.

But this time, she had a face.

Ned Justine's heart skipped a beat. He started to rise from his cot.

"Please don't get up, Ned," Elaine Hopkins said. Concern showed in her deep blue eyes, belying the smile that dimpled smooth cheeks below the halo of blond hair. "You shouldn't be trying to move much just yet. How are you feeling?"

Justine settled back on the cot. "Much better, thank you, ma'am." He became aware of the scratchy stubble on his jaw and cheeks, that his uncombed hair splayed in all directions, and he blushed in total embarrassment. At least he was fully clothed, albeit rumpled and with one sleeve of an old tunic still dangling empty at his side.

"It is so nice to see you sitting up," she said. "You *are* looking better. Your color is returning. Are you in pain?"

"No, ma'am. Not much." It wasn't exactly a small lie. More like a big one. He lowered his gaze, aware of the warmth that flooded his cheeks. "I apologize for my appearance, Mrs. Hopkins—"

"Nonsense," she said brightly. "You've been bedridden with your wounds for several days. Besides, this is no formal inspection of the troops. I suppose I should have warned you, but I had the opportunity for an impromptu visit. And I simply *had* to check on my patient."

Justine lifted his gaze, saw the twinkle that had replaced the worry in her eyes. "Your patient?"

"Why, yes. I have a bit of training as a nurse. I often lend a hand at the hospital here. Many of the other ladies on the post do the same. Don't you recall my earlier visits?"

Justine swallowed. His mouth had gone dry. "Yes, I suppose I do. Vaguely. I thought . . . Well, I remember one time in particular. I thought . . ." He hesitated for a moment, then the words came in a rush. "I thought I had been visited by an angel with a golden halo." The heat grew in his cheeks. He instantly regretted the statement; a common soldier did not say such things to an officer's wife. Especially one who made it hard to breathe each time she came near.

Her laugh was musical, throaty, and genuine. "Why, thank you, sir." She curtsied slightly, creating small folds in her floor-length dress, a pale blue that seemed to deepen the color of her near-indigo eyes. "I'm most flattered. I've never been mistaken for an angel before."

"I'm sorry, ma'am. I shouldn't have said that."

Her lips pursed in a pretend pout. "Don't tell me you're going to take it back?"

"No, ma'am. It just . . . it wasn't a seemly thing to say. To a lady."

"But was it the truth?" At Justine's nod, her smile returned with a warmth and brilliance that further scrambled his brain. "Then I accept the compliment and reject the denial. Perhaps you *have* seen an angel—a true one. I have prayed to the Virgin Mary every day for your recovery. But are you truly doing well? Don't lie to your nurse, Corporal Justine." She reached out and placed a hand on his cheek; he instinctively flinched and drew back. A flicker of hurt danced in her eyes.

"I am much better, thank you, ma'am."

"Your fever seems to be gone." She lowered her voice to a near whisper. "Why do you recoil from my touch, Ned?"

"Ma'am, please don't be offended. It's just that . . .

well, it isn't proper. I mean, you're an officer's wife. . . ." His voice trailed away in embarrassment.

"If it makes you uncomfortable, I apologize, Ned. However, I will remind you that I have a first name. It's Elaine, in case you've forgotten."

"I haven't forgotten—Elaine," he said apologetically, still uneasy at using her first name. "And I truly appreciate your being here, for being concerned." He ran his left hand through his unruly hair, then over his scratchy chin. "It's I who should apologize. The last thing I wanted to do was inadvertently offend you."

"No offense taken. I just think you're overly sensitive about this officer's wife thing. After all, we *are* friends. You were very kind to me when I arrived here. And on other occasions."

The look in her eyes added to Justine's discomfort. It seemed to say, *We could be more than just friends.* Was it a hint? She was out of his reach, and always would be, he reminded himself.

She seemed to sense his unease and smiled in reassurance. She placed a small, delicate hand on his left forearm. This time he didn't wince or withdraw. The warmth of her touch flooded through him.

"I heard what you did in the McClellan Creek battle, Ned, and I'm so very proud of you," she said. "I must go soon. Is there anything I can do? Anything I can get for you?"

Justine found himself all but drowning in those dark blue eyes. "Yes, there is one thing," he said. "Would you mind seeing if one of the post barbers could come here? I can't shave with my left hand and I feel scruffy as a molting prairie dog. If I don't get rid of these whiskers soon, I'm going to lose what thin grasp I still have on sanity."

She chuckled softly. "Consider it done." She removed her hand. "Honestly, I'm so relieved that you are recovering well. All of us were terribly worried. When you're able to take short walks without much discomfort, I would be delighted to lend you an arm." A slight flush colored her pale cheeks. "With a proper escort, of course. An orderly, perhaps?"

Justine nodded. "I'd like that very much, ma'am—Elaine."

"Ah, Corporal Justine," a voice from behind Elaine said, "glad to see you're sitting up." Lieutenant Carter removed his hat and bowed slightly to Elaine. "Mrs. Hopkins. I hope I'm not interrupting?"

"Not at all, Mr. Carter," Elaine said. "I was just leaving after a quick check on the patient."

As he watched her leave, Justine wondered: Was he afraid of the fact that Elaine Hopkins was an officer's wife? Or was it more than that? That he was afraid of himself, what he might do to ruin three lives, if he let his guard down for an instant?

Carter toed a camp stool alongside Justine's cot. "I suspect you're tired of hearing this, Ned, but I've got to ask how you're feeling."

"A bit battered, but much better, sir," Justine said, beginning to relax. He realized with a bit of a start that he found talking to an officer was, compared to talking to Elaine Hopkins, a mild breeze instead of a whirlwind.

"Good. Glad to hear that. You will, of course, remain on the inactive roster until you've recovered sufficiently to assume minor duties." Carter glanced around, as if to make sure no one else remained in earshot. "I'd like to ask you a few questions about McClellan Creek, Ned."

"Yes, sir?"

"There have been questions raised about Lieutenant Hopkins's efficiency in that engagement. The colonel has asked me to quietly investigate those issues and report back to him. This is not a formal inquiry, so please feel free to give your honest answers, to the best of your knowledge. You knew Company I was assigned to the arroyo to cut off the Indians' escape route."

"Yes, sir. I was there when the colonel gave the order."

"And you know Company I didn't arrive until most of

the fighting had ended. Do you know why Hopkins's troopers didn't get to their assigned post on time?"

"No, sir. All I know is that they weren't there, and that the Indians held the arroyo."

"And that's when you led the squad up the canyon wall and directed fire to rout the Indians?"

"Yes, sir. Something had to be done." Justine sighed and shook his head. "I'm afraid that's about all I can tell you, Lieutenant. I blacked out soon after we reached the top."

Carter nodded. "You scouted the west side of the valley the day before the attack?"

"Yes, sir. Mr. Thompson scouted the other."

"And you delivered a remarkably detailed account of the terrain, as I recall. Do you remember crossing a deep wash a half mile before reaching the arroyo?"

Justine thought for a moment, then shook his head. "No, sir. Not a deep one. There was one place, a tributary streambed. But the sides weren't steep, sir. I crossed with no problem. At a trot, in fact."

"Lieutenant Hopkins's report to Colonel Mackenzie asserted that the company's way was blocked by a deep ravine. That he had to lead his men more than a mile around the ravine. That your scouting report was in error."

Justine fought back a surge of anger at the accusation. He held Carter's steady gaze. "Sir, it is not the place of an enlisted man to imply that an officer misled his commander. Perhaps there was another reason, but it wasn't any deep cut in the terrain. My report was accurate."

Carter nodded. "Your account tallies with what others, including some of Hopkins's own men, have said." He rose from the stool. "Thanks for your help, Justine."

As the officer turned for the door, Justine said, "Lieutenant Carter?"

"Yes?"

"Will I be expected to repeat what I told you before some official board, or the colonel himself?"

"No, not at all. As I said, this is not a formal inquiry.

The information is for the colonel's use only. Put your mind at ease about that."

Justine sighed in relief. "Thank you, sir. Sorry I couldn't offer more."

Carter smiled. "You offered plenty, Ned. Your actions in leading that squad up the canyon wall and into position saved the lives of a lot of good men. My company alone most likely would have taken heavy casualties if the Indians had kept control of that arroyo. For that, you have my personal thanks and respect. And that of Colonel Mackenzie." Carter snapped a salute, then turned and strode from the hospital.

Justine didn't have much time to wonder if Lieutenant Hopkins might be in serious trouble. One of the civilian post barbers strode in, a small bag in hand, looked around, and said to Justine:

"You must be that prairie dog I was told about."

The boy knelt as he had for the past hour, his gaze steady on the small mound of earth four strides away, a short throwing arrow gripped in his right hand.

Badger squatted beneath a nearby cottonwood tree, the sunlight turned even more golden as it filtered through the yellow leaves overhead, his breast warm with pride as he watched the child.

For one so young and so constantly in motion, the boy's patience on the hunt—his careful stalk of the earth mound, and now waiting without movement for such a long time, at least in a child's world—was but part of the warmth in Badger's heart.

On the hunt, at least, the boy seemed to have already outgrown the rather whimsical title bestowed upon him by the giver of names—Pihpitz, or Horsefly, who seemed to buzz constantly about the sprawling Comanche camp in the remote canyon. He will be a great hunter and warrior, Badger thought. But for the whiteness of his skin, which seemed never to darken but to turn red, and then peel away like the snake sheds its skin, he was Comanche.

Watching the boy brought back memories of Badger's own youth when he himself stalked the rabbit, the prairie dog, the small bird. It was a time of serious work, but also one of laughter and freedom and games. Badger had been fortunate. His father had been a gentle teacher, polite and wise. He vowed to do the same for Horsefly and the child who grew in Star's belly.

There was much to do in the short time between the turning of the leaves and the time of snows, but nothing so important to Badger as watching his son grow and learn. Badger realized with a touch of surprise that he no longer thought of Pihpitz as his "already-son." Only as his son—

The child's arm flicked out as a small, dark head peeked from the mound. The throwing arrow arched little as it sped just past the prairie dog's head. The small animal ducked back into its burrow as the arrow fluttered to the earth a few strides beyond the mound.

Horsefly leapt to his feet and hurried to retrieve his throwing arrow. It was the boy's most prized possession, made by his father's own hand. Soon, Badger mused, Horsefly would require better arrows than his father could make. Among Quanah's band were two skilled arrow makers. Their work was not cheap, but the straight, strong shafts and true flight was worth the extra price.

Badger remained seated as Horsefly strode toward him, his gait more that of an older boy than the awkward steps of one of so few summers.

"How goes the hunt, my son?" Badger asked, as if he did not know.

Small frown lines creased the sunburned skin of Horsefly's forehead. "Not well. I missed."

"But not by much. It was a good throw. Soon there will be no prairie dog safe from the arrows of Pihpitz. All will shiver in fear and dread at the very mention of his name."

The boy's face brightened at the calm reassurance; his

blue eyes seemed to sparkle in delight at the mental image of quaking prairie dogs as the nervous animals squeaked to warn each other of his approach.

Badger placed an arm around the youth's shoulders. "You do well, Horsefly. I could ask for no finer son. Let us return to our lodge now. Your mother will be pleased to hear of your hunt."

"Even though I bring no meat back to camp?" The Comanche words fell easily from the boy's tongue. He learned quickly. Once he was told the name of a thing, it need not be repeated.

"Not all hunts end in success. It is the way of things. Perhaps we shall have more luck tomorrow."

The boy's face brightened. "We?"

"I would be honored if you would accompany me on the hunt," Badger said solemnly, "if you have nothing else of importance planned. It is time you introduced your brown pony to the ways of the trail outside this canyon."

"Will Mother let me go?" The boy's voice quavered in barely suppressed excitement.

"We will ask. It is the only way to find out." Badger smiled and winked at his son. "I can teach you many things, Horsefly, but not the workings of a woman's mind. So we will ask. With dignity, of course. Not pleading. A hunter and warrior must not display such weakness before his woman, whether she be his mother or his wife. But it is a wise man who seeks the counsel of his woman in such matters."

Horsefly nodded solemnly. The two walked without speaking until they reached the edge of the sprawling village. Then the boy said, "Father, I have seen other men beat their wives. But you have never struck Mother."

"Not all men are as fortunate as you and I, to have such a fine wife and mother. Some who mistreat their women have a reason to do so. Star has never given me reason. A few men beat their wives without reason except that they are simply cruel husbands, or perhaps when they drink *poisabá,* white man's whiskey. Such men as those are looked upon with scorn by The People." Badger's toned softened. "There is another reason I treat your mother with respect and gentleness. You will understand that reason when you are older."

Horsefly nodded, satisfied with the answer. "I have much to learn."

Badger patted his son's shoulder. "We all do, son. It is said a wise man is one who never stops learning, even though his face wrinkles, his eyes fail, and his hair grays. It is why we respect and honor our elders. They have the wisdom of many summers. We learn much from them, if we but listen to their words. How it was that the buffalo and the horse came to The People. Why Coyote is known as the Trickster, why we follow certain rules. Many valuable things."

"Will you tell me of these things?"

"The elders tell them better and with more wisdom, Horsefly. Visit their lodges when you would hear such stories. Now, let us eat something and discuss our planned hunt with your mother."

It seemed to Badger that little Horsefly was long in going to sleep that night, caught up in the excitement of the coming hunt. Badger understood. He had felt such eagerness before his first real hunt at his own father's side.

Sleep did not come soon to Badger, either.

The sense of loss in the horse soldiers' attack had diminished somewhat, though his heart still ached from the death of his friends who had fallen in battle. The fight had cost him his own lodge, most of his and Star's personal belongings. But Yellowfish had saved his two most prized possessions—Star and the boy. Star in turn had saved his third most prized, his war shield. All else could be replaced.

The women of Quanah's band had made the lodge in which they now lived, within a few suns of their arrival. The robes they slept on also were given to them. The new lodge was smaller than the one Bad Hand had burned. When the baby came, they would need a larger home. But they would know no empty bellies, even if Badger's own hunts failed. The Comanche were a generous people, even more so than his own Kiowa had been.

Badger was no longer wealthy, but neither was he poor. His pony herd still numbered more than fifty, even after trading one good horse for a quiver of fine arrows, another as a gift for the giver of names, a few others for special comforts for his family, a rifle to replace the one lost in battle, and twenty of the stubby little shells for the weapon. When the grass greened, he and Yellowfish, who also had lost most of his wealth in the attack, would again ride to the raid. They would replace that which had been taken from them.

Star snuggled against his side beneath the buffalo robe, her slow, deep breaths soft on his shoulder. She had not yet begun to show the child she carried; her belly was only slightly rounded to his touch. Soon, he knew, he must begin looking for a second wife as Yellowfish had said. Star would need the extra pair of hands to help as the family grew.

Badger traced a finger softly beneath the curve of her cheek. Yes, he would need another wife. But he would not, could not, have the same feelings for a second wife.

There could be only one Star.

The breeze against Justine's cheek carried a sharp hint of the coming winter, but even though he wore no coat, he didn't feel the wind's chill. He did feel the sharp stab of pain from his hip joint at each step, felt the dull click as his foot swung forward.

The cold itself was no problem. The warmth of the slender form at his side heated him from bootsole to hatband. Elaine Hopkins cradled his upper arm in her hand, seemingly unaware that her breast brushed against Justine's arm every few steps and sent a tingle through his spine.

"Are you sure you're strong enough for such a long walk already, Ned?" Elaine asked. The breeze whipped a strand of gold hair across her cheek.

"We can head back anytime you say, Corporal," said the orderly whose arm around Justine's waist gave additional support.

Justine smiled at Elaine and nodded to the orderly. "I'm fine so far. I thought I was never going to get out of that stockade called a hospital. I was at the brink of total insanity before Dr. Patsky gave in." He wondered if he actually had gone insane; no enlisted man in his right mind would be walking around in broad daylight with an officer's wife rubbing her breast against his arm. Especially *this* officer's wife.

"When you start to get tired, just say so," the orderly named Preston said in the slow Carolina drawl that disguised the young man's quick mind. "But I reckon I know how you feel about getting out of there, even for just a short walk. Gotta keep you on a short rein, though, or the doc'll chew my—" Preston glanced at Elaine, his cheeks reddening. "He'll fuss at me something fierce."

"We can't let that happen, Mr. Preston," Elaine said, barely suppressing a giggle. "One sore backside is enough for this post." She promptly blushed at her own brashness. "Besides, I have to make sure my patient doesn't overdo it and wind up back on the operating table."

"No," Justine said with a wince, "we certainly don't want *that* to happen." The muscles of his buttock still pained him from the bullet wound, and the ache in his shoulder often turned sharp when he moved. The bullet hole and arrow slash itched almost constantly now. Patsky said that was a good sign. It meant he was healing nicely. And with the constricting bandage confined now to his chest and back, he had his right arm free. It had lost strength, but if he moved with care he could use it again. At least he would be able to write home instead of having Preston or someone else do it for him.

As they reached the midpoint of the parade ground,

Justine realized his strength was beginning to fade, his breathing becoming labored. The mind might be willing, but the body ignored its orders. Already his thigh muscles and knee joints trembled. "I don't really want to, but maybe we'd better start back now," he said.

Elaine caught the disappointment and reluctance in his tone and gave his upper arm a reassuring squeeze. The action pressed her soft breast against him. "This is enough for your first time out, Ned."

Justine glanced at the orderly, certain he would see a frown of disapproval at Elaine's casual use of his first name, the way she walked so close to his side. If Preston noticed the hint of intimacy, he kept it to himself. The orderly merely nodded his agreement. "Might be a good idea at that," Preston said. "It's almost mail call, anyway."

Elaine's hand lingered on Justine's forearm for a moment at the front door of the hospital ward. "Tomorrow, and each day afterward, we will do it again. Walk a bit farther each time, and before you know it you'll be strong as an ox again."

"I doubt that," Justine said with a wan smile. "I wasn't exactly blessed in the strength department."

"Nonsense again. A man's strength isn't measured in muscle. You, Corporal Justine, are living proof of that. We're all so very proud of you." Justine couldn't help but wonder at her references to being proud of him. How could anyone be proud of a soldier who'd gotten himself in the way of a bullet and arrow? "Now, if you'll excuse me, I'll take my leave. Until tomorrow."

She gave his arm a parting squeeze, another brush of breast. Justine watched her walk away, trim hips swaying, her strides fluid and confident. He knew he shouldn't stare. But he couldn't take his eyes from her.

"Nice lady," Preston said. "Too classy to be wasted on that man she's married to. Hopkins must have bought his commission." The orderly's tone turned bitter. "That man's yellow to the core, Ned. No guts. The colonel should have brought him up on charges after the McClellan Creek fight."

Justine glanced around, grateful that no one else was within earshot. He liked Preston. He didn't want to see the man face disciplinary action. An enlisted man who openly challenged an officer's courage was inviting a trip to the guardhouse.

"Frank, you'd better be careful with that kind of talk," Justine said.

The orderly spat in disdain. "Hell, every trooper on the post knows it. I've talked to a bunch of the I Company boys. Hopkins didn't just use that little gully as an excuse. When his company finally got close to the fight, Hopkins's horse all of a sudden came up lame. Sergeant Hawthorne led the men while Hopkins lollygagged behind until the fight was over. Never fired a shot."

"But Lieutenant Carter conducted an inquiry—"

"And Mackenzie ignored it. Formally, at least," Preston interrupted. "I hear he chewed Hopkins's butt out in private, but that's all that ever come of it. Nothing we can do about it except hope he doesn't get a whole company wiped out. He's sure as hell not going to get close enough to an Injun to do us all a favor and catch an arrow." The orderly sighed. The bitterness faded from his tone. "Come along, Corporal. Time to rest up."

An hour later, Justine sat on the edge of his cot, reading the latest letter from back home, written in his mother's fluid, looping hand. The news from Maine was about the same as her last letter, the tone as breezy as her penmanship, first expressing relief that he was recovering from his wounds, then that friends and family were fine, the fall harvest had gone well, and a brief discourse on the first major snowfall of the year.

Justine reread her closing paragraphs:

Your father sends his regards. He is so terribly proud of you, son. You know your father; he can't bring himself to come right out and say so, of course, but he must have read the nice letter from your Lt. Carter a dozen times. But, young man, if you were still nine years old, I would have to bend you over my knee. Shame on you for not telling us how badly you were hurt, that you almost died, or the brave thing you did at that battle with the enemy at the place called McClellan Creek.

I know you did not want us to worry, and that you have never been one to boast of your exploits, even as a child. But, dearest Ned, you must never again mislead us so. You must write the full truth in the future. As for myself and your sisters, we shall not rest comfortably until you are again safe at home. It must be terribly dangerous out there on the frontier, so promise me you will take no more unnecessary risks. The tradition of the Justine name includes coming home once your military service is completed.

I must admit such acts as you performed in the McClellan Creek battle came as a surprise to me personally; it seems so out of character for such a gentle soul. That said, I also add that I am very, very proud of you, my dearest son.

Your Loving Mother,
Mary Walker Justine.

Justine fought back a slight twinge of aggravation at Carter for having written his family such details of the battle. He had no wish—or right, as he saw it—to be seen as some sort of heroic uniformed figure on horseback, leading men into battle. But the damage was done. And why was everybody always saying they were so damned proud of him? He hadn't done anything special.

He folded the letter with care and stowed it in his footlocker along with the others.

Sorry, Mother, he thought, but I can't bring myself to tell you the truth. That I'm anything but a brave hero.

That I'm a frightened man who, most un-Justine-like, almost wets his pants every time he rides into battle. A soldier who yet may one day panic in the face of the enemy and bring disgrace to the hallowed Justine tradition. . . .

15

JUSTINE HUNCHED OVER the footlocker that served as his desk, the nub of his quill pen scratching intermittently on his latest letter to home.

The smell of bootblack, leather, gun grease, and sweat that he had once found rather offensive now seemed refreshing, even pleasant. He wasn't sure he could ever get the scent of the post hospital completely from his nostrils. A month in that place was a long time.

He had regained much of his strength. The hip joint still clicked when he walked, and the dull ache at times turned sharp. He still didn't have full range of movement in his shoulder. The reddish ridge of scar tissue remained tender, and lifting his right hand above his shoulder brought a stinging reminder that he was a few weeks away from full recuperation.

The only problem was the length of the days. The post surgeon refused to remove him from inactive duty. The enforced idleness wore on his nerves. He felt confident he could handle light details, but Patsky disagreed. Mackenzie might be commander of the Fourth Regiment, but the surgeon was the boss where a trooper's illness or injury were concerned.

What made the hours so long was that he no longer walked with Elaine Hopkins, but alone, with his limp and the cane Preston had purloined from somewhere. That Justine had been the one to suggest an end to the daily ritual didn't heal the empty spot he had come to identify as loneliness. But it had been necessary. There had been too many suspicious looks cast in their direction during the outings with Elaine.

He turned his attention back to the paper and the pen poised above it. The words to his mother did not come easily; there was no real news to report. Once he had assured her he was well on the road to recovery, expressed his hope that all was well back home, and given the obligatory weather report, there seemed nothing more to say.

He couldn't tell her he had fallen in love with a married woman. An officer's wife. And a devout Catholic, forbidden by Church doctrine from ever leaving her marriage.

This time, the weather had furnished two whole paragraphs. The seasons seemed to have become confused. A Christmas norther, bitterly cold but dry, had passed, as had the New Year's Day ice storm. The first week of February seemed more like spring, sunny and unseasonably warm. Several of the Texas frontier veterans assured him winter would be back, that what they called the "February thaw" would soon end with a vengeance.

In Maine, there was no February thaw, at least not that Justine could remember. In his mind's eye, he gazed from his second-floor room at home over waist-deep snow that shortened the height of towering maples and weighted down the boughs of evergreens. At night, thick tree limbs cracked like rifle shots, splintered by sub-zero cold. To venture outdoors meant donning layer after layer of clothes and strapping on the latticework of snowshoes.

He shook away the vision. North Texas offered no resemblance to home.

At least the frontier was quiet now. Indians did not raid in the dead of winter, when food was scarce and their ponies thin and weak from lack of graze. Justine knew that would change with the coming of spring. The army held some leverage over the Comanches now, thanks to Mackenzie's defeat of Mow-way's band last fall and the subsequent capture of more than a hundred of their people. The Comanches were forced to behave, to negotiate for the exchange of their own.

The Kiowas were under no such restraints. Even the "goodwill" commutation of death sentences for Big Tree and Satanta, to life in prison instead of hanging, did little to mollify the Kiowas. When spring came they would ride the war trail with a fury honed over a winter of forced idleness and nursed anger.

Justine dreaded the coming of green grass. All hell could break loose on the frontier then—

"Corporal Justine."

Justine glanced up from the paper, brows raised toward Lieutenant Carter, and stiffly rose. "Yes, sir?"

"Best bib and tucker, Ned. General assembly, formal, two hours, all troops on the parade ground. Full-dress uniform, sabers, polished buttons, the whole bit. You can bring the cane, though."

Justine blinked in surprise. Mackenzie might penalize a man for slovenly dress on post, but the colonel put little stock in spit-and-polish inspections. Justine could remember only two since his posting with the Fourth. Those had been cursory at best.

"If you need help getting into dress uniform, I'll have someone lend a hand," Carter said.

"I can handle it, sir."

"Very well. Considering that your shoulder hasn't mended yet, don't try to snap off any flashy salutes. Colonel's orders." Carter turned to leave.

"Sir, may I ask why general assembly now? Are we having a change of command?"

Carter's eyes seemed to twinkle. "No change of command. Mackenzie's still the boss. You'll have the answer to your question in a couple of hours."

Precisely two hours later, Justine stood at attention in the second rank as the final bugle notes faded in the mild, windless air. He had never seen so much gold braid, glistening brass, and polished silver in his brief army career. The parade ground seemed a sea of crisp, freshly pressed blue uniforms. New flags and company guidons hung from staffs in the hands of the color guard.

Behind the low makeshift reviewing stand and dressed in their finest gowns, the wives of officers, noncoms, and enlisted men waited patiently, chatting. Justine had to struggle to keep his gaze straight ahead, to avoid eye contact with Elaine Hopkins, who sat smiling a few chairs from the reviewing stand.

Mackenzie stepped onto the stand to face the assembled troops. He did not speak until the regimental sergeant major turned to him and barked, "All troops not standing duty apost or afield present and accounted for, sir!"

"Very well. Carry on, Sergeant Major."

The highest ranking noncom of the Fourth Regiment did a crisp about-face to address the assembled troops. "The following officers and enlisted men will step forward, front and center, when their names are called!"

The booming baritone of the career army veteran carried well in the quiet air as he called out the names and ranks of two enlisted men and one officer.

"Nathaniel Edward Justine, Corporal!"

Justine started at the sound of his name. What in heaven was going on? he wondered. Confused and nervous, his heart hammering against his ribs, he limped forward and joined the other three waiting men facing the reviewing stand. He began to sweat, but his fingers chilled as if he were about to go into battle. A quick surge of fear flicked across his brain—some sort of disciplinary action? He offered up a silent prayer. The guardhouse, or worse—court-martial or dishonorable discharge—would devastate his family. If he were brought up on charges for consorting with an officer's wife, it would bring censure down upon on Elaine Hopkins's head. It was a thought painful beyond belief.

"Olaf Svenson, Trooper!" the sergeant major bellowed.

The call added to Justine's confusion. Svenson couldn't answer. His remains lay in a shallow grave two miles from the valley in McClellan Creek.

"Here, Sergeant Major!"

The response came from Captain Wirt Davis.

The roll call continued until eight men stood at attention before Mackenzie. An empty space between the last two men would have been Svenson's spot.

The sergeant major about-faced to Mackenzie and snapped a crisp salute. "All present and accounted for, sir!"

"Thank you, Sergeant Major." Mackenzie's voice was no match for the senior noncom's in volume, but his words carried well in the unnerving silence. The colonel gazed over the assembled regiment for a moment, then cleared his throat.

"Gentlemen of the Fourth Cavalry Regiment, we are gathered here today for a special occasion. I speak to you as a representative not only of the Cavalry branch of the United States Army, but also on behalf of the Congress and the President of this great nation." He held out a hand. "Lieutenant Carter, if you please." Carter handed the colonel a small wooden box.

Mackenzie stepped from the makeshift platform, Carter at his side, and stood before the men called from the ranks. His gaze rested for several heartbeats on each face. Justine swallowed nervously as the colonel's attention seemed to linger on him.

"Corporal Justine, step forward," Mackenzie said.

Justine blinked in surprise, quickly regained a measure of composure, and took two shaky strides forward. Sweat beaded on his brow. His heart beat even faster.

"It is my personal honor, on behalf of a grateful nation, to at this time express our deep appreciation for your actions at McClellan Creek, Corporal Justine." Mackenzie unfolded a slip of paper from the small wooden box in his hand.

"This citation reads as follows: 'For valor above and beyond the call of duty, and despite being twice wounded by enemy fire, on September twenty-ninth, eighteen hundred and sixty-two, in the Battle of McClellan Creek, Trooper Nathaniel Edward Justine at great personal peril rallied a small squad of men who turned the tide of battle, saving the lives of many of his comrades in arms.' "

Mackenzie paused to lift a beribboned bit of metal from the wooden box.

"In recognition of your valor in the service of your country, Corporal Justine, it gives me great pleasure to present to you at this time, before your assembled fellow soldiers of the Fourth Regiment, the Congressional Medal of Honor."

Justine's heart all but stopped. For an instant he stood immobilized in disbelief. This couldn't be happening. Not to him—

"Lower your head a bit, son," Mackenzie said quietly. A moment later Justine felt the soft ribbon around his neck, the slight weight of the metal emblem against his chest. "Thank you, Corporal. Don't try to salute back, son. You must take care of that shoulder." The colonel stepped back, snapped a crisp salute, then offered a hand. His grip was firm despite the missing fingers. Mackenzie called the next man forward.

Justine barely heard the rest of the ceremony, similar in tone though varied in the accounts of the action of each man during the battle in the valley. Individual words rattled against the whir and clatter of disbelief and confusion in Justine's brain, the sensation that he had once again stepped outside his own body and now watched through the eyes of a stranger as the presentations unfolded. For a tense moment he feared he would be physically ill. The brief touch of nervous nausea passed.

When Captain Davis accepted the posthumously awarded medal on Olaf Svenson's behalf, Mackenzie said, "About-face, gentlemen, and accept the salutes of your comrades in arms. Honors squad, prepare to fire!"

Seven Spencer carbines barked into the sky, three times each. A twenty-one-gun salute, the ultimate honor. Justine's vision blurred as he stared at the wash of faces before him, each man at attention, the entire regiment saluting eight men and one vacant spot in the short line.

It all seemed unreal; this couldn't be happening, he thought. A dream. He'd wake up and—

"At ease, gentlemen." Mackenzie waited until the rustle of cloth subsided, then said, "The ladies of the post have prepared a reception in the mess hall for those honored here today. All who wish to attend are invited, regardless of rank. Sergeant Major, you may dismiss the regiment."

Well after retreat had sounded that night, Justine lay on his bunk, staring at the darkened ceiling, the medal and citation stored in its small wooden box in his footlocker. He couldn't shake the feeling of shocked detachment. He still stood outside his own body.

His hand ached. It seemed he had shaken the hand of every man on the post, from Mackenzie to the lowest green recruit. Except for Lieutenant Hopkins. His only recollection of Hopkins's even being at the reception was the disdainful way the lieutenant glared at Justine. For a moment, the hard stare sent a chill through Justine. If the lieutenant suspected, or had heard rumors—but then, Hopkins looked at every enlisted man as if he were watching a tumblebug roll a ball of dung across his dinner plate.

The only thing Justine fully remembered was Elaine Hopkins's soft hand on his forearm, her muttered "Ned, I'm so very, very proud of you."

Justine had no idea why he suddenly was a hero. In his own mind he had done nothing to deserve the nation's highest military honor. Any man would have done the same under the circumstances. He knew he should be thrilled and proud. He wasn't.

None of it made sense.

Why should any man be given a medal for shooting other men? Where was the logic of that? There was no glory in blood and human suffering and death.

He would gladly trade the medal in his footlocker for freedom from the recurring nightmares—an Indian face exploding in red mist at the muzzle of his revolver, an old man bashing an infant's brains out.

Justine knew he would live with the dreams forever.

➤ ➤ ➤

The night vision would not retreat even after Badger opened his eyes; his heart still thumped in excitement against his ribs.

A true vision, or simply a recurring dream?

Badger did not know. He had sought no medicine vision. The images came to him at night, in his lodge, not as he sat fasting atop the rim of the canyon. Still, he wondered, would a mere dream repeat itself so often? Could it in fact be a true vision?

The scenes still played across his mind, as vivid as if unfolding before his eyes in the darkness of his lodge. Row upon row of blue-clad horse soldiers falling before his bullets and arrows until none remained. And always, the last to fall was the young warrior who had shot him in Mow-way's village.

On some nights, the falling figures were not horse soldiers, but the long-haired white men with big guns who destroyed the buffalo; and when they all had fallen, a great hole opened in the earth and the buffalo poured fourth in numbers too many to count.

And always, after either night battle fought beneath blankets and robes, Badger awakened with heart pounding, almost with a victory cry on his lips. Should he seek the counsel of wiser men and women, the dream readers, to search for an answer? Or keep the night battles to himself, in case they should actually be true spirit medicine and not simply dreams sprouted from the seed planted by Yellowfish's visions?

He did not know.

He lay awake for a long time, listening to the wind rustle the new leaves on the chinaberry and cottonwood trees outside his lodge, the sleepy call of Owl, who hunted on silent wings, and the yelps and wails of Coyote.

Though the time of greening grass had come, the earth nourished by warm sun and plentiful rains, Badger was now reluctant to leave his lodge on the hunt. He had chosen not to ride with Quanah on the raid into Mexico, as had Yellowfish and many others of Quanah's band.

Star's belly was swollen, her breasts stretched full and tight until he dared not touch them and cause her pain. Her time was near. Badger could not be at her side as the child was born. That was not permitted. But he could remain here, only a short walk from the special lodge the village women had built for her, where the baby would first see its mother's eyes and wail its first cry.

At his side, Star grunted in sudden discomfort through her soft snores. Badger smiled. The child was a hard kicker. He had felt it himself, the sharp jab against his hand on her belly, its skin now tight as the head of the ceremonial drums.

The first rays of the new sun showed through the flap of the lodge when Star suddenly gasped aloud. Her hands went to her belly.

"Mother, what is it?" Horsefly muttered sleepily from his own robes.

"Your brother, Pihpitz," Star said. She lifted her gaze to Badger. "It is time"—she gasped again—"that I go to the lodge beside the water."

Badger's heart pounded harder than it had in his dream vision. He helped Star to her feet and escorted her to the entrance of the temporary lodge made of brush. He could not enter. The only male permitted inside would be a maker of medicine with special powers, and only then if the birth were long and difficult. Badger silently prayed to the spirits that no medicine man would be needed for this child.

He would not see her again until after the baby came and she had regained her strength, then bathed in the purifying running waters of the stream. He went to summon the women who would serve as Star's midwives, then to tell Holds-His-Horses that his daughter had entered the brush lodge. The grandfather was not allowed to enter the lodge, but when the child was born Holds-His-Horses would stand in front of the temporary shelter to learn the sex of his grandchild.

There was nothing for Badger to do now but wait and worry for Star. At least he had Horsefly to keep him company. He could see the concern in the boy's eyes, knew it was reflected in his own.

"Will Mother be all right?" the boy asked.

"That is up to the spirits to decide, Pihpitz."

Throughout the day and night, the wails and chants of the women attending Star mingled with the scent of sage burning in the birth lodge. Badger did not sleep that night.

Why, he wondered, had the Great Spirit not made an easier way to bring a child into the world? Would there not have been a way to make such a thing less painful to the woman, and less dangerous? He quickly banished the question from his mind. One did not question the leader of all spirit beings in such matters.

It was the way of things.

Badger rose, picked up his ceremonial pipe, and strode into the clear night air beneath its blanket of stars. He filled the bowl and lit the tobacco with a twig brought from the lodge fire. He held the pipe to the four winds, then to Mother Earth and Father Sky, and prayed to the spirits for Star's safety and the health of the child soon to come.

As the sun rose on the following day, Holds-His-Horses strode to the brush lodge after a baby's wail sounded in the clear air. He spoke briefly with the aged woman who served as Star's primary midwife. Badger, honing a knife edge already keen enough to split a single hair, could only wait as the new grandfather slowly ambled toward Badger's lodge.

For a long time, Holds-His-Horses stood in silence, the frown lines deep in his forehead, shoulders slumped. He was either teasing Badger, or he was the true bearer of bad news. Badger had to test the limits of his own patience, to try to still the rapid thump of his heart, and ask no questions; the new grandfather would speak when he wished.

Finally, the frown lines faded from the older man's face. His shoulders lifted. A smile spread. Pride glinted in his eyes. Holds-His-Horses said, "It is your close friend."

Badger's heart leapt in joy. A son. "And Star?"

"She is well. For a first child, the birth was an easy one, the old woman says." Holds-His-Horses casually rumpled Horsefly's red hair. "You have a brother, Pih-pitz."

Horsefly's young chest swelled with pride, but the expression on his freckled face did not change. He nodded solemnly. "That is good. I will teach him to become a great hunter, horse thief, and warrior."

Badger placed a hand on his first son's shoulder. "Yes, Horsefly. It shall be so. And when your mother returns and we have met our new friend, you and I must ride to the hunt. Our lodge will be in need of fine, soft new skins, and I know of a place but two suns' ride from here where an elk's tribe lives."

Excitement danced in Horsefly's blue eyes. "Who will go with us, Father?"

"Only you and I. Two of The People's finest hunters will be more than a match for the elk whose band awaits us."

Horsefly's face broke into a wide smile. "It is so. I will go now and see to our ponies."

Badger nodded. "Beware of *pasinugia,* the snake. It is the time of seasons when he first slithers from his winter bed. He will be angry that his sleep has ended."

"Yes, Father. I will be watchful." The boy scurried away, running toward the horse herd held downstream from the village.

The boy grows quickly, Badger thought, his heart threatening to burst with pride. He grows tall and strong, in spirit and mind as well as body. Badger could not ask for a finer companion and friend.

And now, he had a second friend.

Badger sighed in contentment.

It was a good time to be a proud father. It was a good time to be young.

That night, Badger again smoked to the spirits, offering his gratitude for the great gifts bestowed upon him.

He did not dream.

Two suns later, Star returned to the lodge, her hair still damp from her bath in the cool waters of the creek, bearing a small bundle wrapped in rabbit fur. She seemed a bit weak from her ordeal, but strong in spirit. He read her joy in the twinkle of her eyes.

"Horsefly," Badger called from the flap of the lodge, "it is time for you to meet your brother."

The boy arrived moments later, breathless from the run from the arrow-and-hoop game, his eyes wide and eager.

Badger gently lifted the fold of soft fur that covered the baby's face. He could have sworn the tiny mouth smiled at him.

"He is a perfect son, Star." Badger heard the warmth and pride in his words.

Star flashed a dazzling smile. "Yes, he is. But then, he has a perfect father."

"And a perfect mother."

"He is very small," Horsefly said in awe.

"You were once very small, Horsefly. He will grow into a strong young man, just as you have. You two will have plenty of time to get acquainted. Return to your contest now, before someone beats you."

"No one beats me in the arrow game, Father," Horsefly said. The red-haired boy paused at the lodge flap, brows raised. "What shall we call our new friend?"

"We shall give this careful thought, you and I," Badger said solemnly. "With our combined wisdom, he will have a fine name until he is old enough for the formal naming by a wise medicine man, as were you."

Horsefly nodded and left. Seconds later, the baby whimpered, then cut loose a lusty wail.

"Your son is always hungry," Star said as she slipped her loose-fitting deerskin dress down past a shoulder. She nuzzled the baby's face against a swollen breast. The baby's lips quickly closed on her nipple.

Badger placed a gentle arm about his wife's shoulders as the baby nursed. "Now I must begin to seriously search for a second wife. It would not be fair to you, so much work for only one pair of hands."

She smiled at Badger. "Thank you, husband. I had planned to mention that very thing soon. But as usual, your thoughts read mine."

"I only regret that you have no unmarried sister."

"Yes, that would be best." After a time, Star shifted the baby to the other breast; the child's brief wail of protest ended when he again found a nipple. She turned her gaze back to Badger. "It is not my place to choose for you, husband, but Turns-Over-Turtles has been much like a sister to me. Her husband died in the fight with the horse soldiers in Mow-way's village. He had no brother."

Badger thought for a moment, then nodded. "It is true. She will need someone to provide for her."

Star said, "Her mourning time will end soon. She is but three summers older than I. She has beauty and is a hard worker."

Badger pondered the suggestion. Turns-Over-Turtles was attractive and of sunny disposition when not in mourning. She had earned her name from her habit of righting any overturned turtle or terrapin unfortunate enough to have somehow wound up on its back, helpless. He saw no reason why she would not be a fine second wife. She and Star would get along with each other. His lodge would be filled with laughter.

He nodded. "What you say is true, Star. When her grieving time has ended, I will call on her." He placed his fingertips on the back of her bared shoulder. "But I shall have only one favorite wife, Star. As long as the heart beats in my breast."

16

"LEFT WHEEL, AT the gallop!"

Justine watched with mixed amusement and understanding as the squad of recruits turned a reasonably straight line into a ragged tangle.

A horse in the center of the line squealed, ducked its head, and started pitching. The rider stayed in the saddle for two jumps, then went high in the air, made a half-somersault, and landed hard on his butt.

These boys had a lot to learn, Justine mused.

So had he, when he first reported for duty with the Fourth. He wasn't sure he had learned all that much, but at least he could now execute the basic parade ground drills. Not that they meant that much when it came to fighting Indians. No formal maneuver-countermaneuver applied to their armies. Indians had their own rules of battle.

He trotted his sorrel over to the downed trooper, who quickly stood, face flushed in embarrassment, as he dusted off the seat of his newly issued field uniform.

"Are you all right, Merriweather?" Justine asked.

"Yes, sir. I wasn't expecting—he caught me off guard."

"Don't call me 'sir,' trooper. Save that for officers. I'm just a corporal." Justine shouted instructions to two other recruits to bring back the still-pitching horse.

"Sorry, s—Corporal," Merriweather said. "I've never been on a horse before. As if you couldn't tell."

"No need to apologize, trooper. We all get bucked off. I've tasted dirt more than a few times myself. Believe me, it's worse if you land in a pile of rocks or a cactus patch. It's just a matter of getting back on and trying it again. Don't let the horse know you're scared of him. They can sense it. Just makes them harder to handle."

Justine waited until the troopers led the snorting horse back and Merriweather cautiously remounted. "Form up, men. Let's do it again until we get it right." He kept his tone civil. He remembered from his own experience that yelling at green recruits didn't teach them a thing except the fear of making a mistake.

"Merriweather, take the pivot this time. That horse is only half-broke to saddle. Keep the reins snug. Don't let him get his head down. He can't buck if his head's up."

He rode off to the side and gave the left wheel order again. The execution was still ragged, but a bit better; at least they didn't wind up scattered all over the drill field. He didn't expect much. These boys would serve as mounted infantry, not cavalry. If they went into battle, they would dismount and fight on foot.

Justine didn't understand why mounted infantry had to know horseback battle maneuvers. Their primary role was in escort or supply train duty. When they were called upon to fight, their mounts were simply a mode of transportation to the battle site. In the swirl of clashes with mounted Indians, trained cavalrymen might have a chance up against Comanches and Kiowas, the finest horsemen the world had ever seen. But, for the near future, mounted infantry seemed the only option available to protect the frontier. There were few experienced horse soldiers available now.

Mackenzie had led most of the Fourth south for the campaign against the Apaches and the Mexican livestock thieves along the Rio Grande. The only seasoned men available to protect the northwest frontier around Jacksboro at the moment were two companies of cavalry, three of infantry or mounted infantry, and two artillery batteries. The cannons were all but useless in the field. The artillery's job was to protect the fort itself.

Justine put his squad through the drill a third, then a fourth, time. Such training duty should have belonged to a more experienced noncom. Mackenzie had taken all but a handful of such men with him, so Justine drew the assignment.

The best thing about training detail was that it allowed him to be on horseback again. The hip and shoulder wounds still pained him from time to time, but seemed to hurt less with each passing day. The scars were all but healed now, reduced to red, angry whelps. In a couple more weeks he would be up to patrol fitness.

The bad part about it was that I Company was one of those left at the post. Which meant Hopkins was now his immediate senior officer. God help us, Justine thought, if we have to actually fight Indians with that man in command.

Hopkins seemed to be ignoring the fact that the Kiowas again raided frequently, and viciously, along the frontier, from the reservation to the north all the way to the Concho River country to the south. And when the few experienced trackers Mackenzie left behind did find fresh Indian sign, Hopkins seemed to go to great lengths to avoid finding the raiders.

Justine still didn't like the way the lieutenant looked at him. He wasn't sure if the officer's disdain was for him personally because of his proximity to Elaine Hopkins during his convalescence, or if it simply extended toward all enlisted men. Justine had gone to considerable length to avoid Elaine since his hospital stay. He didn't trust himself to control the impulses that surged through him when she was near. But in a relatively small garrison, it was impossible not to run into her from time to time, when she was on her way to Mass or the hospital. He did wish she could break her habit of touching his hand or arm on those chance meetings. The glances that brought made him uncomfortable.

He shook the thoughts away.

"Form up! By the fours!" he called. The recruits of Gray Squad had had enough for one day.

He sat aboard the sorrel for a moment facing the young men, aware of—and somehow resenting—the look of awe on their faces, as if a piece of ribbon and a small chunk of metal made him into some kind of god. He never wore it, but they knew.

"You're doing better, men," he told the group. "We'll call it a day. Dismissed. Tend to your mounts, then clean up for mess and mail call. I urge those of you who haven't written home lately to do so this evening. If any of you need pen and paper, let me know. The mail coach goes out tomorrow afternoon."

He reined his horse back toward the post.

Merriweather drew alongside him. The sandy-haired trooper with the boyish moon face said, "Corporal, can I ask you something?"

"Sure."

"What's it like? Fighting Indians, I mean?"

Justine frowned. "I may not be the right one to ask. I'm not exactly an old veteran." He sighed. "It's like any battle, I suppose. Dirty, bloody, dangerous, frightening, and confusing. Facing a man and knowing you have to kill him or be killed yourself, or get some of your friends killed, is the worst feeling a man can have. But that's only the way I see it. Others view it differently."

Merriweather fell silent for a moment, then said, "Corporal, I think I can trust you to keep this just between us. A lot of these men are actually eager to fight. But me—well, I'm not sure I can—that I have the courage. I worry that I'll panic. Freeze up, or even break and run."

"I felt the same way when I first came out here, trooper," Justine said. "I still do. I almost wet my pants every time."

"Even when you won the Medal of Honor?"

"Especially then. I still don't think I deserved it. Just try to remember you have to overcome the fear and do your duty. Otherwise, you'll put the lives of your fellow soldiers at risk."

"I've never killed a man. Or even been in a fistfight. At least since my schoolboy days."

"Neither had I, Merriweather," Justine said. "Don't worry about it. If the time does come, you'll do fine. And you have my word, this conversation will remain confidential."

Merriweather touched the brim of his field cap, not a salute so much as a gesture of appreciation. "Thanks, Corporal. I feel better just having just talked on it."

"Any time, trooper—" Justine abruptly reined in a hundred yards from the fort. Anger and disgust flooded his cheeks as a familiar figure trotted toward them astride a sweaty gray. "Go ahead, Merriweather," he said through clenched teeth. "I'll be along shortly."

Elijah Thompson stopped the gray nose-to-tail with Justine's sorrel. "Good to see you up and about, Ned," Thompson said. "Hear you turned out to be one hell of a hero." He held out a weathered hand. "Gonna be mighty fine to ride with you again."

Justine ignored the hand.

"What do you want, you son of a bitch?" Justine's words were cold and tight; his right hand involuntarily clenched into a fist.

Thompson's gaze turned as cold as Justine's. His offered hand slowly dropped. "What's eatin' you, Justine?"

"You, Thompson. 'We' won't be riding again. I don't ride with baby killers and woman shooters."

"What the hell you talkin' about?"

"I'm talking about how you shot that girl in the back at McClellan Creek, that's what." Justine's words quavered in rage and the effort it took to keep from yelling them out. "About how you picked her baby up and bashed its brains out."

Thompson didn't reply for a moment, as he reached into a pocket for a twist of tobacco and bit off a chew, but his eyes narrowed and a blood vessel in his forehead bulged. "That all?"

"It's enough."

"You still got a lot to learn, Justine."

"Not from you I don't."

"Don't count on it, you little holier-than-thou whelp," Thompson growled. "As far as that papoose goes, you know what the Comanches' favorite game is? Tossin' a white sucklin' infant up in the air and catchin' it on a spear point. Or maybe tyin' a rope to one foot and draggin' it through rocks and cactus 'til there's nothin' left but little pieces."

Justine shook his head. "I don't believe you."

"You damn sure would if you ever spent half a day pickin' up pieces of a white baby scattered all over hell and gone. Ever hear the ol' Ranger sayin' 'Nits grow into lice'? That nit I bashed ain't never goin' to grow up to drag no white baby to death, laughin' and cacklin' while the child tears into little chunks. And the woman? Take out the breedin' stock and the damn Injuns can't grow no replacement herd, can they?"

Justine shuddered inwardly, partly in rage, partly in revulsion. "That doesn't make it right." He snorted. "*You* call *them* uncivilized savages? You're no better than they are."

The old scout grimaced in disgust. "Never figgered you to turn into no damn Injun-lover, Justine. Reckon they done give that high-powered medal to the wrong man."

"I reckon they did, Thompson. I never asked for the damn thing. And I didn't kill any women and babies."

"That a fact? You willin' to bet your soul you didn't maybe shoot a squaw in all that dust and confusion? Maybe run down and trample a kid yourself?"

Justine hesitated. No, he had to admit, he couldn't be sure. "If I did, it wasn't a deliberate, cold-blooded act. Dammit, Thompson, Indians are people, too."

Thompson rolled his chew into the other cheek and spat. "You don't know 'em, Justine. I do. Now, before you aggravate me into gettin' down off this hoss and whuppin' your butt—which I could damn well do despite spottin' you a passel of years—you answer a few questions for me."

Justine gritted his teeth to hold his anger in check and resist the challenge, but he didn't speak. Finally, he nodded grudgingly.

"Good. I didn't want to bust you up anyway, on account of I need you, Injun-lover or not. Now, listen careful. After you hear me out, if you still got that burr up your butt we'll settle it any way you want."

The old scout shifted his weight in the saddle and pinned that hard gaze back on Justine. "I know you seen what them savages do to white men. You was at Salt Creek. But you ever ride up to what was left of white women and girls been raped by thirty or forty of them savages, then split from crotch to gullet with a knife when they was done with 'em? With both tits cut off while they was still alive? White woman's tits make big medicine pouches for a redskin. Sometimes the younger ones lift the pelt between their legs for a different sort of scalp. Maybe you ain't seen it, Justine, but I damn sure have. What was left of it. The woman was my wife. The girl was my oldest daughter. She'd just turned thirteen."

Justine's rage faded. He didn't want to believe Thompson. But he had to. The pain that showed through that icy stare told Justine the old man was telling the truth.

"It took me half a day to find enough of my baby girl to bury after them bastards dragged her to pieces," Thompson said. "Never did find one arm. Or one foot."

Justine lowered his gaze. "I . . . I didn't know. I'm sorry."

"Well, now you do know. This here's a rough game we're playin', Justine. There ain't no rules. Not a damn one except do our job out here. Find and kill Injuns. We don't do that job, the butcherin' goes on another fifty, hundred years. Now, you with me, or not?"

Justine swallowed against the tightness in his throat.

"I'm with you, Mr. Thompson. If Lieutenant Hopkins agrees."

"Don't matter whether Hopkins does or don't. Bad Hand left the papers before he pulled out for the Rio. Told him I wanted you and Al Duggan, and he could keep his damned Tonk scouts. Said that'd be fine with him." Thompson spat again. "You up to forkin' a hoss? For long stretches, not this pissant drill ground stuff. Serious ridin'."

Justine had no choice. Not if Mackenzie had signed the orders. "If the post surgeon doesn't say otherwise, I can be ready in an hour."

"Don't have to be that soon. Me and this hoss are a tad tuckered out, and Duggan's still payin' the price for his regular payday bout with Old Headacher. We'll hang around a few days before we move out." He held out his hand again. "Still partners?"

This time, Justine took the hand. "You're right, Mr. Thompson. I've still got a lot to learn. Still partners."

"Then drop the 'Mr. Thompson' horse apples, Ned. My name's Lige, in case you forgot. Let's head for the barn. Be mess call soon. Army grub's a sight better'n what I've had of late."

Badger chewed on a strip of beef broiled over the fireplace of the white man's house and ignored the chill gust of air through the doorway. He made no effort to move the mutilated body of the settler so he could close the door and shut out the swirling wind and its flecks of stinging sleet and snowflakes.

It had been a good raid, despite the difficulties of organization. The first problem had been finding ponies—even from among his own herd—strong enough to mount the eleven warriors chosen to come with him from the winter camp in the Place of the Chinaberry Trees, many days' ride from this place.

Raiding in the time of snows was difficult at best.

The ponies were gaunt and weak from lack of grass. For the past moon the horses had subsisted on bits of cottonwood bark peeled from the stands of trees along the creeks that fed into the canyon. In such times as these, men naturally were reluctant to leave the comfort of warm lodges and warmer wives.

This time, he had no problem finding followers. Only in mounting them.

Through the gray mist of sleet and snow flurries beyond the open doorway, he saw the hazy shapes of the sacred Medicine Mounds looming south of the Red River. When a wanderer brought word the two white families had settled almost within rifle shot of the sacred hills, Badger had many warriors eager to smoke the war pipe. He could mount but eleven and himself. On such a mission, Badger would field only a war party consisting of multiples of four, the sacred number.

His medicine had been good.

So, he had to admit with some reluctance, was the taste of the white men's beef. It would never replace the buffalo, or even the meat of the mule. But it had been waiting for them, dripping fat into the fireplace coals, when they entered the house. After an extended diet of dried buffalo and pemmican, any fresh meat was welcome.

He squatted for another moment, finishing the strip carved from the slab, and listened to the cries of the other members of the party. He would summon them to share the beef when the excitement of the victory ebbed.

They had struck at first light, when the white men remained groggy from sleep and their bladders full. The whites had gone down quickly, unprepared, not expecting an attack during the time of snows. Three men, a boy of perhaps twelve summers, two women, and an infant lay dead.

Badger regretted the death of the baby, now having one of his own. But there had been no other choice. There was no way to feed the infant on the long ride back to the camp, and no woman there making enough milk to nurse the child. Falls-Down-Hills bashed the baby's head against the corner of the house. That the infant was a girl child helped ease Badger's regret at seeing it killed.

Badger's party suffered but one death, though it was one that cut into his heart. A settler's rifle ball had passed through the calf of Yellowfish's left leg and killed Yellowfish's prized paint war pony, Tuaahtaqui.

Yellowfish now knelt a few yards outside the front door, beside the body of the paint pony, rocking back and forth in grief. The loss of a beloved horse tore at a man's heart as deeply as the death of a close friend.

Badger couldn't make up the loss, but he could provide Yellowfish and the others strong new horses from the white settlers' herd. The animals were big, well cared for, grain-fed, in good condition despite the harshness of the season.

Badger wiped his hands on his leggings, stepped into the wind-whipped sleet, and strode to Yellowfish's side. The cloth hurriedly tied around Yellowfish's lower leg was bright with fresh blood. Badger slipped an arm around his brother's shoulders. "Go inside now," he said softly. "Eat while I tend to your wound. I grieve with you for your Cricket."

"He was a good friend," Yellowfish said. "I will never again have such a fine horse."

Badger helped Yellowfish into the warmth of the white man's house and tightened the bandage around Yellowfish's leg as his brother ate. Satisfied the bleeding had stopped, Badger went outside to the others.

Falls-Down-Hills finished lashing the final sack onto one of the six mules in the white man's corral. The dried corn would help ease the bellies of their own horses back in the village, as well as feed their own cooking pots. The white man's guns, blankets, iron pots, bolts of cloth, and other goods taken in the raid would be welcome in many Quahadi lodges.

"We burn the white man's lodge now?" Falls-Down-Hills asked.

Badger shook his head. "The smoke might draw the attention of horse soldiers. The going home will be slow. We will not chance pursuit."

Falls-Down-Hills grimaced in disappointment, but nodded. "Your words make sense, Badger."

Badger clapped the stocky Comanche on a muscular shoulder. "You did well here, my friend. I will vouch for you at council. You and the others go and eat now. The white man's woman left meat on the fire. We leave as soon as all have eaten."

The compliment and reassurance that his deeds would be verified, along with the prospect of fresh meat, smoothed the frown from Falls-Down-Hills's face. "It was a good raid, Badger. Many good things here. And now our sacred Medicine Mounds are safe from the bad spirits of the white man."

"And that," Badger said, "was the point of this raid. Go. Enjoy the meat and warmth."

As he waited, Badger switched his saddle from his ribby sorrel to the back of a big, powerful bay from the white man's herd. The bay snorted nervously and pawed the ground, frightened at Badger's unfamiliar scent. Badger spoke softly to the animal, praising it, letting the big horse become accustomed to his scent and touch, making a new friend. After a time the bay stopped fretting and lowered its head.

Badger cupped the horse's chin and blew softly into the bay's nostrils. The breath would complete the bond between horse and new owner.

He selected a stocky buckskin that looked like it would have an easy gait and led it to Yellowfish's dead paint. After a brief struggle he freed Yellowfish's saddle and swung it onto the buckskin's back.

He led the buckskin back to the corral and waited patiently for the other members of the raiding party to emerge from the house of stone slabs and wood.

As he waited, he idly wondered where Quanah might be at this moment. The Quahadi war chief would not have left his people for such a long time without good reason.

Badger wondered what it was like, being a war chief. Would the honor of the shield and feathered bonnet rest lightly on a man's arm and head? Or would the weight of responsibility for so many people make the symbols too heavy for one man to carry?

He shrugged aside the wonder. One did not set out to become a chief. War chiefs and peace chiefs were not elected, not like the white man's way. Among The People, such things just happened.

The sleet pellets and snow flurries gave way to a cold, drizzling rain as Badger led his party and its many prizes from the white man's lodge. He pulled his winter buffalo robe more snugly about his shoulders, but never relaxed his vigilance. Even though Bad Hand Mackenzie had taken most of his warriors south, and though the chief of horse soldiers left behind at Fort Richardson seemed unwilling to find Indians, the chance remained that a scout party might stumble across their trail. He must remain alert to danger at all times. The goods and horses taken in the raid were too valuable to Quanah's band to lose.

It was going to be a long, cold ride home, Badger thought.

Lige Thompson knelt on one knee, Ned Justine beside him, on the ice-fringed east bank of Wolf Creek, half a day's ride into the western edge of the Indian Nation reservation lands.

The frigid late February wind numbed Justine's cheeks and ruffled the long silver hair that flowed from beneath Thompson's battered hat. The scout glanced at Justine. "What's your read on it, Ned?"

"I make it a hunting party. Only four warriors. Kiowas. Three of the pony tracks match those we've been looking for." He poked a finger through the ashes of the small camp fire. The sand beneath was noticeably warm. "They camped here between eight and twelve hours ago."

The weathered scout nodded. "Damn me if you ain't gettin' near as good as me on the hunt, son." He rose to his feet, a bit stiffly; Justine suspected the man was in pain from an old arrow wound in the knee, made worse over the years by rheumatism, but Thompson tried never to let it show outwardly. "Whose band?"

"Scar Nose's."

"Yep. It's that murderin' red son of a bitch, sure enough. And he's close." Thompson stared toward the north. "Half a day's ride at the outside. He'll be camped in Wild Horse Canyon, figurin' he's safe there. Not more'n twenty-five, thirty bucks with him."

Thompson turned to the third man in the scout detail. "Al, fetch Hopkins. If the dumb bastard ain't got hisself lost again, he oughtta be no more'n five, six miles back. Tell 'im we got a chance to put this bunch of butchers down for keeps. Ned and me'll scout out their camp. Shouldn't be no more'n five miles or so up, where this creek runs out of the canyon breaks."

Duggan spat a stream of tobacco juice and nodded. "Reckon one company'll be enough, Lige?"

"Hell, even I Company ought to be able to handle this little bunch," Thompson said sarcastically. "Damn sight rather have Davis or Carter. Or near anybody else. But we're stuck with Hopkins. At least he's got a couple decent noncoms to see the job gets done."

Duggan nodded and reined his mount back in the direction they had come.

Despite the weight of miles that heavied his shoulders and ached his hip, Justine's heartbeat picked up; his teeth no longer chattered, but the cold seemed to sink deeper into his belly with the realization the long hunt was near its end.

Almost three weeks ago, Scar Nose's renegade Kiowas had ambushed a small band of settlers almost within cannon shot of Jacksboro. Three white men and two women lay dead, the bodies stripped and mutilated almost beyond recognition. Ned had found the lone survivor, a terrified girl about eleven years old who had huddled in a tangle of berry vines as her family and friends were butchered. Justine didn't want to imagine what she had seen.

The girl hadn't spoken a word since. She just stared straight ahead, her eyes dull and lifeless.

The timing of the raid puzzled Justine. Normally, Indians did not stray from the reservation during the harsh winter months except to hunt, not to raid and kill. But Scar Nose was as unpredictable as he was brutal. He didn't follow the tradition of holing up on the reservation to ride out the winter. That made him one dangerous Indian.

Justine knew conditions were tough on the reservation. The Indians there weren't receiving adequate food, blankets, or medicine. The so-called Indian Ring back East didn't care if women and children starved—especially red ones—as long as they could fatten their own purses with government payments for goods not delivered and sell the promised cattle and other necessities of life to their money-hungry friends and associates.

In his heart, Justine honestly couldn't blame the Indians all that much. When a man's family faced starvation, he did something about it. If he wasn't too drunk on white man's whiskey to take action. But was that an excuse to do what they did to settlers who wandered too far from the safety of the forts? Was this much brutality necessary?

The question had plagued Justine since he'd first ridden up on the Salt Creek massacre site.

He still had no answer.

The long scouts he, Thompson, and Duggan had made over the past year and a half had mostly come up empty, yielding nothing but exhausted, sore-backed horses, and men too tired to eat.

Even this one, with a hot trail to begin with, almost had gone down the river along with the cold, drenching rains mixed with sleet and snow. Only Thompson's bulldog determination and Indian savvy had brought them back to it.

Thompson snugged up the saddle cinch on his gaunt buckskin. "Better check your weapons again, Ned. Ain't plannin' on Scar Nose spottin' us, but best be ready. Expect the worst and you're set for it; if it works out better'n you expect, that there's just a bonus."

Justine examined the new firearms the army had issued only a few months ago. The Springfield trapdoor carbine in .45–70 caliber was a single shot, but its additional range and stopping power made it more valuable than the seven-shot Spencer. The new Colt's Single Action Army model revolver now in his holster, a solid, strong, .45-caliber metallic cartridge handgun, was a monumental improvement over the old cap-and-ball Dragoon that took forever to reload under fire. And it packed a lot more wallop.

Satisfied that all was ready, he tightened his saddle cinch and nodded.

"All right, son," Thompson said, his eyes narrow and cold, whiskered jaw set firm, "let's go find Scar Nose and bring back that bastard's balls back in his own medicine pouch."

17

THE THIN LAYER of ice on Justine's coat crackled with each movement as he stood beside Thompson in the small group gathered in a half circle before Lieutenant Hopkins.

Hopkins had his back to the wind and his coat collar turned up, leaving his subordinates to face the freezing drizzle and sleet. Prints left by boot or hoof only moments before already sprouted rims of ice and collected miniature drifts of sleet.

Justine had long since passed the shivering stage. His teeth no longer chattered. The only feeling in his toes, gloved fingers, and injured hip joint was a constant ache from the bone-chilling cold. He had had to physically pry the fingers of his left hand from the reins before dismounting for the parley with Hopkins and the ranking noncoms of I Company.

The only man in the group who seemed not to feel the cold stood at Justine's side.

"Scar Nose's village, sure enough," Lige Thompson said, his tone as bitter as the wind. Ice crusted the old scout's beard and eyebrows. "Ten years now I been hopin' for a shot at that ugly bastard. Now we got it. He's ripe for the pickin', Hopkins. No lookouts posted, every damn redskin snug in their lodges. We couldn't have set him up better if we'd laid his camp out ourselves."

Indecision flickered in the lieutenant's eyes. "I don't know, Mr. Thompson. The prudent course would be to send for reinforcements before attacking. My company is not at full strength."

Thompson's eyes narrowed into slits. "Dammit, Hopkins! Scar Nose ain't got but twenty, twenty-five fightin' men! You got sixty-odd troopers here! Hit him now—and I mean *now*—and we've got 'em outnumbered by plenty. Sit here on your butt and wait for help, he'll spot us and clear out."

"Mind your tone of voice, Thompson! You're speaking to an officer."

"Look, *Lieutenant* Hopkins"—venom practically dripped from the old scout's tongue—"if you don't hit Scar Nose now, Bad Hand's gonna want to know why. And, by God, I'll tell him."

"That's enough, Thompson! I won't stand for—"

"Excuse me, Lieutenant Hopkins," the senior sergeant, a burly Irishman named O'Grady, interrupted with a warning glance at Thompson. "If I might offer a suggestion, sir, quarreling among ourselves is not going to get the job done." O'Grady ignored the icy glare Hopkins turned on him. "I believe Lige is right. Scar Nose is one bad Indian. The worst of the litter. If we can wipe him out, even his own people would hold a victory dance. With all due respect, sir."

Ned braced himself for the explosion.

It never came.

Instead, Hopkins turned his normal bug-in-his-soup disdain toward Justine. "Is that your evaluation of the situation, Corporal Justine?"

"Yes, sir, it is. We will never have a better opportunity." He swallowed, then jumped in with both feet on the only way he knew to persuade Hopkins not to turn tail. "Sir, the unit that brings down Scar Nose will have the gratitude of the entire chain of command of the army, not to mention that of the settlers on the frontier." He didn't add that Hopkins just might get a promotion, at least a brevet rank. Hopkins would know that.

The lieutenant dropped his gaze and stroked his chin for a moment, then shook his head. "The terrain isn't all that favorable. If we skirt the village and attack from the north, our chances for complete success will be better." The indecision had returned to Hopkins's expression. Justine knew the lieutenant was stalling, unwilling to go into battle.

Justine glanced at Thompson, saw the barely controlled rage in the frontiersman's eyes, then said to Hopkins, "Sir, I'm no trained tactician. It seems to me that ordinarily such a plan would be sound. However, I personally believe we don't have the time to execute such a maneuver. It would take most of the day. By then the ground will be completely frozen and coated with an inch or more of glare ice. The horses could easily lose their footing."

"The corporal's right, sir," O'Grady said with a nod. "We could lose more men to falls by mounts than at the hands of the Indians."

Justine thought he saw a flicker of fear in Hopkins's eyes. After a moment, the officer nodded. "Very well. We'll stage a frontal assault. Sergeant, take four squads and lead the charge. Corporal Kincaid will take one squad past the village and capture the pony herd. I'll keep a squad of five of our best riflemen in reserve, to go where we're needed as the situation dictates. Any questions?"

Justine knew one big question existed. Why Hopkins didn't lead the charge himself. There was no need to ask. Every trooper in I Company knew the answer.

"Have the men see to their mounts, tighten girths, and check weapons, Sergeant," Hopkins said to O'Grady. "Make sure every man understands his assignment. We move out in twenty minutes."

"One more thing, O'Grady," Thompson said, pointedly not addressing his comments to the commanding officer, "there's a man in that village I'd as soon not see killed if it can be helped. Mexican captive. Name's Amarillo Castañada. One of my spies. Wears a red serape over an old Navy peacoat, wolf-skin cap. Keep him alive if you can. I owe him. And I think he's got some information for me."

O'Grady nodded and strode toward the troopers standing at horse, shivering in the cold, a few yards from the parley.

Thompson fell into step beside Justine as they strode toward the remounts to change horses.

"You handled that yellow-bellied ass pretty smooth, Ned," Thompson said. "I was near deckin' the bastard 'til you and O'Grady stepped in."

Justine shrugged. "Hopkins is a glory hound. Provided somebody else takes the risks. I just played that against him. Now I'm beginning to wonder if maybe I shouldn't have."

Thompson snorted in disgust. "Maybe we'll get lucky and some redskin'll do us a favor. Lift the incompetent sumbitch's scalp for us. Ain't likely, though. Hopkins'll run like a rabbit if the fight gets too close to him."

Justine didn't reply. An enlisted man didn't make such comments about an officer, even in confidence. And Justine wasn't sure whether his dislike of Hopkins stemmed more from the lieutenant's incompetence as a field commander or the fact that he was Elaine Hopkins's husband. The barrier that stood between him and the woman he had grown to love—

"Reckon Hopkins was payin' attention when we warned him about that box canyon?" Thompson's question shattered Justine's mental picture of blond hair shimmering in sunlight. "Wouldn't bother me none to see Hopkins get suckered into it. I'm half a mind to lift his scalp myself and blame it on Scar Nose."

They saddled fresh horses and mounted. For a minute or so, the big bay under Justine threatened to buck, his back humped, ears laid flat against muscled neck. Justine managed to talk the horse out of the notion as he and Thompson rode back toward the main body of troopers, who were now forming up by the fours.

Justine reined in alongside Merriweather, in the front rank. "Scared, Merriweather?"

"Real scared. Close to peeing in my pants." The young trooper's teeth chattered, slurring his words. "You?"

"I always am before a fight. Any sane man would be."

Merriweather glanced toward the aging scout, who had reined his steel gray to a stop before the troopers. "Thompson doesn't seem to be scared."

"He isn't. In addition to being an old hand at this job, he's too filled with hate to be scared. No other emotion drives him, Merriweather, and I pray to God neither of us turns into Elijah Thompson." Justine sighed and forced a reassuring smile. "Just stick close to the sergeant. O'Grady's a veteran at this business. He knows what he's doing. Good luck, Merriweather."

"You, too, Corporal."

Justine kneed his mount alongside Thompson's steel gray. The icy knot in his belly wasn't from the cold. "Just once, Lige, I wish you'd let someone else be first to the fight."

"Ain't gonna miss out on this fun. There ain't no Injun alive I'd rather get in my sights than that bastard Scar Nose." Thompson fell silent for a moment, then said, "Ned, it's up to you, me, and O'Grady to see these boys through. You know Hopkins ain't gonna be no help." He glanced back at the cavalrymen waiting in formation, lifted a hand, and waved the troopers forward. "Let's get movin'. It's time to go stomp us some red snakes."

The hour's ride to the spot where the charge would begin seemed to last forever, yet at the same to speed by, as Justine's gaze constantly swept the rocky hills grayed and blurred through steady, freezing rain. He knew this fight was going to be up close—red warrior and white trooper looking into each other's eyes.

It wasn't a comfortable feeling.

Justine fought back the wave of nausea that churned up from his gut. He followed Thompson's lead, pulled the Colt from his flap holster, and rotated the cylinder for a final check. The cylinder he normally carried empty beneath the hammer now held a sixth round. The extra shot could mean the difference between life and death.

Thompson reined in just short of the bend in the valley

floor, the smell of the Indian camp borne to their nostrils by the stiff north breeze. The mud beneath the horse's feet was freezing rapidly, covered with a sheen of ice that crunched beneath hooves. Another hour or two and a full-out charge would be impossible.

Thompson flashed a series of hand signals, then acknowledged the answering signs from Sergeant O'Grady. Not a word sounded from the ranks. No guidons fluttered, no bugle calls sounded. There was no glint of light on polished sabers, no flash and glory here, Justine thought. Just a bunch of men fanning out in a skirmish line, about to charge an enemy village. To kill or be killed, to spill blood or see their own stain the frozen mud of the valley floor—

"Well, Ned," Thompson all but whispered, "this here's what it's all about. Watch your hair, son." He rammed spurs to the iron gray.

The front ranks were within a hundred yards of the nearest lodge before the first warning cry sounded from the village. Moments later, Thompson and Justine were among the lodges, picking their targets as they thumbed the hammer for the next shot. Bedlam broke out in the village as the first wave of soldiers swept through, the powerful new handguns dropping Indians as they tried to flee their lodges. The charge had caught them completely by surprise.

A lance whirred between Justine and Thompson. Ned shot the swarthy Indian who had thrown it and saw the man drop straight down, dead before he hit the ground. Thompson yelped a shrill Rebel yell, yanked his gray to Justine's left, and fired point-blank into the broad, dark face of a stocky Indian. The remaining half of the Indian's nose exploded in a red mist. Thompson whooped in triumph.

The charge carried Justine beyond the last lodge. A rifle ball whirred past his ear as he spun the big bay on its haunches for another pass. At the corner of his vision he saw Corporal Kincaid's squad bear down on the unguarded pony herd and sweep the spooked horses away to the north, up the valley.

Justine felt a tap against his cheekbone at the same instant the close-range muzzle blast numbed his ears. He snapped a quick shot at a crouching Indian, missed, and then was back in the middle of the swarming melee in the village.

The powerful bay's shoulder rammed into an Indian, knocked the man sprawling. A trooper shot the downed warrior before Justine could react.

Justine's horse carried him back through the confusion and powder smoke. On the east side of the village the bay bore down on a crouching figure. Justine stopped just short of pulling the trigger. The man wore a red poncho-like garment over a faded blue coat, a wolf's head cap pulled over his ears. Justine gestured with the barrel of the Colt toward a nearby jumble of rocks and low junipers, and turned in the saddle to watch the man scramble out of sight.

He reined the bay to a stop in the cover of a stand of stunted post oaks, ejected the spent cartridges, and reloaded. His fingers shook so violently the brass cartridges clattered against the steel chambers. He snapped the loading gate shut, started to rein the bay back toward the battle—and froze at the sudden rattle of gunfire from nearby. From the direction of the box canyon.

He forced himself to take a deep breath, let his gaze flick over the battle swirling below, then toward the spot where Hopkins and his squad were supposed to be holding in reserve.

He saw no one.

He knew immediately what had happened. On his last pass through the village, he'd caught a quick glimpse of two mounted Indians followed by several on foot, running toward the box canyon, all carrying rifles. Hopkins had followed. It had to have been that way. No one else would be that stupid. A thought flashed through Justine's mind:

All he had to do was sit tight and let the Indians kill Hopkins. Elaine would be free . . .

He pushed the notion aside as quickly as it had formed. He couldn't leave a man to the savages. Even Hopkins. Especially when there were five troopers with him. He spun the bay toward the edge of the battle below.

Through the fog of gunpowder and smoke from lodges already torched, he caught a glimpse of Al Duggan and spurred toward him. "Hopkins rode into a trap in the box canyon!" Justine shouted. "Grab as many men as you can! We've got to get them out!"

Justine didn't wait for others. He leaned over the bay's neck and spurred for more speed. The big horse slipped on the frozen ground, almost went down, but regained its footing. Minutes later Justine yanked the horse to a stop, his fears confirmed.

Five men in blue lay or knelt in a shallow depression, three behind the bodies of downed horses. Powder smoke bloomed from all three sides of the box canyon walls. Justine bailed from the saddle, holstered his handgun, and yanked the .45–70 carbine from its saddle sling. He grabbed a leather ammunition pouch and scrambled up the side of the canyon.

He flung himself behind a big boulder, chest heaving as he gasped for air. He forced himself to take his time as he cocked the Springfield and picked his target. Partway up the slope and just over a hundred yards off, an Indian crouched behind a juniper, rifle pointed toward the soldiers trapped below.

Justine drew a deep breath and squeezed the trigger. The carbine stock slammed against his shoulder. Through the boil of smoke from the muzzle he saw the rifleman spin and fall.

He fumbled with the trapdoor, finally sprung it open, ejected the spent cartridge, reloaded, fired again. The slug spanged from a rock a foot short of the mark, but glanced off to hammer into the second Indian's ribs. The rifle fell from the Indian's hands.

The troopers pinned in the depression below returned the Indians' fire, but were shooting blind and uphill, with no clear targets. Justine knew time was running out for the men even as he thumbed a third cartridge into the carbine.

He fired toward an exposed leather-clad hip and leg across the canyon, saw the ice and dirt kick as the slug fell a yard short, heard the Indian's faint yelp of surprise. A rifle ball spanged off rock a foot from his shoulder.

Then a rattle of carbine fire sounded from behind Justine, on both north and south walls of the canyon; another Indian stood, then flopped facedown in the rocks. He glanced over his shoulder. Duggan and another trooper held the high ground on Justine's right; two more Springfields cracked at his left.

The remaining Indians gave up the fight, clawing their way up the canyon walls. Two of them didn't make it, downed by the accurate fire of Duggan and his men.

Through the ringing in his ears, Justine became aware that the distant firing in the village had stopped. Moments later the clatter of hooves sounded. Lige Thompson and a dozen or so troopers spurred into the mouth of the box canyon.

Justine let his cheek drop to his forearm, too fatigued to move, battling the nausea that churned his gut. After a few moments he heard someone call his name, became aware that all firing had stopped except for an occasional distant gunshot. He glanced at his forearm. Blood stained the coat sleeve where his head had rested.

"Up here, Lige!" he yelled. He was afraid his voice, weak and shaky, wouldn't carry far enough. He tried to stand. His knees buckled. He had to lean against the boulder to stay upright. He lifted his hand to his cheek. His fingers came away bloody.

Moments later, Thompson stood beside Justine.

"You hit bad, Ned?" Thompson asked.

"Not . . . bad. Nicked . . . just tired."

Thompson's wiry arm slid beneath Justine's shoulders.

"Got to get you down off this hill, son. Might be an Injun who can shoot up there on the rim with a long gun. O'Grady's mopping up at the village. Duggan's took over here."

"Anybody dead?"

"A mess of Injuns. No white men." Thompson sounded disappointed. "What the hell you go and pull Hopkins's butt out of the fire for? Seems to me you'd want him dead worse'n any man in this outfit."

Justine winced inwardly. He'd never mentioned Elaine to Thompson, but the old man knew. Was he that transparent? he wondered. "Have to admit—I thought about it," Justine said as Thompson guided him down the steep, rocky slope. "But the other boys. Couldn't let the Indians have them."

"Reckon you done all right at that, hoss. Been me, I mighta been willin' to make the trade."

"How did we make out in the village?"

"Just fine. Maybe eight, nine Injun bucks got away. We got the rest of 'em. And I got to put a slug right where the other half of Scar Nose's beak was. Brightened my whole day, that did. We didn't get nobody hurt bad. And we got the whole damn Injun pony herd."

Justine recovered most of his wind and a bit more strength by the time they reached the floor of the box canyon. "By the way, Lige, I know where your Mexican spy's hiding, if he hasn't moved. I came within a whisker of shooting him." Justine told Thompson where he should find his man.

Thompson nodded. "I know Amarillo Casteñada. He'll be right where you left him. Much obliged. I'll fetch your horse and we'll go sort things out."

Justine leaned against his bedroll beside the fire and sipped from a cup of bitter camp coffee. The freezing rain had given way to fat, heavy snowflakes. The wind had eased. He almost had feeling back in his feet now.

Hopkins had avoided Justine since the fight, for which Ned thanked his lucky stars. The farther he could stay from the lieutenant, the better.

He touched the gash on his left cheek. Another unwanted scar of battle. But it could have been a lot worse. A few inches toward his nose and he would have been one dead trooper. The bitter cold helped stop the bleeding. The gouge didn't even hurt much. He doubted the bone beneath it was broken or even cracked.

The attack had been a solid success. Scar Nose and most of his warriors were dead, the few survivors on foot and without food or clothing, their lodges and personal possessions burned. Hopkins picked a few of the better horses from the Indian herd for cavalry remounts and had the others herded into the box canyon and shot. Justine was glad to have been spared that duty.

He idly wondered how close to the truth Hopkins's official report of the battle would be. If he were prone to lay bets, he'd have to wager it wouldn't look on paper like the fight he had gone through. It certainly wouldn't mention that the lieutenant commanding I Company had spent the time cowering behind a dead horse and never fired a shot.

"Warmed up yet, partner?" Lige Thompson seemed to have appeared at Justine's side from nowhere. One minute he wasn't there, the next minute he was. Justine knew he should be accustomed to that by now. He wasn't.

"I'm working on it as hard as I can," Justine said.

Thompson squatted beside him. "Reckon you earned it, son. You done mighty good out there today." The scout fished his pipe from his pocket and clamped it, unfilled, between his teeth. "Just had me a tolerable long parley with Casteñada. What he had to say ain't no particular surprise, but I was hopin' otherwise."

Justine sat up a bit straighter. "What's going on? You look a little worried, Lige."

"More'n a *little* worried, Ned. I'm frettin' like hell."

Thompson chewed on the pipe stem, staring toward the north. "Big doin's up on the Wichita headwaters here lately. Comanche Sun Dance last summer."

Justine lifted an eyebrow. "I didn't know the Comanches held Sun Dances."

"They don't. And that's what's got me fretted up. Mean's somethin's afoot. Somethin' big. Somethin' you and me gotta go find out about."

Justine's spirits sank. "Now?"

"Nah. We'll go back to Richardson, get re-outfitted and rested up first. Too much cold weather ridin' aches up my ol' bones somethin' fierce. When she warms up a bit, we'll see what we can find." Thompson rose and rubbed his backside. "Reckon I'll go see if there's any of that chow left. I done missed mess call."

Badger fished a morsel of boiled buffalo meat from the iron pot suspended above the coals of the lodge fire, popped it into his mouth, wiped his fingers on his leggings as he chewed, and listened in contentment to the sounds of home and family.

Outside, the gentle breeze ruffled recently opened leaves on the cottonwood and chinaberry trees. The greening time had come early. Ponies already had begun to shed their heavy winter coats, their bellies swollen with tender new grass.

Star and Turns-Over-Turtles chatted and giggled constantly as they worked. Hearing their laughter again reminded Badger he was a lucky man, to have two wives who got along so well. As Star had said, they seemed more like sisters than two women related by only a lifetime of friendship and now by marriage.

It made the white man's notion that one wife was all a man could be allowed even more absurd. Why should one woman be required to do all the work, when two did it more efficiently and enjoyed each other's company?

Badger had spent enough time around the white tribe's religious leaders during his visits to the reservation to have at least a vague idea of their beliefs. Those who wore the cross around their necks were horrified at the thought that a man should sleep with more than one wife. But then, the white man was greedy, possessive. They even had a word for it.

Jealousy.

There was no such disease among the Comanches. Star felt no resentment when Badger and Turns-Over-Turtles shared sleeping robes; why should the whites?

It was one of many puzzles posed by these people who called themselves Christians. They preached love and kindness but made bloody and violent war against those who did not share their beliefs down to the last word, even among their own people.

Most confusing of all was their concept of a single deity, a benevolent but wrathful one. How could a benevolent supreme being wear two faces? A gentle, kind, loving deity did not bring hunger and sickness and misery to his children. The Great Spirit of the Comanches could not; to inflict suffering was the realm of evil spirits, not good ones.

There was no figuring the white man. To try only made one's head hurt.

Badger felt a tug at his sleeve and smiled down at his youngest son, then picked the boy up and plopped him onto a knee. Within moments they played at some kind of finger game that had no meaning except the boy's enjoyment. That was enough meaning.

The child was almost two summers now, constantly in motion, curious, poking into any and every thing that caught his fancy. The giver of names had known him since the boy's birth. He promptly named him Ecapusia, the Flea.

The name fit, except that the child was no pest. He was a delight to those around him, healthy, happy, good-natured, growing like a weed at the edge of a water seep.

Already he rode with Star on her horse when the camp moved or she went to gather edible plant roots. Soon, Badger must select a gentle mare and begin to teach the boy the riding skills he would need.

Horsefly also had grown, tall and straight, his chest and legs thickening with muscle, an accomplished rider and hunter, and a fine companion. Badger knew that sometimes white brothers fought and snapped at each other, but Horsefly doted on Flea. When Horsefly wasn't with others of his age group or riding to the hunt with his father, he and Flea were inseparable.

Badger could not recall a happier time, other than when Star's father had accepted his bride price. He knew his heart would never soar higher than it had on that day.

A soft summons from outside the lodge interrupted the finger game. Badger plucked Ecapusia from his knee, told the child to go to his mothers, and stepped out into the warm sunshine.

"Greetings, brother," Yellowfish said, his normally jovial face solemn. He had been even more jovial the last six moons, since Badger had acted as Yellowfish's intermediary to secure the hand of Runs-With-Antelope.

"Something troubles you, Yellowfish?"

Yellowfish shook his head. "Not troubles, exactly. A short time ago, a messenger arrived. Quanah returns from the north with the next sun. He has called a council for the second sun after his arrival. He specifically asked that you and I attend."

Badger frowned as he nodded. "Quanah does not call such councils lightly, nor with such haste. He does not ride long distances in the time of snows or stay gone from his people so many moons without reason. Something important must ride with the wind. Of course I will be there. And you, brother?"

"I will attend."

"Good. Come inside. There is meat."

"Perhaps later. Now I must help spread the word among the others, the most senior warriors and wisest of the elders." Yellowfish strode away, the puckered scar on his left calf still showing white above the top of his moccasin.

Badger realized that he and his brother had accumulated more than a few scars during the years since their first raid, when Yellowfish was a mere holder of horses and Badger had lifted his first scalp. Most seasoned warriors wore such scars, either from battle or from the hunt.

Yellowfish's climb through the unofficial ranks to the status of respected warrior had been almost as rapid, and as well deserved, as Badger's had been. Badger's pride in his brother's courage swelled his breast, along with lingering gratitude that Yellowfish had forgone the battle with Bad Hand's horse soldiers to see Star and Horsefly to safety.

That their views were now sought in council as senior warriors was the ultimate honor Quanah could bestow. It was yet another bond of their brotherhood. The warmth of that bond turned away cold winds and slaked thirst when the sun bore down hard upon them. The bond also reassured each that if he were to fall, his family would pass into the caring hands of the surviving brother.

Badger returned to his lodge. Star and Turns-Over-Turtles must be told of the upcoming council.

They would know soon enough what Quanah had in mind.

18

BADGER STOOD IN the first row behind the seated elders in the crowded council lodge, holding his curiosity in check as the sacred pipe ceremony neared its end.

The temporary council house, quickly erected from chinaberry and cottonwood timbers overlaid with willow branches and fragrant juniper boughs, would be dismantled after this meeting. Not even Quanah's lodge, the largest in the village, could accommodate such a gathering.

Wisps of warm breeze drifted into the lodge. The drafts gained more heat from the assembled bodies and the ceremonial fire.

Quanah sat in the center of the first row, flanked by the elders of the band. Senior warriors such as Yellowfish and Badger stood behind Quanah. Fighting men of lesser standing formed other rows behind the senior ranks. A number of women who had gained stature through wisdom and medicine power lined the walls behind the men.

The absence of older children, normally admitted as observers, told Badger this was to be a serious council. Not a simple meeting to decide when to begin the buffalo hunt or to move the village.

It had all the trappings of a war council.

No one needed to be reminded of etiquette, or of the solemnity of such a council; personal conduct in such a gathering had been ingrained in them since childhood. It was the way of The People. Quanah would speak first, then others of descending rank, until all who wished to do so had the opportunity to express an opinion. None would be so discourteous as to interrupt or ridicule a speaker.

The opening ceremony completed, Quanah returned the sacred pipe to its soft deerskin pouch. His deliberate and careful actions reflected the honor due such a powerful instrument.

Only the whisper of breeze rustling the freshly cut juniper boughs and the faint crackle of the council fire broke the silence of the gathering. After a time, Quanah stood tall, his back straight, head held erect, a proud and respected man. His gaze moved around the gathering, lingering for a moment on Badger and others of high standing.

Finally, he began to speak; though his voice was strong, many of the elders whose hearing was no longer sharp cocked their heads to absorb each word. Many squinted through eyes clouded with age or by the strange sickness that so often came to blur the vision of The People.

"My friends," Quanah said solemnly, "you know I have been gone for many moons, traveling the lands to the north. While my heart sings to once again be among my people, it is heavy with the news I bring. At the same time, it grows hot with anger."

Quanah paused for a moment to let the solemnity of his words register with those who listened.

"On the reservation lands the white man set aside for red people there is great hunger. Children's bellies swell and they cry from want. The milk of infants' mothers dries in their breasts. Those who do not starve shiver in bitter cold in the times of snows." Quanah's tone itself grew cold as the breath of the old man of the north.

"They suffer because the white man does not distribute enough food, or warm blankets, or the numbers of promised cattle to feed them. They suffer because their men, once proud warriors, hide themselves in a river of *poisabá,* the white man's whiskey."

Badger sensed the outrage already building in the council house. The same emotions stirred in his own breast.

"Yet," Quanah continued, "this is not the only reason my heart is heavy, my spirit dark. During my journey, I rode many suns through the plains beyond the Arkansas River. The buffalo are gone."

An involuntary gasp of astonishment burst from the lungs of the listeners. The hairs on Badger's neck prickled. A cold hand closed around his heart. It was not possible, he thought. The Great Spirit had promised The People the buffalo would be there for them, for all time.

Quanah glanced at Badger. "Yes," he said as if reading Badger's mind, "it is true. For one full moon I rode the northern lands. In all that time, the number of living buffalo I saw I could count on my two hands. For one full moon I saw nothing but rotting carcasses or bones.

"Had I not seen this with my own eyes, I would not believe. It is the work of the white hunters who kill for hides only. They leave the meat, the sinews, the very soul of our brother the buffalo to rot on the prairie, to fatten only scavengers. The great northern herd no longer exists."

Quanah paused again, to let the enormity of his words settle firmly in the minds of those gathered.

"Not only do the white hunters destroy the buffalo; when they see one whose skin is not white, they fire upon him without warning or provocation. Comanche, Kiowa, Pawnee, Cheyenne—it does not matter to them to what band a man or woman belongs. They simply shoot at all red people unfortunate enough to appear before their guns."

Badger shifted his gaze from the speaker and glanced around the gathering. The brows of men and women alike furrowed in angry scowls, mirroring his own. A few snorted or grunted in outrage. The air inside the council lodge grew heavy with wrath.

"The horse soldiers at Forts Sill and Dodge make no effort to stop the slaughter of buffalo or the hunters' attacks on red people. They make no effort to stop the white bandits who raid the horse herds of those fortunate enough to still own ponies. These outlaws steal the horses not for honor, as in the Comanche tradition. They do this to exchange the stolen animals for white man's gold." Quanah's words remained calm, but Badger sensed the tight control the war chief held on his emotions.

"These bandits kill the herders of horses, young men, old men, women and children, who stand in their way. Among the ranks of the thieves are many whose skin is red but whose hearts have been poisoned against their own people by walking the white man's road.

"The American soldiers pledged by treaty to protect the reservation Indians do little or nothing to find and punish these killers and thieves who strike without honor. And now, even as we speak here, it grows worse."

Quanah paused again, to allow his people to prepare for the hearing of more bad words. The chill of dread in Badger's belly did little to bank the glowing coals of his anger.

"Some suns ago, a band of buffalo slayers—a great train of wagons, many men bearing long guns—left the village called Dodge. With no more buffalo to hunt in the north, they have crossed the Arkansas River. Now they make war on the buffalo on Quahadi land. On *our* hunting grounds."

The announcement struck the council house as if it were a lightning bolt. The shocked disbelief gave way in a heartbeat to outrage that seemed to crackle in the air.

"They build lodges of sod and timber on the river they call the Canadian, near the place where our fathers fought Short Chief Carson many summers ago," Quanah continued.

"Their long rifles kill many buffalo on hunting ground reserved for the red man in the papers signed at Medicine Lodge, papers the Quahadi did not sign, yet which the white man would impose upon us anyway. If there are those among you who doubt my words, those who rode with me can vouch that I speak the truth."

An audible murmur swept through the gathering. The

mutter held an ominous undertone. The Quahadis needed no one to vouch for Quanah's words. Quanah did not lie. His words and heart were straight and pure. It showed in his eyes, in the set of his jaw.

"The white hunters call this place Adobe Walls. It is from that village that they war on the great southern herd. The white soldier chiefs will not put an end to it. In fact, they encourage the slayers to wipe out all the buffalo—the animals given to The People by the Great Spirit.

"And it is there, in that village in that valley along that river, where the slaughter must be stopped, while the white men are few. Before they kill all our buffalo as they did those of the north. Those white hunters must be slain, must be driven from our lands, or The People will cease to exist."

Badger felt the surge of raw rage in the lodge. It was a thing he could almost touch, a mirror of the fury that boiled in his own breast.

Quanah said, "When the grass grows tall, a great band of warriors—more than ever before assembled—will gather where the waters of the Washita River begin to flow. From there we ride to the place called Adobe Walls and kill the white hunters. I have visited many villages—Comanche, Cheyenne, Kiowa, Arapaho—since the great Sun Dance. This visit to my home village and my people is the last such stop before this great band gathers to slay the hide hunters. Soon, the war pipe will be passed among you."

Quanah sat, the signal that the floor now was open for other speakers to voice their views.

Afraid-of-His-Shadow, stooped by age and infirmities of the bones, was the first to struggle to his feet. His name misled many who did not know him; the aged one-time war chief was not afraid of his shadow. His enemies were.

The old man stood for a moment in silence. The gaze from his clouded eyes swept the gathering.

"Once, many summers ago, I was a young man, and strong," Afraid-of-His-Shadow said solemnly. "Now I am old. At this moment I but wish I were again young, for Quanah speaks the truth. If I could, I would smoke his pipe and ride with him.

"I have seen in a vision what Quanah speaks. Quanah, a powerful young medicine man from the north"—the hazy gaze shifted to Badger for an moment—"and Tabi unuu, a great warrior from our own band, lead many man to a great victory over the whites in a valley along a river."

The old man's words jolted Badger. It was the same vision Yellowfish had seen. That Badger himself had seen in the night. It must be not a recurring dream, but a true vision, one that had come to many others.

"That is all I have to say." Afraid-of-His Shadow sat, assisted by the strong hands of those who stood behind him.

After a moment another elderly man stood. Calls-Ravens had ridden with Afraid-of-His-Shadow and Peta Nacona, Quanah's father, against many enemies. Among the Quahadi his reputation as a warrior was exceeded only by the power of his medicine accumulated over many winters. Now he served as principal peace chief of the band. Calls-Ravens's eyes remained bright, his vision and other senses keen though his muscles withered.

Badger expected Calls-Ravens to object, or at least to question the wisdom of a massive raid which joined together warriors from many bands. Even among the Comanche, some bands did not get along well. Often, The People had gone to war against the other tribes Quanah had mentioned; could former enemies join ranks against the white man? To Badger's knowledge, it had never been done.

Calls-Ravens surprised him. "I have heard stories of this young medicine man's powers. But his magic is untested. I would hear more of him if he is to ride with Quanah and Badger." Calls-Ravens sat, yielding the speaker's role to Quanah.

"His name is Isatai," Quanah said, rising. "His medicine

is the most powerful I have ever seen. He has climbed above the clouds and spoken with the Great Spirit. He has brought life back to the dead. He predicted the star with long tail feathers, the thing the whites call a comet, that rode across the sky but twelve moons ago. It was a thing of great wonder, seen by all."

Many heads nodded in agreement. The star with tail feathers had been a topic of much conversation and speculation among the bands. It had enthralled and mystified Badger himself.

"Isatai also predicted the great dry spell that followed the star with tail feathers." Quanah paused, waiting patiently until the involuntary murmur of astonishment faded. "There is more to Isatai's medicine. I have seen him belch forth cartridges and swallow them again, enough to keep hot the barrels of many warriors' rifles. He has magic which will keep the white man's guns from firing at our warriors."

Quanah sat, awaiting more comments or questions.

There were few.

The entire council lasted but three handspans of the sun before Quanah produced the revered war pipe. He tossed a bit of tobacco and crumbled sage into the lodge fire, lit the pipe with a coal, and made the offerings to the four winds, the earth and sky. His first offering of the pipe was to Badger. "Will you smoke, Tabi unuu?"

"I will smoke." Badger took the pipe, smoked, and passed it to his right to Yellowfish, standing alongside. Yellowfish smoked, then handed it to the man at his right. By the time the pipe returned to Quanah, almost every man of fighting age had smoked.

"It is good," Quanah said. "We leave for the great warrior gathering at the Washita in two suns."

➣ ➣ ➣

Justine knelt beside the ashes of the big council fire in the valley at the headwaters of the Washita, the heat of the late June sun heavy against his shoulders.

"Well, partner," Thompson, still astride his sweaty horse, said, "reckon we know now where all them trails we cut was headed. What's your make on it?"

Justine wiped a sleeve across his brow. Butterflies flickered to life in his belly. "War party. The biggest I've ever seen. They left here four days ago, I'd say. Comanche, Kiowa, Cheyenne, Pawnee, a few other tribes. I've never heard of that many different Indian bands getting together in one war party."

Thompson leaned in the saddle and spat. The amber tobacco stream splatted against the head of a greenish-gray lizard, sending the animal on a leg-blurring dash for cover. "You never heard of it 'cause it ain't never happened before, Ned. What we got here is one heap big bunch Injuns. And I got a feelin' I know what's afoot with that many savages."

"What might that be?"

"Adobe Walls." The old scout's tone was flat, matter of fact. "Reckon about thirty or so buffalo hunters gonna wake up soon lookin' at the biggest mess of savages the southern plains country ever seen. Two fifty, three hunnerd fightin' men. Maybe more, judgin' from the size of this camp."

Justine swung into the saddle. "We've got to warn them, Lige."

Thompson shrugged. "Too late, son. Even if we could get there in time, we'd still have to ride through a swarm of redskins to do it. I ain't ready just yet to shake ol' Satan's hand." He stared off toward the hunters' post. "Two more guns wouldn't help them hide men much, anyway."

"Then we have to alert the army. Fort Sill—"

"We'll do that, but it's too late. Troops couldn't get there in time to help. Even if the soldiers paid us any mind, they wouldn't be just real anxious to tangle with that many Injuns."

Justine fought back a surge of irritation. "So we do nothing? Just let a bunch of white men be butchered?"

"We don't do nothin', Ned, on account of there ain't nothin' we *can* do, 'cept light a shuck out of here before we lose our own hair. Go the long way round, keep quiet, maybe we'll get clear. We get to Sill, let the boss soldier there know there's one helluva Injun uprisin' in the works."

"Then?"

"We re-outfit for a mighty long ride, Ned. While them savages are busy at Adobe Wall, we go huntin'. See can we find where the Injuns winter. Then we go back to Concho and tell Bad Hand where to find 'em when he gets back. He'll by-damn do somethin' about 'em."

"So we just ride off and forget about the hide hunters?"

Thompson rolled the tobacco chew to his other cheek and stared off toward the south. "Ned, I been huntin' Injuns for many a year, and I learnt one thing sure. There's a time to fight and a time to sneak off. This here's sneakin' time. Them boys down at the Walls are on their own, I reckon."

Badger and Yellowfish squatted at the base of the bluffs on the east side of the hide hunters' village awaiting the first faint light before sunrise.

Almost three hundred other warriors also waited out the darkness, smoking, praying to their own spirits, talking softly among themselves. The barely constrained eagerness for battle and a great victory was a thing Badger could almost gather in his hand with a single swipe through the cool, late night air.

To a man, they wore war paint, mostly Isatai's magic yellow that would stop the white mans' guns from firing at them.

Badger studied at the tall figure standing arm's length away in the starlight. Moments ago, Quanah had donned his elaborate war bonnet. The long fall of feathers brushed his knees, rippling in the faint sigh of a light breeze.

All was ready.

The most difficult job facing Quanah and the other leaders was to keep the younger, more eager warriors in check, to await the proper time for the attack. Soft voices, the rustle of clothing, and the muted sounds of weapons checked and rechecked, reflected the restlessness. Even the horses seemed anxious, snorting and stamping. The throng of warriors spread out, braided reins of their best war ponies in hand, along the base of the bluffs.

Peering toward the darker blobs of buildings in the valley, Badger refreshed his memory of the layout of the hunters' camp. He had studied it at length the previous day.

The white man's houses lay roughly in a line from north to south on the flat ground of the north side of the Canadian River. The buildings were few, only as many as he could count on one hand, made of sod and slender poles in this land of scarce timber. They would not burn well. It would take considerable effort to reduce the village to ashes.

Badger sensed Yellowfish's taut eagerness and put his hand on the younger man's shoulder. "Patience, brother," Badger said softly. "I share your excitement for the kill, but we must wait for Quanah's signal."

Yellowfish sighed. The muscles beneath Badger's hand softened. "It seems this night will never end."

Badger glanced over his shoulder toward the sky visible above the bluffs that blotted out the lower stars of the eastern sky. "It will not be long, Yellowfish. Sun soon wakes from his sleep."

He turned his attention back to the settlement below. Two places in particular fanned the cold rage in Badger's breast. On the north and south sides of the camp lay stacks of drying hides, all that remained of more than enough buffalo to fill the needs of many families for many winters. Wagons parked seemingly without plan dotted the open spaces around the white man's lodges. There were no signs of movement, no sentries posted.

The hated hide hunters remained in their blankets, as Isatai had promised. Badger found that reassuring. If the magic were false, the white men would be alert and watchful, for within a few miles of this village three groups of white hunters already had fallen before Indian bullets and arrows over the last two suns. Yet the main body of whites seemed unconcerned. It was as if they did not know of the existence of the largest band of warriors ever assembled in the big grass country.

They soon would see the error of their ways. With Isatai's magic and Quanah's plan of attack, it would be a simple thing to eliminate the unsuspecting killers of buffalo who now slept in the village below. Despite his tightly controlled hate for the the white hunters and the itch of muscles anxious to spring into action, Badger's spirit lay calm.

After a time, he again glanced at the top of the bluffs. The first sign of the coming dawn had begun to wash stars from the eastern sky.

Quanah said, "The time nears. Pass the word among the others. Remind them again not to run their horses until the cry is raised."

By the time Badger and Yellowfish again took their positions at Quanah's side, their best war ponies snorting and fidgeting beneath them, the sky had brightened until a faint gray light lay upon the settlement.

At the base of the bluff, Isatai, naked, his body covered in yellow paint, sat astride his horse with two other medicine men. Isatai would not join the battle; from here, he would make the magic that would wipe out the white men.

Quanah lifted his feathered war lance high overhead, paused for a moment, then swept the lance point toward the white man's village.

The Indian line moved forward, first at a brisk walk, then at a trot. Badger still saw no movement in the village. His spirits soared. They would slay the white men while they still slept in their blankets.

Muted calls from the leaders to stay the pace fell on

anxious ears until finally Quanah yelled, "All right, go ahead!"

The line of warriors kneed and quirted mounts into a run. A moment later a lone white man appeared near the hunters' horse herd. He stood for a moment, stared toward them. Then fire lanced from the muzzle of the white man's gun. The shot hit nothing. The white man turned and ran as fast as his feet would carry him toward the nearest building. Another white man caught outside paused long enough to tie his horse to a wagon wheel and fire one wild shot before running to the safety of another lodge.

A hundred horse strides from the scattered buildings, the shrill war cries of different tribes split the sound of thunder from the hooves of the charging ponies.

Badger's heart soared high in triumph. It would be an easy victory—

A young Comanche riding a few feet from Badger suddenly tumbled over his horse's rump. A heartbeat later the heavy muzzle blast of a big-bore rifle sounded. This is not right, Badger thought; Isatai had said the white man's guns would not fire at the protective yellow paint. Then he had no time to reflect on the bad omen.

The wave of warriors swarmed into the buildings, some firing handguns, others rifles. Most wielded lances, bows and arrows, war axes. Several yelling warriors swarmed over a wagon parked before one building.

The flat bark of handguns and deafening blasts of big rifles from inside the buildings and the screams of wounded men and horses battered Badger's ears as the dust and gun smoke began to cloud the morning sky. In the swirl of battle he found himself in front of one of the big lodges, its door closed, probably barred. He spun his war horse around and backed the strong animal into the wooden door, trying to break it open. The door did not yield to the pony's weight and powerful muscles.

A bullet stung the point of his shoulder. Another buzzed past his ear. Through the blur of battle he saw horses and men stagger or fall, their screams shrill in his ears now ringing from close-range muzzle blasts. Within moments he knew the surprise attack had failed. Bodies of warriors, horses, and oxen littered the open spaces between buildings.

He kneed his horse away from the door, flung his short lance through an opening in the wall in rage and futility, and cast a quick glance for a safe haven from which to fight.

Others had dismounted to fight on foot, but soon found themselves pinned down by the gunfire of the buffalo hunters. Still others broke off the attack, quirting their mounts back toward the safety of the bluffs.

At the edge of his vision he caught a glimpse of a flowing headdress, saw Quanah fall from his horse, then scramble on hands and knees toward the scant cover of a berry thicket a short distance away. Badger forgot the fight; saving Quanah was more important. He slammed his heels into his pony's ribs.

Bullets sang past his head, kicked dust beneath his pony's feet. A familiar figure drew alongside. Yellowfish also had seen Quanah go down. Leaning over the necks of their ponies, Badger and Yellowfish raced side by side, only a few feet separating them.

Badger leaned to his right, Yellowfish to the left side of his horse, as Quanah stumbled to his feet, blood pouring down his chest and side. The two rescuers grabbed Quanah beneath the armpits, carried him between them for a hundred pony strides. Then Badger swung Quanah up behind him and urged his tiring horse toward the sheltering bluffs.

The first attack had failed miserably. The war party paid a heavy price for the scalps of but three white men. The sun had barely cleared a hand span of the eastern sky before the surviving attackers reassembled at the base of the bluffs.

Despite his wounds, Quanah slid from his seat behind Badger without waiting for assistance.

"I will find a healer," Badger said.

"No. That will wait. Gather the other leaders. We must decide what to do now."

Throughout that day, and the next, the warriors attacked—in small groups and large bands—and accomplished nothing except the loss of more dead and wounded. They did manage to retrieve many of their injured and the bodies of most of their dead. They could not reach those who lay within the shadow of the white man's walls.

On the afternoon of the third day, Quanah and Badger were forced to acknowledge defeat. Only an extended siege could wear down the white men. Such was not the Comanche way. They had lost many men to the big guns of the buffalo hunters, who in the awed words of one warrior, "shoot at us today and the bullet kills us tomorrow."

Healers moved among the wounded. Badger waved them away. His wounds, and those of Yellowfish, were slight. Quanah finally had relented and let the healer treat his gunshot wound late in the first day. Despite the pain, Quanah continued to lead. Badger knew the events at Adobe Walls had sapped the chief's spirit. The quiet confidence in Quanah's eyes had given way to a bleak look of despair, the heavy weight of failure.

Badger shared that despair.

He, Yellowfish, and Quanah now squatted twenty strides from where Isatai and two others, one a Cheyenne and one a Kiowa, sat astride their horses atop a bluff overlooking the battlefield. Swarms of black flies covered the bloated corpses of horses and oxen that littered the place called Adobe Walls.

Badger heard a thump, a sudden grunt, and glanced up in time to see the Cheyenne at Isatai's side tumble from his horse. More than two heartbeats later he heard the faint report of a rifle. Badger and Yellowfish stared at each other in shocked disbelief.

The slug that downed the Cheyenne had been fired from

an incredible distance, more than half a white man's mile. No gun the two had ever heard of could shoot so far.

Quanah's jaw muscles twitched. He rose and strode toward Isatai and the group of astonished men gathered around the fallen Cheyenne.

"Where is your magic, Isatai?" Quanah's words were tight with rage. "The white men were supposed to be asleep. Their guns were not to fire. Your magic paint that would stop their bullets is nothing more than a color."

"It was a Cheyenne brave who broke the magic," Isatai said with a defiance that seemed forced. "He killed a skunk the night before the attack."

Surly murmurs rose from the crowd around the medicine man.

"Isatai should be whipped! Or better, killed!" one man shouted as he reached for his knife.

Quanah raised his uninjured arm. "No. Isatai is disgraced enough. It would be a more fitting punishment that he live with his failure the rest of his days."

The warrior's hand dropped from the knife.

"What is done is done," Quanah said, his tone heavy. "We cannot win this battle. It is over. But the whites shall still feel our anger. We go find other whites. On them we take our revenge for our dead."

19

To Justine, the return of the Fourth Cavalry to Fort Concho seemed as much a family reunion as a massing of troops.

Many of the men he had not seen since the McClellan Creek battle in the fall of 1872, almost two years ago. Three days after the arrival of the last company, his knuckles still ached from all the handshakes.

His closest friends had survived the Rio Grande campaign.

Given the Fourth's success on the southern border, the atmosphere at the fort held an almost festive air.

The Fourth Cavalry now had a new nickname. Mackenzie's Raiders. According to the stories the returning troopers told, the colonel's brash crossing of the Rio Grande in pursuit of marauding Indians and livestock thieves had almost caused an outbreak of apoplexy among the nation's politicians.

"Some say Mackenzie's a touch crazy," one of the veteran troopers had said, "but, by God, the man's a *soldier.* He got the job done. If he wants to pitch a temper fit from time to time, fine by me. If the generals and politicians would give him free rein, we'd end the Indian war in two shakes of a mare's tail in fly time."

Mackenzie's raid hadn't caused a war with Mexico, though it had come close. What it had done was win the war for the Rio Grande country.

John Charlton's sleeve had sprouted a third stripe. Justine thought the chief of scout's sergeant rank long overdue.

Even Al Duggan had arrived in Concho from Richardson, recovered from the bout of what the surgeons called dust pneumonia for lack of a definite medical diagnosis—the illness that had sent him to a hospital cot instead of on the long scout in the southern Staked Plains with Justine and Thompson. Duggan seemed chipper enough, considering he hadn't yet completely shaken the effects of the illness.

Of all the officers, Justine had been most relieved to find Lieutenant Carter and Captain Davis hale and hearty. Justine still felt out of place in the company of officers, but Carter and Davis were different. Those two actually saw the enlisted ranks as men, not ignorant pawns to be expended in battle to advance their own careers. Like Mackenzie, they *cared* for their men. They didn't relish bloodshed. But they never dodged a fight, never invented excuses not to be in the forefront of the charge. That was the difference that set the Carters and Davises and Mackenzies apart from the Hopkinses of the army.

One development relieved Justine, and at the same time left a part of him empty.

Elaine Hopkins had not accompanied her husband to Fort Concho. Justine would be spared the ache of seeing her on the post, blond hair glinting in the sun, the quick, warm flash of her smile, the way her hips moved as she strode toward the chapel for daily Mass. And the invitation, unspoken but never far beneath the surface of her eyes and in the touch of her hand when they chanced to meet.

Out of sight, but never out of mind, Justine thought; of all the women in the world, he had to turn into a weak-kneed puppy in the presence of one woman he couldn't have—

"Something bothering you, Ned?" Charlton's words jarred Justine from his reverie. He realized in embarrassment he had been standing in the knee-deep waters of the

Concho, boots off and trousers rolled up, staring into the distance for quite a while.

"No, not really," Justine said self-consciously. "Just woolgathering, I guess."

"We could all stand to do more of it when we have time. At least for now, we can afford to daydream a minute or two without the chance of losing our hair," Charlton said. "I think I know what's on your mind, Ned. I'd feel the same way in your boots. I'm not sure I'd have your self-control. I might be tempted to take the chance. She's quite a girl."

Justine didn't reply. Dammit, he wondered, did everybody in the whole army know? How could it possibly have been *that* obvious when he'd gone to such pain and effort to hide it?

To cover the sudden flush in his cheeks, he returned to probing the bottom for the sweetwater mussels of the Concho. The shellfish were an unexpected life form out here in what seemed to be mostly near-desert constantly scoured by hot, dry wind. Their meat, sweet and succulent, provided a welcome break in the unimaginative army chow, a treat that reminded him of home and long-ago visits to the Maine shoreline on clam digs.

Already, Justine had accumulated a sizeable number of freshwater pearls, small pebbles in a rainbow of colors. He intended to have them made into a necklace for his mother when his tour of duty ended with the dawn of the coming year.

That dawn couldn't come too soon.

"Justine!"

Ned glanced up at the call from the bank of the Concho. "Yes, Captain Carter?"

"Hate to interrupt your fishing, but Colonel Mackenzie wants to see you," Carter said. "His quarters."

Justine's nerves twanged taut. "Yes, sir. As soon as I can change into uniform," he said as he waded to the bank.

"Don't bother. I think the colonel meant he wants to see you *now.*"

Justine hurriedly dried his legs and feet, pulled on his socks and boots, and strode toward the post, feeling out of place in the civilian clothes he wore when off duty. He paused for a moment on the crude boardwalk outside Mackenzie's quarters, wiped the sweat from the brutal August sun off his face as best he could, then knocked softly. At Mackenzie's call to enter, he removed his battered hat and stepped inside.

Mackenzie stood behind a table strewn with papers, his brow furrowed in thought, studying a map tacked against a wall. Except for Comanchero roads snaking from Caprock into New Mexico, and a couple of trails Justine and Thompson had located, most of the map of the Staked Plains remained marked "Unknown."

"Corporal Justine reporting, sir," Ned said, snapping his best salute as Mackenzie glanced up. "Captain Carter said you wanted to see me."

"Ah, yes. Come in, Corporal." Mackenzie waved his damaged hand toward a chair across from the desk. "Have a seat." The colonel propped a hip on the edge of the desk, half sitting and half leaning, as Justine sat, back straight, boot soles flat on the floor.

"At ease, Justine. Relax. I haven't summoned you here to bite an ear off."

Justine relaxed as best he could, but the knot in his gut tied itself tighter. Enlisted men didn't get summoned to the regimental commander's office unless they were due a butt chewing that their company officers couldn't deliver with the proper emphasis.

Mackenzie didn't speak for a moment, idly tapping the nub of a pencil against his thigh, staring at the map. Then he said, "I need you to answer a few questions for me, Justine. In confidence."

"Yes, sir."

"I need to ask you, outside of Elijah Thompson's presence, to again confirm the information the two of you forwarded to me at Fort Clark after your lengthy scout across the Staked Plains."

Justine felt a sudden thirst. It always came when he recalled the swollen tongue, cracked lips, raging sun and scouring wind, and the body's agonized screams for water, during those two long months afield.

The tap of pencil stub on thigh stopped. Mackenzie lifted an eyebrow. "It isn't that I disbelieve Thompson's observations. He's a superb scout. But at times, his hatred of Indians seems to cloud his judgment.

"Now to the heart of the matter. Do you personally, based on your own observations during that scout, believe that a major band of Comanches and their allies will be wintering somewhere along the headwaters of the Red River?"

"Yes, sir, I do," Justine said. He was surprised that his voice didn't quaver.

"Yet you saw no signs of any large bands."

"No, sir. What we observed were many old trails, obviously well used over the years—perhaps for generations—all leading toward the northeast of our route, in the general direction of the Red River's source. The few reasonably fresh tracks we did find also pointed in that direction, both on the southern Staked Plains and in the breaks below the Caprock itself."

"I see," Mackenzie said thoughtfully, "and how do you account for the apparent absence of any large Indian bodies on the move?"

"It is my opinion, Colonel, that the major bands were all to the north and northeast at the time, raiding along the Arkansas and beyond, taking revenge for their defeat at Adobe Walls. Only a few smaller bands have attacked settlers and wagons on the upper Brazos watershed in the last few months."

Mackenzie nodded. "That jibes with other reports of atrocities forwarded to me. It's strange, but the Indians may not realize their defeat at Adobe Walls was, in fact, a tactical victory. The buffalo hunters have all withdrawn from the Panhandle. Fear of Indian depredations has pushed the frontier back almost to Jacksboro."

Mackenzie paused for a moment, studying the map. "Now for the big question. Can you and Mr. Thompson, supplemented by a larger band of scouts, locate the Indians' winter camp?"

Justine paused for a moment, lips pursed, then shook his head. "I can't promise that, sir. Perhaps we could, perhaps not. The Red River watershed is a big country. The Staked Plains are laced with many unexpected canyons, deep arroyos, and numerous tributaries flowing into Red River. To date, only a fraction of that country has been scouted. Or even seen by a white man's eyes."

Mackenzie started tapping the pencil again, then nodded. "I appreciate your candor, Corporal Justine. Had you blithely said, 'We can damn sure find it,' as did Mr. Thompson, I might have had to question your judgment. As I do his, in that particular regard."

Mackenzie eased away from the desk and began pacing. For several minutes, Justine wondered if he had been dismissed without realizing it. He decided the best course of action was to sit and wait. Mackenzie would tell him to leave when he wanted him out.

After a time, Mackenzie turned to Justine. "Now, Ned"—the colonel's use of his first name startled Justine—"what I'm about to tell you is not to leave this room. I must ask you to keep it totally confidential until final plans are firmed."

"Of course, sir."

The colonel started pacing again. "The Quaker policy of Indian pacification has failed miserably, as I suspected it would. The problem has now been turned over to the army, and the Fourth has been assigned a major portion of that problem.

"We—the whole of the Department of the Missouri forces—are to open a four-pronged offensive against the Indians. A fall and winter campaign, when the Indians will not be expecting such a move. General Miles will lead a column south from Fort Dodge. Colonel Davidson will drive west from Fort Sill, Major Price east from Fort Bascom in New Mexico. The Fourth will move north from Fort Concho. The idea is to put pressure on the Indians, squeeze them into a small area where they can be decisively whipped. This war must be brought to an end."

Mackenzie stopped pacing and fixed a steady gaze on Justine. "I want you and Thompson, working with Charlton and his scouts, to find that winter camp. If you have no questions, that will be all for now."

"Yes, sir." Justine stood, hesitated for a moment, then decided to take the gamble, whether it earned him a scathing tongue-lashing or not. "Colonel, I do have one question. Why are you telling me this? I'm only a corporal, not a student of field tactics."

"Because I want you to fully grasp the importance of your assignment. And to assure you that I have the utmost faith in your abilities, Ned. You've established a proven record as an honest man with a cool head and gained a reputation as a warrior of the first rank."

"Begging the colonel's pardon and with thanks, sir, but I see myself only as a common soldier doing his duty. As a reluctant warrior at best."

Mackenzie placed an almost fatherly hand on Justine's shoulder. "Give me a thousand such reluctant warriors and I'll give back ten thousand glory hounds—and win this war with that one thousand." The hand fell away.

"This campaign isn't about just killing Indians. It's about forcing them to end hostilities by any means possible. I intend to borrow a page from General Sherman's book. A scorched earth policy to leave the Indians afoot, with no food, clothing, or shelter. That will end the Red River War with as little loss of life as possible on either side." Mackenzie returned to his desk and sat.

Justine assumed he had been dismissed and turned for the door.

"Ned?"

"Yes, sir?"

"One more item. Your enlistment is up at the end of the year. I hate to lose a good man. Any chance I can talk you into staying with the Fourth?"

Justine sighed and shook his head. "Sorry, sir. I just want to go home, go to college, study engineering. I want to learn how to build, not destroy."

Mackenzie half smiled. "Engineering. A most laudable profession." The colonel's voice softened. "If you change your mind, you have a home in the Fourth. Go back to gathering your shellfish, son. We won't have much spare time before we begin preparations to move out. Might as well take advantage of it."

"Thank you, sir."

As he stepped from the doorway into the bright white summer sunlight, Justine realized he had been sweating even more profusely inside the colonel's office.

He knew he should feel honored and flattered that the commanding officer, a full colonel and a war hero brevet general, would confide in a mere corporal.

All he could truly feel was relief at being dismissed. And the first glimmer of that familiar cold spot in his belly. . . .

Badger squatted in the shade cast by his black buffalo hunting pony, honing the skinning knife dulled by peeling many hides, and smiled in satisfaction as Star stripped buffalo entrails with her fingers and fed pieces of the delicacy to Ecapusia.

Pihpitz sat at Badger's side, trying his best to look stoic and calm, but unable to hide the pride that swelled his chest.

It was a time to be proud. For both father and son.

Young Horsefly had made his first kill on this hunt. He placed the arrow well, driven deep between the ribs of a yearling buffalo. The boy's immediate prize had been a choice chunk of liver flavored with bile. His second prize would come later, when his father and others stood before the entire band and vouched for his prowess as a hunter.

The youth's face glowed from more than just pride, Badger noted. The harsh sun on the rolling plains miles west of the river the white man called the Pecos had again burned his fair skin. Horsefly lost his hat during the chase, and it wasn't until much later that they had a chance to return for the leather headgear with its floppy sunshade brim.

Pihpitz's skin refused to darken. His white heritage showed in the red hair and constant peeling of his freckled cheeks and nose. But not in his heart. Horsefly was Comanche where it counted.

Badger glanced up as Yellowfish reined in, his own hunting pony lathered, its gaunt flanks heaving.

"The chase is ended?" Badger asked.

Yellowfish nodded. "It ends well. If Quanah's hunt in the falling leaf time goes as well, there will be no empty bellies among our people." Yellowfish dismounted, the fluid movement belying his awkward gait afoot. He squatted beside Pihpitz and clapped a hand on the boy's shoulder. "I saw. Horsefly has proven himself a great hunter today. I shall speak on his behalf at the harvest feast."

The boy's grin grew even wider. He said, "I would be honored," and then set off on the extended tale of how Pamo, his paint hunting pony, had run alongside the buffalo to give him a clean bow shot, then whirled aside to barely escape the stubby horns as the mortally wounded animal thrust its head at the pony's ribs. "Tobacco is a fine horse, wise for his years," Horsefly concluded.

Both adults listened in silent respect to the somewhat lengthy story, then nodded in unison.

"Pamo will carry you to many kills, Horsefly," Yellowfish said. "You must continue to treat him with the kindness and care you show a best friend."

The trio sat for a time in silence, watching Star and Turns-Over-Turtles finish butchering the buffalo nearby, listening to the squeals of delight from younger children as their mothers carved up and handed out choice morsels.

Badger saw other women, little more than specks in the distance, at work around larger, darker specks. The hunting party was spread over quite some distance. This small herd had bolted more quickly than others.

That the hunt had been difficult and dangerous, or that they had to travel much farther toward the sun's bed, into the land the whites called New Mexico, to find the animals, did not matter now. Buffalo went where water and grass were to be had. The rains had come late to the big grass country.

This particular hunt had been early, beneath the hot rays of the sun. These hides would be far from prime. The buffalo still wore summer hair instead of long, shaggy winter coats. The resulting robes would not be as warm when the cold winds came from the north. But the hides would serve adequately as lodge covers, for repairs, and to make new winter dwellings for many poor families who came almost with each sun, seeking refuge with the Quahadis. The skin of younger animals such as Horsefly's would provide clothing to those in need.

The unseasonable hunt had been necessary. Meat was the greatest need as Quanah's band grew. The flesh would be less succulent and tender, given the lack of fat on the animals. But it would fill bellies.

Badger gestured toward the distant figures. "Runs-With-Antelope works among them?" he asked Yellowfish.

"Yes. Her husband managed to find a few buffalo who had stumbled, fallen, and broken their necks," Yellowfish said solemnly.

The two men and the boy chuckled at Yellowfish's small joke. The slender Comanche was one of the better hunters of the band, as competent as Badger himself.

"Her time nears," Badger said, squinting toward the distant figures.

"Yes. Soon after the time of falling leaves."

"The child will be your new friend. I saw in a night vision, a dream. A fine, healthy young boy."

Yellowfish's eyes brightened. "I have seen this same night vision, so it must be so, brother." After a moment, the gleam faded. "The last few moons have been a difficult time."

Badger nodded, his brow furrowed.

It had been a difficult summer. The defeat at the hands of the hide hunters at their river village seemed to have angered the spirits. The memory of the Adobe Walls disaster brought the bitter taste back to Badger's mouth. Isatai should have suffered more than loss of prestige and banishment for his inept magic.

But what was done was done. It could not be undone.

Raids against the Texans and their white cousins to the north provided a measure of revenge for the losses at Adobe Walls. But since that painful battle, game had been even more scarce than Badger could remember. The People had wandered far in search of buffalo, elk, and even deer and antelope.

There had been no chance to raid into Mexico for captives, horses, and other plunder. The soldier chief Bad Hand and his warriors prowled the lands along the big river. Had it been any soldier chief but Bad Hand, it wouldn't have mattered. They would have gone anyway. Since it was Bad Hand, it would have been too great a risk.

Bad Hand had made other problems for The People.

The number of Comanchero traders now willing to venture into Quahadi lands had sharply dwindled for fear of the soldier chief. That source of much needed supplies, once a river, narrowed to a scant trickle, like the streams in the big grass country in times of little rain like these.

"Your spirit is troubled, brother."

Badger glanced at Yellowfish and shrugged. "It is nothing."

"I, too, worry about the future, Badger. I fear no man. But those who dismiss Bad Hand as but a fleeting shadow may find themselves walking the darkness. He becomes more Indian than white with the changing of the seasons, and thus more dangerous to The People."

Yellowfish's words again startled Badger. It seemed that Yellowfish could read his own heart, hear his own thoughts.

"I am concerned not just about the coming time of snows, but beyond," Yellowfish continued as he peered into the distance. Then he turned to Badger and smiled. "But this is no time for shadows. Let us listen to the cries of happiness from the children, the laughter of women, and let our spirits be at peace."

Badger nodded. "It is so, my brother. By the time of turning leaves we will be in the Place of Chinaberry Trees. Our women, children, and elders will be safe there, where we will welcome your new friend."

Yellowfish's smile widened. "Yes, we will be safe there, our lodges warm. Bad Hand will not find us. The Great Spirit gave The People that place, and will turn away those who would intrude." The expression in his eyes turned wistful. "It will gladden my heart to welcome my new friend into the world in such a place of magic."

Badger cocked an eyebrow at Yellowfish, a slight smile lifting his own lips. "Once you wisely told me, brother, when Star's time neared, that I should search for a second wife to ease her labor. Have you followed your own advice?"

"I have. Blushes-Often, the younger sister of Runs-With-Antelope."

Badger nodded in approval. "It is good. Sisters make the best wives. Blushes-Often is young and strong." He winked at Yellowfish. "She does not hurt the eyes when one looks upon her, either. When the time comes, if you wish, I would be honored to speak with Para-a-Coom on your behalf."

Yellowfish frowned. "It will be a hard trade. Her father will ask a high price."

"Not that hard. I have come to know his weaknesses." Badger clapped Yellowfish on the shoulder. "You will not be left a poor man, brother. Trust me in this matter." He rose. "Now, let us get back to present business. We will camp at Sweet Spring until the meat harvested here has been racked and dried and the hides scraped."

He placed his other hand on Horsefly's shoulder and again was somewhat startled at the solid muscles, the chest more broad and strong than most youths his age. "At Sweet Spring during the feast honoring this hunt, I shall tell The People of my pride in my son, Pihpitz, and of his bravery and skill on the hunt. Today, he ceased to be a boy. He is a man."

Horsefly's chest swelled even more. Try as he might, the boy could not remain solemn. He couldn't hold back a broad grin.

"The horses have rested," Badger said, "and the butchering is nearly finished. Come, Horsefly. Help me find saplings in the stand of trees in the distance. We will need travois to carry the cured meat and our other fruits of the hunt. With the next fat moon we begin our return to the Place of the Chinaberry Trees."

20

JUSTINE STARTED AT the touch on his shoulder and realized he had been dozing in the saddle again.

"Stay sharp, son," Lige Thompson said. "We could ride into a nest of Injuns any minute now."

Justine shook his head, trying to chase the fog from his brain. "Sorry, Lige."

"I'm a tad tuckered myself, but this ain't no time for nappin'. We're close. We know it. Worse yet, they know it." The old frontiersman's leathery face and alert eyes showed no outward sign of his professed exhaustion. Thompson's nostrils flared as he tested the cold north wind. "We're so close I can damn near smell 'em."

Justine lifted his face into the wind, hoping the cold would jolt his scratchy lids fully open and restore his senses. He couldn't remember the last time he had slept. The wind didn't clear his mind as much as Thompson's reminder that survival depended upon who spotted who first. He knew Indians were nearby. And that for now the Indians held the high hole card.

They knew where the soldiers were.

A couple of minor skirmishes and one major clash within the last week had established that fact. Six days ago Charlton and his band of Seminole Negro scouts had traded shots with a mixed band of Kiowas and Comanches. The Seminoles killed one Indian in another skirmish. And less than forty-eight hours back, a war party tried to raid Mackenzie's horse herd. Company A fought off the attack. At least fifteen warriors died in the battle. Pursuit of the raiders did nothing but wear down cavalry horses. The Indians simply disappeared from the treeless prairie as if swallowed by the flat earth itself.

So far Mackenzie's command had suffered no casualties other than a few wounded horses. But if the Indians attacked in force, Bad Hand might be in serious trouble. A blinding rainstorm three days past had turned the big grass country of the lower Texas Panhandle into a quagmire, all but impassable. The quartermaster corps managed to get only one wagon through the muck. The rest of the supply train lagged far behind under the guard of infantry troops.

Mackenzie had made one decision that lifted the morale of the weary, storm-battered troopers. He left Lieutenant Hopkins in command of the infantry guarding the wagon train. Mackenzie obviously was aware of the disdain the soldiers felt toward the gutless Hopkins. Why the colonel hadn't cashiered the lieutenant for cowardice, only Mackenzie knew. It was enough that he now kept Hopkins away from any situation where he might get men killed.

Which, Justine reminded himself, might happen at any time. So far, luck and the Plains Indian concept of warfare had kept the campaign from being a complete failure and possibly a rout of Mackenzie's command. Several times on this long campaign, Bad Hand's column had been strung out in scattered units, fighting its way through deep mud, soldiers half-asleep in the saddle, vulnerable to any massive attack.

Such an attack had never come.

The Plains tribes might be the finest guerrilla fighters and best light cavalry to ever straddle a horse, but their culture had been built for generation upon generation of quick, slashing raids that carried maximum odds of success with minimum losses. By nature and training, they were reluctant to mount a mass assault on a large enemy force. The battering they had taken at Adobe Walls reinforced that belief.

That there had to be a sizeable Indian camp somewhere

nearby was equally obvious. Justine, Thompson, and their band of Tonkawa scouts had cut sign on many fresh trails before and after the storms—trails that varied from one rider to as many as twenty or thirty sets of pony tracks. Charlton and his Seminoles, veterans of the Apache campaign along the Rio Grande, had found similar sign. Most of the trails led northeast.

Justine shivered under the bite of the late September wind. He had been on the Staked Plains many times, but the vagaries of weather still caught him by surprise. At noon they might ride through heat waves under a cloudless, brassy sky; two hours later through cold, blustery, wet northers or booming thunderstorms. It should have been the end of summer, but nights out here felt more like the dead of winter—

A shrill whistle cut through Justine's dark musings. He glanced to his left. Two hundred yards away, Whiskey Pete waved his hat above his head.

Thompson stared toward the Tonkawa for a moment, then grunted. "Looks like that damn useless Tonk's stumbled onto somethin' accidental-like. Reckon we better see what's got the heathen's breechclout in a knot."

Moments later, the two reined in beside Pete at the edge of a wide swath of trampled grass churned into mud by the passage of hundreds, maybe thousands, of hooves. Individual moccasin prints, dog tracks, and the distinctive gouges left by travois poles told Justine this was no small band of raiders. It was the movement of a large village, women and children included, the biggest Indian trail he had ever seen. Justine's heart leapt into his throat, his exhaustion forgotten for the moment.

"You want Injun, Butt Kicker, you got 'im." Whiskey Pete slipped into the pidgin dialect he adopted when he wanted to rile Thompson. "Heap bunch Injuns up ahead. Peel creaky old scout's pale skin first, cook 'im later. Feed to camp dogs, make dogs heap sick. Mebbe so dogs die."

Thompson glanced up, anger flashing in his eyes.

"Mind your tongue, you heathen bastard, or I'll lift your scalp first!"

"Pete not squaw or papoose," the scout said with a laconic shrug. "Not so easy Kicker lift Pete's hair. Mebbe so Pete save other Injuns trouble."

The old frontiersman glared hard at the Tonkawa for a moment, then snorted in dismissal. "I'll kick your rusty butt later. Right now I ain't got the time. 'Pears you somehow stumbled onto somethin' for once in your misbegot life." Thompson turned to one of the other scouts. "Job, get your red ass in gear and fetch Charlton. Tell 'im it looks like we found his Injuns."

Badger stood just inside the lodge entrance and struggled to control his growing anger toward the man seated across the way.

Badger had made no attempt to clean the dried blood from his upper arm where a rifle ball gouged out a chunk of muscle during the futile attempt to steal the horse soldier's pony herd.

O-ha-ma-tai, the leader of the largest Comanche band remaining in the camp in the Place of the Chinaberry Trees, again shook his head as he puffed on his pipe.

"Tabi unuu frets like an old woman." The sarcastic tone of O-ha-ma-tai's words added a sting to the rebuke. "The horse soldiers will never find us here."

A muscle twitched in Badger's jaw. "They will find us. Their chiefs of scouts, the soldier Charlton, the ancient one called Thompson, and the young warrior who rides with the old one are like the wolf on the trail of a crippled buffalo."

The Comanche chief waved his pipe stem as if dismissing a pesky fly. "The Great Spirit will turn their ponies aside. It has always been so in this place."

Badger forced himself to unclench his fist. He had to try at least one more time. "O-ha-ma-tai, think back on

Mow-way. He, too, made the mistake of underestimating this white war chief. Bad Hand's scouts will find us. He will attack."

"You have such powerful medicine visions as to foretell the future?"

"What I have seen the last few days is no vision. Bad Hand comes with many men, four times four more than we have to stop him." Badger's anger almost boiled to the surface as the skeptical expression remained on the chief's face.

"It will not happen. The Great Spirit has spoken of this to many chiefs of much power." O-ha-ma-tai bent his head to concentrate on refilling his pipe.

"Then at least double the lookouts." Badger was pleading now. Logic had not worked. "Send word for the warriors to prepare their weapons and stand ready. Post our best rifle shooters along the canyon walls. Move the main pony herd, the women, children, and old ones back to a place of greater safety, with all the supplies they can quickly gather."

O-ha-ma-tai didn't bother to look up. "There is no need. It will not happen."

Badger's heart sank into a dark pit. This stubborn chief had just pronounced a death sentence upon the village. He spun on a heel and stalked from the lodge, ignoring the leave-taking ritual as O-ha-ma-tai had ignored his warning.

If only Quanah were here, Badger thought, perhaps at least some lives might be saved. But Quanah was far away, with most of the warriors of his Quahadi band, on the annual hunt in the time of turning leaves. Of Quanah's best fighting men, only Badger, Yellowfish, and a handful of others had stayed behind.

None of the other chiefs—Iron Shirt of the Southern Cheyennes, Maman-ti of the Kiowas—would listen. They believed O-ha-ma-tai. Because they wished to believe, Badger thought bitterly. He squared his shoulders. If O-ha-ma-tai would not save his people, at least Badger's own might survive. If he acted quickly.

He found Yellowfish rubbing bear grease and crushed sage into a shallow bullet crease along his war pony's upper leg, another legacy of the failed attempt to stampede Bad Hand's horses.

Yellowfish glanced up, an unasked question in his eyes.

Badger shook his head. "He would not listen, my brother. O-ha-ma-tai sacrifices his people on the stone ledge of his stubborn beliefs. His eyes are blind and his ears deaf." He placed a hand on his brother's shoulder.

"You must save our families and those of our wives. Runs-With-Antelope's time is but a few suns away. You must take her to a place of safety, far from here. Quickly, before Moon raises his face, strike our lodges. Have the women pack as much as they can. Take our own horses. Leave two of my best war ponies for me and take the rest. Flee before Bad Hand comes."

"But you, my brother—"

"I stay. O-ha-ma-tai will not organize a fight against the horse soldiers. Someone must hold them back as long as possible. Some of the warriors here will believe my words."

A quick stab of inner pain flickered in Yellowfish's dark eyes. "You will join us later?"

"If the spirits will it so." Badger said solemnly. "If I die here, take Star, my sons, and Turns-Over-Turtles into your lodge. Add my ponies to your herd." Yellowfish started to protest. Badger cut him off. "There is no time to argue. We must begin immediately if our families are to live."

Yellowfish finally nodded. "Where should we go that Bad Hand will not track us down?"

"To any place safe from the horse soldiers." Badger took a deep breath, then said the unthinkable. "Even to the reservation lands, should you feel it necessary. I ask much of you, Yellowfish, as I did once before. Again I ask you to save my family and yours. It is more to ask than an honorable death on the field of battle. For this my heart is heavy."

"Come with us, Badger."

"No. I must stay. There is much to be done. The horse soldiers will be here soon."

Justine crabbed on hands and knees to the edge of the deep chasm he had almost ridden into in the near darkness. The sun didn't slowly sink into the west out here. Night slammed down with an almost audible thud.

He heard his own soft gasp of surprise echoed by Charlton, the quiet grunt of satisfaction from Whiskey Pete, and the grating of Lige Thompson's teeth.

Barely visible in the deepening gloom, a string of lodges lined the narrow stream of the Prairie Dog Town Fork of the Red River five hundred feet below. The lodges stretched as far as the eye could see. Ponies staked beside some lodges were but small dots of deeper shadow. Justine saw no sign of individual Indians moving about, only the pale glow of fading fires.

"There's your Injuns, Kicker," Pete said, his words little more than a whisper. "Heap bunch dirty heathen redskins."

"You got that much right, you damned cannibal," Thompson growled. "What you make of it, Ned?"

Justine squinted into the darkness. "Like Pete said, heap bunch redskins. Probably more than two hundred lodges. Judging from the way the village is laid out, I'd say Comanche, Kiowa, a few Cheyennes. Big pony herd, maybe a couple thousand animals."

"Pretty fair job of lookin' for a greenhorn," Thompson said. "Funny. You and me'd've found this place last summer if we'd rode just another fifty miles or so north, Ned. Now, what's the biggest problem gettin' to these Injuns?"

"Just that. Getting to them. The only way in appears to be from the south, through the canyon valley. If we went in that way, they could make it tough. Maybe wipe us out if they've got lookouts posted. There has to be a trail down from the other end of the canyon, but it would take days to circle around. They could easily spot any massive troop movements like that. Your opinion, Sergeant?"

Charlton didn't answer for a moment as he studied the extended line of lodges, then sighed. "You nailed the tactical problem, Ned—getting troops down there without losing the element of surprise."

After a moment, Charlton waved the scouts back from the lip of the canyon, to where Job, the scout who spoke the best English among the Seminoles, held the horses. "Job, get to Colonel Mackenzie. Tell him what we've found. And that by the time he gets here, we'll have found a way down."

Job mounted and disappeared into the night.

"Lige, you and Ned scout north from here," Charlton said. "Pete and I'll ride south. Look for any passable trail down. In a quarter hour we'll have decent starlight, later a moon. We have to find that trail before Mackenzie gets here. That should be an hour or two before dawn."

The next few hours seemed to be the longest that Justine had ever spent.

The ticking of the clock in his head compounded the weight on his shoulders and the heaviness in his legs. His hip hurt from the cold and from walking, leading the horses, unwilling to risk being skylined, or crouching over to peer at the ground in the blackness. Several times they were forced to mount and ride around deep arroyos or juniper-choked feeder canyons.

Twice they had doubled back, retracing their steps in pale moonlight and inky black shadows as the search carried them too far north of the main body of lodges below.

Justine glanced at the sky. The cold fist of desperation tightened its grip on the cold spot in his belly. The stars said they were running out of time—

"Ned." Thompson's soft voice from the canyon rim a few feet away held a note of satisfaction. "We got it. Rode right past it a few hours back. Ease over here and take a look."

Justine limped to the juniper stand where the old scout squatted. "Here she is," Thompson said.

Ned studied the narrow game trail that angled down the sheer canyon wall. "You've got to be kidding, Lige," he said after a moment. "A goat would have trouble with that. We'd have to go single file—"

"No time to find nothin' better, even if there is one. Was I one of them Injuns down there, I'd never figure horse soldiers to come down this trail." His tone tightened. "Ain't gonna have a better chance to wipe out them savages once and for all. We'll pick up Charlton and let Bad Hand know there's a way to get down there."

"Lige, they could pick us off on the way down. Half a dozen good shots would have us cold on that trail."

"Maybe they could if they was smart enough to know we'd take the hard way. But they know the white man's lazy, likes to do things without puttin' out much effort. Take another look, son. You see any signs of this here trail bein' used lately?"

Justine didn't.

"Then likely them Injuns don't even know it's here, or forgot about it. Let's mount up. Bad Hand ain't gonna be far off by now."

Sunrise was still two hours away as the group of scouts knelt beside Mackenzie, who squatted in the mud and studied the map scratched into a slab of saddle skirting leather. The tracings of Thompson's knife point were barely visible in the weak light of a half-shield camp lantern.

The jangle of bits, creak of saddle leather, snorting and pawing of cavalry mounts, the soft murmurs of muted conversations among the troops seemed loud to Justine—loud enough that, in his state of heightened tension, it seemed the Indians camped below could hear every word. He knew that wasn't possible, not with the wind in their faces and the distance involved. The knowledge didn't warm the chill of dread in his belly.

"Very well, gentlemen," Mackenzie said calmly. "We attack in at first light. Sergeant Charlton, you will take your scouts down and open the fight."

"Ned and me'll lead the way," Thompson said.

Mackenzie nodded. "As you wish. I'll bring Second Battalion down immediately behind the scouts. First Battalion will remain on the flats above to cut off any Indian retreat or provide reinforcements for us if necessary." The colonel glanced at each of the officers gathered around. "Remind your men that a silent approach is our best weapon. Inform the buglers there will be no calls sounded until the enemy is fully engaged, and then only at my order. Understood?"

At the ensuing nods, Mackenzie rolled the stiff leather sketch and tucked it beneath his arm. "It must be a swift and decisive attack, gentlemen. The initial charge must sweep through and decimate the Indian ranks."

The colonel paused for a moment. "We may never again be presented with such an opportunity to end the Indian resistance with a single such stroke, gentlemen. Let's make it count."

Badger sat behind the cluster of boulders, his rifle barrel resting across a rolled blanket, his bow and quiver slung across his back and his medicine bag around his neck. He tried to calm the spirits warring in his breast.

His fingertips brushed against the soft elkskin sash tied around his waist. Though he now considered himself Comanche, his Kiowa blood flickered to life soon after his vigil began.

Badger knew he would die here. He knew as surely as if the Great Spirit had spoken directly in his ear.

He would die as a Koisenko. When the final stand came, he would drive an arrow through the trailing end of the elkskin sash into the ground—the final gesture of the great Kiowa warrior society. He knew there would be no one to pull the arrow free and release him from the Koisenko vow.

Already he had spoken with the spirit of his father. He knew Hawk Chaser looked down upon him with pride.

His own pending death was of little consequence; it did not stir his troubled spirit. Yet a feeling of sadness remained, the lingering sensation of the final embraces of his sons and wives and his brother Yellowfish. The sadness warred with anger and disgust and dismay. Anger at the stubborn chiefs who refused to see danger. Disgust at the many men who scoffed at his warnings and went to the warm comfort of their robes and their women. Dismay that he had failed to stir so many from their apathy, their certainty that no white man would ever find the Place of the Chinaberry Trees. Pain at the coming end of so many lives. Perhaps the end of The People themselves.

His arguments and pleadings had gained but a handful of believers. No more than thirty warriors now slept with war ponies roped to wrists or staked outside lodges, weapons within easy reach. Just seven young men, all unproven in battle, watched over the pony herd in the side canyon. Only two veteran warriors agreed with Badger on the need to establish lookouts.

When Bad Hand came, the village was his.

All Badger could hope for was to fight a delaying action. To give the women, children, and elders a chance to escape.

It was not much of a hope. It was all he had. That, and to kill as many of the horse soldiers as possible before his final stand. And if the spirits willed, one chance to rip away the scalp of the hated old man with long gray hair. The scout named Thompson, who had stalked and slain The People for so many years.

Badger idly wondered if he would again face Thompson's young friend, the man who had wounded him and been wounded by Badger during the fight for Mow-way's village. He hoped so. If the spirits so willed, it seemed only fitting that they should again face each other. One or the other, but not both, would ride away from this Place of the Chinaberry Trees.

It was as if Badger could sense the presence of the old scout and the young warrior. As if their gaze already rested upon him.

He prayed it was so. To die in such a sacred place as this, in the defense of his people, would be an assurance of admission to the afterlife.

Badger's own preparations for battle were complete, his war paint applied, half his face now as black as the night sky, the other half streaked and dotted in yellow and vermillion, his long hair pulled into a single braid and tied with a red ribbon from Star's favorite dress. A similar red ribbon fluttered from the forelock of his war horse, a sturdy gelding the color of the sun. At times the yellow horse nudged Badger's back or shoulder as if to reassure his friend of the bravery of both. The feathers, scalp locks, and tufts of horsehair ringing Badger's war shield rippled in the cold wind.

He was prepared.

Overhead, the stars continued their ride across the sky. The sliver of moon had gone to its sleeping robes, leaving the shadows blobs of impenetrable darkness, even for one whose night sight was as keen as Badger's.

He did not need sunlight to know Bad Hand was nearby.

The first faint streaks of gray brushed the eastern horizon as Justine and Thompson reined in at the edge of the canyon and the beginning of the narrow trail down the steep wall.

Justine fumbled for a moment while pulling the girth tight on his horse, the stiff chill in his fingers unrelated to the bite of the wind. He fought back the sudden lurch of nausea that threatened to well up into his throat, nodded to Thompson, and glanced around the scout troop.

They were veterans, this mixture of Tonkawa red men, dark-skinned Seminoles, and white scouts. The kind of seasoned fighters a man wanted at his side when he rode into battle. Behind the scout company the black mass of Mackenzie's Raiders, Second Battalion, silently tightened girths and checked weapons.

After what seemed to be hours and a fleeting instant at the same time, Mackenzie reined his horse to a stop facing Thompson, Justine, Charlton, and Whiskey Pete.

"Gentlemen, lead the way," the colonel said.

21

LIGE THOMPSON SEEMED to drop off the edge of the earth.

A heartbeat after the old scout spurred his horse over the lip of the canyon, Justine could no longer see man or mount. He did hear the faint hiss of sand and shale beneath the horse's hooves and Thompson's muttered curse as a dislodged stone ticked down the steep canyon wall.

Justine took a deep breath and kneed his own mount over the rim onto the narrow, twisting trail, barely visible in the pale gray light. He could see only a few feet; below his right stirrup the trail seemed to drop straight down into a black hole of nothingness. A misstep, a stumble, or a slip on a smooth rock would send both man and mount tumbling to sure death down the almost vertical cliff.

Justine gave the buckskin its head and leaned back, his weight forward against the narrow stirrups of the McClellan saddle. His heart lurched at each slight slip of the buckskin's hooves. The horse fluttered its nostrils, head held low as if studying its next step. Justine realized he had been holding his breath. He gasped in a lungful of the sharp morning air and forced himself to breathe as naturally as he could.

A small avalanche of soil, shale, and pebbles slid past him as other riders followed. The narrow trail allowed passage of only one horse at a time. Each creak of saddle leather, snort of a nervous horse, jangle of bit or curb strap, clink of shod hoof, or clatter of a dislodged stone tightened Justine's throat. The muted sounds seemed to build to a tumultuous racket in his ears.

He tried not to dwell on all that could go wrong during the long, agonizingly slow descent. A falling horse, an inadvertent, startled yelp from a rider, the accidental discharge of a rifle or handgun, a cry from an Indian lookout in the camp below, and the men on the canyon wall would be easy targets for any riflemen waiting in ambush.

The far wall of the canyon, a black mass looming against the pale gray of the eastern sky, lay more than five hundred yards away—too far for accurate shooting from that vantage point. The real hazard lay below, where fallen boulders, rock outcrops, piles of driftwood, and brush clumps provided cover and a good field of fire for any waiting Indian.

Justine realized his palms had begun to sweat, heated by sizzling nerves. He could only pray that Thompson was right, that the Indians would not be expecting an attacking force to come down the side of the canyon, but up the valley from the south. Or that they would not anticipate an attack at all, secure in their belief the soldiers would never find the secluded winter camp. If the old frontiersman was wrong, a lot of good men would die on the side of this canyon.

The muscles of Justine's jaws, buttocks, belly, and thighs yelped from tension and raw fear as his buckskin passed the midpoint of the descent. He chanced a quick glance over his shoulder. The long line of horsemen behind him snaked all the way to the top of the rim, with another appearing every few heartbeats. Justine knew the better part of an hour would pass before the last of the sixty riders in the scout troop reached the canyon floor. Longer for Mackenzie's Second Battalion. And the light seemed to grow brighter with each skidding step of the buckskin's hooves—

A distant yell and a single rifle shot all but stopped Justine's heart.

They had been spotted.

He braced himself for a storm of lead to rake the column snaking its way down the canyon wall. . . .

➣ ➣ ➣

The warning shot and cry sent a bolt of alarm through Badger's veins.

For a few heartbeats he thought the warning might have been a false alarm; from his lookout post partway up the east canyon wall, he saw nothing but emptiness in the valley to the south, from where he expected any attack to come.

At the edge of his vision he caught a glimpse of movement across the canyon. The small dark shapes of many horsemen, riding one behind the other, snapped into focus. The white men had come down the *side* of the canyon. The shadowy blobs stretched from near the valley floor to the top of the wall, a line of ants on the march.

Badger levered a cartridge into his rifle, though the range was too great for the weapon. He tore his gaze from the distant line of ants and stared toward the village.

There was no sign of movement. Not a single man emerged from his lodge or hurried to horse. It was as if the entire camp still slept.

Badger barked an oath even as his heart sank in his chest. If only they had listened. Half a dozen good rifle shots could have dropped the lead horses, blocked the trail, and the soldiers could have been picked off one at a time. Now it was too late. All he could do was try to rally enough men to fight a rear guard, to give the women and children time to escape.

He vaulted onto the back of the palomino and kicked the horse into a run toward the village, shouting orders as he rode.

➣ ➣ ➣

A sense of relief momentarily warmed the cold knot of fear in Justine's belly as his buckskin reached the bottom of the steep trail.

Despite the warning cry and gunshot, no storm of lead had engulfed them on the way down. Even now there were few Indians stirring in the first of the three villages strung out along the shallow stream ahead. Why hadn't they counterattacked? There had to be a sizeable force of fighting men in more than two hundred lodges, yet only a handful had rallied to the alarm.

"Grab iron, son," Thompson growled at Justine's side. "We're about to open this here dance."

Justine pulled his extra revolver from its pommel holster, tucked the weapon beneath his belt, and palmed the Colt Single Action Army .45 from the flapped holster at his hip. The initial charge would be handgun work. The single-shot Springfield carbines were more a hindrance than a help in close-quarter fighting on horseback.

By the time Justine readied his weapons, most of the scout troop had finished the descent and formed into a ragged skirmish line. He cast a quick glance at Whiskey Pete, now at his left, revolver in hand. Pete caught the glance and winked.

"Heap Injuns up there, old man," the Tonkawa said to Thompson. "Mebbe so six-year-old Comanche take Kicker's scalp today."

"Shut up, you heathen bastard!" Thompson snapped. "Mebbe so I skin you alive after this! Right now we got *real* Injuns to fight, not lazy Tonks!" The aged scout lifted his old Remington percussion revolver overhead and dropped his arm forward.

Within a heartbeat the thunder of hooves and the piercing war cries of Tonkawas and Seminoles echoed from the canyon walls. In the last hundred yards Justine chanced a quick glance back at the trail. The first group of Second Battalion troopers, Mackenzie in the lead, had almost reached bottom.

A rifle ball hummed high above Justine's head. A second staggered a Seminole's pony, but the game animal kept its feet. Then pandemonium broke loose as the scout company swept into the first line of lodges. Handguns thumped as the Indian scouts fired into tepees, not waiting for clear targets.

One man darted from a lodge, raised his rifle. Justine snapped a quick shot. The Indian stumbled and went to his knees. Thompson's familiar Rebel yell and the blast of his old cap-and-ball revolver sounded above the crackle of gunfire.

Several Seminoles shook out hemp ropes, tossed loops over the tops of lodges, and yanked the skin shelters to the ground. Other Indian scouts bashed in the heads of the exposed men and women with war axes or clubs.

One young woman burst from a lodge directly ahead of Justine, a baby in her arms, eyes wide with terror. She ran a few strides, then dropped the infant to run for her life; Justine tried to yank his mount aside, but too late. His heart skidded at the solid thud of his horse's hoof against the small, blanket-wrapped bundle.

Justine, Thompson, and Whiskey Pete charged head-on into the first real resistance, half a dozen warriors kneeling to draw bows or aim rifles. The three thundered into and through the knot of Indian men, handguns cracking; Justine glanced back to see four of the warriors sprawled in the dust as the other two darted about, desperately seeking cover, before a haze of powder smoke and dust obscured the view behind him.

Justine emptied his first revolver and yanked the second Colt from beneath his belt as his horse raced through the second group of lodges. He snapped a quick shot at an Indian whose breast was covered by a latticework of chain mail, but doubted the slug had found its mark. An arrow buzzed above his horse's mane. A slug ripped past his ear.

Justine heard the distinct slap of lead against flesh, then Thompson's guttural grunt. He glanced at the old frontiersman, saw the bullet hole dark against Thompson's shirt. He started to rein in. The old man shook his head and spurred ahead.

Justine had no way of knowing what was going on behind him, and no time to find out. He did see puffs of powder smoke from the canyon walls to either side and realized a number of Indian riflemen had scaled the rocks to fire at the soldiers below. He heard a series of bugle calls from the dust and smoke cloud behind him, the steady crackle of carbines and handguns, the agonized cries of wounded men, women, and horses.

Although he couldn't see the entire field of battle, he knew the worst of the fighting lay ahead, beyond the final village with its lodges marked by Kiowa symbols. The Indians were regrouping there, falling back to cover the retreat of families fleeing the sweep of horse soldiers. Justine caught a quick glimpse of an Indian mounted on a palomino, his back to Justine as he shouted at a small band of warriors. Justine felt a tingle of recognition.

He had seen that Indian before—

Justine's tiring horse began to falter, its sides heaving, flecks of lather blowing from its neck. The steep descent and hard run through two miles of villages on the canyon floor had sapped the tough gelding's stamina.

"Ned! Over there!" Thompson shouted. He waved his handgun toward a deadfall, a jumble of downed trees that provided at least some cover. "Rein in and reload!"

Justine spurred toward the deadfall and saw an Indian rise from behind a tree trunk, bow drawn. He thumbed the hammer twice as quickly as he could. The Indian went down, the arrow wobbling harmlessly to the ground.

Justine vaulted from the saddle at the same time Thompson dismounted. The old scout's knees buckled as his boots touched the ground. Crimson ringed the dark hole in Thompson's shirt.

"Lige, you're hit!" Justine said.

"Noticed that right off," Thompson said. His eyes glittered, but in rage, not pain. "Ain't bad." By the time he had the words out, Thompson had removed the empty cylinder from the old Remington and replaced it with a fresh one, loaded and capped.

Chips of deadwood and fragments of twigs spat from the deadfall, spraying Justine's head. One slug tugged at the brim of his hat. He instinctively ducked.

Thompson ignored the shower of debris. "Better feed some more brass to them sidearms of yours, son. This ain't over by no long shot." He glanced over his shoulder. "Where's that worthless son-of-a-bitchin' heathen redskin Pete? Damn his thievin' soul, he ain't never around when we need 'im."

Justine ejected spent brass from both revolvers and fumbled fresh cartridges into the cylinders. "Think I saw his horse go down a ways back. Don't know if Pete got free or not."

"Don't matter. One dead Injun's like another." Thompson peered over the top of the deadfall. "You nailed that one, son. Right in the windpipe. Good shootin' from a runnin' hoss."

"Blind luck," Justine said as he swallowed against the bile in the back of his throat and tried to calm his racing heart. "What now, Lige?" More chips flew from the dead trees.

"Up ahead a hundred yards or so. Damn Injun on the yeller hoss got hisself a fair-to-middlin' rear guard set up behind them rocks. Gonna be tough to dig 'em out. Red bastards up there shoot better'n most."

"How do we go about that?"

"Same way we got here, son. Butt in the saddle and spurs to the ponies, straight-ahead charge. Likely they'll break and run 'fore they can get any lead in us."

Justine glared in disbelief at the frontiersman. "The two of us? Against a dozen or more Indians?"

"Help's comin'. Charlton and a few of his boys is right behind."

Justine glanced over his shoulder and saw a knot of horsemen break through the smoke and dust less than two hundred yards back, horses in a dead run, revolvers in hand.

"How'd you know?"

"Charlton's always where he need be." Thompson tugged his hat down. "All set?"

"Hell, no."

"Close enough. Let's go git 'em."

From his post behind a sandstone rockslide, Badger lined his sights on the chest of the horse soldier riding in the lead. He squeezed the trigger—and heard only the dull metallic click as the hammer fell on an empty chamber. He had fired his last round a heartbeat before.

He tossed the now-useless rifle aside, grabbed his bow, and nocked an arrow. The first shot from the approaching horsemen sent a lance of stone shard into his cheekbone. At his side a young Cheyenne paled, then turned tail and ran. Another followed, then a third.

"No!" Badger yelled. "Stay! We must hold here!"

His cries fell on deaf ears. All but one, a Kiowa shot through the ribs, fled. Badger's heart sank into a cold, black emptiness. Few of the surviving men, women, and children who struggled toward the north passage to safety, stumbling in exhaustion, could hope to escape now. The rear guard was shattered.

Badger's eyes narrowed as the charging horsemen drew near, close enough now in the growing light to distinguish individual riders. At Badger's left, gray hair flying in the wind, rode the hated scout Thompson; beside him, the young man Badger had twice before faced in battle. The white warrior who had shot him and had in turn taken Badger's arrow in his back.

Badger knew he had but moments to act.

He tied one end of the soft leather sash around his waist, stood, and drove an arrow through the trailing elk-skin into the ground. He raised his gaze briefly to the skies.

"Father, hear my words," he muttered aloud. "Here I stand, as Koisenko. Here I die." The beat of his heart steadied as he nocked a second arrow, drew the bow, and loosed the shaft. The arrow flew true. It sank deep into the chest of the man called Thompson.

He felt a blow against his side at the same time smoke billowed from the handgun in the young warrior's fist. There was no pain. A serene calm settled over Badger. He nocked a second arrow and drew the bow, aiming for the young warrior's chest—

Justine almost froze in the saddle as he recognized the face behind the arrow swinging toward him—half painted black, the other half streaked and dotted in different colors. The face he had seen twice before.

The shock of surprise lasted less than a heartbeat before he yanked his winded horse sharply to one side; the warrior's arrow whistled past his shirtsleeve. Justine reined his mount to a skidding halt, thumbed back the hammer of the Colt, laid the front sight on the Indian's chest, and fired. Dust puffed from the front of the sash trailing from the warrior's waist. The man didn't go down. Instead of falling, he pulled another arrow from his quiver. Justine fired again; a black dot on the Indian's chest marked the impact of the heavy .45-caliber slug.

The Indian sank to his knees, still attempting to draw the bow. Justine again lined the sight and fired. Through the cloud of blue-white powder smoke he saw the man go down. He reined his horse around, let Charlton and the other men pass in pursuit of the fleeing Indians, and rode back to where Thompson had fallen. He flung himself from the saddle and knelt in the dust beside the old man.

The arrow had buried itself deep in Thompson's upper chest. Pink bubbles at the corners of the old man's mouth told Justine the arrowhead had pierced a lung.

Justine slipped a hand behind Thompson's head and gently cradled it above the sandy soil of the canyon floor. Justine's eyes stung. The old frontiersman grabbed his Justine's sleeve in a gnarled fist.

"Reckon the—bastard—got me." Thompson's words

came out a hoarse gurgle. "Been—expectin' it. Ned—" The words ended in a choking cough and spray of pink spittle.

"Take it easy, Lige. We'll get you to the surgeon—"

"Won't—help—none." Thompson's grip on Justine's sleeve weakened. "Ned, find—my boy—and girl—for me. Tell 'em—" The gurgled words faded; Justine leaned his ear near the old man's mouth.

"Tell them what, Lige?" Justine asked through a sudden, painful tightness in his throat.

"Not—*tell* 'em. *Kill* 'em. . . ."

"Lige, I—" Justine didn't finish the comment. Thompson couldn't hear. His eyes were open but they didn't see. His chest stopped moving.

Justine lowered the old man's head to the earth. He became aware of a presence. He glanced up at Whiskey Pete, who had just dismounted from an Indian pony. Blood trickled down Pete's cheek and dripped from his chin. The look of sadness in the Tonkawa's eyes surprised Justine, stilled the angry rebuke that tried to form on his tongue. The distant rattle of gunfire, shouts, and bugle calls ceased to exist for a moment.

"So an Injun finally killed Kicker," Pete said, his voice soft. "Damn shame, in a way. Kicker was mean as a scorpion, but one helluva fighter. I'll miss the cranky old bastard."

"Me, too, Pete," Justine croaked past the painful constriction in his throat.

"Can't help the old man now," Pete said, staring at the downed Indian's body. "This man was Koisenko. Top Kiowa warrior. You take his scalp now. You earned it."

Justine didn't really have the heart to look at the face of the man he had confronted for the final time in battle. But he knew he must.

The Indian still clung to a faint spark of life as Justine and Pete strode to him. One glance was enough to tell Justine the warrior wasn't long for this world.

The youthfulness of the face beneath the war paint surprised Justine; the man appeared to be about his own age. Something about the expression in the warrior's eyes stirred Justine. He did not see the anticipated hatred there, or pain—merely a calm acceptance.

The Indian muttered something in Comanche. Justine didn't understand. His grasp of the tongue was meager, even if the speaker had been strong of voice.

Whiskey Pete glanced at Justine. "He says his name is Tabi unuu—Badger. He would know yours."

Justine knelt beside the man called Badger. For the first time, he realized the Indian's eyes weren't black or dark brown. They were a deep hazel color, greenish-brown speckled with gold.

"I am called Justine. Ned Justine," he said to the Indian.

Badger drew a labored breath. He muttered something else, a phrase that sounded to Justine like a name. His gaze lifted toward the sky. A moment later the hazel eyes glazed.

"What did he say just before he died?" Justine asked.

"A name. Maybe that of his wife or mother. *Tiesuat tatzinupi.* Small Star in English." Pete pulled the knife from his sheath and offered it, grip forward, to Justine.

Justine shook his head. "I can't do it, Pete. And I can't let you scalp him, either. Not this man."

Pete shrugged. "You'll never make a good Injun, Justine, but you fight well. For a white man." He reluctantly sheathed the knife. "Maybe you're right. This one was too brave to scalp. Even lazy thieving cannibal Tonk heathen savages admire courage in a man. Kicker say something to you before he died?"

"He asked me to find his son and daughter. And kill them."

"Sounds like Kicker. Half your job's already done."

"What?"

Pete nodded toward the body. "This man Badger was Elijah Thompson's son."

A chill whipped up Justine's spine. "You knew? And never told Lige?"

Pete shrugged. "It wasn't my fight. It was his." The Tonkawa stood and listened for a moment. Justine again became aware of the sound of battle in the canyon behind them, then to the thunder of many hooves heading back downstream.

"Sounds like Company A got the pony herd," Pete said. "We'll take Kicker's body back with us and see if we can help out Bad Hand. Got one little thing yet to do."

"What's that?"

"Get out of this canyon without getting ourselves killed, white man. In the words of the late Kicker Thompson, this here little fracas ain't over just yet."

Justine sagged against his bedroll in Mackenzie's camp in Tule Canyon, several miles south of the Palo Duro battle site.

Despite having spent almost fifty hours in the saddle with no more than three hours' sleep and having just eaten his first real meal in almost that long, Justine found himself fighting to keep his eyes open.

He knew that when he slept the nightmares would return. He also knew he would never escape them. They were his for life. Dreams of a red face exploding at the touch of the muzzle flash from his handgun. Of the sickening thud as his horse's hooves trampled the life from an Indian infant. Of a white teamster roasted alive over a slow fire, mouth open in a silent scream. Of Lige Thompson's bashing an Indian baby's brains out.

Now there would be other nightmares. Seeing the arrow driving deep into Thompson's chest. Trying to make sense of Lige's last request. Why would a father want to kill his own children? Of standing over Thompson's unmarked grave on the flats above the rim of Palo Duro Canyon.

"Lige," Justine had said as the others drifted away from the freshly turned sod, "I rode with you for three years, off and on. And I still don't know what to make of you."

He found little solace in the fact that the Palo Duro Canyon campaign had been a solid success, and with a limited loss of life on either side. Thompson had been the only man killed in Mackenzie's command. A few others were injured, only one seriously, and the surgeon said he would survive.

Less than half a dozen Indian bodies had been recovered. Even Badger's body disappeared before the fight finally ended, carried away by retreating tribesmen. Ned figured the true number of casualties the Indians had sustained would never be known.

Pete had been right. Getting out of that canyon had been even tougher than getting into it. For hours, Indians hidden on the rocky walls fired toward the soldiers. Justine still couldn't believe so few of Mackenzie's men had been hit.

Considering the amount of ammunition expended during the fight, which lasted from first dawn until early afternoon, the scant number of known dead seemed impossible.

Justine would never forget the devastation Mackenzie's force left behind in the canyon. The entire campsite and many trails left by fleeing Indians were littered with personal goods, bundles of food, supplies, robes—all gathered into piles and put to the torch by troopers, along with more than two hundred lodges.

Most painful of the mopping-up operation to Justine, and another nightmare he felt sure he could never escape, was the wholesale slaughter of captured Indian ponies. Of almost fifteen hundred head taken by the Fourth, Mackenzie kept some four hundred for remounts and as rewards to the Tonkawa and Seminole scouts. The others were herded into a canyon near this camp and shot.

The screams of wounded animals and the steady crackle of carbines still echoed in Justine's ears. He had become physically ill as horses dropped beneath his Springfield's sights. Shooting an innocent horse was not the same as killing a man who was trying to kill you. He couldn't question Mackenzie's logic in destroying the horse herd. Indian raiders couldn't recover what no longer lived.

With the onset of winter, afoot, with little food, no shelter or extra clothing, the Indian presence on the Southern Plains was doomed. It was only a matter of time, Justine knew. The Indians had no choice if they were to survive. They had to report to the reservations, as Mow-way's band already had done, or face lingering death from starvation or freezing.

The knowledge that Mackenzie's scorched-earth policy had been necessary and would prove successful didn't lessen the ache of the suffering it would cause innocent women and children. Or Justine's part in it. Or the nightmares. Including the frequent dream in which a beautiful, slender, blond woman with sparkling blue eyes and blinding smile stood just out of arm's reach before him. When he tried to touch her, he couldn't; no matter how quickly he moved or ran toward her, she was always just beyond reach—

"Justine?"

Ned glanced up at Charlton. "Yes, Sergeant?"

"Colonel Mackenzie asked me to have a word with you." Charlton, coffee cup in hand, his face lined beyond his years by fatigue, squatted before Ned. "He said to pass along his compliments. He would do so himself, but he's more than a tad busy at the moment. Personally speaking, I can say you—and Lige and the others—did one hell of a job out there."

Justine sighed. "The others, maybe. I just sort of tagged along."

"Always the reluctant warrior," Charlton said with a weary half grin. "Mackenzie also wanted me to ask you something. Your enlistment's up in a couple of weeks, Ned. The colonel asked me to try one last time to talk you into staying with us. The Fourth needs good men. If you agree to re-enlist, there's a promotion to sergeant waiting. And the colonel will do his best to get you an appointment to a school where you could earn an officer's commission. That shouldn't be hard to do for a Medal of Honor winner."

Justine shook his head. "Sorry, Sergeant. A career in the army isn't for me. As far as I'm concerned, the medal I never sought or asked for is just a piece of tin and ribbon to remind me of those I've killed."

Charlton's slight grin faded. "Don't belittle the medal, Ned. It's the nation's highest honor, the ultimate tribute to a soldier's courage under fire."

"I'm not belittling the symbol itself, Sergeant," Justine said. "Lord knows there are hundreds—thousands—of men who deserve it more than I do. I'm just saying that what it represents is too heavy for me, personally, to wear."

Charlton frowned for a moment, then nodded. "I guess I see your point, Ned. So, what will you do once you've gotten your discharge papers? Head back home?"

"In time. I still have one job to do. A job I can only do as a civilian."

"Mind if I ask what it is?"

"To find Lige Thompson's daughter. As he asked me to with his last breath."

"And tell her what?"

Justine sighed. "I haven't the faintest idea."

22

SAYING GOOD-BYE TO the United States Army didn't bother Ned Justine all that much.

Saying the same to his friends in uniform was a lot tougher.

By the time he had made his rounds and said his farewells, his right hand was swollen and swore. He could barely close his fingers into a fist.

Justine couldn't help feeling a sense of personal loss beneath his rediscovered civilian freedom. The bond of friendships forged in barracks, on drill fields, long rides, forced marches, and battlefields would endure the separation of miles and years. He would never again see the vast majority of these men, Justine knew. In time, names would fade. Mental images of individual faces would blur or fade entirely. But he wouldn't forget them.

Was this, he wondered, the true reason men donned uniforms and went to war? For the brotherhood of soldiers, not the quest for glory and honor or sense of duty to cause, country, flag, or family? Or did each go for a different reason?

Justine's quest for his father's approval and acceptance had forked onto a different road somewhere amid the Indian trails crisscrossing the Red River country and the Staked Plains. He felt as if he had been studying a painting while standing too close. Then at some point—he couldn't say when—he no longer saw individual brush strokes. He saw the entire canvas.

The painting wasn't pretty. But now it was complete.

For the first time, Justine felt he had begun to understand his father. The man's aloof, stern demeanor, his inability to show even a glimmer of approval—or love—could be rooted in a stiff-necked personal pride, a belief that any such show of affection was a display of unmanly weakness. Or it could be a reluctance to form strong bonds, a reluctance born in blood on battlefields.

It simply hurt too much when a friend fell.

Justine wondered if the new understanding came from common experiences shared by two soldiers. Or was it simply a matter that the son had grown from a boy into a man, out here in the wild emptiness of the western frontier? That the boy-turned-man had finally come to realize there was more to life than a parent's approval? That it was *his* life to live? That approval and acceptance came from within himself, not handed out by someone else?

What event or events had finally finished the painting?

Justine didn't have all the answers, not yet. But, he vowed, if ever he had children of his own, he would hold nothing of himself back from them. Should he someday father a son, the Justine family tradition ended with that generation. That child would have not have to ride into war to know his worth in the eyes of his father. Should the boy choose to serve of his own free will, Justine wouldn't stand in his way. He would not, could not, force the boy into battle, bloodshed, death, terror, and hatred for men he didn't even know.

Justine tradition be damned.

The thought jarred Ned a bit. He didn't know if the idea sprang from newfound courage and conviction, or from a resentful defiance that had been bubbling in some dark corner of his mind.

He pushed the musings aside. He wasn't finished here yet.

Whiskey Pete was the last man of the scout troop Justine sought out. The white man and the Tonkawa grasped each other's forearm in the formal Plains Indian greeting.

"Can't say it's all been fun, Ned, but at least it's been interesting," Pete said.

"No, it hasn't been fun. I'm going to miss you, Pete. You're a good man to ride with." Justine had to force the words past the lump in his throat.

"Nice thing for a white man to say to a dirty shiftless thieving savage heathen redskin cannibal Tonk Injun." Pete's eyes seemed to glitter in a strange mix of amusement and sadness. "Smooth trails, brother. May your spirit find peace."

Justine released his grip. "Pete, I need one last favor. Tell me where to start looking for Lige Thompson's daughter."

"Gonna scalp squaw like Kicker want?"

"You know better than that."

Pete grinned. "Didn't think so. You won't need me, Ned. She won't be that hard to find. She's on the Kiowa reservation. She's not Sarah Thompson now. She's Quill Weaver Woman. Look up a skinny old Injun name of John Mule Walker. Hangs out around Fort Sill headquarters, knows everybody from the Red River to the Arkansas, speaks every Indian dialect west of the Mississippi. He'll take you to her."

"Would you take me there? The army wouldn't go out of business if you take a few days off."

"A Tonkawa going onto Comanche and Kiowa reservation land might not be such a real good idea, Ned. I'd last about as long as a half pint of whiskey in a hide hunter camp."

"Oh." Justine's cheeks warmed. "Guess you're right at that. I never even thought about it."

Pete chuckled. "Not half a day a civilian, and already you start forgetting everything I taught you about Injuns, white boy." The Tonkawa scout put a hand on Justine's shoulder. "Keep your hair on, partner."

"You, too, Pete."

"No man livin's hoss enough to take this Injun's scalp, Ned. At least I haven't met him yet. Won't believe it 'til

I do. Take care of yourself, brother." The Tonkawa turned and strode away, waddling on stocky, bowed legs.

Justine fought back the almost overwhelming urge to just saddle up and ride out now.

He had one last call to make. A call that filled him with more dread than facing a mounted band of painted warriors. A call he didn't want to make. But he owed her at least that courtesy, even if it did rip out his own heart.

She waited for him in the narrow space between two cabins that served as officers' quarters, her golden hair tossed and teased by the chill, swirling wind.

Justine touched fingers to his hat brim. "Elaine," he said softly.

She reached out, tried to come into his arm, embrace him; he grabbed her shoulders gently, held her at arm's length, and shook his head. "Not now, Elaine. Not after all these months and years of resisting the impulse. If I took you in my arms now, I'd ruin four lives before I could stop myself."

She clutched his coat sleeve. "Ned, please tell me it isn't true. Tell me that you're not really leaving." She made no effort to stop the tears. The roundness of her belly, swollen with the child she carried, bulged her long coat and drove a fresh stake into Justine's heart. Under other circumstances, it could have been his child. Their child.

"It's true, Elaine." He had to push the words through the pain and tightness in his throat. "I'm riding out within the hour."

"Please—I . . . I'll go with you, Ned. Anywhere you want." Her words held an edge of desperation, the sharp pain of loss and want. Tears spilled down her cheeks. "I'll leave him. I'll just walk away . . . with you—"

"No, Elaine. I can't let you do that."

"Because of the baby? Or because you don't love me as I love you?"

"I do love you, Elaine. I've loved you since I first laid eyes on you at the stage stop in Jacksboro. If we had met a few short years ago . . ." His voice trailed away, the words stuck in his throat.

"Ned—please. I . . . I beg you. If it's the baby, we could raise the child as yours. It need never know. . . ."

"That isn't it at all," Justine said, his voice hoarse. "Elaine, if you walk out on your husband, you'll be excommunicated from the church, condemned forever. Your child can never be baptized. You and the baby would be shunned."

"God would understand—"

"The Catholic Church wouldn't. In your own heart, neither would you. Your faith is too strong, Elaine. I know how much the church means to you. I can't let you throw your faith, your soul, your life, away like that."

"I could ask for an annulment. Then we could be—"

"It would never be granted. I'm no student of Catholicism, but on what grounds?" When she didn't answer, Justine gently removed her hand from his arm. "No matter what you and I want, it simply can't be. It's too late. I'm sorry. For both of us."

He turned and strode away before she saw the tears spill down his own cheeks. It was time to leave.

Fifteen minutes later, Justine rode from the post.

He didn't look back.

He sat the civilian saddle he'd bought from a passing traveler, a used but comfortable Spanish-style rig, astride Lige Thompson's iron gray and leading a brown pack mule. The mule's pack wasn't heavily laden.

The personal stuff Justine wouldn't be needing for a while was already on its way back to Maine, packed in a single small trunk and shipped out on the morning stage. The piece of beribboned metal lay in the very bottom of the trunk, beneath the folded tunic with the corporal's stripes, a few books and journals, individual and unit letters of commendation, a couple of souvenirs, and other flotsam accumulated over four years.

Also in the trunk was his father's old percussion Army Colt revolver, still in its original belt and holster, honorably retired from service and replaced by the engraved .45 Colt now at his hip. The new handgun was a gift to him from the officers and men of the Fourth Cavalry Regiment.

They hadn't had to do that.

But they had. The brief presentation ceremony had raised yet another painful lump in Justine's throat. The backstrap engraving listed his name, rank, and dates of service; along one side of the barrel was the simple reminder, "Mackenzie's Raiders."

Ned hoped he never had to fire the new revolver in anger.

Justine tucked his chin into the collar of the knee-length bearskin coat to turn the late February wind and reined the gray to a stop at the crest of the timbered ridge.

In the village below, wisps of smoke drifted from chimneys of crude stone-and-log homes, little more than hovels, and from the vent holes of a couple of buffalo-skin lodges.

He could only hope the remote village held less misery than others he had seen in his ride through the reservation lands.

The sights and sounds of poverty, want, and abject despair cut into his heart like wind-driven sleet. It hurt even more to realize he was partly to blame for these people's suffering.

The vacant stares of young children with bellies swollen from hunger, without the energy to even play games, haunted him most. They stared blankly at the white man without hatred or curiosity. And without hope.

The stoic emptiness in the children's eyes reflected that of the adults. The tears of young women grieving the death of infants who died when their mother's breasts dried and stopped producing milk, the slack-jawed stupor of adult men in the grip of illegal whiskey, seemed to accuse Justine at every stop. Even the gaunt, ribby ponies that had so far escaped the cooking pot stood disinterested, hipshot and heads down, as he rode past.

The sudden influx of hundreds of defeated Southern Plains bands, forced onto reservations by cold and starvation after the battle of Palo Duro Canyon, overtaxed already inadequate supply lines.

A brutally cold, wet winter left the few government supply trains mired miles from the reservations. Even when promised rations did arrive, the flour held more weevils than substance, the beef was stringy and tough, sugar and salt almost unknown, housing and blankets inadequate against the bitter winds.

It seemed the white man had not been satisfied to merely crush the Southern Plains Indians. He now appeared bent on starving them to death. To the last man, woman, and child.

Justine found no solace in the knowledge that the defeated always suffered at the hands of the victors. It had been so throughout history. It would be so through the remainder of history, as long as men followed different cultures, worshipped different deities, or coveted the land or possessions of other tribes. In that respect, the color of their skin was immaterial.

He found no solace in the knowledge that even before the white man came, tribes conquered by others of copper skin had suffered equally—or worse.

He tried without success to quiet the lingering, morbid guilt in his breast, reminded himself he had only done his duty, that the duty had ended. He was a civilian now, not a soldier. No longer an enemy to these people. Just a man riding on one last mission.

Justine turned to the slightly built, stoop-shouldered old man at his side. "This is the village?" he asked, blinking against the sting of sleet daggers born on the knife-edged wind.

John Mule Walker, his guide and interpreter, nodded. "She is here, along with others of her band. Quill Weaver

Woman lives in the stone half-dugout nearest the pine ridge. She may choose not to speak with you."

"I wouldn't blame her," Justine said heavily, "but I have to try." He kneed the gray toward the dugout, John Mule Walker close behind on his sorrel mustang, a mount whose legs were barely longer than its rider's.

The two reined in. John Mule Walker dismounted, ignoring the yapping of scrawny camp dogs. Justine waited in the saddle, still not completely sure what he would say, as John went into the lodge.

A few minutes later the guide emerged, a woman at his side. "This is Quill Weaver Woman," John said. "She has agreed to speak with you."

Justine dismounted, respectfully removed his felt plainsman's hat, and nodded to the woman. She seemed older than Justine expected. Deep wrinkles lined her narrow face. Strands of gray streaked her short, grease-coated dark hair. Thin shoulders hunched beneath a threadbare blanket made her seem not only old, but brittle. The eyes told Justine he had found the woman he sought.

They were a deep hazel, flecked with gold.

"I'm sorry to disturb you," Justine said. "My name is Ned Justine." He waited for John to translate. The guide stood silent.

"What is it you wish?" she asked in surprisingly good English.

"Are you Sarah Thompson?"

For a moment, confusion flickered in her hazel eyes. Then she nodded. "My name was Sarah long ago. When I was only six years old."

"You had a younger brother?"

"Yes." Sadness flickered in the deep hazel eyes. "I cannot speak his name. He was killed in a fight with horse soldiers in the Place of the Chinaberry Trees."

"I know," Justine said softly. "I came to tell you that your brother died courageously. He gave up his own life that others might live. He made his last stand as Koisenko."

The woman nodded. "It is good to know this. You saw his death?"

Justine lowered his gaze. "Yes, ma'am. I was the horse soldier who killed him."

"Then you must be a great warrior and a brave man, for only such a man could have bested my brother in battle." There seemed to be no bitterness, no hatred toward him, in her tone. "Thank you for telling me he died well. His spirit, and mine, now will rest more easily."

Justine blinked against the sudden burn in his lids and lifted his gaze back to her. "There is something else I must tell you. Your birth father, Elijah Thompson. He also died in the same battle."

He didn't tell her that her brother had killed her natural father. Lige Thompson and Badger had not known each other—at least not as father and son—at the time. There was no point in driving yet another stake into this woman's pain.

She shook her head. "It does not matter. My true father was Kiowa, a brave warrior. A Koisenko, like my brother. Of this white man you name I remember only shadows."

"After you and your brother were taken, he spent the rest of his days searching for the two of you. With his last words, he asked me to find you. He wanted me to"—Justine decided against telling her the full truth; sometimes a few details could be omitted—"to tell you something."

"What is this something?"

"That he never stopped looking. There was something else he tried to say, but I don't know what. He died before he could tell me."

To Justine's surprise, Quill Weaver Woman smiled. "That, too, is of no consequence. If his words are meant to reach me, the spirits will send them in a dream."

Justine hesitated for a moment, then said, "Your brother mentioned a name. Small Star. It was on his lips when he died."

"His wife. A lovely, gentle girl, the mother of his two

children. She makes her home now with the family of Yellowfish, my brother's brother," the woman said. "As is Comanche custom, when her time of grieving ends she will become Yellowfish's wife. As will my brother's second wife, Turns-Over-Turtles. Their village is not far, perhaps two hours' ride beyond the ridge to the west."

John Mule Walker nodded. "I know where it is."

"Will you call on her, to tell her how her husband died? The knowledge would comfort her in her grief."

Justine hesitated, not knowing if he had the will to face the wife—wives—and children of the man he had killed. He feared it could only make his lingering guilt a heavier burden. But the expression in the hazel eyes gazing into his swayed his decision.

"Yes. I would be honored."

"Good. Will you come inside? There is food."

Justine shook his head, knowing that to do so would take food from the mouths of her family and touched by the offer made despite that certain knowledge. "No, thank you. Your hospitality is deeply appreciated, but John and I must be on our way." He replaced his hat, toed the stirrup, and mounted. Before reining the gray around, he asked, "Will you forgive me?"

"For what? My brother's death? There is nothing to forgive. Two brave men met in battle. One lived, one died. It is the way of things. Let your heart be still, not heavy, Ned Justine."

"It won't be easy. But I'll try." Justine waited until John Mule Walker mounted, then nodded to the old man. "Take me to her," he said.

Darkness had fallen before the lights of Fort Sill appeared in the distance, tiny dots flickering through the snow.

Justine hadn't noticed the cold. Nor had he spoken since he and John Mule Walker rode away from Yellowfish's lodge.

Justine couldn't shake the overwhelming sense of sadness. Or forget the serene beauty of the young woman named Small Star. It showed through the hair cropped close in mourning, the healing scars where she had slashed her flesh. It was a beauty almost, but not quite, reflected in Badger's second wife, Turns-Over-Turtles.

The faces of the children also haunted him, the tall, strong youngster called Pihpitz, or Horsefly, with his fiery red hair and sunburn even in the dead of winter, or the young Ecapusia, the Flea, not long past the toddler stage.

Yellowfish had been a gracious host. He seemed to bear no ill will toward the horse soldier who had killed his brother; nor did Badger's wives or children. The prevailing emotion beneath the grief was one of pride.

Yellowfish had told him it was Badger's intelligence, foresight, and courage that allowed both families, which soon would be one, to escape the carnage in the canyon. They had fled with most of their valuables intact, including a sizeable pony herd. By reservation standards, they were well off, even wealthy. Justine sensed that had conditions been different, he, Yellowfish, and the others of the family might have been friends.

As they parted, Yellowfish told Justine that Quanah soon would be bringing his band of Quahadis to the reservation, "to follow the white man's road."

The Red River Indian War was over. At the cost of more than just lives. It had cost an entire race its culture, perhaps even its very existence.

"What will you do now, Ned?" John Mule Walker asked as the lights of Fort Sill grew brighter through the swirling flurries.

"Go home. Go back to school. Learn to build buildings instead of burning them."

"It is a good plan. The world needs more of those who build and fewer of those who destroy. And perhaps in your new world you will find peace within yourself."

Justine wondered if that day would ever come. If he

would ever be free of the nightmares, the lingering sadness and guilt.

The whole thing wasn't fair.

The Indian called Badger had everything a man could want. Two beautiful, gentle wives, two fine children, a brother and friend who rode at his side and shared his joys and sorrows. A man trained since birth for his role as a killer, a man whose entire life was built around warfare. Yet, though his world was so much different as to be alien to Justine, Badger had been a man of courage and principles. He fought for his family, for his heritage, for his beliefs, his religion, his freedom, his land.

And he had been killed by one who had nothing.

A man who loved a woman he could never have. A man who had no children, no true home to call his own. A man who didn't want to fight, who never rode toward a battle without almost wetting his pants in raw terror. A man who fought for the wrong reason, a quest for approval, and who finally gained that approval with blood on his hands, a piece of metal on a ribbon packed away, and two stripes on his uniform sleeve.

The price of that approval had been too high.

Justine started inwardly at the sudden realization: that his need for approval and acceptance, a need that had gone unsatisfied for years, meant nothing in the overall scheme of things.

As brutal as it had been, the last four years had been a time when Ned Justine changed from boy to man.

He had not become his father. He had not become Elijah Thompson. He had become Ned Justine.

And he was no longer afraid.

He no longer feared that his courage would be found wanting. He no longer feared trying, even if it meant risking failure. He no longer feared men who outranked him socially, politically, or economically.

He no longer feared his father.

He understood now that his quest hadn't been for approval. It had been a quest to find himself, to find freedom from fear.

Quill Weaver Woman's parting words flashed into his mind: *Let your heart be still, Ned Justine.*

"It won't be easy," Justine repeated to himself, "but I'll try."

The wind didn't seem so cold now.